P9-DGZ-721

LA MAGDALENA

Also by William M. Valtos

RESURRECTION

THE AUTHENTICATOR

LA MAGDALENA

William M. Valtos

HAMPTON ROADS
PUBLISHING COMPANY, INC.
for the evolving human spirit

Copyright © 2002
by William M. Valtos

All rights reserved, including the right to reproduce this
work in any form whatsoever, without permission
in writing from the publisher, except for brief passages
in connection with a review.

Cover photographs: Digital Imagery (c) 2002 PhotoDisc, Inc.
Cover design by Grace Pedalino

Hampton Roads Publishing Company, Inc.
1125 Stoney Ridge Road
Charlottesville, VA 22902

434-296-2772
fax: 434-296-5096
e-mail: hrpc@hrpub.com
www.hrpub.com

If you are unable to order this book from your local
bookseller, you may order directly from the publisher.
Call 1-800-766-8009, toll-free.

Library of Congress Cataloging-in-Publication Data

Valtos, William M.
La Magdalena : a Theo Nikonos mystery / William M. Valtos.
p. cm.
ISBN 1-57174-278-6 (alk. paper)
1. Private investigators--Spain--Fiction. 2.
Americans--Spain--Fiction. 3. Valencia (Spain)--Fiction. 4.
Reincarnation--Fiction. 5. Bombings--Fiction. 6. Nuns--Fiction. I.
Title.
PS3572.A4135 L3 2002
813'.6--dc21

2002013094

10 9 8 7 6 5 4 3 2 1
Printed on acid-free paper in Canada

FOR MY
BELOVED
GRACE
AND
CHLOE

"DURING PETER'S STAY IN ROME, (MARK) WROTE
OF THE LORD'S DOINGS, NOT, HOWEVER, DECLARING
ALL, NOR YET HINTING AT THE SECRET, BUT SELECTING
THOSE HE THOUGHT MOST USEFUL . . . FOR NOT ALL
TRUE THINGS ARE TO BE SAID TO ALL MEN."

—Clement of Alexandria

Deep beneath the massive stone walls of the Vatican Library, in a secret chamber originally built as a bomb shelter for the Roman Catholic popes, lies a specially constructed vault whose very existence is one of the Vatican's most closely guarded secrets. Only the Pontiff himself is permitted to enter the vault.

The vault houses a single object: a gleaming metal cube that measures exactly 60 centimeters (about 24 inches) on each side. The shell of the cube, it is said, is made of a special blend of titanium and non-radioactive depleted uranium, an alloy strong enough to withstand a nuclear explosion. Lining the inner walls of the cube is a special heat shield developed for the American Space Shuttles that has a protective rating that exceeds 1,500 degrees Celsius (about 2,700 degrees Fahrenheit).

Nestled in black velvet in the center of the cube's heavily padded interior is an object reputed to be an ancient relic. In front of this mysterious object are two silver tubes containing hair samples. Between the tubes is a silver plaque, on which is engraved the results of a carbon-dating test of the relic and a mitochondrial DNA analysis of the two hair samples.

This is the story of how those objects came into the possession of the Vatican, and why their very existence has been kept secret. Until now.

One

IT WAS IN the great Cathedral of Valencia, just outside the entrance to the Chapel of the Holy Grail, where the lovely young Spanish nun's left breast pressed itself softly against the back of my right hand.

At the time, I thought it was accidental. But the events that flowed from that first contact soon made me believe otherwise.

The touch of the nun's breast sent a violent tremor through my body, much like the shock I felt a year earlier when electric defibrillator paddles jolted my heart back to life.

She withdrew immediately, staring at me with eyes that revealed both fear and disapproval. For a moment, neither of us dared breathe. Her cheeks, which were framed by a starched white linen wimple, turned bright red. She seemed bewildered, torn between shame and the dread of imminent divine punishment.

"I'm sorry," I managed to mumble.

In most countries, where nuns have given up their traditional robes for more conventional clothing, such incidents might be cause for amused embarrassment. But this was Spain, the land of Torquemada, where the queen who launched the Spanish Inquisition is still venerated. In this most rigidly conservative Catholic country in the world, nuns are still considered "Brides of Christ," who behave and dress according to rules laid down centuries ago by the founders of their specific orders. Any affront to their dignity is considered a serious offense by the local police, if not the *Guardia Civil*.

What made my transgression seem even more sinful was the sanctity of the environment in which it occurred. The thirteenth-century Cathedral of Valencia is one of Christendom's most important sites, a pilgrimage church which attracts thousands of visitors every day. They are drawn to the magnificently gloomy Gothic structure, as I was, by nothing less than what is reputed to be the legendary Holy Grail. In the most popular retelling of its history, the Holy Grail was the chalice from which Jesus Christ drank at the Last Supper, and was later used to collect his blood at the foot of the cross.

The mystical vessel inspired Mallory's *Morte d'Arthur* and has been the object of untold generations of fictional and real treasure seekers, from Sir Launcelot and Parsifal to the Crusaders and more recently, that notorious Nazi collector of religious relics, Heinrich Himmler.

My own interest in the Valencia Grail was based on curiosity more than reverence. I knew of at least twelve "Holy Grails" circulating in Europe, but this particular Grail had the best pedigree, and was the only one considered authentic by the Vatican. It is an agate chalice with gold handles and jeweled bands. According to brochures in the cathedral, it was originally taken by Saint Peter to Rome, where it remained in the possession of the Bishop of Rome until the third century, when the beleaguered Pope Sixtus, through his disciple, sent it to Aragon for safekeeping. It remained hidden in a mountain sanctuary until 1399, when King Martin brought it to Valencia.

It was while I was reaching for an informational brochure that the nun's breast pressed against my hand. What I felt first was the rough serge fabric of her robe, that shapeless garment designed to shield a nun's figure from curious eyes. But then, unmistakably, came the warmth of a fully formed breast, which yielded softly as it pressed against my hand.

I had touched the untouchable, and it would change my life forever.

Two

OUR EYES MET during that brief, erotic moment before she withdrew.

She was a lovely young woman, in her early twenties, with a face which, although it was totally devoid of makeup, radiated a beauty that seemed eerily familiar. Although we had never met, I was convinced I had seen that face before. It wasn't until later that I realized where: in religious paintings and church statuary, in gilded Russian icons and illuminated manuscripts. She was Our Lady of Guadalupe, St. Therese of Lisoux, Madonna with Child, Veronica Wiping the Face of Jesus, and dozens of other saintly representations, all of whom had surprisingly similar features. They were invariably portrayed with the same sad eyes, graceful lips and elegant contours of chin and cheek that I saw before me. Even now, knowing what I do about her, I still find it remarkable that through some inexplicable coincidence of aesthetic determinism, this lovely nun's face had been immortalized by artists who painted her image centuries before she was born.

She exuded an aura of virginity that made me feel ashamed of the unexpectedly intimate contact. I probably should have been asking myself why she had allowed her body to come so perilously close to mine. Instead, I wondered whether I was the first man who had ever touched her in this way. How would she react? Would she scream and alert the crowds of faithful pilgrims that some foreigner had committed the unpardonable sin of fondling a nun in church?

"I knew you'd find me," she said in a hushed voice.

"Excuse me?"

"Say nothing," she whispered. "We are being watched."

She cast her eyes modestly downward and turned partially away from me.

I started to apologize again, but she made a motion with her hand commanding me to silence. The hand darted quickly beneath her habit and extracted a small white envelope. She pressed it into my hand.

"Take this to Padre Serrano," she said.

Was it her hand that trembled?

Or was it mine?

"But who is . . .?"

"His address is on the envelope," she whispered. "Be sure you give it to no one but Padre Serrano."

By now I could no longer see her face. She had turned completely away, apparently to shield the conversation. "I beg you, be careful. You may be in danger. There are watchers everywhere."

Danger? Watchers everywhere? I knew of the Spanish penchant for melodrama and intrigue, but this was ridiculous. I had touched a nun inappropriately, but what was the "danger" in that? Who were the mysterious "watchers"? A harsher psychologist than I would have immediately diagnosed the nun as paranoid and delusional, possibly incipient schizophrenic. Certainly she was using the language of those disorders, and the way she passed the envelope, the whispering to avoid being overheard, were also symptomatic of a paranoid personality. But the events of the last year had taught me to be more compassionate in my evaluation of others, and I knew there were less severe explanations for her behavior:

3

an overwrought imagination perhaps, certainly not unusual for someone whose days were spent in the isolation of convent life, or a minor phobia or an irrational fear, triggered by lack of contact with the outside world.

And, of course, there was always the possibility that she suffered from no mental disorder whatsoever, that her warnings had a basis in fact, that we really were being watched.

I turned slowly, trying to make the action seem casual, as if I was looking for a friend. Most of the crowd that surrounded us was intent on entering the passageway that led to the shadowy chapel where the Grail was on display. They shuffled slowly past, without any of them giving me a second glance. What was I looking for? A suspicious face? A shadowy figure? An angry glare?

There were a hundred people or more in this part of the cathedral, everything from beggars and backpackers to camera-toting tourists and the elegantly dressed local women, come for the midday Mass. If there were any "watchers" among them, it was impossible for me to tell who they might be. The most desperate of stalkers could have been standing right next to me, without revealing himself.

Fifty meters away, just inside the main entrance of the cathedral, a smaller crowd was gathered around the Gift Shop where Grail replicas, postcards, rosaries, and other religious souvenirs were sold. None of the shoppers seemed to be showing any interest whatsoever in me.

The only person whose eyes met mine was an ancient priest, a man so old he could in no way be considered a threat, much less be assigned to follow anyone. I guessed him to be perhaps ninety years old, although he could easily have been over a hundred. He was unusually tall, even for a Spaniard, towering above the *mantilla*-clad heads of the women. But age had eaten away at his spine, bending his head and neck until they seemed to be bowed down in eternal prayer. Unable to raise his chin from his chest, he was forced to turn his head sideways to look at me. His eyes had long ago retreated deep into their sockets. His lips, when they parted, were paper-thin. With what seemed to be great effort, he managed to smile at me. It was a friendly, impersonal smile, the kind priests offer to unknown parishioners at the end of Mass.

Behind me, I heard a rustle of rosary beads, and when I turned, the nun was gone.

I pushed past the crowd into the Grail chapel, where I assumed she went. Three nuns were inside, kneeling at the altar railing. The Chapel of the Holy Grail is not a place where people push and twist to force their way to the altar, but that's what I did, making myself totally obnoxious, I'm sure. Some of the tourists pushed back, the locals muttered *"Basta!"* and worse, but all I cared about was reaching the young nun. She wasn't one of the three nuns at the altar. The squared-off corners of their wimples indicated that they didn't even belong to the same order. She was gone. The only link I had to her identity was the envelope she had given me. Ignoring the angry stares of the people I had pushed past on the way in, I threaded my way more carefully outside.

I looked for the old priest, thinking he might have recognized the robes of the nun, and could tell me where to find her convent. But he was gone, too. Shuffled off, I assumed, to some sanctuary within the cathedral where he could rest his ancient body.

There was no point in searching for her outside. It was market day, and the *Plaza de la Reina* had been taken over by vendors. Carts had been pushed into place, canvas awnings erected, and the huge *plaza* had been converted into a confusing warren of narrow lanes jammed with shoppers and tourists and, according to my guidebook, pickpockets.

I stepped into the shelter of a doorway, out of the way of the crowds, to look at the envelope she had given me. It was of a type I had never seen before. The paper was heavy, with a luxurious creamy finish that suggested it was hand-laid. A white ribbon circled the envelope, the ends held in place by a red wax seal that fastened the back flap. The name of Padre Javier Serrano and an address were inscribed on the face of the envelope in a delicate calligraphy. In the upper left-hand corner, where the return address would be, the same elegant script spelled out the words *La Magdalena*.

The Magdalene.

Was it her name?

If so, I thought at the time, it was a very unusual way for a Spanish nun to identify herself.

To be named after Mary Magdalene was not unusual for a nun. But I was puzzled by the absence of the name of Mary, which was not only the Magdalene's given name, but is also adopted by all nuns as a way of honoring the mother of Christ. Missing in addition was the standard honorific of *Hermana* (Sister in English) identifying her religious status. The correct signature should have been *Hermana Maria Magdalena*. Not La Magdalena. It seemed a curious affectation.

I walked around to the shady side of the cathedral, where I found a place to sit while I studied my Michelin map to find my way to the address where I was to deliver the envelope. *Calle Nueva Ecija* didn't look far away, perhaps a five-minute walk from the *Plaza*. The shortest route seemed to be through the middle of the market. I was halfway down the cathedral steps when I was rudely bumped and sent sprawling by someone in a terrible hurry. He looked like one of the tourists I had seen inside the cathedral: a middle-aged man wearing a photographer's vest, wraparound sunglasses and one of those floppy, wide-brimmed Tilly hats that are supposed to protect the traveler from the harmful effects of the sun's rays. I noticed the hat, because even when he hit the ground, it remained firmly attached to his head, the wide brim masking most of his face. He apologized quickly, dusted himself off and disappeared into the crowd, in apparent pursuit of his tour group.

In fact, as I soon discovered, he had run off with the envelope the nun had given me.

Three

"ARE YOU ALL right?" asked a voice from behind me.

"I think so," I murmured.

I felt for my wallet. It was still safely buttoned up in my trouser pocket. The Michelin map was lying at my feet, trampled by my assailant in his rush to get away. The only thing missing was the envelope. Why would a mugger take the envelope and not go after my money, I wondered. It didn't make sense. Unless the envelope had been his target all along.

"Allow me to help you up," the voice behind me said.

Turning to thank him, I recognized my Good Samaritan as the ancient priest from inside the cathedral. He slipped his bony hands under my arms and lifted me easily to my feet. It was a display of strength I found amazing for so cadaverous a figure.

"These markets can be quite dangerous," he said. His accent sounded more French than Spanish, his wording formal. "Are you certain you suffered no injury?"

"I'm fine, thanks." I brushed the dirt off my shirt. "Except for a little bump on my elbow." There was also a curious red mark on the back of my hand, but I paid little attention to it at the time.

"Did you see his face?"

"No."

"Pity. Did he get your wallet?"

"No."

"Perhaps it was something else he sought?"

That was one question too many, I thought, suddenly suspicious. My instincts as an investigator, dormant for so long, were apparently still functional.

"No," I lied. And immediately wondered whether the priest had seen the nun slip the envelope into my hand.

Was he one of the "watchers" she had warned me about?

I backed up, out of reach of those powerful arms. He immediately seemed to sense my distrust, and his thin lips parted in a sad, knowing smile.

"I leave you now, my son. You still have work to do," he whispered as he backed away. "But remember, believe not everything you hear."

I stared after him as he disappeared into the cathedral. Work? What was he talking about? I had no work. My career as a near-death investigator was over, ended in a spectacular shoot-out that left me with what the doctors called "phantom pains" where the bullet tore through my chest. They explained it was probably caused by a damaged nerve, but I preferred to think it was the pain of a broken heart, still aching over the death of the woman I loved.

I had come to Europe to escape the media frenzy that surrounded my trial. By the time reporters from the National Enquirer and Fox News tried to find me, I had disappeared temporarily into the monastic life on Mount Athos. I found solace there in ancient manuscripts and metaphysical studies. And I vowed never to return to investigative work.

But old habits die hard, and I couldn't help feeling curious about the contents of the missing envelope. What secret did it contain? A theft in broad daylight on the steps of the cathedral, in full view of pilgrims and shoppers, suggested a message of great importance to someone.

But if that was so, why was the missive entrusted to me? Why did the young nun single me out to be her messenger? I was, after all, a stranger. Worse yet, a foreigner, and apparently a clumsy one at that. And what about this Padre Serrano to whom the envelope was addressed? Even in a cloistered existence, there had to be more efficient ways for a nun to communicate with a priest. Was I chosen to be the innocent go-between for some illicit love affair? And was that affair about to be revealed as a result of my carelessness?

I had no moral obligation to alert the padre that the envelope had been stolen. I could have gone about my sightseeing, writing off the incident as one of those unfortunate misadventures that all tourists eventually encounter.

Except for the words of the old priest.

"You still have work to do."

I had heard those words before. Not in this world, I thought with a shiver, but in the land of the dead.

Four

THOSE OF US who have returned from the dead are unlike ordinary mortals.

We may walk in the world of the living. We may eat, drink, live, and love like ordinary human beings. But we are haunted forever by our journey into the afterlife, where some of us have actually looked upon the face of God. Why, we wonder, were we chosen from among the countless others who died at the exact moment we did, to return to our earthly bodies?

"It is not yet your time," I was told. "You still have work to do."

And almost instantly, I was returned to my earthly body, to be greeted by a smiling paramedic who thought it was his defibrillator paddles that brought me back to life. "Welcome back, buddy," he said. "We thought we lost you for a while."

I didn't want to come back, I protested. I wanted to stay on the other side with my beloved Laura. But they took me to the hospital, where the doctors repaired my chest and told me how close I had come to dying. They dismissed the story of my afterlife journey as a delusion, and trotted out tired old medical explanations that had long ago been debunked. It wasn't until my murder trial that I was able to convince anyone that my near-death experience was in fact a brief visit to the afterlife.

But I was still haunted by the words that sent me back.

"You still have work to do."

What work?

What possible mission on Earth could be significant enough to require my presence?

I was not an important person. My ability to influence others was negligible. Despite a promising academic future, I never achieved any of the goals I planned for myself. I abandoned my psychology studies before achieving a Ph.D. My only marriage ended in divorce. I was fired from my job as an insurance investigator. And my career as a private investigator specializing in near-death experiences was ended by that bullet in my chest.

The only positive thing I had accomplished, other than being acquitted of double-murder charges, was the book I wrote about my NDE, which flirted briefly with the best-seller lists. Unfortunately, it only added to my notoriety. Tabloid TV turned me into what they called a "ghost hunter" rather than the objective scientific investigator I really was.

Getting away to Europe at first seemed like a good idea. The media soon forgot about me, and the stay on Mount Athos was ideal for a man of my academic interests. The particular monastery at which I stayed, one of more than 4,000 on the island, was founded in the fourth century. I was assigned a spiritual mentor, Brother Kyriakis. For a year he translated ancient manuscripts for me, teaching me more about the true history of Christianity than I could ever learn by relying solely on the canonical Gospels. He led me through the "secret" Gospels, which were suppressed by Clement with the startling statement that "not all true things are to be said to all men." And he speculated about the nature of the secret teachings of Christ, which were hinted at in the Gospels of Luke and Mark, the letter of Paul to the Romans, and a number of apocryphal sources. But as fascinating as this theological tutoring was, I didn't feel that studying fragile manuscripts in a fourth-century monastery on an island populated only by men was the work I was sent back to Earth to finish. With the encouragement of Brother Kyriakis, I set out like a modern Siddhartha on a search for enlightenment.

I traveled throughout Europe, visiting famous churches and sacred sites such as Glastonbury and Stonehenge, Lourdes and St. Peter's, where I questioned priests and self-proclaimed holy men. All I ever heard in response were the banalities and platitudes of men whose knowledge of life after death came solely from books.

Until that aging priest in Valencia lifted me to my feet and spoke the words that I last heard in the afterlife.

"You still have work to do."

A coincidence? Not likely. As an investigator, I learned not to believe in coincidence.

My mind raced. Was it possible, I thought? Was it possible that some cosmic convergence of events had ordained my presence in Europe, brought me to Valencia, and deposited me on these steps so that I might hear those words again?

But why?

The answer, I realized, might well lie with Padre Serrano.

Five

FORTUNATELY, I WAS in the process of marking Serrano's address on my tourist map when the thief struck. It was less than two kilometers from the cathedral, and not very hard to find.

Calle Nueva Ecija was probably a fashionable street three or four hundred years ago, back when incredible amounts of gold flowed from the New World to Spain. But the days of glory were over for this narrow cobblestone street. The buildings that lined its sides were uniformly gray, with none of the flowing bougainvillea or giant hibiscus planters that adorned the more sunlit sections of town. The windows were all shuttered, the entrances all barred by wooden doors, most of them faded and cracked from decades of neglect. Every available inch of sidewalk space was taken up by parked cars, forcing pedestrians into the street, where motor scooters and cars took turns honking their horns at anyone who dared get in their way.

A set of massive double doors, large enough to admit a horse-drawn *calesa*, guarded the entrance to *Casa Alonzo*. Beneath the rusted iron bell that hung over the doors was a polished brass plaque that identified the building as the Jesuit *Residencia*. I was tempted to ring the rusty bell, but opted instead for the shiny buzzer. As I pressed the buzzer, I again noticed the strange red mark of the back of my right hand.

Almost immediately a woman's voice responded from a small speaker that was cut into the wall.

"Quien es, por favor?"

Even I knew enough Spanish to understand the question.

"I'm looking for Padre Serrano," I replied in English.

"Cómo?"

"Habla inglés?" I asked.

"Sí."

"Padre Serrano," I repeated. "I want to speak to Padre Serrano."

"Padre Serrano. Si. Un momento, por favor."

After a short wait, I head footsteps approaching from an inner court-yard. A round peephole opened, allowing a bloodshot brown eye to examine me.

"Qué?" A man's voice this time.

I smiled and tried to look non-threatening.

"Are you Padre Serrano?"

Behind the doors, I heard a metal bar being removed from its slot. A small servant's door opened just enough for me to see the man inside.

"Sí. I am Padre Serrano."

As soon as I saw him, any thoughts of a romantic liaison between the nun and this priest evaporated. Padre Serrano was a Friar Tuck sort of priest, short and fat, with plump cheeks and a bulbous nose. The top of his head was crowned with a small bald circle. I remember feeling a vague sense of relief that this portly priest with the tired, bloodshot eyes wasn't the handsome young lothario I had expected.

"What is it you want?" he asked, snapping me out of my reverie.

"I was given a letter for you . . . ," I started to say.

He glanced down at my empty hands.

"A letter? From whom?"

"A young nun, in the cathedral . . ."

Startled by my comment, he drew back from the door, as if not wanting to be seen.

"Give it to me," he said, his voice dropping to a whisper.

"I don't have it anymore."

"What do you mean?"

"It was stolen."

"Dios mío! By whom?"

"I don't know. It happened right outside the cathedral. Somebody knocked me over and took off with the letter."

"Leave here!" he said. "Quickly, before you are seen."

He tried to close the door, but I blocked it with my foot.

"No," I said. "I want to know what's going on."

"It is nothing that concerns you."

He pushed harder against the door. Although shorter than I, he was a heavier man, and I had to press my shoulder against the door to keep him from crushing my foot. This was strange behavior for a priest, I thought, and my curiosity, already aroused, grew stronger.

"I didn't come here to cause any trouble," I said. "I didn't have to come here at all. But I was knocked down, and someone stole a letter that was addressed to you. I thought you'd want to know about it. Now my elbow hurts, and I'm tired, and you're crushing my foot, and I'd like to find out what's going on."

"I'm sorry you were hurt," he responded. "I appreciate your efforts, but I have nothing to say. Now please go."

The harder he pushed, the more determined I became. My foot was growing numb, but I wasn't ready to give up. I pushed back with all my strength.

"If you don't talk to me," I threatened. "I'm going to have to talk to the other priest."

I planned to have a talk with the other priest anyway, but my threat worked with Serrano. I felt his pressure on the door momentarily relent.

"What other priest?" came his harsh whisper.

"The priest at the cathedral. He saw the thief, and I think he saw the envelope being given to me by the nun . . . by *La Magdalena.*" When I spoke the name aloud, it seemed such an awkwardly formal pseudonym, but it had an immediate effect.

The pressure on my foot stopped. The door eased open. Padre Serrano's face was flushed from the exertion. Beyond him, I could see a peaceful courtyard with a lovely garden and fountain.

"She told you her name?" He couldn't conceal his surprise. "She actually spoke to you?"

"We talked." It wasn't really a lie, although I knew her name only from the envelope. But I wanted to give him the impression that more had passed between us than just a few words. "She said she was worried about me, worried that I was being watched."

"We are all being watched."

"She said I could trust you." Now that was an outright lie, of course. But the most effective lies are always those which are surrounded by small truths. Padre Serrano was apparently as concerned about the mysterious "watchers" as the nun who called herself La Magdalena had been. And using the name she signed had given me instant credibility. "But now I'm not so sure about you," I bluffed. "Maybe the other priest . . ."

"No! You mustn't tell anyone about the envelope! Especially a priest. You don't understand what's involved."

When he said that, I knew I had him.

"Then perhaps you should tell me," I said.

"We can't talk here." He looked up and down the street again, and surprised me by checking the courtyard behind him, as if he expected some eavesdropper to be lurking in the bushes. The grounds were lush and green, complete with fountains and espaliered orange trees. It was typical of Spanish architecture to hide such beautifully landscaped vistas behind grim outer walls, reflecting the secretive nature of the Spanish people themselves.

Padre Serrano whispered an address and a time for us to meet. A part of town, he said, where no one would know him. He cautioned me to travel there by a roundabout route, warning me to be certain I wasn't followed. After checking the street one last time, he closed the door and slid the metal bar back into place.

I have to admit I was unnerved by his behavior. The cobblestone street suddenly seemed narrower, frighteningly confining, as if the walls had moved closer together, trapping me in a grim corridor from which the only escape could be cut off easily. I was beginning to feel the first delicate tendrils of paranoia beginning to grow within me. Was that the sound of footsteps I heard behind me? Was someone watching from behind the shuttered windows? Was that a figure reflected in the side mirror of a parked car? Of course, whenever I turned, no one was in sight. If anyone had been there at all, they were well hidden.

I was worried about being followed, when in retrospect, I should have worried more about what lay ahead. As I headed up the street, I rubbed the back of my right hand. The red mark that I thought at first was a scrape was beginning to feel more like a burn.

Six

I MET PADRE Serrano at seven that evening. The Spanish dinner hour is notoriously late, and most restaurants don't open until eight or nine or even ten p.m. So we met in a place called Naranjas, one of the small non-alcoholic juice bars so popular in Valencia. It was located on a quiet street near the Museo De Bellas Artes, on the other side of the Jardín del Turia.

The priest was already waiting for me, sitting in a corner where he could watch the street as well as see anyone who entered. He seemed nervous, as if unaccustomed to being away from the protective confines of the *Residencia*. He recommended I order an *horchata*, the local specialty, which turned out to be a semi-frozen drink tasting of almonds and served with crunchy wafer sticks.

"Now, exactly who are you?" he asked, wasting no further time on small talk.

"My name is Theophanes Nikonos."

"You are Greek?"

"Greek-American. My friends call me Theo."

"May I see your passport?"

I handed it over.

"All right, Theo," he said, as he compared my face with the passport photo. "What is your interest here? What business do you have in Europe?"

"I'm just a tourist, seeing the sights," I said.

"I think not." He waved my passport at me. "Tourists visit for a week, a month, sometimes a little longer. But according to the Immigration stamps, you have been in Europe for well over a year."

"You sound more like a detective than a priest."

"I am merely being careful. Please answer the question."

Reluctant to reveal too much about myself to a stranger, I decided to go with an edited version of the truth, omitting any reference to my trial.

"All right," I said. "Originally, I came over to visit my father. My mother passed away years ago, and when my father retired he decided to move back to Greece, where he was born. I stayed with him for a few weeks, until we got on each other's nerves, and since then I've sort of been wandering around. I spent some time in a monastery on Mount Athos . . ."

"Why Mount Athos?" he interrupted.

"Curiosity, I guess. Not about monastic life, but about myself. I had been through some difficult times and I wanted some solitude . . . I needed time to look inside myself."

"And what did you see when you looked inside?"

I shrugged.

"Memories. The past. Mistakes I made. No great revelations. I ended up spending my time discussing theology and church history with the monks. It was an Eastern Orthodox monastery, my father's religion. They had an amazing library. Some of the books and manuscripts went back to the days before Constantine. It gave me a chance to brush up on my Greek, as well as religious history."

Padre Serrano fell silent, and I followed his bloodshot eyes to a young man who had entered the juice bar. The newcomer was in his early twenties, I guessed. He was lightly bearded and was wearing the usual college student's uniform: a loose T-shirt and faded jeans, a blue nylon backpack draped over one shoulder, and headphones attached to an audio player that was turned up loud enough for us to hear the overflow. The young man ignored us. He ordered a glass of orange juice and sat a table near the entrance. Padre Serrano turned his reddened eyes back to me.

"You are interested in Church history?" he asked. "Are you a religious person?"

"I believe in God, if that's what you mean. But I don't belong to any organized religion. Not since I was a child."

"Is that not what you call in America a cop-out? Trying to have it both ways?"

"I'm making progress," I smiled. "Two years ago, I was an agnostic. At least now I'm back on your side of the fence."

The answer seemed to amuse him.

"And what attracted you to Valencia?"

"I wanted to taste the oranges, see if they really were as sweet as they're supposed to be. And eat some authentic *paella Valenciana.*"

"And see the Holy Grail," he added.

"Well, at least Valencia's version of the Holy Grail."

"You may no longer be an agnostic, but you are still a skeptic, I think."

"I'm a psychologist. I was trained to separate perception from reality."

"And I myself am a psychiatrist. And I've learned that perception can create reality." He looked around the juice bar, his eyes once again settling on the young man who sat near the entrance. Then he leaned forward and whispered, as if he feared the young man might overhear, "What is your interest in La Magdalena? Why are you so curious about her?"

I couldn't very well tell him that I had felt the weight of her breast in the cathedral. How the wonderful softness of her flesh had stirred forbidden emotions within me. The very idea of such intimate contact with a nun would almost certainly offend him. And he would probably resist any attempt of mine to meet her again.

I stared down at the narrow streak of reddened skin on the back of my hand. She had left her mark on me. Whether it was from an allergic reaction to something in her garment, or from some form of psychosomatic response suggesting how deeply the incident affected me, I didn't know. I moved my hand out of sight, under the table, lest he question me about it.

"It's not La Magdalena that I'm curious about," I lied. "It's the contents of the envelope she gave me. What was so important that a thief would steal it in broad daylight?"

"What was in the envelope is a private matter," he whispered. "And please keep your voice down."

I couldn't figure out why he kept whispering. No one was within twenty feet of us. The counter clerk was absorbed in squeezing oranges, and the young man near the entrance was paying us no attention. No sound escaped the CD player now, but he was still wearing his headphones. From that distance, I was sure he couldn't hear anything except his music.

"I'm sorry," I said softly. "You're right, of course. Under normal circumstances, her message to you should remain private. But when she gave me the envelope, she warned me of danger. Now the envelope's been stolen, and you seem very frightened. What's going on?"

The priest didn't respond.

"Whatever's going on between you two, I didn't ask to get involved," I said. "If the message was so important, why did she entrust it to me? Why hand it over to a complete stranger? I'm sure she knew others who could have carried the message to you. Why choose me?"

He stared at me for a long moment, as if he were trying to figure it out himself. When he finally responded, instead of answering my question, he posed one of his own.

"Do you believe in reincarnation?" he asked.

Seven

THE QUESTION WAS delivered in a conspiratorial tone of voice, with Serrano leaning forward, his eyes nervously darting from side to side to be certain no one overheard, and then locking on mine with an expression that seemed to beg me to take him seriously. There was something in his manner, the vulnerability in his face, that reminded me of those hundreds of near-death experiencers I interviewed. So many of them were accustomed to having their accounts of the afterlife journey ridiculed that they were hesitant to discuss the matter with others. Not wishing to offend this earnest-looking priest, I responded with as much seriousness as his question was posed.

"That depends on how you define reincarnation," I said.

"But you know a little about the subject, don't you?"

A little? As an academic, I bridled at the suggestion.

"It depends," I said. "It depends on whether you're talking about reincarnation in the Vedantic sense, in which humans are supposedly reborn as animals and vice versa, or if you mean reincarnation in the Talmudic sense, in which God created a limited number of souls which are continually reincarnated until the time of the Final Judgment. I find both of those concepts difficult to accept. I believe in an afterlife, certainly. And the immortality of the soul. But that doesn't automatically mean I believe old souls can be poured into new bodies."

Seeing that I had his full attention, I continued. There are times when I can't resist a bit of intellectual grandstanding. The urge usually strikes when I detect a patronizing attitude in others, or, as in this case, when I feel a need to establish my credentials.

"Still, the idea of reincarnation has been around as long as mankind," I continued. "So it shouldn't be lightly dismissed. After all, every major religion has strains of reincarnation theory woven through its beliefs. Not just the Hindus and Buddhists, but the mainstream religions, too."

I took a sip of my drink. The ice crystals had still not melted.

"You can trace reincarnation beliefs through Jewish thought back to the third century B.C.," I elaborated. "And hear it today from the most conservative Hasidic rabbis. It's been called the Lost Chord of Christianity because of the prominence it enjoyed in the early Christian Church. As a Catholic priest, I'm sure you're aware of Saint Gregory's teaching that it can take more than one lifetime for a soul to be purified and healed. That's remarkably similar to the Eastern philosophy of the path to enlightenment and the Great Wheel of Karma, and the beliefs of the Druse and Sufi Muslims."

The way he listened, the way he allowed me to continue uninterrupted, reminded me of the Master's Program at NYU, where we were regularly subjected to oral tests to determine whether we had truly mastered the required course material.

"There's a lot of anecdotal evidence that certain individuals have memories of previous lives," I said. "As a psychologist, I personally lean more towards Carl Jung's theory of psychic heredity and the residual memories of ancestral life to explain such events. But I know there are more people in the world who believe in reincarnation than in Jesus Christ, so I'm willing to be convinced."

His stunned expression pleased me, because I had long ago tired of priests who act as if they alone are the receptacles of all spiritual knowledge.

"I'm impressed," he said. "I didn't know they taught such things in American psychology classes."

"They don't," I replied. "Except as examples of illogical thinking. Which is one reason why I'll never get my Ph.D."

While some might have been put off by my long-winded response to a simple question, Serrano apparently saw within me a kindred spirit. We were, after all, two academics who had pursued similar fields of study with dramatically different professional outcomes. Soon we were relaxed and chatting like old friends on some college campus. Reincarnation theory was set aside for what seemed like a concerted effort on Serrano's part to get to know me better. He quizzed me on every detail of my *curriculum vitae,* not only the Psych courses, but the comparative religion and Eastern mysticism and archeology classes that I took simply because I enjoyed them. He got me talking about my love of research, and how my failed marriage sidetracked me into a job as an insurance investigator. But he seemed particularly interested in the work I did as an NDE investigator for Professor Pierre DeBray. Normally I find the clergy tend to ridicule any discussion of the near-death experience, which is unusual when you consider that life after death is the bedrock of Christian belief. But Padre Serrano was fascinated by the subject. He was especially curious about my investigative techniques, and how I could possibly establish whether anyone who claimed to have come back from the dead was telling the truth.

He did a good job of drawing me out. I was soon telling him about my own NDE, and the subsequent murder trial in which I portrayed myself as an "authenticator" of life after death. He seemed positively enthralled with my description of the Other World. I told him about my book on the subject, which I submitted as my doctoral dissertation, only to have it rejected as "undeserving of academic recognition."

"You must have been disappointed," he said.

"Not really. After what I've been through, a Ph.D. doesn't seem very important anymore."

"You have a fascinating background," he said. "Perhaps it was karma that brought you to Valencia."

"I didn't know Catholic priests believed in karma."

"Jesus Christ was sent to Earth specifically to die for our sins. That was a classic case of karma, was it not?"

I responded with a shrug. I didn't want to be drawn into a discussion of comparative religions right now.

"Let's get back to La Magdalena and the envelope," I said.

"Ah yes, La Magdalena." Padre Serrano leaned forward in his conspiratorial mode again. "She is a very special creature. A rare flower who has been sheltered and protected from outside influences. She has known no life except that of the convents, where she has lived since she was an infant. She is an innocent, a pure and unsophisticated child whom I believe incapable of lying. But she speaks of things, some of them terrible secrets, that were known only to Christ's Apostles."

He let that sink in while he took a slow sip of his *horchata*. I think he was trying to decide exactly how much to tell me.

"She was a patient of mine. I was her psychotherapist. Unfortunately, that is no longer true. The vicar general's office has terminated my work with her. They have confiscated my notes and correspondence, and forbidden me from any further contact with La Magdalena." He tilted his head and looked at me with renewed curiosity. "But now you come along, a foreigner who has investigative experience with metaphysical matters. Perhaps you were sent to succeed where I have failed."

"Succeed?" I asked. "Succeed in what?"

"In bringing her story to light. It is an astounding account, one which challenges the most cherished Christian beliefs."

He paused.

"If it is true."

He paused again.

"And if you live to write about it."

Eight

"YOU'RE TRYING TO scare me," I said with a smile.

"To the contrary. From what you've told me, I don't think you scare easily. But I would be remiss if I didn't give you my assessment of the situation. I was warned from the outset that La Magdalena's case was an extremely sensitive affair. That I must be discreet. Like you, I was skeptical. After all, this was not some criminal enterprise I was investigating. I am a priest. A Jesuit. A psychiatrist. I was counseling a nun. It was a Church matter. But troubling things began to happen. I was followed wherever I went. My room was regularly searched in my absence. One evening in the cathedral, a man behind me . . . I think he was a priest, warned me to be careful, that my life was in danger."

"Who was he?"

"I don't know. He told me not to turn around."

"What makes you think he was a priest?"

"Something about his voice. It seemed the voice of an old man. I thought I recognized it. But I can't be sure. And he was wearing black. I'm sure of that, because I turned a little when he was entering the pew behind me. Imagine that," Serrano shuddered. "To be threatened in the cathedral."

"Did anybody try to follow through on the threat?"

"Not yet. But my meetings with La Magdalena were restricted, and, finally, cut off completely. I was warned that I must discuss the results of my investigation with no one, under pain of excommunication. For the vicar general's office to intervene . . . to cut off contact between a psychiatrist and his patient in so heavy-handed a manner . . . I never would have believed it possible."

"With all due respect, Padre," I tried to calm him down. "Maybe they just wanted a different psychiatrist to work with her."

"But that is not the case. I have learned through some of the other nuns that no psychiatrist has replaced me." He half-rose, as if he recognized someone on the street outside. "The church authorities have conducted tests on her, both physical and psychological examinations. But the results of those tests are closely guarded secrets, as carefully shielded as those of the confessional. I believe Cardinal Herrera is in Rome at this very moment discussing the matter with his counterparts in the Curia. Meanwhile, I am permitted no contact with her. I am followed wherever I go. And my room is still being searched in my absence. These cannot be the doings of the vicar general's office, at least not without pressure from outside. There must be other, more powerful people who have taken an interest in this case. And in Spain, such situations can quickly turn nasty. That worries me greatly, Mr. Nikonos. I am finding it difficult to sleep, not knowing what the next day will bring."

Simply by talking to me about the nun, Padre Serrano apparently felt he was putting himself at risk. That would explain his edgy behavior at the gate, the fatigue in his eyes, the choice of this obscure meeting place, the way he kept glancing nervously at the young man near the entrance. But what was really going on here? Did he suspect the bearded backpacker was some sort of ecclesiastical spy, detailed to follow him and perhaps compile a dossier that would lead to excommunication?

Or was I being manipulated by this priest, slowly getting sucked into some mysterious scheme, in which case the young man with the headphones was there as an observer, to be sure things went according to plan? It may sound overly dramatic, but the history of the Church in Spain is an epic saga of intrigue and betrayal, of priests plotting with kings and rebels, of unbelievable acts of inhumanity committed in the name of God. While much of that was in the past, it was no secret that some of today's priests are allied with the Basque and Catalan independence movements. I didn't want to get involved, however tangentially, in someone else's war.

Yet my curiosity was aroused.

"What are we really talking about here?" I asked. "Is this young nun in some sort of danger?"

"No, not her. Not La Magdalena." I noticed he pronounced her name with an almost loving reverence. "She is being watched . . . she has been watched all her life, and she is certainly in no danger. But as for us . . ." he let out a long, resigned sigh. "I'm afraid our fate has already been decided."

"Now wait a minute," I protested. "I'm just an innocent bystander. Why would I be in any kind of danger?"

"I'm sure you've already been identified. The fact that a thief stole the envelope from you suggests that you were seen talking to La Magdalena in the cathedral."

"Identified by whom?"

"The people who are watching her, of course."

The "watchers" again. I sighed. "And who are those people?"

"I don't know. I'm sure they're not acting on their own, but I don't know whom they represent. All I know for certain is that sometime during the past six months, some sort of surveillance has been set up around the young nun. The man who stole her note was almost certainly one of them."

"This is crazy," I said, unable to keep the frustration out of my voice. "So I spoke to a nun. Is that a crime?"

"Not a crime, no. But the fact that La Magdalena chose to speak to you . . . well, to the best of my knowledge, this is the first time she has ever spoken to a secular. It was bound to be noticed."

He was talking in circles. I tried a different approach.

"What about the envelope?" I asked. "Just what exactly was so important about the envelope?"

"It contained . . ." he started to say, and then went back and carefully rephrased his words. "I believe it might have contained extremely sensitive information."

"About what?" I tried to laugh it off. "Did she find out the Cardinal was dipping into church funds? Or having an affair with some nun?"

"Please," he said. "I believe this young nun knows secrets that could shake the foundations of Christianity. Information that has been kept secret for two thousand years."

"You're kidding me," I said. "We're talking about a young nun in a sequestered convent. What sort of secret information could she possibly possess?"

He didn't answer immediately, and we ended up glaring at each other. He was probably still struggling with the question of whether he could completely trust me with information that he apparently thought was terribly important. And I probably should have been more understanding. But it was so difficult getting information out of him. It reminded me of my trial, where my attorney had to work hard to get hostile witnesses to part with the tiniest scraps of information that might prove helpful to my case.

"I don't like this little game you're playing," I complained. "If you don't tell me what's going on, I'll find out some other way."

"Please keep your voice down," Padre Serrano repeated his earlier warnings, glancing again at the young man. "You must understand, much of what I know about this matter was told to me as part of my psychiatric evaluation of the nun. I am ethically constrained from revealing any of that information. I will tell you what I have learned outside of those sessions, but you must promise to reveal none of it unless she personally grants you permission to do so."

"I'm not sure I can make that promise."

"Then you can walk out of here right now and face your fate in ignorance."

His eyes remained locked on mine. He stared unblinking, daring me to accept his challenge.

"This business about the danger . . . ," I murmured, rubbing the back of my hand beneath the table. "You wouldn't be just kidding about that . . . would you?"

He shook his head slowly.

"But you do know the source of the danger?" I asked. "Maybe not names, but what I should watch out for?"

He kept his lips closed in a grim line, suggesting he wasn't going to say another word unless I agreed to his condition.

"Will I get the chance to talk to the nun again?"

He shrugged his shoulders.

I could see I was getting nowhere, so I finally gave in. "Well, I guess there's no harm in listening. All right, I agree. I won't reveal anything you tell me, unless she grants permission . . . or if I learn about it from other sources."

"Fair enough," Padre Serrano said, his tired face breaking into a relieved smile. "You don't know how glad I am to finally be able to talk to somebody about this."

"I'm listening."

"Magdalena is nineteen years old."

"She looked older to me," I interrupted, remembering our encounter at the cathedral. "Although maybe that was because of the nun's clothing."

"Yes, well, there are times when she seems older, much older," he said. "And it has nothing to do with the wimple and veil." He shook his head and let out a long sigh. "I first met La Magdalena almost fourteen months ago, when I was asked to evaluate her by the mother superior of the *Convento de las Hermanas del Sangreal* . . . that's the Convent of the Sisters of the Holy Grail," he needlessly translated. "As a psychiatrist and a priest, I am often called upon when a member of any of the religious orders in Valencia exhibits symptoms of mental problems. The diocese is very sensitive about such cases, especially when a nun is involved."

"I can understand that."

"Magdalena was a model novice and nun until her eighteenth birthday, when during a Solemn High Mass, as the sacred host was being elevated, she began to scream and cry uncontrollably. She complained of horrifying images flashing through her mind. She was quickly removed from the chapel. After a brief examination, a local doctor suggested she was suffering from stress, and simply needed rest and quiet. Easy to do in a convent, *no?*"

I nodded, keeping the back of my hand out of sight, under the table.

"She went into seclusion for a period of time, perhaps six weeks of minimal contact with the other nuns. Exactly what the doctor ordered. But after that, she was never the same. The images returned, growing stronger and stronger. Her behavior deteriorated. Or at least it changed, when compared to what you might expect the behavior of a nun to be.

"Her behavior became disruptive of the convent life. She spoke of things a cloistered nun should not know. She would sometimes make long speeches, in a language that was completely unintelligible to anyone who heard her. She questioned the rules of obedience and refused to accept the authority of the priests. In chapel, she made comments about the liturgy that some of the other nuns considered blasphemous. The mother superior was convinced that some evil creature had taken possession of the young girl's soul."

The burning sensation on the back of my hand seemed to grow more intense.

"The mother superior was thinking spirit possession," Padre Serrano continued. "And I was thinking schizophrenia. But after a few sessions, I found we were both wrong. La Magdalena was a wonderful, level-headed, eminently sane person whose unusual behavior had a simple explanation."

"Such as?"

"I think she was having glimpses of a past life."

"You're joking."

"I wish I were," Padre Serrano said. "My life . . . perhaps I should say my faith . . . would be safer if I could treat this all as some enormous joke. A fraud not to be believed."

"That's certainly possible. I'm sure you've come across patients who tried to deceive you."

"Yes, I have. Some patients even deceive themselves. But even the most clever patients can maintain their deception for only a short time. I spent nearly three months working with La Magdalena, talking to her, observing her, corroborating her stories with independent research. I am convinced she's not deceiving me. I've done a lot of work with amnesiacs, suppressed memory cases, patients with false repressed memories. But I've never had a patient like her.

"At times, she exhibits flashes of episodic recall, images as powerful and vivid as those which are normally associated with post-traumatic stress syndrome, but with a stronger spatio-temporal context. What Atkinson called "autobiographical" memory. At other times, she experiences longer interludes of what we know as "semantic" memory, a store of general knowledge, which includes factual material, language, customs and cultural rules. But all these memories are of another time, a time of antiquity. They appear to be not her own memories, but those of another person, a person who lived two thousand years ago."

"And who is this person?"

"That's what makes it so incredible. That's probably why I was taken off the case."

"Who are we talking about?" I persisted. "Who does she think she is?"

"Mary Magdalene," he said softly. "This nineteen-year-old nun believes that she is the reincarnation of Mary Magdalene."

He let that sink in while he took a slow sip of his drink.

"And in my considered professional opinion, as impossible as it might sound, I believe that it just might be true."

Nine

IT WAS A diagnosis I never thought I would hear from a psychiatrist.

The secular reductionism that pervades modern psychiatric academia contends that metaphysical beliefs are merely forms of delusion or wishful thinking. Beliefs in guardian angels, miracles, apparitions, and the like are generally considered to be the often harmless imaginings of the overly religious, although sometimes the intensity of the belief may be indicative of serious mental disorders.

While an ordained Catholic psychiatrist might be more willing to accept religious beliefs as part of normal behavioral thought processes, a clinical endorsement of reincarnation was astonishing. His priestly vows, after all, would have bound him forever to the accepted beliefs of the Catholic Church, which spoke of a single life on Earth to be followed by the resurrection of the body on Judgment Day.

"You're probably surprised to be hearing such a diagnosis from a Catholic priest . . . especially a Jesuit," he said, as if reading my thoughts.

"It does seem odd," I replied. "After all, the Church turned away from those early teachings about reincarnation sometime in the sixth century."

"The Church turned away from a number of early teachings," he said with a note of sadness in his voice. "You're probably referring to the Council of Constantinople, which was called in 543 and declared Origen's teachings on reincarnation to be anathema, and its followers subject to excommunication."

"And after that, the atmosphere turned hostile," I said.

"More than just hostile," Serrano quietly responded. "Belief in reincarnation was one of the so-called heresies that was used to justify the Albigensian Crusade, which wiped out much of the population in the South of France during the fourteenth century. And the mere mention of reincarnation would have been enough to have the offender burned at the stake during the Inquisition."

Those events had taken place half a millennium ago. But this priest was talking in such hushed tones, it seemed as if some vestigial fear of persecution might still be gnawing at his mind.

"Nevertheless there were always dissenters," he continued in his whispered voice. "The Council of Constantinople, for example, was called by the Emperor Justinian, not the pope. And Pope Vergilius not only didn't attend, but refused to endorse its conclusions, including the anathema against Origen. Interestingly, there has never been a papal encyclical forbidding belief in reincarnation. The transmigration of souls was embraced by a long line of Catholic leaders, including St. Francis of Assisi, St. Jerome, St. Augustine of Hippo. Even Pope Pius XII, one of our more conservative popes, seriously considered granting official recognition to the doctrine."

It sounded to me as if Serrano was going through a process of rationalization, trying to justify his diagnosis as somehow acceptable for a Catholic priest. But for every reincarnationist he cited, I knew there were probably dozens of edicts, anathemas and warnings handed down over the centuries by Vatican theologians who were sworn to preserve the existing dogma. That might explain why he had been removed from the nun's case. But it didn't explain why, despite knowing the Church's position on such matters, he still held to his original, controversial diagnosis. A diagnosis which, at least in part, sounded unbelievable.

"Frankly, it sounds a little too Hollywood to me," I said.

"I don't understand."

"This business about a nun claiming to have been Mary Magdalene in some past life . . . even if I bought into the reincarnation hypothesis, it reminds me of those movie stars and show-business celebrities who like to talk about their past lives. They always claim to be Cleopatra or a Roman general, or some other important person. They never talk about having lived as migrant workers or criminals or the common people who make up the vast bulk of the population in any era. It's always somebody glamorous."

"There's nothing of what you call "Hollywood" about La Magdalena," Serrano protested. "To the best of my knowledge, she has never even seen a movie. She is a simple, honest girl . . ."

" . . . making an outrageous claim," I said. "I'd be more likely to believe her if she claimed to be a housewife or a fish peddler or a schoolteacher in her past life. That's what made the Stevenson research so credible. All of his cases were ordinary people who claimed to have lived previous lives as . . . ordinary people."

I was referring to Doctor Ian Stevenson, the director of the University of Virginia's Department of Medicine, who researched and documented more than two thousand cases of alleged reincarnation. His book *Twenty Cases Suggestive of Reincarnation* remains the classic in the field, a work of scientific methodology and objectivity that earned grudging praise even from skeptics.

"She didn't choose to be the reincarnation of a woman as celebrated as Mary Magdalene," Padre Serrano contended. "That decision was made by a Higher Power."

"I'm just saying the celebrity aspect makes it harder to believe."

"But what if it's true?" he asked, leaning forward. "What if her memories of a life lived two thousand years ago are genuine? I think that's what the Church authorities suspect. I think that's why I was removed from the case. There is something in those memories about Jesus Christ and the founding of Christianity that many people don't want revealed."

"*If* it's true." I shrugged.

"You are a doubter," Padre Serrano sighed. "Why she chose a doubter like you to be her messenger is puzzling to me. But she must have sensed something about you." He studied my face quizzically, as if he expected to find some answer there.

"You realize how ridiculous this all sounds," I said.

"Oh, I know. It's absolutely incredible. That's what the vicar general said when I was told not to discuss it with anyone. Don't think I haven't had second thoughts, that I haven't questioned my diagnosis. I'm already suffering the consequences for having formed so outrageous an opinion. They've put me in a kind of professional purgatory, with no patients, no duties, nothing but my books to keep me occupied. But I stand by my diagnosis, Mr. Nikonos. My reputation may be in shambles, but I stand by my diagnosis."

He was really serious, I could see. This wasn't some off-the-cuff, spur-of-the-moment evaluation of a patient by an ambitious psychiatrist hoping to cause a stir. Something about the young nun had touched him so deeply, he was willing to defy his superiors at great cost to himself.

"With all due respect," I said. "Proving or disproving a case of reincarnation is a very difficult matter. Have you considered this might all be some sort of fraud?"

I knew I was being blunt, but if we were going to have a serious discussion about this young woman, there were certain questions we had to get out of the way. Fraud, whether intentional or unconscious fraud, was one of the first possibilities any paranormal researcher must consider.

"I considered it, yes," he said. "But I found no evidence of fraud, no motive, and never once caught her in a lie or a contradiction or anything in her past-life memories that couldn't be proven from independent sources."

"Those memories . . . how did they emerge? Was it under hypnotic regression?" That was a loaded question. I was referring to the technique originally used in the famous Bridey Murphy case and now a major fad among New Age devotees. Although it has some vocal adherents, hypnotic regression has an equal number of critics, including Dr. Stevenson.

"Definitely not! I am a psychiatrist, not a hypnotist," Serrano said. "I know the flaws and weaknesses of hypnotic regression, the "phantom memories" that can be created by subjects who are eager to please or deceive the hypnotist. I didn't hypnotize La Magdalena. I didn't use any drugs. She was entirely conscious when she spoke to me. She described her life as Mary Magdalene in much the same way you would describe events that you might recall from an earlier time in your own life."

"You said you considered schizophrenia?"

"Yes. And rejected it. She presents none of the symptoms."

"Multiple personality disorder?"

"That was one of the first possibilities I considered. But I quickly ruled it out. Those cases normally involve a change of vocal characteristics, facial expressions and attitude. La Magdalena never adopted a different personality."

"What about spirit possession?" I was going through the same checklist Dr. Stevenson normally followed in his protocols. Only after eliminating every possible alternative explanation did Stevenson feel reincarnation could be seriously considered. "You said the mother superior thought she was possessed by an evil spirit."

"That one was easy to dismiss," Serrano said. "In the first place, there is nothing inherently evil about La Magdalena's outbursts. When she raises objections to the gospel or church rituals, she doesn't spew obscenities, exhibit psychokinetic abilities or any of the other paranormal manifestations normally associated with spirit possession. She appears upset at times, yes, but her complaints are well-mannered, and well within the bounds of her normal personality.

"Cases of possession normally involve the visiting spirit taking complete control of the physical organism. I saw no evidence of such control or personality changes. When La Magdalena speaks of her past life, she appears to be a normal young woman remembering events that happened earlier."

"You said she never mentioned that past life until her eighteenth birthday? Isn't that unusual? Most of the best-documented reincarnation cases involve children."

Typical of such cases was the three-year-old girl in India who, as soon as she could talk, began to describe a past life in a town hundreds of miles away, where she had supposedly been married and lived in a small whitewashed house with a red door. Taken to the town by her dubious parents, she led them to the whitewashed house with the red door, recognized by name all the relatives from her former life, and as a final proof, confronted her former husband with details of her married life that were of so personal and intimate a nature, they were unknown to others in the same house, much less a small child who lived hundreds of miles away.

"Late-onset spontaneous recall of past lives is unusual," Padre Serrano agreed. "But not unknown. It's possible that she remembered some of it when she was younger, but was too frightened or embarrassed to tell anyone. Remember, she was raised in a convent. Thinking of the outside world, even the world of two thousand years ago, is not encouraged."

As a psychologist, I long ago learned not to trust what others told me, no matter how intelligent or well-meaning they might be. The padre seemed trustworthy and apparently believed what he was telling me, but I remained skeptical. Having at least satisfied myself that he had considered some of the various alternate explanations for his case of "reincarnation," I sat back and let him tell the story the way he wanted.

"Her name, the one given to her at the convent, is Mariamme, which is the Greek form of the Hebrew Miriam, which in its anglicized version is Mary. The other nuns started calling her La Magdalena when she began talking about her past life," Serrano explained. "At first they did it as a joke, a way of making fun of her. But now they use the name because they believe that she truly is the reborn Magdalene."

I took a sip of my *horchata*, which had grown warm while we talked.

"I went in assuming I would probably be dealing with a religious hysteric," Serrano continued. "That was based primarily on the mother superior's description of the way La Magdalena would sometimes speak in what appeared to be a totally incomprehensible language. The fundamentalists call it "speaking in tongues.""

"*Glossolalia,*" I murmured, feeling the need to remind him that I wasn't a neophyte when it came to understanding the eccentricities of the human mind.

"That's right. *Glossolalia.* In clinical terms, it's the use of an invented language known only to the speaker, or an uncontrolled outburst of gibberish, usually a symptom of hysterical compulsion or religious frenzy. But La Magdalena's version seemed more structured and had more of a natural rhythm than similar verbal outbursts from other patients I had treated. So I made a tape and sent it to a friend of mine, Professor Naghib

Abramakian, a specialist in Semitic languages and linguistics at Lebanon University. According to him, the language on the tape was Aramaic, a version of Hebrew used in Judea at the time of Christ."

This was getting more interesting. Unusual linguistic ability was one of the reincarnation "markers" Professor Stevenson reported in some of his most convincing cases. But like Stevenson, I searched for alternate explanations.

"She might have learned it at the convent," I said.

"I checked. No one in the convent speaks Hebrew, and there are no Hebrew dictionaries or language textbooks in the library. Collectively, the nuns speak Spanish, French, English, Italian, and have some understanding of Latin. But none speak Hebrew, much less the particular dialect of Aramaic, which hasn't been spoken for nearly two thousand years."

"The language didn't exactly disappear," I attempted to correct him. "Some of the Dead Sea Scrolls, as I recall, were written in Aramaic. Which means scholars can still read it."

"Yes, but that is the written language. And as anyone who studied French knows, the written language can be dramatically different from the spoken language. It's true that Jewish religious education still involves Aramaic, since there are Aramaic passages in the Old Testament, and it is the language of many other religious texts, including the Jerusalem Talmud. But to give you an idea of how obscure this language is, the version of Aramaic used in most of these ancient religious works is normally written in Hebrew script, not Aramaic script."

"And that makes it even more difficult to determine the way it was spoken," I said, following along.

"Exactly! In addition, according to Abramakian, the problem in studying the language today is further complicated by the number of distinct dialects that evolved. By the time of Christ's birth, so many dialects were spoken that they are now classified under the broad headings of 'East Aramaic' and 'West Aramaic.' Jewish Palestinian Aramaic, the language of Jesus, was one of dialects of 'West Aramaic.'"

"And supposedly, this language the young nun is speaking . . ."

"One of a number of languages she speaks," Serrano interrupted.

"This Jewish Palestinian Aramaic she supposedly speaks . . . is a language no longer spoken by anyone?"

"It is extinct, according to Abramakian. It is not only dead, but is no longer in existence in its original phonetic form . . . and hasn't been spoken in that form for nearly two thousand years."

"Well, if that's so," I wondered. "Then how can this Professor Abramakian even understand it?"

"That's a wonderful story in itself," Serrano said, clearly enjoying the way he was slowly unraveling what he thought was the cleverness of his own detective work. "It was not by accident that I contacted Professor Abramakian. He is not only one of the preeminent experts in Semitic languages, he speaks many of them fluently. Because he grew up in Lebanon, Arabic was his mother tongue, and Hebrew was an important second language. These two languages provided a linguistic entree to dozens of dialects spoken in nearby countries, which he studied during his travels in the region. One of those dialects is Syriac, which is spoken today by perhaps 200,000 people in Iraq, Turkey, Iran, and Syria. That dialect, according to Abramakian, is the closest modern phonetic link to ancient Aramaic, although the link is through Eastern, rather than Western Aramaic. Not a perfect linguistic lineage, perhaps, but good enough for our purposes. He said he was stunned when he received the tape. He said he had never actually heard any of the ancient Aramaic tongues spoken with the fluency and inflection, and what appeared to be idiomatic expressions, that he heard on the tape."

"There must be a reasonable explanation," I said. "It may not be readily apparent, but I'm sure there's an explanation."

"For one ancient language, perhaps. But she also speaks biblical Hebrew from the late period, as well as Latin."

"I assume biblical Hebrew and Aramaic are similar and there's nothing unusual about a Roman Catholic nun with a knowledge of Latin."

"I studied Latin," he said. "And I know some of the older priests who speak Latin. But she speaks the language with the facility and casual ease of someone speaking her mother tongue."

"Obviously, the result of practice," I said.

"Yes, practice would be necessary," he said. "With any language, practice is necessary to retain the facility. But where would she practice? And with whom? Since Vatican II, even the Roman Catholic Mass is no longer conducted in Latin. Our new priests have little knowledge of it. She also speaks Hellenistic Greek. Not the Greek of modern times, the one you may be familiar with, but the Greek spoken in Judea and Samaria."

"She could have picked up some words from a careful reading of the original text of the New Testaments," I said, continuing to reach for rationalizations. "The original was written in Hellenistic Greek. She could have taught herself by comparing it with English or Spanish texts."

I could see my continued disbelief was irritating Serrano.

"Then how do you explain her knowledge of what appears to be Proto-Provençal?" he asked. "Not the Provençal spoken in the South of

France today, with the addition of so many modern words, but the ancient tongue, the language used in southern Gaul under Roman occupation, before it became part of France."

"So she's multilingual."

"Please, Mr. Nikonos. Listen to what I am saying. Of course, the young woman is multilingual. She speaks the modern Spanish and English, as many of us do. But she also speaks five of what are called the 'dead tongues.' Dormant languages. The vocabularies in those four languages are frozen in ancient time. She claims to know no word in Aramaic or Latin or Greek or biblical Hebrew or Proto-Provençal for anything that was invented or discovered by the civilized world in the last two thousand years. Not just things like computers and television and airplanes and automobiles. But older concepts, such as movable type and windmills and gunpowder. This is the material of linguistic archeology. Professor Abramakian was so excited, he wanted to fly here to meet her, but of course, that was out of the question."

In spite of my professions of incredulity, I was fascinated by Serrano's story. Even if I didn't quite believe in reincarnation, there might be other mysteries here worth investigating.

"Tell me more about the disruptive behavior," I said.

"She was discovered on more than one occasion tearing pages out of the bibles in the chapel. She continues to interrupt the Mass to argue with the priest's reading of the Gospel. She refuses to pray before the crucifix, refuses to make the Sign of the Cross, refuses to wear the crucifix that is part of the order's vestment. She was once found attempting to destroy a crucifix."

"That sounds like the old Cathar heresy," I mused. "The Cathars reject the veneration of the cross and the crucifix as holy symbols. They also believe in reincarnation. Do you think she might have had access to some cache of Cathar literature?"

"I doubt it. She strongly believes in one God, that Jesus Christ was his son, that he became man. She also claims that she witnessed his Crucifixion. Those are all mainline Christian beliefs that the Cathars rejected."

"Yet she destroys the crucifix, the very symbol of her faith."

"She abhors the sight of a cross or crucifix. But she loves to tell the other nuns stories about Jesus, and about her life in Magdala and Jerusalem and the Galilee. Actually, she attracted a regular group, who have now become her loyal supporters."

"Perhaps this is all part of a plan. Maybe she wants to leave the convent, and she's trying to upset the order of things so they'll kick her out."

"Oh no, not at all. In all my interviews, she seemed perfectly content with convent life. She claims to enjoy the seclusion, the prayer, the contemplative atmosphere."

"It could be a subconscious acting-out of some repressed desire," I said, slipping into psychological jargon.

"Not that I could determine. She admitted she was fully aware of what she was doing and why. She claimed her actions were simply attempts to correct errors in the bible. Certain chapters were made up, according to her, and not based on fact. The meaning of other chapters was changed when certain contextual elements were eliminated. And many of the words of Jesus, according to her, were fabrications."

"There are a lot of modern theologians who would agree with her," I pointed out. "According to the Jesus Commission, eighty-two percent of the words attributed to Jesus Christ in the New Testament were invented."

"You and I may be aware of that. But in the convent, La Magdalena had no access to the writings of those theologians. Inside the convent walls, all modern revisionism is suppressed. Even the mother superior seems unaware of many of the theories of today's theological revisionists. Yet La Magdalena's comments on specific chapters and events in the New Testament go far beyond what even the most radical theologians dare to contend."

"And the mother superior puts up with her? Why didn't she expel her from the convent?"

"That was my question also, since I thought at first many of her actions verged on blasphemy. The mother superior tried, of course. But she told me the head of the order refused to consider turning out La Magdalena. You see, there was no place for the young woman to go."

"What about her parents? Surely she has some family on the outside?"

"No one seems to know. Apparently she was brought to the convent as an infant. Perhaps her mother was unmarried and unwilling to bear the shame of raising a child outside of wedlock. In any event, no birth certificate seems to exist. La Magdalena's ancestry is completely unknown."

Ten

THE MYSTERY WAS deepening, and with it my interest.

"There must be a record of her birth somewhere," I persisted.

"Not necessarily," Serrano replied. "She could have been born in one of the *barrios* or in the mountains, where there are no doctors. Many of the midwives in remote areas are illiterate, and can't fill out the proper forms."

"But didn't the nuns ask any questions at the time? Anyone taking in a child would want some sort of documentation. For their own legal protection, if not the child's."

"According to what I was told, the child was found in a basket on the convent doorstep."

"Like Moses in the bullrushes," I couldn't help smiling. "Do you really believe that?"

Serrano shrugged. "Leaving a child at the convent was a common tradition in medieval times. Not so much today, with all the social service programs available to poor mothers. But it happens. There is no reason to disbelieve it."

"Why didn't the nuns turn the child over to the proper authorities?"

"The Sisters of the Holy Grail live by rules which do not permit them to turn away foundlings entrusted to their care. Their charter dates back to the twelfth century, and their behavior is still quite medieval. They have little knowledge of the ways of the outside world, and no desire to participate in it. Most of their day is spent in prayer. They leave their convent only to visit the cathedral, where they meditate before the Holy Grail. When they found the newborn girl on their doorstep, they must have considered her a gift from God."

As he continued his explanation, his voice grew gentler, more sympathetic. "Can you imagine the impact such an event must have had on their austere world? Here you have a closed society of women, shut off from all contact with their loved ones. Their vows forbid them to even contemplate the possibility of motherhood. And suddenly a child appears in their midst. How they must have welcomed her. To have a child's laughter inside the convent; tiny feet running up and down the dark corridors; an innocent child smelling of powder and soap to hold and to kiss . . . it must have brought great joy to their lives."

There was a far-away look in his eyes as he spoke, as if he could visualize the young Magdalena playing her little-girl games under the watchful eyes of the black-robed surrogate mothers.

"Magdalena is a child of that world," he said. "She was raised by the nuns of one of the most restrictive orders in Spain. She must have brought great pleasure into their otherwise barren lives as they played with her and taught her their ways. But now that she is grown, she knows no other life. Perhaps the fear is that, like a rare bird suddenly released from its cage, she would be unable to survive in the outside world."

"You said perhaps."

"Yes. Perhaps. Perhaps there is some other reason, also. I find it very peculiar that the church authorities refused to take any action against her. Instead, their action was directed exclusively against me."

That was an intriguing point, and perhaps I should have pursued it, but I was interested in hearing more about the incidents of outrageous behavior. It certainly wouldn't be the first time that a child raised according to a strict moral ethic grew up into a rebellious, outspoken young woman like the one Padre Serrano described.

"You said she actually stood up and corrected the priests during Mass?"

"According to the other nuns, her favorite expression was 'That's not the way I remember it.' The priests, of course, were taken aback. But they couldn't very well forbid her from attending Mass."

"Pretty daring behavior for a nun," I said. "To openly challenge the priests like that. And during a church service, of all times."

"For a young nun, yes, it was daring. Even inconceivable. But for someone like Mary Magdalene, it would be entirely predictable. Especially when she hears the priests describe the original Magdalene as a fallen woman. That sort of language totally infuriates her. For centuries, Catholic priests have been characterizing Mary Magdalene as a harlot or a whore. Yet nowhere in the New Testament is there any language to support that claim."

"There's a reference to Jesus casting seven demons out of her," I agreed. "But that's a far cry from calling a woman a whore."

"Exactly. Today most biblical scholars and theologians agree that the "seven devils" actually referred to a mental disorder. The characterization of Mary Magdalene as a reformed prostitute seems to have originated in the second and third centuries, when for some reason certain church leaders decided it was important to destroy the Magdalene's reputation. Pope Gregory the Great made it official in the sixth century when he proclaimed that she was the "sinful woman" in Luke's Gospel, that the "seven devils" were the seven sins, and that she perfumed her flesh for sinful acts. Rome reversed Gregory's edict in 1966, but the stain remains. Of course, our little nun has no recollection of events that happened after the death of Mary Magdalene. But she assumes the criticism started with Peter."

"Peter? The apostle Peter?"

Padre Serrano nodded. "Apparently he was very jealous of her close relationship to Jesus. The way she tells it, she and Peter had some terrible rows. She's convinced he was the one who set in motion the attack on her character. As far as she's concerned, it was all part of a successful effort to exclude women from the Church hierarchy. And there's a lot of truth to that. In the early Church, women and men served as equals, following the instructions of Christ. Starting in the second century, however, men began to take over the ministries. Women were once again being relegated to the same inferior positions they occupied in the Jewish temples before the coming of Christ. Tertullian issued his order that women were not allowed to speak in church.

Women were being portrayed as the bearers of original sin. And the male leaders began to tell the most awful scandalous lies about Mary Magdalene's character. So when Magdalena says it was all part of the effort to ensure male dominance of the hierarchy, she has a point."

"So now we have Mary Magdalene, reincarnated as a feminist," I smiled.

"What she says can't be dismissed as modern feminism," Serrano insisted. "Her disputes with Peter go to the very heart of what it meant to follow Christ. She was quite specific about the discussions and arguments that took place, especially after the death and resurrection of Christ, when the Apostles were dispirited and confused. She spoke of matters that were never recorded in the canonical gospels."

"Such as the secret teachings that Jesus revealed only to her," I said.

"Yes. That's right."

"And the refusal of Peter and Andrew to believe that Jesus would not have revealed those secrets to the other apostles."

"Yes, yes. How did you know?"

"Because that particular argument between Mary Magdalene and Peter was reported, almost verbatim, in the *Berlin Codex*."

Serrano's eyes narrowed.

"Where did you hear about the *Codex*?"

"From a monk in the monastery on Mount Athos."

While most of the world's attention has been focused on the Dead Sea Scrolls, a totally separate series of discoveries, with far more direct relevance to the development of the early Christian Church, was also being studied by scholars. This was the *Nag Hammadi* Library. The *Berlin*

Codex, to which I had referred, predated the discovery of these ancient Coptic texts. It appeared suddenly in Cairo in 1896, where it was put up for sale, and made its way by a circuitous route to Berlin, where it was labeled *Papyrus Berolinensis 8502.* It purported to be the lost Gospel of Mary. It wasn't until 1945, when thirteen "books" were found in an earthenware jar in the Nag Hammadi region of Upper Egypt, that scholars were able to validate the *Berlin Codex.* The *Nag Hammadi* discovery consisted of fifty-two tractates, including The Gospel of Thomas, The Gospel of Philip, The Gospel of Truth, and fragments of the previously discovered Gospel of Mary. They proved to be fourth-century Coptic copies of lost Greek manuscripts, the originals of which dated back to the first and second centuries. The *Nag Hammadi* texts, translations of which I was permitted to read at Mount Athos, presented a far more intimate portrait of the interplay between Jesus and his followers than the traditional gospels of Matthew, Mark, Luke, and John.

"It's possible," I pointed out, "that she might have had access to some of the *Nag Hammadi* material. That would explain her knowledge of the discussions and arguments that followed Christ's death and resurrection."

If so, I realized, it would also account for her anger with Peter. Because in the Gospels, Peter continually expressed his frustration that Mary Magdalene was closer to Jesus than any of the other apostles.

"You surprise me with your knowledge," Padre Serrano said. "But surely, you know many of those second-century Greek texts were condemned by Athanasius and other early Church fathers as heretical expressions that were particularly dangerous to the Faith. They were supposed to have been destroyed. No monastery or convent was allowed to possess copies of those documents, under pain of excommunication."

"Perhaps because they emphasize the pivotal role of women in the formation of the early Catholic Church," I suggested. "Because they might challenge the traditional role of men as priests. Maybe that was why some unknown scribe was forced to hide his painfully transcribed documents in an earthenware jar in the desert."

Padre Serrano sighed and shook his head sadly.

"You think it's as simple as that," he said. "You think this is a case of a young nun who happened to read some forbidden documents and has invented a *faux persona?*"

"It's certainly a possibility," I responded.

Actually I thought it was much more than a mere possibility. Although reincarnation beliefs date back to the dim mists of prehistory, the growing interest in New Age theories has produced a bumper crop of false prophets proclaiming their existence in past lives. Some are innocent victims of their own delusions, while others practice deliberate fraud for monetary gain. The real problem, as Professor Stevenson and other researchers admit, is that past lives are almost as easy to fabricate as false credit identities.

"Perhaps you are right to be skeptical," he said. "At first your attitude troubled me, but now I think I understand. A good investigator must examine every possibility, *no*? I think you are a very good investigator. And I think that is why God sent you to me."

"Excuse me?"

"I have been praying for your arrival," he explained. "I didn't know who you would be, but I had faith you would come."

"You're back to that karma thing again."

"Call it karma, predestination, fate, whatever term you like. It's just another way of saying you were sent to me by a higher power. You came knocking at my gate when I needed you most."

"I pressed the buzzer at your gate because I was given a letter addressed to you."

"Exactly!" the priest exclaimed. He slapped his hands on the table between us, as if I had just proved his point. The backpacker had left and the counterman was noisily cleaning out the juice machine, so there was no longer a reason to fear being overheard. "And why do you think La Magdalena chose to entrust that letter to you? Out of all the people in Valencia, why would she select you to be her courier?"

"An accident." I said. "I'm just a tourist."

"Freud said there are no accidents," he reminded me. "You are a tourist who happens to be a trained investigator, who holds a master's degree in psychology, and is knowledgeable about theological matters. I would say La Magdalena made the perfect choice. You are exactly the right person for the job."

"What job?"

Even as I asked the question, I was afraid I knew what he had in mind. He adjusted his glasses and smiled.

"You are here to take over my investigation," he said. "I believe that is why you were sent to me."

"You want me to authenticate that Mary Magdalene was reincarnated as a Spanish nun?" I chuckled at the idea. "I don't think so."

"But . . . but why won't you? You are ideally suited for the assignment. You have the academic and professional background this type of case would require. I'll be glad to turn over my books and other research materials to you. I have compiled a very good library on the matter."

Serrano made it all sound so simple. But I knew that authenticating a case of reincarnation is far more difficult than it might seem. Part of the problem is that many of the indicators isolated by Stevenson and Moody and others appear to be part of the universal life experience and therefore too easily dismissed or explained away. How many of us have not experienced feelings of *déjà vu,* possess a skill that seems to "just come naturally," or have been told our behavior reminds someone of a long-dead relative? How often do we read about little children who can read or play the piano or perform complex mathematical equations while others their age are still playing with blocks?

Serrano frowned and adjusted his glasses. "If it's money you're worried about, I can assure you I will compensate you for your work. I have certain funds available, and I can get more from my family. What sort of fee do you charge?"

"It's not the money," I said. "I'm just not sure I want to get back into investigative work . . . and especially not into investigating reincarnation."

"But surely you recognize the importance of this case," he pleaded. "Can you imagine the impact of what she might remember from her past life . . . the significance to the Church and to future generations? How can I describe the enormity of it all?"

"If it's true," I pointed out. "And that's a very big *if.*"

"Of course, of course. And that's why it is so important that the matter be pursued. To discover the truth. Please, Mr. Nikonos, You must do this."

Did Serrano really think that, after two thousand years of distortion, suppression, and in some cases, outright character assassination by priests, scholars, and even popes—did he really think that anyone today could ever hope to discover enough of the truth about Mary Magdalene?

In recent times, she had become a symbol for women, an icon for Catholic feminists struggling to gain what they considered their rightful place in the Church. But the cult of the Magdalene was nothing new. The woman who was so often derided as a sinner and a whore had been an object of veneration throughout Europe, and particularly in the South of France, for centuries. The most famous of the churches dedicated to her memory was La Madeleine in Paris. But many other shrines to her memory were scattered throughout Europe. Each seemed to have a legend attached. Some of the memorials border on the grotesque, such as the procession through the streets of Provence every year on July 22, in which a human skull reputed to be that of the Magdalene is displayed to cheering crowds. Others are more benign, such as the cave at Sainte Baume, where the Magdalene was reported to have prayed in her final years. One thing they all had in common, however, was the apparent inability of archeological theologians to ever corroborate the truth about this woman who had become by now a truly mythical figure.

And if no one knew the truth about Mary Magdalene, how would it ever be possible to authenticate any claim the young nun might make about her reputed past life?

"So what do you think?" the priest asked. "Will you take the case?"

"I'm flattered that you believe I can help," I said. "And I'll admit I'm intrigued by your story. But that's all it is. A story. Everything you've told me about La Magdalena has a logical explanation."

"Ah, but I haven't told you everything. Perhaps when you see what I brought with me, you'll change your mind."

He reached under the table, lifted his robe, and from between his ankles, pulled out a battered brown briefcase.

"The vicar general thinks he has all my documents. But I saved the most important ones." He ran his hand lovingly along the top of the leather case. "I have them all here. Photographs. Maps. Tape recordings. Including Magdalena's version of the missing portion of the Gospel of Mary."

He said it so casually, I almost missed it. I had to stop for a moment and consider the importance of what he just said. Portions of all the documents in the *Nag Hammadi* had deteriorated over the centuries, leaving small gaps in the text that could only be guessed at. But something different had happened to the Gospel of Mary. Sometime during the previous millennium, someone had removed an entire section of the Gospel. It was the part that dealt with the secret teachings of Christ. All that was left behind was the introduction to the section, which suggested that it explained how Jesus Christ performed his miracles.

"Are you saying she claims to know the secret teachings of Christ?" I asked.

My sudden interest brought a smile to his face.

"Well, of course she does," Serrano said. "If she didn't, I wouldn't believe she was the re-embodied Mary Magdalene, would I? After all, she was described in the Gospel of Philip as "the woman who knew the All." And I believe that knowledge is what she was sent back to reveal to the world. "

After scanning the room once again, to be certain no one was watching, he lifted a heavy briefcase onto the table. He fitted it carefully between our beverage glasses and spread his hands over the leather surface as if it contained some great treasure.

"The Cardinal's office thinks they have all my notes," he whispered. "But what I have in here is the first half of the True Gospel of Jesus Christ, which she has been dictating to me. If I am correct about this nun being the reincarnation of Mary Magdalene, this represents the only eyewitness account of Christ's ministry. It includes part of the secret teachings of Christ, which the Gospel of Mark claims Jesus shared privately with his disciples, and which Paul claims to have learned, also." Serrano worked the combination locks with his pudgy fingers. "But the most amazing revelation it contains . . ."

When the case snapped open, the action knocked over my glass of *horchata*. I jumped up and tried to get out of the way, but it was too late. The white liquid quickly spread across the table and ran over the side, where it dripped onto my trousers.

"I'm sorry! *Lo siento!* Excuse me, how clumsy!" Padre Serrano tried to soak up the liquid with a stack of paper napkins, and offered a handful to me for my trousers.

The liquid soaked me in an embarrassing place. Fortunately, there wasn't anyone in the juice bar to notice other than the clerk. The young backpacker had disappeared.

"You'd better wash it off," Padre Serrano said. "If you don't wash it immediately, you'll have a terrible stain. I'm sorry. Really, I'm sorry."

I headed to the door marked *caballeros,* noticing, in some quirk of observation, that the young man had left his blue backpack behind.

I hardly had time to turn on the faucet when an enormous blast sent the restroom wall crashing against me. Plasterboard and two-by-fours slammed me up against the mirror on the facing wall. A powerful concussion sucked the air out of my lungs and exploded inside my ears.

Eleven

I DON'T KNOW how long I was unconscious.

When I came to, my mouth was filled with wet plaster dust. The greasy after-odor of spent explosives hung in the air. I could hear water shooting out of broken pipes around me. Insulation from the collapsed wall formed a heavy protective blanket over my back. Pieces of shattered wallboard, ceiling tile, Formica, and rolls of toilet tissue floated in the water collecting around me. My ears ached, but I could hear the sounds of the emergency sirens, faint at first but growing louder. My initial thought was to be grateful my eardrums hadn't been damaged. Slowly I flexed my fingers, moved my toes, tried to ascertain that my body parts were still in working order. The water was rising around me, collecting around my mouth.

My first two attempts to pull myself up failed. The broken wall with its framework of two-by-fours was too heavy to move. My arms kept slipping out from under me. I tried calling for help, but my throat didn't seem to want to function. It was the water that helped me to finally extricate myself. Combined with the dust and plaster and probably even the remnants of the broken soap dispenser, it formed a lubricating slurry that helped me slide out from beneath the debris.

When I at last pulled free, I was a filthy mess on shaky legs, covered with mud and dust and probably looking a lot worse than I felt. But I didn't seem to have any broken bones, and I didn't see any signs of blood on me. By some lucky stroke, I had managed to avoid getting slashed by the broken mirror. When I looked out through the shattered framing timbers, I realized just how much of a miracle it was that I had survived.

The entire interior of the juice bar had been obliterated. All that remained was a blackened cavern, soot and smoke still hanging in the air. The ceiling had been stripped of its tiles. Wires hung down from the rafters. The windows and front door were gone. The bomb, for that was what it must have been, had probably been placed near the entrance, because all the furnishings had been blasted back towards the rear, where I stood. I had to thread my way through a clutter of broken chairs and tables and pieces of the counter to search for Padre Serrano.

All that was left of him was a blood-soaked lump that had been blown into a corner, identifiable only by his brown robe. Another broken corpse was nearby, the white shirt identifying him as the counter boy.

Two local policemen rushed in, immaculate blue uniforms and highly polished shoes seeming so horribly out of place amid the wreckage. When they saw me, they immediately took me by the arms and led me outside. A crowd had already gathered, drawn by the dark impulse that always draws people to scenes of human tragedy. For a moment I thought I saw, in a doorway on the other side of the street, a familiar tall figure. But the police quickly blocked my view. I assumed they were interrogating me, but they spoke no English, and I couldn't make out what they were asking.

Soon the paramedics arrived. One went inside, while the other attended to me. He asked me a few questions in Spanish, which I didn't under-stand. Then shaking his head impatiently, he flashed a penlight in my eyes. I was familiar with the test for shock, so I followed his finger from side to side without moving my head. He checked my pulse, took my blood pres-sure, examined my scalp, and unbuttoned my shirt to check me with a stethoscope.

"You have been involved in violence before?" asked a voice in thickly accented English.

It was a deep, authoritative voice, and when I looked up, I saw it came from a distinguished-looking man in civilian clothes. He was immaculate-ly groomed, his upper lip outlined by a pencil mustache, his pomaded black hair flecked with silver at the temples. He was staring at the scar on the left side of my chest, my permanent reminder of Harrison Duquesne's attempt to kill me.

"It's not something I enjoy," I murmured.

"And where is the man who shot you?"

"He's dead."

"You must be a very lucky man," he said. "You survive a gunshot to the chest, and now you survive a terrorist bomb attack. I think I would like to talk to you further."

He made a sharp motion with his hand, and the paramedic withdrew, allowing one of the policemen to lead me to a small black van. He pushed me into the back, handcuffed me, sat me down and shackled my legs to a pipe that ran beneath the seat.

"May I have your passport please?" the distinguished-looking man said. By now I realized he was probably some high-ranking law-enforcement official. He seemed too elegant, his bearing too assured, to be an ordinary plainclothes detective.

I handed over my sodden passport. He checked to be sure my face matched the photo in the passport, and then examined the passport itself, turning it at various angles in the sunlight, as if he suspected it might have been doctored.

"What were you doing here?" he asked.

"I saw the man who left the bomb," I told him. "I'm sure I could iden-tify him if I saw him again."

The interrogator stared at me.

"How did you know the dead man . . . the one in the priest's robe?"

Something in my subconscious, some signal it was picking up from the questioner's tone of voice, warned me to be cautious in my answer.

"I didn't know him at all," I lied.

"But you were talking together."

My questioner must have a witness, I thought. But how was that possible, since he had time to speak to no one except me?

"It was just a casual conversation," I replied. "I'm a tourist, and I was asking directions."

"Directions to where?"

"To the cathedral." It was all I could think of.

"You were in the bathroom when the bomb was detonated . . ."

"Yes. A drink spilled on my pants, and I had to clean it off."

He looked down at my pants, and shook his head. With the water and dirt that had soaked into my trousers, I realized there would be no way to corroborate that part of my story.

"You talk with the priest, then you get up and go to the bathroom, and he is killed by a bomb."

"Basically, yes. That's what happened. But there was another person here. A young man with a blue backpack. The bomb must have been in the backpack."

"And where is this other person?"

"He left."

"Yes. And you went to the bathroom. Isn't that, *como se dice,* very convenient? Perhaps you went to the bathroom to hide from the explosion."

"I wasn't hiding!" I knew it wasn't a good idea to raise my voice, but I didn't like where he was going with this. "If you have a police artist, I can give him a description of the man who left the backpack. He was young and thin and had a small beard. The bomb must have been in the backpack he left out front, because all the furniture was blown into the back of the room."

"You know something about bombs, do you?"

"It's just . . . common sense," I said. "Anyway, I already told you, the young man left before I went to the bathroom."

"But if you did not go to the bathroom, you would be dead also, is that not so?"

"Well, yes, but . . ."

"Take him away," he told the policeman. "I'll talk to him later."

Twelve

I WAS TAKEN to the Valencia headquarters of the *Guardia Civil*, the Spanish national police force. There is no precise American counterpart to this unit, which handles matters of public order considered too important or too sensitive for local law-enforcement officials

I didn't question or protest the action. I allowed myself to be led along, the shock of the bombing rendering me temporarily docile. My brain attempted to avoid dealing with the horror I had just witnessed, a classic example of a psychological defense mechanism at work. Rather than dwell on the death of Padre Serrano and my own narrow escape, my brain concentrated instead on the minutiae of my surroundings: the outdated computers on the *Guardia* desks, the portrait of King Juan Carlos on the wall, the beautifully carved arm of the chair to which I was handcuffed, the vague smell of cigar smoke that lingered in a room where no one appeared to be smoking.

What helped bring me out of my state of fugue was my surprising discovery of the quality of the coffee the Spanish police enjoy at work. Handcuffed to a chair in a busy police station, I was served what was probably the finest cup of coffee I ever tasted. Unlike the warm brown liquid that masquerades as coffee in most American restaurants and offices, the rich and aromatic brew that I was offered seemed to be pure Arabica. Although it came in a plastic cup, it had a topping of luxurious pale brown froth. Along with the coffee came an accompanying cup half-filled with real cream, and four paper-wrapped sugar cubes on the side. For a moment, I imagined myself back at my local Starbucks, loading up on my favorite flavor of caffeine. But I was quickly brought back to reality by a guard who led me away to be fingerprinted and photographed.

Although I suspected most of the *Guardia* I encountered spoke at least some English, they seemed to go out of their way to pretend they didn't. They directed me through a combination of sign language and simple words that any tourist should know: *Sí. . . no . . . por favor . . . está aquí . . . prohibido . . .* plus a lot of arm waving and finger pointing. I assumed it was one of their interrogation techniques, a trick they used in the hope they might overhear some vital admission from an unsuspecting English-speaking prisoner.

After being fingerprinted and photographed, I was taken to a narrow room where an attractive young woman waited behind a table that contained a small rectangular vat of waxy-smelling liquid. With the smile of someone who enjoyed her work, she immediately plunged my hands into the scalding liquid and held them there for what seemed a horribly long time, but was probably only ten or fifteen seconds. The liquid turned out to be melted paraffin. Not quite as hot as boiling water, but intense enough to be painful. My hands came out with a pale white glove-like coating of wax. The procedure was repeated four times, until the layer of wax was thick enough for her to peel off a cast of each hand. It would be examined, I assumed, for evidence of some sort.

From there, I was led to another room, where a bored guard ordered me to remove my *"camiseta y pantalones y zapatos, por favor."*

"Para evidencia," he explained.

Judging my size (correctly, it turned out) he reached under a long counter and brought out a T-shirt, a pair of neatly pressed grey slacks, socks, and plastic bedroom slippers. I was thankful that they had no need for my undershorts.

Another guard led me to what appeared to be a high-security holding area. It was a long corridor lined on both sides with windowless steel doors. Each door had a peephole at eye level, and a narrow slot near the floor which I assumed was for meal trays. The cell to which I was led contained a single cot, a toilet, a sink, and a small table and chair. A single overhead light, protected by a grid of metal bars, provided meager illumination. There was no switch on the wall, which suggested the light was controlled from some central location. The physical layout wasn't much different from my prison cell at Riker's Island. But when the guard's footsteps disappeared down the long corridor, I felt far more frightened than I ever did at Riker's. I was an American in a foreign jail, maybe a more civilized jail than those Turkish prisons demonized by Hollywood scriptwriters, but still a place where a prisoner's rights often start and end with his jailer's moods. The game here was played according to Spanish rules, and although Generalissimo Franco was long gone from the scene, the old dictator's spirit still ruled the *Guardia Civil*.

There was no point in screaming or banging on the door and demanding to see the American Consul General. With the guards pretending not to speak any English, all my requests were dismissed with a shrug: *"No hablo Ingles."*

I was allowed no phone call, given no opportunity to contact a lawyer.

All I could do was wait.

Stare at the walls.

And think.

Eight hours earlier, I was just another American tourist seeing the sights of Valencia. Now, two men were dead, I had been mugged, narrowly missed being killed myself, and here I was, sitting in jail apparently as a suspect in a terrorist bombing. I hoped I would quickly be released as an innocent bystander, but there was much about this society and its customs that I didn't understand.

Serrano was frightened long before I ever met him. He spoke of important people who had taken an interest in La Magdalena's case and seemed to almost expect an attack on his life. But what, really, was he worried about? His work with a young nun claiming to be the reincarnation of Mary Magdalene? A controversial case for a Jesuit psychiatrist, perhaps, but certainly nothing that would merit killing him.

What of La Magdalena herself? She warned me of danger, too. By what chance of fate did she select me to be her messenger? Why did I not walk away when her breast insinuated itself against my hand? Was it because it was really I who subconsciously placed my hand in position to touch the forbidden fruit?

And where did the old priest at the cathedral fit into all of this?

His last words to me were an eerily exact repetition of the last words that were spoken to me during my near-death experience.

If the work I was supposedly sent back from the dead to finish was so important, then why were the powers that sent me back allowing me to sit here in jail?

Anwar Sadat, Nelson Mandela, and others have eloquently described the almost mystical insights that were visited upon them during their periods of solitary confinement, but no such enlightenment seemed to await me that night. When the cell door closed and the lights went out, I was confused, frightened, and exhausted. All I wanted was some sleep. My mind was too tired to seek any insight other than to wonder when I might be released.

The only thing I knew for certain was that I would probably be summoned for further interrogation in the middle of the night. It was a standard technique, perfected by jailers over the centuries. In those desolate hours before dawn comes the moment of weakest psychological resistance. It is the time when our biological clock is at its nadir, leaving the strongest of us feeling most vulnerable. It is the time when the night demons prowl, waking the healthiest of us to worries that we manage to suppress during the daylight hours. For a prisoner in solitary confinement, whose body is crying out for rest, the predawn hours are the time when jailers know that careful questioning produces the best results.

Knowing the psychology behind middle-of-the-night interrogations didn't help me very much when the guard opened my cell door. I was exhausted, fearful, and compliant.

He led me to a brightly lit room which was bare except for two heavy wooden chairs that were bolted to the floor. The walls were grey, as was the metal door. A small two-way mirror was set into one wall. Waiting for me was the neatly groomed plainclothes officer from the bombing site.

"I am *Coronel* Fulgencio Velarde," he said. "I am sorry to disturb your sleep. But I have some questions to ask of you."

I slumped down in one of the chairs and closed my eyes. With luck, I thought, I could doze off during the interview.

My captor kicked the chair.

"You will please to remain awake while I am talking."

"Some coffee would help," I said. It wasn't that I really wanted to stay awake, but a desire to feign a lack of fear. "Or maybe this close to morning, I should be ordering hot chocolate and *churros*."

"Perhaps when we are finished here," he said. He stood directly behind me. I didn't give him the courtesy of turning to face him. "You suffered no injuries from the explosion, except for a small burn on the back of your right hand."

He reached down and turned over my hand so that he could examine the reddened flesh for himself. The mark had taken on the shape of a vertical slash, wider in the middle and pointed at both ends.

"Insignificant," he sneered, dropping my hand. "I'm sure you don't even notice it."

I shrugged, trying to feign disinterest.

"Two men are dead," he went on. "Disfigured so badly that identification has to be made from the papers they carried. Yet you sustain only a minor red mark on the back of your hand. How do you explain that?"

"I already told you, I went to the men's comfort room. I spilled some *horchata* on my trousers, and I had to wash it off."

"You were sharing drinks with the priest," the *Coronel* said. "What were you discussing?"

"The typical tourist questions," I replied, desperately trying to remember what I had told him at the scene. That was another reason for middle-of-the-night interrogations: fatigue makes it harder to remember any lies told earlier. "I was asking him about the cathedral."

"*Sí, sí* . . . the cathedral. You were there earlier in the day."

Had I told him that? I didn't remember.

"There was an incident outside the cathedral," he said. He moved around to the front of me, probably to look for some signals in my face that would reveal when I was lying. "You were accosted by someone . . . a man with a wide-brimmed hat."

I tried to cover my surprise by faking anger. "That stupid bastard," I muttered. "A clumsy tourist in a rush . . . he knocked me over and didn't even have the courtesy to apologize."

"You never met him before?"

"No. And I hope I never bump into him again."

"That is a pun." The *Coronel* gave me a frozen smile. "You have an odd sense of humor, Mr. Nikonos. After you see two men die, you are still able to make the joke?"

"I didn't mean it as a joke."

He placed his hands on the arms of the chair and leaned in closer, so close I could smell the floral fragrance of his after-shave lotion.

"Did anything change hands during your encounter with the clumsy tourist? Did you give him anything?"

Of course that was part of the central question I had been puzzling over in my cell. The envelope that was stolen was intended for Padre Serrano. Could the message in the envelope have somehow precipitated his death?

"No." I lied as convincingly as I could. "Nothing changed hands."

"No document? No piece of paper?"

"Absolutely not," I had learned to lie with authority on the Duquesne case, and how to divert uncomfortable questions. "Speaking of documents," I countered. "Padre Serrano had a briefcase with him. What happened to it?"

"Why do you care?" The *Coronel* asked. "You said you hardly knew him."

"It might be evidence. He acted as if he had important documents in the briefcase. That might be a motive for the bombing."

"I doubt it," the *Coronel* sniffed.

"Then why is the briefcase missing?"

"You tell me."

"Maybe it was stolen by the man who set the bomb."

"And maybe it was taken by you, Mr. Nikonos."

It was a ridiculous charge, but I couldn't be sure whether he was being serious or not. Standard interrogation technique is to throw a steady stream of charges at the subject, partly to intimidate, partly in the hope that one of the charges will elicit an admission.

"And maybe it was taken by the police," I responded.

His face remained impassive. He sat down in the chair facing me.

"According to Interpol, you were arrested for murdering two people in New York," he said.

"I was acquitted."

"That does not mean you were innocent," he argued. "It simply means there was not enough evidence to convict you."

"The jury was polled after the trial, and every one of them said I was not guilty."

"You had a very good lawyer."

"The only one who would take the case was my ex-wife's husband."

"It was an interesting defense strategy. Your lawyer claimed you couldn't have killed them because you were dead at the time."

"Interpol supplies trial reports, too?" I asked.

"No," he said with a smile. "I accessed the *New York Times* archives on the Internet. Apparently your whole defense revolved around a near-death experience."

"The paramedics revived me. They said I was dead for at least six and a half minutes."

"And the jury believed them," he said with a sneer.

"There was a lot more to the case than that," I said.

"Yes. The location of the gun and the money. You knew the bank account numbers, the total balances, and you told the police where to find the murder weapon. That proves you were guilty."

"It was information I brought back from the afterlife. It proves the reality of the near-death experience."

"Yes, of course. That was your defense. But the issue of credibility remains."

We were parrying, neither of us trusting the other, each of us hoping to extract some insight into the other's motives. Contrary to what I'm sure he expected, I seemed to grow stronger, more alert as the questioning went on. Perhaps it was his probing of the Duquesne case that got my adrenaline flowing. The memory of that tragic investigation, never far from the surface, continued to stir powerful emotions within me.

"If you want to know the truth about the Duquesne case, read my book," I snapped. "Now let's talk about the bombing. Why don't you bring in a sketch artist, so I can give him a description of the young man with the backpack?"

We went on like this for an hour, the *Coronel* ignoring my theory of the bombing, seeming more interested in my background. I assumed he was making a case against me, and after a while, I became less combative, less talkative. I retreated into a careful pattern of one-word answers and nods of the head. Talking less, I observed more. He was a man who was very careful about his appearance. I could see that the silver hair that adorned his temples was an artistic choice rather than an accident of nature: barely discernible grey roots on the top of his head suggested it would soon be time for another bout of hair coloring. His fingernails were freshly manicured. A coat of clear polish glistened in the light. His thin mustache gleamed with wax. Was it dyed, also?

In the top buttonhole of his right lapel was a tiny gold pin. At first, I had thought it was some sort of *Guardia Civil* decoration. Perhaps an award or medal of merit. But closer examination revealed the design to be a circle, in the center of which were two mounted knights on a single horse, each carrying a shield and sharing a single upraised lance.

I had seen that symbol before.

Never on a pin. Never on an actual member. I had seen it in books and research documents, in museums and carved into the walls and over the entrances of some of Europe's greatest cathedrals. Two men, knights in armor, astride a single horse, bearing a single lance. It was the symbol of an ancient brotherhood: a secret society that I assumed had long ago passed into oblivion.

The *Coronel* caught me staring at the tiny pin.

Our eyes locked in a moment of recognition.

He immediately rose and announced the interrogation was over.

Thirteen

I DREAMT OF Laura Duquesne that night.

It was my usual dream, the one where I watch in slow motion as she steps in front of a bullet that is meant for me. I am lying on the floor, already shot once in the chest. The second bullet, the one she takes, is aimed at my head. She lets out a grunt as the bullet tears through her stomach. I watch helplessly for perhaps the thousandth time as Laura throws herself against the gunman, knocking him off balance. As he crashes through the window, his hand reaches out in one last desperate effort to save himself. He grabs at Laura's arm, succeeding only in pulling her out the window with him. The dream ends, as it always does, with me left behind to die while the only woman I ever truly loved falls eight stories to her own death atop a parked van.

The dream never shows what happened after my death: how I traveled across the astral plane into the afterlife, where an incorporeal Laura took my hand and guided me into the loving presence of the Being of Light. The Laura who lives on in the afterlife never appears in my dream. The Laura who is waiting there now for me, my beloved otherworld Laura who until today was the only woman who occupied my waking thoughts . . . that Laura remains just beyond the reach of my deepest REM dreams. For reasons I fully understand, but can yet do nothing about, the part of my brain responsible for creating dream images cannot normally break itself loose from the central fact of those horrifying moments: Laura died that I might live.

And always, when I awaken, the first question in my mind is whether her sacrifice was worth it.

Before my trial, a court-appointed psychiatrist explained to me that the dream never moves beyond the moment of Laura's death because I had not yet successfully worked through the grieving process.

I knew the psychology of grieving as well as the court-appointed psychiatrist, and I knew his diagnosis was correct. That knowledge didn't help me, however. There seemed to be nothing I could do. Until I found a way to break the psychological block, the dream would continue to unfold in the same manner.

The knowledge that Laura was waiting for me on the Other Side was little consolation. Why did she leave me behind? Why give up her life to save me, knowing the grief I would feel at her loss? Those were the questions that haunted me, the questions I asked myself every night and at odd, unbidden moments during the day.

Fourteen

THEY CAME FOR me in the morning.

Two guards opened my cell door just as I was dipping my last *churro* into the thick hot chocolate I was served for breakfast. They led me not to the interrogation room, but to the office of *Coronel* Velarde. It was a small, somber chamber, with heavy black chairs and an antique desk that was notably free of clutter. His full name, Fulgencio Victor Velarde, was etched in large letters on a bronze nameplate from which two pens protruded. A small bottle of ink, with a blotter nearby, indicated that the pens were the old-fashioned dipping variety. On the wall behind the desk was the usual color photograph of King Juan Carlos, as well as a lithograph of the Duke of Ahomada, a silvery-haired member of the nobility whom I would later learn was the founder of the *Guardia Civil*.

The guards waited with me until *Coronel* Velarde entered the room and dismissed them with a barely perceptible nod of his head. The *Coronel* looked tired, although he appeared freshly shaved and as carefully groomed as ever. His dark blue suit had been changed to a pale blue pinstripe, so I assumed he had managed to go home and get a little rest. The gold lapel pin was absent from his new suit. Was it the oversight of a tired policeman? Or was it a belated attempt to conceal his membership in the mysterious society?

The *Coronel* sat down behind his desk and made a show of examining his papers, signing his name to some, dropping others in the wastebasket.

"The paraffin test was negative," he said at last, as if noticing my presence for the first time. "And there were no traces of explosive residue found on your clothing. That does not mean you had nothing to do with the bombing. It simply means the bomb was constructed by someone other than yourself."

It was typically circular police logic, I thought. No different from the flawed reasoning that led to my indictment in New York.

"The man you met in the juice bar, the man you claim was Padre Javier Serrano, how did you come to know him?"

I had already lied once, to protect the identity of La Magdalena. I had no choice but to continue with the lie.

"I told you last night, I'm a tourist. I was just asking directions."

"You met him twice. At the juice bar, and earlier at the Jesuit *Residencia* on *Calle Nueva Ecija*. What sort of directions did you need that required two meetings?"

Lying to a policeman is like playing chess. It requires thinking two falsehoods ahead, and anticipating the direction the questioning might take. Fortunately, I had already learned from the interrogation last night that I had been under surveillance outside the cathedral. That I would have been followed to *Calle Nueva Ecija* came as no surprise, and I was prepared with an easy answer.

"I was lost," I said with a shrug. "The guy who knocked me over at the cathedral trampled my Michelin map. It was dirty and torn, so I threw it away. I got lost in the narrow streets, so I knocked on a door to ask directions."

Part of it was true. The map was trampled when I was knocked over, and I eventually did throw it away, and the police surveillance report would document that I did indeed ring the doorbell at the *Residencia*. The blending of fact with falsehood has long been recognized by behaviorists as the most effective method of achieving the illusion of truth.

"There was a struggle at the door," the *Coronel* said. "You tried to push your way in."

"The door was stuck," I lied, having already anticipated that the argument would have been observed. "Padre Serrano asked me to help him push it back and forth until the hinge loosened."

The questioning continued for a while, in a more or less perfunctory manner. My nervousness lessened, and I began to relax. Velarde seemed to accept my answers without challenge, apparently more interested in the contents of the folder before him. In fact, as I soon discovered, he was lulling me into a false sense of confidence. I should have seen it coming when *Coronel* Velarde finally looked up at me and smiled.

"Why do you keep calling him Padre Serrano?" he asked. "You know perfectly well that the man who was killed by the bomb was not Padre Javier Serrano."

Fifteen

"THE MAN WHO was killed in the explosion, the one wearing a priest's robes, was not the man you claim he was," the *Coronel* elaborated. "We were able to obtain Padre Serrano's records from the archdiocese. He is not in Valencia at the moment. He is currently on leave, traveling somewhere in South America. According to his medical records, which we obtained, the real Padre Serrano is 157 centimeters tall, weighs 78 kilos, has an appendectomy scar on his navel and has type O negative blood. It required little more than a cursory examination to establish the fact that the dead man is not Padre Serrano."

I was dumbfounded.

"Perhaps mistaken identity . . ." I struggled for an explanation. "Maybe there's another Padre Serrano."

"Not in Valencia," *Coronel* Velarde said. "Either you are lying, or you have been deceived."

I had been lying, of course, lying to protect La Magdalena; but not lying about my belief that the man I met was Padre Javier Serrano. It was inconceivable to me that I had been deceived. The man had sounded so genuine, so knowledgeable, so careful about establishing my identity. Why had I not been as careful about his identification? For someone who prided himself on his research capabilities, I had acted foolishly.

"Perhaps you are now prepared to tell me the truth," the *Coronel* said. "Who was this man?"

"All I know is that he called himself Padre Serrano. He said he was a Jesuit."

"And you believed him?"

"I had no reason not to. I'm not a policeman. I don't make it a practice of asking people to prove their identity."

The *Coronel* studied me carefully. Although the research shows that some facial clues such as pupil dilation can, in fact, reveal inner tensions, there are no universal physical indicators of untruthfulness. Nevertheless, *Coronel* Velarde kept his dark eyes trained on me, as if the intensity of his gaze would force my face to reveal some telltale sign of deception.

If he saw anything, it was probably my confusion as my mind tried to cope with his revelation. If the man claiming to be Padre Serrano was an imposter, then it called into question everything he told me about La Magdalena. All that business about her belief that she was the reincarnated Magdalene, her knowledge of ancient languages, her strange behavior in chapel, and the following she had developed among the other nuns: was it all a fiction?

And if so, why?

Suddenly, I was questioning everything. If Serrano wasn't a priest, was La Magdalena really a nun? Or was she an accomplice in some incredible fraud? But fraud, as my insurance investigative work taught me, was always tied to money. Where was the profit in pretending to be Mary Magdalene? Was it intended to be part of some sort of religious blackmail? Perhaps an attack on the Church hierarchy? They were questions without answers. The only thing I knew for certain was that two men were dead, and it was a matter of pure luck that I was still alive.

I snapped out of my reverie at the sound of *Coronel* Velarde's voice.

"We have determined that the bombing was a terrorist act. No one has yet claimed credit for it, but it appears to be the responsibility of the Basque Separatist group known as ETA."

I had read about the Basque separatists and the bombings they employed to call attention to their cause. But after my experience in New York with policemen who quickly jumped to the easiest conclusion, it sounded a little too convenient an explanation.

"I thought the Basques were up north, along the French border."

"Terrorists do not limit their bombings to their own territory," he said. "There is a history of Basque activity in Valencia. During the Civil War, they held territory on the other side of the river. And recently there was a bombing south of us, in Málaga." As if that wasn't enough, he added, "We have identified your mysterious backpacker as a member of ETA. We know him only as Nestor. But a likeness has been distributed to the press. A nationwide search is under way."

"But a juice bar?" I persisted. "He came all the way down to Valencia to bomb a juice bar? How does that further the Basque cause?"

"When we learn the identity of the man who was impersonating a priest, we will have the answer. Perhaps he was the head of a rival group. Or perhaps . . ." he paused and smiled. "Perhaps the bomb was meant for you."

I stiffened. It was something I hadn't considered. But why? Because of my contact with La Magdalena? Was there something about her so dangerous that anyone who came near her must pay with his life? Was that why the man who called himself Serrano had seemed so frightened?

"Is there anything further you wish to say?" *Coronel* Velarde asked.

"No . . . I don't think so."

"Then we have no reason to hold you any longer." He tossed my passport on his desk, as if happy to be rid of it. No one had bothered to clean the mud off the cover, and water damage had left the pages wrinkled and warped. "You may go now."

I rose slowly. There was still one other item nagging at me.

"I didn't give you much of a description of the backpacker," I said. "And you didn't send any police artists in to see me . . ."

"We already have a sketch of the suspect, which has been released to the press. An eyewitness saw him leave the bar moments before the explosion."

Of course, I thought. The "eyewitness" was undoubtedly the policeman who had been following me. I left the *Coronel*'s office with a greater respect for the efficiency of the *Guardia Civil*.

The good feeling lasted only as far as the nearest newsstand. The headlines blared *"MUERTE!" "ETA BOMBARDE!"* The front pages of all the newspapers displayed photographs of the bombed-out interior of the juice bar, along with the police sketch of the suspected bomber.

He was pictured wearing the traditional Basque beret. He appeared to be a middle-aged man, with a square-cut face, thick eyebrows, a bushy mustache, and a scowling mouth. It was an evil face, the very image of the quintessential terrorist bomber. I could believe him guilty of anything.

The only problem was that I had never seen the man before in my life.

The face that stared back at me from the newspapers, the likeness that had been supplied by the *Guardia Civil*, bore absolutely no resemblance to the thin young backpacker I had seen in the juice bar.

There might be a nationwide search going on, but they were looking for the wrong man.

Sixteen

SOMEONE LESS SUSPICIOUS of police agencies than I might think that such misidentification was an honest mistake, the result of faulty information or some bureaucratic error. But I had spent nearly two hours in the interrogation room with *Coronel* Velarde, and I was convinced he was far too clever to make such a blunder, particularly in a high-profile bombing case.

I wandered through the streets of Valencia, trying to think it through.

Producing the sketch of the man with the beret required the cooperation of a police artist, the production of an obliging eyewitness, and the creation of a paper trail that would inevitably lead back to the *Coronel*. Issuing a nationwide alert based on faulty, if not deceptive, information was a breathtaking risk for a mid-level police official. It made me wonder if others, higher up in the *Guardia*, might be involved.

I bought an ear of roasted sweet corn from a vendor on the *Gran Via,* and nibbled at it as I continued my aimless trek through the city.

It was entirely possible that the *Coronel* truly believed it was an ETA bombing. But if he did, I couldn't understand why he ignored my description of the backpacker; why he refused my request to meet with the police artist; or why he never showed me the sketch of the man with the beret before releasing it to the press. Even the rawest police recruit would have followed those basic procedural steps.

Unless, of course, they were ordered otherwise.

I assumed I was still being followed by one or more of Velarde's men, but I gave no hint that I was aware of their presence. When the time came to evade them, I wanted to take them by surprise.

I ran various scenarios through my mind as I walked. The idea that Velarde's superiors might be involved was intriguing. Padre Serrano had warned me that powerful people were interested in La Magdalena. And who in Spain was more influential than the people at the top of the *Guardia Civil,* who in a breathtaking display of power had once engineered the armed takeover of the entire Spanish parliament?

Lost in thought, I wandered into an unfamiliar part of the city, beyond the borders of the usual tourist district. I happened to glance up at a figure standing behind an upstairs window across the street. There must have been hundreds of other figures in upstairs windows that I had passed without ever looking up. What serendipity caused this particular window to draw my gaze, I still don't know.

The building occupied the entire block, with round castlelike turrets rising above the corners. In the middle of the third floor, at the only window in which the blinds were not drawn, stood a pale figure, her face surrounded with white. I stopped, stunned by what I saw.

The building was the *Convento de las Hermanas del Sangreal.*

The figure in the window was La Magdalena.

There are those who would say it was the working of destiny that brought me to this particular part of town, to this precise place, and moved me to look up at this building at the exact moment that she happened to be looking out the window. I prefer the more mundane explanation: that I had noted the location of the convent on my tourist map when I was looking for Serrano's address, and with my thoughts focused on La Magdalena after I was released from jail, had subconsciously gravitated to the area, where I recognized the fortress-like building as the convent. Looking up was a natural reaction. I have no explanation for why she happened to be at the window looking down at that precise moment, but then, there are many things about La Magdalena that I still can't explain.

Whatever the reason, there she was, staring down at me, our eyes meeting and instantly recognizing each other.

At first, I was frightened. I was certain Velarde had someone following me. And it was obvious that the convent itself was under surveillance. A man leaning in the doorway directly across from the convent glanced at me over the top of his newspaper. The windows of a delivery van parked nearby were masked with black plastic to keep the identity of its passengers secret. How many others were watching her, as she raised her right hand and placed it palm outward against the window, as if she was trying to reach out to me?

Perhaps sensing that she was being observed, she stepped back from the window, to a point in the shadows where she could barely be seen, even by me. She put her left hand under her robe, as she had done in the cathedral, and pantomimed the motion of handing me the envelope.

I understood the charade all too well. She wanted to know if I had delivered her message.

I lowered my eyes, ashamed to look at her. I moved my head from side to side, slowly at first and then faster, no longer caring who was watching, who was following, as I signaled back that I had failed.

She had entrusted me with a simple mission, and I had failed.

A moment of carelessness outside the cathedral had set in motion a dreadful sequence of events. If I had but managed to hold on to her envelope and deliver it to the man for whom it was intended, and then walk away, would I have been able to avert the tragedy that ensued? The priest had warned me that danger awaited anyone involved with the nun who watched me from the window above. Now the priest was dead and only a fortuitous trip to the restroom spared my life.

A rational human being might say that was the moment when I should have walked away . . . put my head down and just continued on my way, leaving the nun, the convent, the *Guardia Civil,* and Valencia behind. It wasn't my problem, I told myself. The safest course of action would be to catch the next flight to Greece, or London, or even back to New York.

But like a jungle creature roused from its sleep by the scent of a passing prey, something inside me was beginning to stir. I could feel the quickening of old instincts and skills that had lain dormant while I recovered from my physical and mental wounds.

Before his death, Padre Serrano had pleaded with me to continue his work, to investigate the mysterious young nun's claims. It was a case I hadn't wanted to take. But now I was beginning to think I had no choice. His death, I was convinced, was connected somehow to her. I might not believe in reincarnation, but I did believe in bringing killers to justice.

When I looked up at the convent window again, the nun known as La Magdalena was gone. The window was empty. The wooden shutters were closed. Had I really seen her, or was it some glassine mirage, an illusion created by a chance reflection of light? And yet, strangely, it didn't matter to me whether she had been there or not.

I was no longer an investigator without a case.

My client was dead, and there was no one to pay me, but I had a mystery to solve.

Seventeen

NOW THAT I was on a case again, I felt like a different person. During my year of idle drifting, I had forgotten the feeling of elation, the heightened sensitivity that comes with living on the edge.

My senses were on full alert. I seemed more aware of my immediate surroundings, more cautious of what awaited me around the corner. I felt energized by the prospect of the chase. Layers of depression and confusion and, yes, even self-doubt fell away, exposing a clarity of thought and purpose. Like some mystical recording tape, my thought processes rolled back twenty-four hours to the scene outside the cathedral, to the image of an ancient priest who came to my assistance.

"You still have work to do, my son," he whispered as he backed away. *"But believe not everything you hear."*

I ran those last words over in my mind again.

" . . . believe not everything you hear."

Velarde had me believing I had been lied to by an imposter.

But I now believed the reverse was true. *Coronel* Velarde was the one who was not to be believed. I was certain that everything he told me from the moment of the bombing was an elaborate and carefully crafted lie. Not just the obvious falsification of the police sketch, but the involvement of the Basques and the ETA group, as well as the identity of the man I met in the juice bar. The *victima no identificada,* as he was described in the newspapers, really was Javier Serrano. The question was why Velarde was lying.

"You still have work to do."

When I heard those words just before I was unwillingly sent back from the dead, I had assumed the "work" I was intended to perform was to focus public attention on the reality of life after death, a work I thought I had completed with the publication of my book, *The Authenticator.* But perhaps, I realized now, perhaps that was the beginning, rather than the end, of the reason I was sent back to Earth. Which meant it was time for me to get on with that work.

I led whoever was following me into the tourist district, to the *Plaza de Toros.* Located beside the RENFRE rail station, the bullring is a natural magnet for out-of-towners, as well as the fifty thousand *afficionados* who regularly show up to cheer on their favorite *matadors.* As a result, the usual agglomeration of vendors remains in almost permanent residence outside its walls.

I bought a bag of freshly roasted peanuts and took my place among the crowd of tourists strolling among the vendors' stalls. I made no attempt to lose my follower. Eventually, hoping to make it seem like a spur-of-the-moment decision, I sat down to have a portrait drawn by a young artist who billed himself as Aquelino Acevida. My reason for choosing Aquelino from the six other artists plying their trade was his facility with English, and his willingness to follow directions. I had him turn his easel to face me, so that I could watch his progress. As I munched my peanuts, I gave him specific directions for the facial characteristics I wanted emphasized in the portrait. Hoping to keep my follower from seeing what I was up to, I made a point of searching the crowd for faces. If he was any good at his assignment, he would blend into the background and avoid coming close enough to see what I was really up to.

Aquelino was a talented artist who did exactly as he was told. Within minutes, he produced a sketch that looked completely unlike me. The likeness he so skillfully captured was that of the backpacker who left the bomb in the juice bar.

I now had my own sketch of the suspect.

My next stop was the Jesuit *Residencia*.

I hadn't yet determined how to make contact with La Magdalena, but I knew I wasn't yet ready for our first encounter. I would have to prepare myself, review reincarnation theory and the relevant psychological, theological, philosophical, and scientific materials, and gather as many facts as possible about the life and times of Mary Magdalene. Only when I was armed with such intellectual weaponry would I feel qualified to meet La Magdalena. I hoped to find what I needed at Padre Serrano's quarters. It would have been the first stop for the *Guardia,* who must have already searched the premises and removed anything they thought pertinent to their investigation. What I sought would probably not have been considered important enough to cart away. The problem, however, was going to be getting past the front gate. For the "*victima no identificada*" fiction to work, the other priests must also have been enlisted in the deception, which meant I would be stopped at the front gate with the *Guardia's* lie that Serrano was alive and well in South America.

How could I possibly talk my way inside?

I always believed my academic background provided the ideal training for a private investigator. I have never handled a gun, and hope I never have to. My weapons of choice were the intellectual variety. I was schooled in logic and analytical thinking. Years of research work had taught me how to find and evaluate the most obscure information, including, in this instance, the names of the individuals who would get me past the front gate.

After two phone calls, I set out for *Calle Nueva Ecija*.

"Quién es?" asked the voice on the other side of the gate.

Using language from a Spanish phrase book, I demanded to see Padre Jose Silva, rector of the *Residencia*. His name had easily been obtained on one of my telephone calls.

The gate opened and I was greeted by a bony woman with severely cropped grey hair. She wore a black mourning dress and her eyes, in confirmation of my belief about Serrano, were swollen from weeping.

"Un momento, por favor," she murmured, bowing her head and motioning for me to wait.

I knew I was being watched, probably from across the street, but possibly from inside the courtyard, too.

The rector looked more like a soldier than a priest, with greying hair cut in the short military style, an angular face, and the stern visage of a man accustomed to giving orders. Under other circumstances, he might have successfully intimidated me. But this wasn't a social call.

"You are Padre Jose Silva?" I tried to sound casual, as if I did this all the time.

"Sí."

"It is my pleasure to meet you." I extended my hand in greeting. "I bring regards from the vicar general, Ernesto Del Pilar." My second telephone call had produced the vicar general's name, as well as the fact that he was in Rome with the cardinal for a meeting with the pope. That meant I could use his name as freely as I chose, without fear of being found out.

The rector shook my hand. "And you are . . .?"

"My name is Nikonos. Theophanes Nikonos. I am here to remove Padre Serrano's books."

The rector told his preprogrammed lie without the slightest hesitation, "Padre Serrano is on vacation." It was the same falsehood I heard from *Coronel* Velarde. "Somewhere in South America, I believe."

"Please, Padre, I know the truth. Padre Serrano was killed yesterday in the bombing."

The statement I thought would have startled the rector drew only a single raised eyebrow in response.

"I met with him yesterday," I continued. "I argued with him at the gate."

If *Coronel* Velarde knew about the argument, then certainly the rector did, too. The housekeeper, whom I was certain was listening to the conversation while she pretended to sweep the area around the fountain, had probably told them all about it. Now it was time for my own lies.

"He was supposed to turn over all his books to me."

"I know nothing of this."

"It has to do with the La Magdalena situation," I said, mixing what little Serrano had told me with the fabrication I concocted on the way over. "We have Serrano's files, but just to be safe, the vicar general's office would also like to have all the books and research materials that might be related to her case. I came here yesterday to recover those materials. But Padre Serrano refused to turn them over to me. That was why we argued."

As I found in the Duquesne case, deception came remarkably easy to me. I felt no guilt in this particular situation, since the rector had been lying, too, and must have been complicit in any searches of Serrano's room.

"I know the *Guardia* has already been here," I continued, certain this would have been the first stop for their investigators. "But the vicar general would like me to examine the padre's room and remove any reference material the police might have left behind."

"But you are not a . . ."

"No, I am not a priest," I quickly responded. "I am a psychologist, working for the vicar general on a confidential basis. This is a very sensitive matter, as you know. Even the *Guardia* is not aware of my role."

Impersonating a police officer was almost certainly as much of a crime in Spain as it was in the United States. Impersonating a priest might also be a crime in this conservative nation. Telling the truth about my profession would be the best defense against any criminal charge *Coronel* Velarde might make when he learned how I gained entry to Padre Serrano's quarters.

The rector opened the door and stepped aside. He led me up a flight of steps and down an open-air corridor to Serrano's room. There was no police seal on the door, which meant I wasn't breaking any laws. The rector unlocked the door and allowed me to enter first. It was a spartan space, reminiscent of those I occupied during my monastic period. Some people claim they can sense the presence of a dead man in the room he once occupied. With me, the reverse was true. What I sensed when I crossed the threshold was not the presence, but the absence of the dead. The possibility of some ghastly spectre lurking in the shadows never entered my mind. What affected me instead were the melancholy remnants of Serrano's solitary life. The bed was neatly made, and protected by a crucifix at its head. Draped over a chair was a faded blue cardigan sweater, waiting in vain for its owner to return. Lined neatly beneath the bed were three pairs of shoes with worn heels, including a pair of black Reeboks whose soft contours had molded themselves to the outlines of Serrano's feet. Behind the door was a bag of laundry that no longer had any purpose in being washed. The faint odor of dried perspiration hung in the closet, along with a brown robe identical to the one he wore yesterday, two black clerical suits, five black shirts, three of which were short-sleeved in deference to the Valencia weather. The only civilian garment in the closet was, oddly enough, a Hawaiian-style shirt overflowing with giant red and yellow hibiscus. It was also the only garment protected with a dry cleaner's plastic sheath.

There was no point in searching the room for any notes or other documents. The *Guardia* would already have gone through every drawer, every box, every item of clothing, including probably checking the linings and seams for any hidden clues. The fact that the room was so neat was a testament to their professionalism. They had, as I expected, already removed the padre's computer and emptied the contents of his filing cabinet. They probably had no idea that diocesan representatives had been there before them.

"There was nothing hidden in the books," the rector said, motioning to the cheap wooden bookcase near the window. "We looked through them carefully, and so did the *Guardia.*"

His comment was a clear confirmation, if I still needed one, that Padre Serrano's claims hadn't been paranoid fantasies.

There were close to a hundred books on the shelves, many of them standard psychology texts. More than half of those volumes were in Spanish, although some were German or French editions. What interested me most, what motivated me to risk coming here, were the books the padre would have used as reference works for his investigation. I tried not to show my excitement as I read the titles. Serrano had put together a small but impressive collection, perhaps four dozen books, that probably contained most of the basic source material on reincarnation theory and the life of Mary Magdalene. Fortunately for me, the majority were in English. Apparently Spain's publishers, whether due to the disapproval of church authorities or the absence of public interest, didn't have much faith in the market for either subject.

Some of the books were old and worn, probably picked up in secondhand bookstores, while others had their original dust jackets and might have been ordered over the Internet. They bore the familiar names of philosophers, mystics, and religious figures such as Edgar Cayce, St. Augustine, the Dalai Lama, and dozens of other important writers from India, China, Japan, Britain, Persia and America. The collection included three different translations of the bible, as well as the Qu'ran, the Bhagavad-gita, the Upanishads, the Tibetan Book of the Dead, the Talmud, the Dead Sea Scrolls, the Nag Hammadi Library, the Pistis Sophia, and the Gnostic Gospels. Analytical works included the minor classics *Study of the Doctrine of Metempsychosis in Greece, Karma and Reincarnation in Hindu Religion and Philosophy, A Reexamination of Jesus, Asian Traditions in Light of Evidence Supporting Reincarnation,* and ten volumes dealing with the life and legends of Mary Magdalene. Scientific books included titles that ranged from *Archeological Discoveries in Biblical Palestine* to *Sociological and Behavioral Factors of the Essenes* to *A History of Alluvial Deposition Patterns in the Rhône Delta,* which volume was unopened, still in its shrink-wrap plastic. On the investigative side, I was happy to see all five volumes of Professor Stevenson's epic examination of 2,000 cases of claimed reincarnation, as well as his casework on xenoglossy, the unexplained acquisition of foreign languages. Serrano also collected the research results of Dr. Erlunder Harroldson of Iceland and Dr. Jurgen Keil of Australia. And veering into the more popular books on the subject, he also had Lenz's *Lifetimes,* Bernstein's famous work on *Bridey Murphy,* and Cott's *Search for Omm Sety.* The contradictory point of view was represented by James Randi, Paul Kurtz, Susan Blackmore, and other skeptics of all things paranormal.

For someone unfamiliar with these works, it would take weeks, if not months, of careful study to master these often tedious materials. But I was already familiar with much of it, at least the portions that dealt with dying, the travels of the soul, and rebirth. It wouldn't take long to get up to speed on reincarnation and Magdalenean mythology. But that wasn't the main reason I wanted Padre Serrano's books. What I wanted was something I was certain the priests and the *Guardia* had overlooked: the Jesuit's marginal notes.

In a classic case of not seeing the forest for the trees, they had searched the books for hidden documents, but left behind what I was convinced was a mother lode of information. Marginal notations are often more revealing about frame of mind or intent than public statements. Such notes, made on memos and speeches, provide an insight that often contradicts the memories of even close advisors. All the way here, I imagined Serrano going through his research material, using the yellow highlighter most academics favor, and making notes in the margins whenever he came across something particularly significant. Although I dared not look for them in the presence of the rector, I was convinced the books were filled with such notations.

Read properly, those markings would almost certainly reveal not only his thought processes but also what had drawn him to become a believer in Sister Mariamme's story. It would be like talking to Padre Serrano beyond the grave.

"Can I get these packed up?" I asked.

"All of them?"

"Might as well." I tried to sound casual, as if bored by my assignment. "I'll need somebody with a handcart. Can you arrange for that, too?"

It went more smoothly than I anticipated. A young servant quickly showed up with boxes and a dolly. I gave him the address of my *pensión* and left him to pack and deliver the books while I took the rector out for a *merienda* of coffee and cake. As I expected, *Coronel* Velarde's agent followed us at a discreet distance, allowing the books to leave the *Residencia* unobserved. I knew the agent would soon report my visit to the *Coronel*. Fearing the wrath of his diocesan superiors more than the *Guardia Civil*, the rector agreed not to tell the *Coronel* about the books. That would buy me some time, at least until the vicar general returned from Rome.

But I had to find a way to protect the books from any sudden search of my hotel room.

Eighteen

ONE OF THE peculiarities of the lodging industry in Europe is the existence of "hotels" and "pensions" that occupy only one or two floors of any given building. A fourteen-story structure might contain four different "hotels," two or three "pensions," a few floors of residential and office space, and on the ground level, the usual mix of storefronts and restaurants.

The *Pensión Adriatico*, where I was staying, was located on the third and fourth floors of a century-old building at 420 *Calle Museo*, well north of the cathedral. Like much of the work of the Spanish architects of that period, the building featured a white limestone exterior whose ornate lintels and curves would have been more appropriate on a wedding cake. But the rooms were clean and cheap, the rotating crew of desk clerks was friendly, and it was within walking distance of most of the Old Quarter.

By the time I got back to the *pensión*, Serrano's books were waiting for me, neatly stacked in four boxes in the fourth-floor lobby. If any of the *Coronel*'s men were watching the building when the boxes were wheeled in, they would have assumed it was another of the dozens of business deliveries made to that address every day. I might have temporarily outwitted the *Guardia*, but I had no illusions about their methods. Although they did a good job of leaving everything almost exactly as they found it, I could tell that my room had been thoroughly searched while I was in custody. It would probably be searched again, particularly when the agent who had been following me reported my visit to the *Residencia*. After my protestations denying that I knew Serrano, I couldn't risk having his books found in my room.

But where could I hide a hundred books in a small hotel room?

The answer lay five floors above me, in the *Pensión Toledano*. It was one of five *pensións* in the building. In the secretive way Spanish business was often conducted, I doubted the managers of the various *pensións* even spoke to each other, which suited my purposes perfectly. I rented a room in the *Toledano,* a corner room where I had a better view of the streets below. Now I had two rooms in the same building, only one of which was known to the *Guardia*. Using the service elevator, I transferred the books from my room in the *Adriatico* to my new hideaway upstairs. To complete the subterfuge, I carried the empty boxes past the lobby desk of the *Adriatico*, pretending to struggle with them as if they were still full. Loading the boxes into the elevator, I told the clerk they had been delivered to me in error, that I was taking them downstairs where they would be picked up later that night. In fact, I collapsed the boxes and left them in a garbage bin in the basement. When the *Guardia* made inquiries about my activities, as I was sure they would, the desk clerk wouldn't send them to my room to search for suspicious cartons.

I was feeling good about myself, better than I had in a long time. The lethargy that enveloped me after the trial had evaporated. My senses were alert. My mind was clear. I was "in the mode," my mental processes working as efficiently as they had at the height of the Duquesne case. The prospect of outmaneuvering not only the church representatives, but the notorious *Guardia Civil* filled me with excitement.

As a further deception, I made a deliberate appearance at my lower-floor *Adriatico* window. I pretended to struggle with the blinds, but my sole purpose was to reassure the *Guardia* observer that I was in my room, and had not eluded him. I managed to get a good view of him. He was a muscular young man, wearing a blue polo shirt and grey trousers, and pretending to be working on a newspaper crossword puzzle. But he might not be the only agent assigned to me.

Retreating out of sight, I made a grid-like sketch of the building across the street, numbering the windows by floor and from left to right. Any window in which a light was visible at night would be marked off with an X. I planned to check the building repeatedly through that night and the following night, when I expected to continue marking off the windows with lights until I had it narrowed down to a few. One of these would have a line of sight into my room. That was where the Guardia's surveillance team would be, afraid to turn on a light that might reveal their presence. I wasn't sure what I would do with that knowledge, but I was attuned to a new, more suspicious sensibility. Self-preservation dictated I gather as much data as possible on the methods being targeted against me.

Closing the blinds and leaving the light on in my room would give the surveillance team something to watch for the next few hours. Later, I would come back and turn off the light to give the illusion I had gone to bed. Only after I was satisfied that I had thought out every possible precaution did I take the service elevator up to my secret hideaway in the *Pensión Toledano*.

It was a small corner room, bare except for a single sagging bed, a battered dresser, and a tiny alcove containing a toilet and sink. An overhead bulb provided the only illumination.

In the solitude of those spartan surroundings, I began my own journey down the path that cost Padre Serrano his life.

Nineteen

I WAS RIGHT about the notations. Serrano was a methodical researcher. He had gone through the books in the interactive pen-and-marker style preferred by academics bent on serious study. Margins were littered with his scribbled comments, sometimes single words, sometimes professional observations. Large sections, often entire pages, were highlighted in yellow. Check marks and exclamation points punctuated phrases and sentences he found particularly significant. Over and over again, the initial *M* appeared, an obvious reference to the subject of his investigation. He had dated the inside front cover of each book, which made it possible for me to arrange them sequentially, and go through them in the same order he did. It was almost as if he was walking me through his thought processes, a teacher guiding a student along the path of discovery.

For three days I remained closeted with the books, venturing out of the building only for food, and to find a soothing salve for the reddened mark on the back of my hand, which was now swelling into a narrow, scar-like ridge. I spent most of my daytime hours in my secret hideaway upstairs, returning downstairs to my original room each night to maintain the illusion of residence. Even on those occasions, I carried a book with me to continue my studying. It wasn't a very glamorous way to begin an investigation. No break-ins, wiretaps, or car chases. Just dogged research, reading until my eyes ached, sometimes falling asleep sitting up, much like my college days cramming for exams. But this was an exam I knew I would never get a chance to retake if I failed.

I started out thinking I already knew quite a bit about reincarnation and the early history of Christianity. But the more I read in Serrano's books, the more I realized I didn't know. The difference, I believe, was that in my days as a near-death investigator I had read many of these books for a different purpose. I had been seeking information about the afterworld. Now that I was confronted with the possibility of someone who might actually have been reborn into this world, each word I read seemed to resonate differently. It was possible, guided by Serrano's notes, to interpret some of the most familiar words of Jesus Christ to support reincarnation theory. As the famed mystic Edgar Cayce once said: "I can read reincarnation into the bible—and you can read it right out again."

Serrano had marked all of the more familiar quotations cited by reincarnationists to prove their case.

He had marked the famous reference in John 9:1-3, which begins when Jesus was asked: *Master, who did sin, this man or his parents, that he was born blind?* The Padre's marginal note pointed out the obvious reference to a previous existence, and the acknowledgment of reincarnation implicit in Jesus' answer.

He marked the ninth chapter of Matthew, in which Jesus identifies John the Baptist as the reincarnation of Elijah.

He marked the Beatitudes. According to Serrano's notes, *As ye reap, so shall ye sow,* was a remarkably clear distillation of karma: the Buddhist belief that the way an individual lives one life will determine the nature of the next life. *The first shall be last, and the last shall be first,* was perfectly consistent with the *Samsara* cycle of existences. Indeed, Christ's Sermon on the Mount, according to Serrano's notes, could have come from the mouth of Buddha himself, with its promise of virtuous action leading to a better state: *Blessed are the sorrowing, for they shall be consoled; Blessed are the lowly, for they shall inherit the land. Blessed are they who hunger and thirst for holiness, they shall have their fill. Blessed are they who show mercy, for mercy shall be theirs.* Serrano's notes pointed out that there is no land to inherit in Heaven, or need for consolation there, so the sayings more logically refer to a subsequent life on Earth.

There were dozens of other highlighted sections, some more explicit in their meaning than others. But what Serrano considered the bible's clearest statement supporting reincarnation, as evidenced by his multiple exclamation points, was found in John 3:6, where Jesus says:

Flesh can only be born of flesh, Spirit can only be born of Spirit.

In his marginal note, Serrano saw the statement as a clear expression of the dualistic view on which the Gnostics based their beliefs in reincarnation. Jesus pointed out, he wrote, that the soul existed independently from the flesh, and since the soul was immortal, it could reside in more than one earthly body.

Granted, there is nothing new in attempting to find references to reincarnation in the bible. Gregory and Clement and Origen and others had been down that path before. But Serrano seemed to be up to more than a simple search for the "Lost Chord of Christianity."

As I went from book to book, following the padre's careful cross-references from the Old Testament to the Qu'ran, from the Kabala to the Laws of Manu, from the Gospel of Q to the Pistis Sophia, from the Upanishads to the Nag Hammadi, I realized that what he had been doing was nothing less than developing a new religious construct. It was breathtaking in its audacity, yet there it was, clearly delineated in his marginal notations, and backed up by the very source material on which it was based: a theology that embraced the similarities between the world's religions rather than isolating them by their differences. Through painstaking research, he had sought out the remarkable parallels that united Buddhism with Christianity with Judaism with Theosophy with Mohammedanism, even with Zoroastrianism and the Coptic and Gnostic sects.

But why? What was the point?

He hadn't seemed like a radical to me. Except for his psychiatric training, he appeared to be a relatively conventional clergyman, a Catholic priest in a Catholic country. He was an intelligent man, a good conversationalist, but didn't appear to be the sort of individual who was capable of launching a new religion. Yet the texts he selected and his marginal comments attacked some of the more cherished tenets of Catholic belief, such as original sin, the primacy of Peter, the role of women, and the hierarchical structure of the Church itself.

These and other dogmas, some of which were never clearly expressed in the bible, had been codified and solidified over the centuries by various Church councils and reaffirmed by a long line of popes. Granted that many of those popes were political appointees, it was nevertheless true that the modern pontiffs had invoked the papal mantle of infallibility to bind Catholics to follow the doctrines of their sometimes illegitimate and corrupt predecessors.

So why would Padre Serrano flirt with heresy?

Could it have something to do with La Magdalena and what he called the "True Gospel of Jesus Christ?" According to him, she had challenged some of those very doctrines herself, had argued with priests and torn offending pages from the New Testament. Whether that behavior was heretical or symptomatic of a disoriented mind had been Serrano's mission to decide, and then treat. Could what started out as a doctor/patient relationship have ended up in a strange form of role reversal? Could the nun, through some strange force of her personality, have converted the priest to her way of thinking?

If so, that might explain why the vicar general had removed him from the case.

It seemed a benign way to deal with a potential heretic priest, much more humane than the death sentences once handed out for such activities. The Church, like Spain itself, had come a long way from those dark times.

And yet, Serrano was dead, as surely as if he had been condemned by some medieval Inquisitor.

Twenty

THE HUMAN MIND has a remarkable ability to keep secrets from itself. Often these are uncomfortable truths that remain buried in the subconscious, where they provide a rich source of income for psychoanalysts and people like me. Those of us who study the workings of the mind are not immune to its peculiarities. It took me three days before my subconscious finally acknowledged what it must have suspected from the very beginning.

It was late afternoon of the third day, and I was deep into the contents of the Pistis Sophia, the Gnostic "bible" which was written shortly after Christ's death. Serrano's marginal notations were becoming harder to decipher. As the marginal notations grew more complex, his handwriting deteriorated into a feverish scribble. If I had not become accustomed to the peculiar characteristics of his penmanship, the hasty scrawls would have been completely unreadable. I was struggling with a particularly incomprehensible phrase, when, unbidden, one of those hidden thoughts bubbled up from my subconscious.

It was a thought I probably would have rejected if I had recognized the signs earlier. Perhaps that was why it waited in the deepest recess of my mind, where it watched and evaluated the material I was studying, until it decided I would be in a more receptive mood.

I sat back, stunned by my own stupidity for not having realized it earlier.

The paranoid behavior, the obsession with his patient, the mysterious files Serrano claimed to carry in his briefcase, the fervent pleas for me to continue his work, were all indications that something had gone terribly wrong in his treatment of the nun. One of the most powerful and potentially dangerous tools in psychotherapy is *transference,* a process in which the patient transfers primal emotions onto the therapist. The emotions can be negative or positive. In many cases the patient idealizes, idolizes, even falls in love with the therapist, who uses this transference of affection as a means of guiding the patient to a new understanding of self. In this case, however, it was apparent that the reverse had occurred. The therapist had projected his own emotions onto the patient, imbuing her with the authority he should have reserved for himself.

The Padre had become a disciple of La Magdalena.

Like the nuns he mentioned in passing, he too had become one of her followers.

It was a fact he had concealed from me during our meeting, an intentional obfuscation of his true relationship with her. But it was clear from his notes and markings that this was the role in which he saw himself. It was an astounding reversal of roles. What strange power did this simple nun possess that could turn a priest into her proselyte, and raise herself in his eyes to the role of prophet?

From a psychological perspective, I knew it was possible for the sheer force of a psychotic personality to overwhelm and dominate a more submissive individual. But Padre Serrano didn't strike me as a submissive type. I was convinced there was something more at work here, some still-unexplained alchemy that, frankly, I was finding a little spooky.

I thought back to my own brief encounters with La Magdalena. At what Jung would have called the *synchronicity* of seeing her at the convent window, the almost telepathic communication as she pressed her hand against the glass and stared down at me. Or the initial encounter at the cathedral, when for some still unexplained reason she had chosen me from among hundreds of others to be her courier. I glanced down at the reddened area on the back of my hand, which seemed to be taking on the characteristics of a permanent blemish. I had somehow been marked by her, I thought. But how and for what reason, I didn't know.

The room suddenly seemed to become unbearably hot and stuffy. I couldn't open the window, because I didn't dare reveal my presence in this upstairs hideaway. The air grew thick and hard to breathe, as if the oxygen level had been depleted. Opening the hallway door didn't help. I felt a need to get out into the streets, where, although the air was as polluted as that of any other large city, at least I wouldn't feel confined.

As I emerged from the building, the Spanish sun assaulted my eyes with its late-afternoon brilliance. Squinting, I found it impossible to see if I was being followed. I did all the usual tricks, using car mirrors and store windows to look behind me, stopping for fake window-shopping, waiting at intersections until the very last second before the light turned red to dash across the street and then turning to see if anyone was careless enough to get caught in the open and reveal himself. It was a game at which my pursuers were far more skilled than I. They remained invisible.

After being cooped up for three days, I was glad to feel the sun's heat on my skin, and decided to take the opportunity to get some much-needed exercise. I headed up the *Gran Via* to the *Jardines del Turia,* the vast expanse of trees and greenery that were planted over what had once been the Turia River. My plan was to follow a circular route that would take me back to my starting point. But somehow I found myself lost in a warren of busy streets near the University. None of them looked familiar until I turned a corner and found myself on *Calle Don Bosco.*

Directly across the street was the block-long *Il Convento de las Hermanas del Sangreal.* And in a third-floor window, looking down at me, was the hooded figure of a nun. Was it La Magdalena? I couldn't tell. The reflection of the setting sun obscured the nun's face. And, I have to admit, I was afraid to make eye contact, afraid that whatever power she exerted over Padre Serrano might somehow be refocused on me. I lowered my head and hurried on.

For the second time, some unexplainable force, whether in my own subconscious or not, had drawn me to this location. A vague and indefinable sense of foreboding crept over me.

If my mind had not been clouded by such thoughts, I probably would have been aware of the black Mercedes that slid quietly to the curb beside me, perhaps been able to escape the two men who suddenly appeared beside me. They wore dark suits and neckties, which at first made me think they were plainclothes policemen.

"Señor Nikonos?" the smaller one asked. He had a narrow, misshapen face, one side of which suggested extensive oral surgery had been performed to reconstruct his jaw. As a result, only the left side of his mouth moved when he spoke.

Before I could answer, the two men each took one of my elbows and guided me into the back seat of the Mercedes, which pulled away without any further instructions to the driver.

Twenty-One

"*Qué pasa?*" I asked, using one of my few phrases of guidebook Spanish. No answer.

My two companions had me wedged between them, the smaller one with bony hips and the larger one with powerfully muscled buttocks. They were both neatly groomed, their hair slicked back with faintly scented pomade. The smaller scar-faced one was pale, his eyes watery, his hands constantly adjusting the crease in his pants and checking the knot in his tie. The larger one was a placid man who stared straight ahead, never once glancing at me after we were in the car. He had the rough, weather-beaten face of a farmer, with bloodshot eyes that drooped at the corners. His fingers were thick and callused, unlike the pickpocket-slim fingers of his companion.

Despite my repeated attempts, it was impossible to get a word out of either of them. The uniformed driver was also unresponsive. If they were policemen, even in Spain their regulations would have required them to declare their intention. On the other hand, their behavior was brusque, but not thuggish. They seemed too disciplined to be ordinary hoodlums.

Pinned between my silent companions, I could only speculate what fate they planned for me.

The Mercedes headed north out of Valencia, up the coastal highway. We passed mile after mile of orange groves, interspersed with stunning views of the Mediterranean on our right and mountain ranges on our left. Ancient castles and battlements, some crumbling, others converted to *paradors* for tourists, rose above the more strategic peaks. At the 25-kilometer mark we passed through the town of Sagunto. It was a town I had planned to visit as a day trip from Valencia, to see the Roman ruins and remains of a Greek Acropolis. According to the guidebooks, it was the place where the first Jews arrived in Spain a hundred years before the birth of Christ, and where Hannibal launched the Second Punic War more than a hundred years before that. I had to settle for a quick glimpse of some ancient columns in the center of town as the Mercedes sped through.

The orange groves continued as we headed up the coast. It wasn't harvest season yet, but the fruit was ripening in the vast orchards we passed, turning the view from the window into a monotonous green and orange blur. The sun soon disappeared behind the mountains. The orange groves grew dark. But a brilliant fisherman's moon lit up the Mediterranean. Except for the circumstance in which I found myself, it was a lovely night. If I had been behind the wheel, I would have opened the car's windows to enjoy the fragrance of the salt air coming in across the orange groves.

We passed through Burriana, Benicasim, and Oropresa, and I began to wonder if they were going to take me all the way to Barcelona. Finally, after about two hours on the road, the driver slowed his steady pace. We were nearing Peniscola, which an overly enthusiastic illuminated sign described as "El Mont San Michelle de España." In the darkness, I couldn't see anything resembling that spectacular French landmark, but moonlight on the water revealed an isthmus connecting the town with the mainland. At the last moment, the driver made a left turn, away from Peniscola, and up into the dark inland hills. The paved road soon turned to gravel, which clattered against the bottom of the vehicle. We stopped at a metal gate. A man with a beret emerged from the gatehouse and came around to speak to the driver and peer into the back seat. The men beside me greeted him in a language I didn't understand. He muttered something and waved us on. As the car pulled away, I noticed another figure waiting in the bushes, out of range of the headlights. Ten minutes and a steep uphill climb later, we passed a second gatehouse, whose guard waved us on. Finally, we arrived at what looked like a seventeenth-century French chateau, a massive stone structure three stories tall and half a city block wide. The castle sat atop its own mountain peak, where it commanded a magnificent view of the town below. The entire front of the building was brilliantly illuminated. Selected specimen trees on both sides were further accented by hidden spotlights. A security guard knelt beside two German shepherds, calming them as the car drove up.

The remnants of an ancient moat had been allowed to go to grass. With the threat of Saracen attack having evaporated centuries ago, the main gate had been converted into a grand entrance, welcoming visitors with a set of sculptured marble stairs that led to massive medieval front doors. A smaller door cut into one of these was opened, not by a butler, but a maid. She was a middle-aged woman, modestly dressed in black with a white apron. She welcomed us in Spanish, and apparently having advance word of my arrival, greeted me by name. The entrance hallway reminded me of Versailles, with its crystal chandelier, broad curving stair-case, and intricate inlaid marble flooring. Ancient battle flags hung from the rafters. Standing guard by an arched doorway beyond the stairs was a suit of armor whose right hand grasped a flagstaff. Hanging from the flagstaff was a faded white silk banner with the fabled red Cross of Lor-raine, the *Rose Croix* carried into battle by the Crusaders in the Middle Ages. A large dent in the helmet and repairs on the breastplate were evi-dence that it had served its owner well. Watching discreetly from the shad-ows was a man who could have been the brother of the sentry who stopped us on the road. He was broad-shouldered and mustached, and stared at me with cold, disinterested eyes.

The smaller of my companions motioned me towards a doorway on the left. It opened to an enormous room, made cozy by a collection of period furniture, artwork, shelves of antique books, and a walk-in fire-place. Seated in a red wing chair was a pale, slender young man, not much older than I. In his lap was a copy of my book. Before greeting me, he carefully compared my face with the photograph on the book jacket.

"Mr. Nikonos," he said when he was sure it was me. "How good of you to come."

"I didn't have much choice."

"I'm terribly sorry about that," he said in elegant French-accented English. "But you were being watched. We had to move quickly." He turned away to ask something of the two men in a rapid burst of Spanish. They replied in the negative. "*Bueno,*" he muttered, and turned back to me with a smile.

"So at last I meet the famous Authenticator," he said. "How fortunate for me that you decided to visit Valencia."

Maybe not very fortunate for me, I was thinking as I watched my two abductors take up positions by the door.

"I am Jean-Claude Flamel DesRosier." He said as he slowly, almost grudgingly, rose from his chair. For a young man, he had an infuriatingly patrician air about him. He had the narrow nose, the receding hairline and the disappearing chin so common on portraits of dissolute eighteenth-century French aristocrats. His wardrobe was what I would call French-dandy style. His blue velvet blazer sported what looked like solid gold buttons and gold thread woven in an intricate design on the breast pocket. A red silk foulard in that pocket matched the red ascot around his neck. Perfectly pressed gray slacks were accessorized with red silk socks and slender black Bally slip-ons. When he offered his hand in greeting, I almost thought he expected me to kiss it. He had mastered the art of speaking without moving his upper lip. "Welcome to my house," he said. "Would you care to join us for dinner?"

"I'd like to know why I'm here."

"Ah, you Americans," he sighed. "You're so abrupt."

"I'm sorry," I said, and instantly wondered why I was apologizing to a man who had me abducted off a street corner. "But I'm sure you didn't bring me here just to invite me to dinner."

"You're right, of course," DesRosier said. "I do have an ulterior motive. But I hoped we could talk about it over dinner. The cook has prepared a traditional Catalan meal for you."

As if some unseen signal had been passed, a set of elaborately carved doors was slowly opened at the far end of the room. Waiting in the doorway was the same black-dressed woman who had greeted me earlier at the front entrance.

"Have you ever eaten true Catalan food?" DesRosier asked as he led me into an enormous formal dining room.

The centerpiece of the room was a table so long that it took two chandeliers to properly light it. The walls were decorated with art that continued the Crusader theme. Hanging above the obligatory fireplace was an enormous oil painting of what looked like Solomon's Temple in Jerusalem, the remnants of which were "liberated" from the Muslims in the First Crusade. Adorning the other walls were portraits of medieval popes and warriors, paintings of savage battle scenes, and renderings of churches, including the Cathedrals of Chartres, Boulogne, and Notre Dame. The manner in which the art was hung presented a disquieting juxtaposition of carnage and Catholicism. The inclusion of the great cathedrals seemed puzzling, since they had little relation to the Crusader theme.

"You have an impressive art collection," I said, trying to find something nice to say about the oddly disturbing display.

"The history of my family," DesRosier explained. "The paintings have been here for hundreds of years."

I paused before a particularly gory painting, which portrayed a knight with an enormous bloody sword slicing the head off what appeared to be a turbaned Moslem. The bearded knight was smiling.

"Your ancestors were Crusaders?" I asked.

"That was centuries ago," he responded modestly. "I am just a businessman."

"Really? What kind of business?" I knew such questions were considered rude in Europe, but so was being snatched off a sidewalk and driven two hours to have dinner with a complete stranger.

"Banks, shipping, computers," he replied. "An airline, diamond mines . . . my ancestors were very fortunate in their investments."

Although there were chairs enough for thirty people at the table, places were set for only four. DesRosier took his place at the head of the table, with me on his right. A bottle of red wine waited, uncorked so it could breathe, for the two of us. A closer glance at the faded label revealed it to be a Chateau Lafite Rothschild, considered by most oenophiles to be the finest of the world's red wines. A more stunning discovery was the smaller vintage label, which dated it to 1941. Since no French wine was exported during the German occupation, the bottle must have come from the legendary "lost vintage" which the most prestigious Bordeaux vintners hid from the Nazis. If such bottles ever came on the open market, their auction price would surely be in multiples of thousands of dollars. Yet, with studied nonchalance, the bottle was permitted to stand alone on the lace tablecloth, without even the benefit of a customary silver cradle. My abductors were seated out of earshot, at the far end of the table. A pitcher of what was probably sangria awaited them. As soon as we were seated, an attractive young woman in a white uniform appeared at DesRosier's side to pour our wine. I watched with anticipation as the precious red liquid coated the side of the crystal glass. After more than six decades, it still retained its rich ruby coloration. Even before swirling it, I could detect the bouquet, a delicate fruity aroma that seemed to mingle black currant, cedar, and, amazingly, a hint of vanilla.

"*Santé,*" DesRosier raised his glass and toasted me in French. And then, peering down the table at his two employees, called out in Spanish, "*Salud!*"

They raised their glasses in response. Slowly, unwilling to hurry the moment of discovery, I took a tiny sip, teasing my tongue with flavors I knew I would never taste again. For a moment, my mouth was transported back to the Medoc countryside, where the long rows of heavy grapes basked in the French sunshine and took on almost magical qualities that allowed their flavors not only to survive, but also to grow and mature inside the bottle until they achieved an almost silken finesse.

"Tito and Manolo will be joining us for dinner, but they have their own matters to discuss," DesRosier said. "In any event, they are not very open with strangers."

"So I noticed."

"They are Basques. It is part of their nature to distrust outsiders. You are perhaps familiar with the Basques?"

"No more than most people," I said cautiously. Of course I had seen news reports about the bombings that were part of the Basque effort to achieve autonomy. But with two Basques watching me from the far end of the table, I decided that topic was too dangerous to get into. "I know about the Bilbao Museum, which sounds spectacular, and I've heard good things about Basque food."

"Then you know very little," DesRosier sniffed. "There is evidence that the Basques are the original Europeans, directly descended from Cro-Magnon man. Their language is extraordinarily complex and dates back to the Stone Age." He lowered his voice to a whisper. "Look at them. Don't they resemble cave men? Look at their bushy eyebrows, their heavy foreheads and long earlobes. These physical characteristics are typical of the Basques."

In America, such comments would be considered offensive. But I found that a matter-of-factness about ethnic differences was still fairly common among Europeans.

"The Basques were great sailors and explorers," DesRosier continued. "Their whaling ships visited your America long before Columbus. They have the finest harbors in Iberia, where they once built and sheltered the mighty Spanish Armada. They were a prosperous people who managed to survive the Romans, the Visigoths and the Moors."

I had learned long ago not to interrupt when someone was expounding on a subject upon which they considered themselves expert. There was always the possibility I might learn something. In any event, I was content to remain silent, savoring the Lafite Rothschild within the confines of my closed mouth.

"But the greatest sins were committed against the Basque people in more modern times," DesRosier went on. "Napoleon divided their country between France and Spain. Hitler allowed the Luftwaffe to practice carpet-bombing techniques on the town of Guernica. And Franco outlawed their language and customs, persecuted them and treated their children as criminals . . . simply for being born Basque. Yet today, they are the most prosperous people in Spain. The Basques control much of Spanish banking and industry. But they will not be happy until they once again have their independence."

"But you're French, and this is Spain. Why do you choose Basques as your bodyguards?"

"Because I can trust them with my life. They are perhaps the most secretive people in the world. And the most fearless." He nodded to the far end of the table. "Tito is a small man by Basque standards. But he once jumped from a second-story window to save a child from the path of the bulls at Pamplona. The bull's horn ripped into the side of his face, but he did not drop the child. Absolutely fearless. That is the kind of man I want as my bodyguard."

DesRosier raised his glass in another toast, this one in a language that resembled neither French nor Spanish.

"*Euskadi Ta Askatasuna,*"

Tito's deformed face broke into a smile. He was joined by the more powerfully built Manolo, and the two men raised their glasses in response.

"*Euskadi Ta Askatasuna,*" they returned the toast.

"Those words are abbreviated as ETA on their banners," DesRosier explained to me. "It means Freedom to the Basques. You see how it makes them smile?" He chuckled, pleased at what he perceived as his facile manipulation of the two men. "They continue to plot and dream of having their own nation again, and are ferociously loyal to those who help their cause."

"Such as you?"

"I contribute to many causes," DesRosier shrugged. "Including *Il Convento de las Hermanas del Sangreal.*"

So there it was, I thought. In the typically roundabout way favored by the French, he was finally beginning to hint at a reason for my presence.

As if on cue, the kitchen door was opened by the middle-aged woman, who apparently served as the chateau's majordomo. Behind her, two young women in white uniforms entered the room. They carried large silver trays that contained a variety of appetizers, which they held before us for our approval. The young woman who had been pouring the wine also explained the dishes to me, a chore my host apparently felt was beneath his dignity.

With her help, I selected *albergines dolce, anxoves fregides, escabetx de colomi,* and *pebrot farci amb anec,* which she explained were eggplant slices fried in honey, crispy deep-fried anchovies, cold pickled pigeon quarters, and a sweet red pepper stuffed with duck. Food has a wonderful way of relieving my anxieties, and along with the help of the superb wine, I relaxed and decided to enjoy my captivity.

"I very much enjoyed your book," DesRosier said between bites.

"Thank you." I wondered exactly how he learned about me or my book.

"You have a very curious occupation, Mr. Nikonos. I know about private investigators, what you Americans call 'private eyes,' but this is something new, is it not?"

"I'm just an investigator," I said. "What I do isn't all that different from what other investigators do."

"Ah, but you call yourself the Authenticator. And the mysteries you deal with are the mysteries of the ages. I never would have believed anyone would have been able to authenticate the existence of life after death. You succeeded where Augustine and Aquinas and so many others failed."

"I was lucky."

"I think more than lucky. I think you have a rare talent for such things. Tell me, do you carry a gun?"

"No."

"And yet, you sometimes find yourself in very dangerous situations. Doesn't it frighten you?"

"At times, yes," I admitted.

"But of course, a gun would have been no help against a bomb," he said.

The tone of his voice remained friendly, but the conversation had taken an ominous turn. I reached for my wine glass, and then, thinking I should keep my head clear, decided to avoid any more alcohol and stick with water.

"You know about the bombing?" I asked.

"Everyone in Spain knows about it. But you seem to have survived without any injury, except of course, for that red mark on the back of your hand. A miracle, is it not?"

The miracle was that he knew details of the bombing that hadn't been released, I thought. Before I could respond, the kitchen door opened again. The three young women returned to refresh our table settings with new plates, silverware and napkins, orange sorbet to cleanse our palates before the next dish arrived, another pitcher of sangria for the Basques, and another bottle of the incredible Lafite Rothschild for us. So far, the food was the best I had eaten since arriving in Spain. Unfortunately, my need for a clear head prevented me from imbibing any more of the extraordinary wine.

"I am not easily impressed, Mr. Nikonos. Particularly by Americans. But you possess fascinating skills, and whether you consider it luck or divine intervention, you seem to have an uncanny ability to survive. I think I should like to hire you."

"Hire me? What for?"

"Why, to conduct an investigation, of course. That is what you do, isn't it?"

"I already have a client."

He didn't look up from his plate.

"I know such matters are often confidential," he said. "But may I ask the identity of this client?"

"His name is Serrano. Padre Javier Serrano."

There was a flicker of reaction in DesRosier's eyes. The first crack in his facade of aristocratic indifference. "But did he not die in the bombing?"

"Who told you that?" I asked.

Realizing his mistake, my host raised his napkin to his mouth, disguising any reaction. By the time he lowered the napkin, he had reassumed his bland expression.

"I guess I made an assumption," he said. "I thought I read somewhere that one of the victims was wearing the robe of a Jesuit priest. Was I mistaken?"

"No, it was Padre Serrano. Although for some reason the *Guardia* would like me to believe otherwise."

"Perhaps it was an imposter."

"The *Guardia* would like me to believe that, too," I said. "But it was Padre Javier Serrano. I have evidence to prove it."

"I see." He sat back and thought about that for a moment. The serving girl immediately removed our empty sorbet cups. "But of course, you are the Authenticator," he said, nodding his head. "You would not be deceived. Still, how can this Padre Serrano be your client if he is dead?"

"I intend to find out who killed him."

"That could be very dangerous. The terrorists could target you as easily as they did him."

"I don't think it was terrorists." I studied DesRosier's face carefully, looking for some sign of guilt, some nonverbal signal that might suggest his involvement. But he was looking beyond me, thinking some faraway thought. "I think the bomber intended to kill me as well as Serrano," I added.

"If that is the case, they may well try again."

The room grew ominously silent, everyone suspended in half-finished actions. The serving girls stared at me. My abductors were watching me. I had the sudden, frightening realization of my absolute vulnerability. I had been abducted off the streets of a foreign city. No one other than the people in this room had any idea of my whereabouts. At the whim of my host, who seemed perfectly capable of such acts, I could be spirited off to some even more remote location and disposed of without a trace. Was that why he asked whether I carried a gun? I waited for him to snap his slender fingers and have me carried away like a soiled plate.

"Well, as you say," I hoped my voice didn't quiver too much. "I seem to have an uncanny ability to survive."

DesRosier smiled, and everyone seemed to relax and behave normally again.

"Bravo, Mr. Nikonos," he said. "Such fearlessness confirms my belief that you are the ideal person for this assignment."

"I told you I already have a client."

"According to you, your client is dead. If indeed he was Padre Serrano, as you claim, then I think you will find we have a remarkable convergence of interests. You knew that Padre Serrano was investigating one of the nuns at the *convento?*"

"Really?" I pretended not to know. "Where did you hear that?"

The serving girls brought out a large silver tureen. One of them placed soup bowls before us. In the bottom of each bowl was a crust of toasted French bread. The second young woman ladled out a thick golden broth laced with chunks of shellfish. The third, who had been serving as my culinary adviser, identified the soup as *caldereta de llagosta*. It was made with the famous spiny lobster from the island of Minorca. A rare treat at this time of year, she explained.

"It's all right, Mr. Nikonos," DesRosier smiled. "We can be open with each other. As a patron of the *convento*, I am well informed about all matters affecting the welfare of our beloved nuns. I knew about Serrano's work. If he is in fact the dead man, then I believe he was murdered because of his involvement with the young nun they call La Magdalena."

Once again, the room fell silent; the only sound came from the end of the table, where the two Basques were noisily enjoying their soup. I stared down at my bowl. My hands were suddenly trembling too much to attempt to lift my spoon.

DesRosier seemed to have no such problem. He took a delicate sip and nodded his approval to the middle-aged woman. She beamed with pleasure.

"Of course, you probably suspected the bombing was somehow connected with the nun, didn't you?" he continued. "A man like you wouldn't be deceived by the *Guardia's* clumsy attempt to blame the Basques."

Was he taunting me? His expression was so bland, it was hard to decipher his intent.

"Obviously, you weren't deceived either," I said. "You already knew the dead man was Serrano, didn't you?"

DesRosier gave a shrug as he munched on a piece of lobster.

"The *caldereta* is quite good," he said to me. "You should have some before it gets cold."

He was right about the *caldereta*. It was rich and aromatic. The consistency was more like a stew than a soup. I could taste onion and garlic and green pepper. But they were simply a background to the incredibly sweet flavor of the lobster.

"The broth is made in the traditional Catalan manner," he explained. "The brain of the lobster is removed, scrambled, and then blended back into the broth as a flavor enhancer."

Normally, I found such descriptions off-putting. But that first spoonful was absolutely addictive. Whatever else I might think of DesRosier, he certainly believed in eating well.

"I'm not asking you to give up your pursuit of the priest's killer," DesRosier said. "I understand that your real motive is probably vengeance. After all, you were almost killed in the bombing that took his life."

It was an interesting attempt at psychological insight, I thought. But he was making a classic mistake of the amateur analyst. He was assuming my motivation would be similar to his, looking at my behavior through the lens of his own character. But unlike the warrior knights whose exploits lined the walls around us, I was seeking justice, not vengeance. I decided not to argue the point.

"You are a man of considerable intellect, Mr. Nikonos. I should like you to apply that intellect to the case of this strange young nun who is disrupting our *convento*."

"What happens inside the convent should be a matter for the Church authorities," I said cautiously. "Why do you feel you should get involved?"

"As I told you earlier, I am a patron of *Il Convento de las Hermanas del Sangreal*. I am interested in anything that affects the welfare of the nuns. It troubles me greatly to think a heresy may be spreading among them. The Church authorities have so far seemed incapable of dealing with the matter. While they delay, a cult following is rapidly developing around this particular individual. Therefore, it is up to others such as me to involve themselves. I believe it is time to bring in an outside investigator."

It seemed reasonable for this self-described patron of the *convento,* to be interested in the matter, yet something about his manner made me feel uneasy.

"I want you to investigate this La Magdalena. Investigate her and expose her claims for the fraud they are."

Twenty-Two

"THAT'S NOT THE way I work," I demurred. "I don't normally approach a case with any preconceived notions. I simply follow the facts, wherever they may lead."

"Very well then, follow the facts. But find out the truth."

"That might not be easy," I demurred again. "As you know, she claims to be the reincarnation of Mary Magdalene, a woman whose very existence is shrouded in myth. A factual trail to either prove or disprove her story simply doesn't exist."

"Which may explain why the Church authorities are having so difficult a time dealing with the case," he conceded. "But there is too much mystery surrounding this La Magdalena. No one knows where she came from. Who her ancestors might have been. Or why she casts such a spell over all who come in contact with her. Perhaps you can start by probing that mystery. Find out who she really is. That may explain why she behaves the way she does. And perhaps help determine what is the source of the power she seems to exert over all who come into contact with her."

I immediately thought of Padre Serrano, and his apparent conversion to her cause.

"Her power probably derives from her claim," I said.

"That she was Mary Magdalene in a previous life?" he snorted his derision. "How could anyone believe such a claim?"

"It's not that unusual for members of a closed society, whether women or men, to embrace notions that might seem outlandish, even bizarre, to the outside world."

"Need I remind you that we're talking about a Roman Catholic convent," he said. "A place of prayer and meditation, not a repository of bizarre religious activity?"

"Catholic convents have produced ecstatics and stigmatics," I responded. "And mystics and prophets and miracle workers, many of whom were elevated to sainthood after careful investigation by the Church. In that kind of environment, a woman who believes she lived a past life might seem particularly blessed, singled out by God for special favors, and thus worthy of veneration."

Finished with his soup, he sat back and touched his lips gently with his napkin. The dish was immediately removed.

"A belief in miracles is central to our Catholic faith," he said. "Reincarnation, however, is anathema."

"I don't think that's really true," I said. I made him wait while I finished my soup before continuing. "If you're referring to the anathema against Origen's teachings, that's been discredited by Catholic theologians who consider it the result of an illegitimate Church Council conducted against the wishes of the pope." My research had confirmed what Serrano had told me. "As a matter of fact, there were many early church leaders in addition to Origen who believed in reincarnation, including Synesius and Justin Martyr, and many later ones, including St. Francis of Assissi and St. Augustine and more recently Archbishop Passavalli and Cardinal Mercier. So it has never really been outside the scope of Christian thought."

"You seem very well informed on the subject," DesRosier said.

That was certainly true. After my conversation with Serrano and three days with his books, there was little I didn't know about just how central reincarnation theory was to Christian history.

"The padre piqued my interest," I said.

As soon as my soup bowl was removed, a parade of serving girls began to fill the table with heavy trays of food.

"Of course, the great flaw to any argument in favor of reincarnation lies in the arithmetic," DesRosier argued.

I was half-listening to him as I hungrily examined the first tray, a large serving of saffron rice, its brilliant yellow decorated with blue and red edible flowers.

"If every person who dies is reborn in another body," he said. "Logic requires that no new person can be born until another person dies. That would dictate a static population. Yet the world population has been growing exponentially, from perhaps two million in the days of my ancestors to its current level of about six billion."

On the second tray were what looked like eels chopped in several pieces. He paused while the serving girl identified the dish as *rabo de toro,* or tail of the bull.

"If every human soul is reincarnated in a new body," he continued. "Where did all these people . . . this extra four billion people . . . come from, unless of course, they don't have souls?"

The third tray placed on the table contained *estofat de bou,* which was Catalan beef stew with orange peel and black olives.

"The simple answer is that God continues to create new souls," I responded. "New souls are coming into the world even while old souls are moving through a succession of lifetimes. It's an additive process."

Finally came a series of trays containing dramatic combinations of fresh and steamed vegetables, some sprinkled with cheese, chopped shrimp and shredded crabmeat. If this was the way DesRosier ate every night, I wondered how he managed to remain so slim.

"There are also more complicated answers to your question," I said. "The Buddhists will tell you it's the result of the transmigration of souls from other living creatures. They believe in an evolutionary process that starts with the simplest creatures and moves up through what they call the Great Wheel of Existence, based on how well the soul performs in each life. A person who is evil might be reborn as a snake or a dog."

"People reborn as animals?" he snorted his derision. "A ridiculous concept."

"Oh, I don't know. There's the classic story of Pythagoras, who recognized the soul of a friend of his in a dog that was being beaten," I said, as the serving girl beside me parceled portions of each of the entrees onto my plate. "And surely you've seen the magnificent stables at Chantilly. They were built by one of your own countrymen, a member of the nobility who believed he would be reincarnated as a horse, and wanted to live his equine life in pampered luxury."

"The French have a history of eccentricity," he said in a dismissive tone. "And I am not an adherent of Buddhist thinking. I am a Christian."

"Then you should read the bible more carefully," I said. "You'll find it contains dozens of references to rebirth, some more obvious than others. And every book of both the Old and the New Testament refers to the immortality of the soul. That's the theological basis the early Christian scholars used as their rationale for reincarnation. If the soul is immortal, it must have some place to go when the flesh decays. At least until the Final Judgment. A new body is the most logical place for the soul to go to wait until then."

Not wanting to be guilty of a faux pas in eating as unfamiliar a dish as a bull's tail, I watched DesRosier expertly separate the meat from bones which resembled vertebrae. It was a feat that I was unable to duplicate without making a mess.

"Any good Christian knows our souls go to Heaven or Hell when we die," DesRosier said.

"Not according to the bible," I replied. "Scripture says the soul's fate must await the day of the Final Judgment. The bible is silent about what happens to the soul between the time of death and Judgment Day. The idea that the soul is immediately consigned to Heaven or Hell, like the concept of Purgatory, was an invention of Catholic theologians who were seeking an explanation for what they saw as a large gap in the biblical explanation of the life and death cycle. The flaw in that thinking, of course, is that any immediate assignment to Heaven or Hell negates the very premise of a Final Judgment." Much of what I was saying came from Serrano's marginal notes. "That gap, incidentally, does not exist in the Gnostic texts, which support the concept of reincarnation as the interim stage before our Final Judgment. They believe, in effect, that our life in the flesh is actually a form of Purgatory."

From the end of the table came the sounds of the two Basques attacking the *rabo de toro*. They made no attempt to imitate DesRosier's effete but effective use of knife and fork, preferring instead to rely on their fingers and teeth to remove the delicious cartilage from the crevices.

"*Rabo de toro* is Tito's favorite dish," DesRosier said. "I think he pretends he is eating the tail of the bull that injured him."

We ate for a while in silence, disturbed only by the ferocity of Tito's appetite for revenge. DesRosier finished before me. His plate instantly removed, he wiped his mouth and sat back in his chair.

"It sounds to me, Mr. Nikonos, as if you believe in reincarnation."

"Not completely. I'm just not as absolute in my disbelief as you seem to be. I try to maintain an open mind on the subject."

"Well said," DesRosier smiled. "Your arguments are very well put, and your objectivity is admirable. But then, I would expect nothing less from a man with your reputation. Shall we discuss your fee?"

"Aren't we getting a little ahead of ourselves here?" I protested. "I don't recall hearing myself agreeing to take the case."

"I am prepared to pay you a fee of $2,000 per week."

"That's a lot of money," I had to admit.

"With a guarantee of $50,000 when you finish your investigation and render your report."

If the amount was intended to take my breath away, he succeeded. I tried desperately to keep from showing my astonishment. I was dealing with a billionaire, I had to remind myself.

"Fifty thousand dollars?" I repeated, just to be sure I heard him right.

"In U.S. dollars," he said, smiling at my reaction. "A fair fee, I think, considering the danger involved."

"Danger?" I repeated the word slowly, tasting the dryness it left in my mouth.

"I will also provide you with a car for your personal use. I assume you will need money for expenses. For hotel rooms, gasoline, bribes, and such things."

"I'm really not sure I want to do this," I murmured.

He motioned to one of the serving girls. She picked up a small silver tray which had been sitting unnoticed until now on a side table. The tray contained a folding wireless telephone, a set of car keys, and a fat white envelope. She placed the tray on the table before me.

"You will find a map and $10,000 in U.S. currency inside the envelope," DesRosier said. "The map will lead you to the location of the car, which is a black Opel Corsa. For security reasons, it is parked outside Valencia, in the suburbs. Although the car cannot be traced to me, please be sure you are not followed when you go to pick it up. The $10,000 is a retainer to cover your first week's fee as well as your initial expenses. The telephone is programmed to call my personal telephone number. To contact me, just press the numeral "1." I will have a similar speed-dial on my phone, using the number "5" to contact you. You may call me directly whenever you have anything to report, or when you run out of money. Keep this phone on your person at all times, and please be sure to charge the battery every night."

It all seemed a bit theatrical. But if it was designed to impress me, the ritual accomplished its purpose. I had never been offered so huge an amount of cash at one time. Nor had payment ever been proffered to me in so formal a manner, dished up on a silver tray like some delicious appetizer, with the promise of more to come. I wanted to reach out and feel the heft of the envelope, open it up and count the cash inside. Instead, I held back, afraid of appearing greedy before this man who displayed an apparent disdain for actually touching money.

"You hesitate," he said. "Why? Is it because of the danger?"

"It's because I haven't decided whether I want to take the job."

Everyone in the room was watching me. Waiting for me to take the money. Waiting to see if I would join their ranks in the employ of this arrogant aristocrat.

He seemed puzzled. "Is $50,000 not enough? What is your usual fee?"

"It's not a question of the money."

"You're afraid," he sneered. "You think it's too dangerous. Thirty minutes ago you were boasting that you intended to find Serrano's killers. And now you are afraid to continue his work."

"I didn't say that."

"Then what are you saying, Mr. Nikonos?"

What I wanted to say was that I didn't like his attitude, the way he presumed he could get me to do his bidding just by throwing money at me. That he wasn't the sort of person for whom I wanted to work.

"I'm not sure I want to get involved . . ." I started to say.

"But you already are involved," he interrupted. "You think the men who killed Serrano don't know your identity? You think they won't come after you when they learn you are investigating his death? The best way to bring them out into the open is to find the truth. I believe the motive for their crime is hidden within the mystery that surrounds the young nun. Solve the mystery of La Magdalena, and you solve the mystery of Padre Serrano's murder."

He was right, of course. I knew he was manipulating me, but his argument made eminent sense. As long as I was going to proceed with my own investigation anyway, there was no reason to reject his offer of money. If it was as dangerous as I thought it might be, $10,000 could buy me some protection.

Reluctantly, I reached out for the white envelope. I could almost feel the relaxation of tension in the room.

"As you can imagine, this will be a very sensitive investigation," DesRosier continued. "It must be conducted with the greatest discretion, for your protection as well as my own. I must insist on absolute confidentiality. You must not reveal my involvement to anyone. And you will communicate your findings to no one but me."

It didn't seem like a particularly unusual request. Most investigators have similar one-on-one agreements with their clients.

"Under normal circumstances, I could provide you with access to the *Convento*, arrange for you to meet with La Magdalena, and possibly make her records available to you," he went on. "But I cannot allow my name to be associated with this investigation in any manner. I assume you will find ways to proceed on your own. And I trust you will move quickly. Time is of the essence in this matter. I'm very anxious to see it brought to a close."

The serving girls brought out plates of fruit and cheese, and placed before each of us a small bowl of *crema catalana*, the famous "burnt cream" of Catalunia. DesRosier finished his *crema* in a few quick spoonfuls.

"Although I don't believe in reincarnation, perhaps you may find an alternative explanation for the young nun's claims," he said. "I would be delighted if you could find any scientifically acceptable explanation for her behavior. But I shall leave the matter in your very capable hands."

His business accomplished, my host seemed to have no further need for my company. He rose and extended a limp hand to me.

"I hope you won't be insulted if I take my leave now," he said. "But I have other matters to deal with tonight. Please relax and enjoy an after-dinner liqueur. When you are ready, Tito and Manolo will drive you back to Valencia."

As we shook hands, my eyes drifted down to the ornate embroidery design on his breast pocket.

Blame it on fatigue. Blame it on the fact that there were so many other fascinating objects to distract my attention since my arrival at the chateau. Whatever the reason, I now realized there was a familiar symbol hidden within the intricate embroidery on his pocket.

In a small circle just below what I assumed was the DesRosier family crest were what appeared to be two knights with a single lance, riding on a single horse.

It was the insignia of a society that was once wealthier and more powerful than all the kings of Europe.

It was the same insignia I had seen on the golden pin worn by *Coronel* Velarde.

Unlike Velarde, however, DesRosier made no attempt to conceal the insignia from me.

Considering the manner in which he had so carefully orchestrated every aspect of my visit, I could only conclude he was displaying the insignia on purpose.

Twenty-Three

THE ENTIRE EVENING, from the moment of my abduction to the sumptuous dinner and DesRosier's hasty departure, was a Machiavellian performance. He had frightened me and flattered me, intimidated me and entertained me, and in the end, he had either hired me or bribed me. I still wasn't sure which. All I knew for certain is that he had learned more about me than I had about him.

The Basques allowed me more hip room on the long drive back to Valencia. We passed through long black stretches of empty countryside and shuttered towns, to which I paid little attention. I was exhausted, but sleep was impossible. My thoughts were dominated by my encounter with my new client. He hired me to solve a mystery, yet he remained a mystery himself. Why would he have me snatched off the street and brought all this way for a meeting that could as easily have been held in Valencia, where a man of his wealth would surely own an apartment? Intimidation, perhaps. A crude display of power. If that was the reason, it certainly worked. He had made the point that he could intervene in my life at any moment he chose. His short lecture on Basque culture was less a history lesson than a reminder that his bodyguards had no affection for foreigners like me. As I ran the evening's conversation through my mind, I realized every word, every action of my host had been carefully chosen.

But what did I really know about the man? Not much, I realized. He was French. He was apparently a very wealthy businessman. He was descended from one of the Crusaders. And the insignia he wore on his breast pocket connected him somehow to *Coronel* Velarde.

It was that emblem, so proudly embroidered in golden thread, that intrigued me most. As with so many other items in the chateau, the design had its origin in the Crusades. It was the insignia of The Order of the Poor Knights of Christ and the Temple of Solomon, the legendary Temple Knights, or Templars, as they are often called. Their exploits were the inspiration for a thousand years of heroic fictional inventions, from Malory's Knights of the Round Table, to Kurosawa's *Seven Samurai* and Sturges's *Magnificent Seven*.

I first heard of these warrior-monks from a committed atheist, one of my college philosophy professors. He used the Templar story to illustrate the Calvinist theory of the "essential depravity" of all men. Even allowing for the anti-religious bias he brought to the subject, it was a fascinating case history of how the noblest of intentions can fall victim to man's evil nature.

In the eleventh century, Pope Urban II seemed to have the purest of motives when he proposed a plan to permit more freedom of movement for Christians visiting the Holy Land. But the altruistic goal quickly degenerated into a desire to control not only the city of Jerusalem, but the entire Holy Land and all ports and points of entry leading to it. As my professor perversely delighted in pointing out, a man devoted to saving souls started a movement that would cost tens of thousands of lives. The Christian warriors of the First Crusade conquered all who opposed their march to Jerusalem, slaughtering all non-Christians along the way. Cities were burned, women raped, children enslaved in a series of battles that were considered among the most bloodthirsty in recorded history. After conquering the city of Antioch, for example, the Crusaders spent a full day methodically butchering every man, woman, and child who remained in the city. By the time Jerusalem was conquered, senseless slaughter appeared to take on the aura of sacred ritual. On the Temple of the Mount, the Crusaders proudly reported to the pope that they rode through blood that came up to the knees of their horses. And in a profane abuse of sacred scripture, one of the priests who took part in the attack described the scene by reciting Psalm 118: "This is the day the Lord has made. Let us be glad and rejoice in it."

But as horrifying as the carnage was, the rewards to the victors were staggering. After the battle of Ascalon alone, the Crusaders captured a treasure of gold, rubies, diamonds, silks, and other loot so vast that an army of twelve thousand men couldn't carry it all to Jerusalem. What couldn't be carted away was burned or otherwise destroyed. Similar wealth flowed from all the conquered territories, and even greater riches awaited in Jerusalem, where the spoils of war reportedly included some of the most venerated religious artifacts of all time: the Ark of the Covenant, the True Cross, and a burial cloth which later became known as the Shroud of Turin.

It was this nightmare of blood and greed that was memorialized by the paintings and antiques at DesRosier's chateau.

The symbol of the two knights embroidered on his pocket presented a different side of the same history.

Disgusted with the growing greed and depravity of his fellow Crusaders, Hugues de Payens convinced eight other knights to join him in a noble cause. They would take vows of poverty, chastity, and obedience. They would become monks in knights' clothing, raising their swords only for the purest of causes, sparing the innocent and protecting the weak. They were the first of the chivalric knights, a clear break with the rapacious armored fighters of their time. The symbol of the two men sharing a single horse and lance represented their vows of poverty and brotherhood.

I remember being entranced by the fairy-tale quality of the story. Even my professor had praise for the ennobling aspects of this small band of warrior-monks who changed the image of knighthood.

The vows they took and their actions to protect even the poorest of pilgrims were unheard of in those days, where plunder and rape were the norm. Baudouin II, who had been installed as king of Jerusalem, was happily astonished at the willingness of the nine knights to defend the Temple. All they asked in return was housing and basic supplies. The king assigned them part of the al-Aqsa Mosque on the Temple Mount. And thus was born the legend of the Templar Knights.

Word of this altruistic band quickly spread back to France, where it caught the public imagination. St. Bernard of Clairvaux created *The Rule,* a code of behavior which governed Templar life. A Papal Bull placed the Templars directly under the pope's own personal authority, freeing them from obeying any orders or laws issued by any government. Knights and nobles were soon vying to become members of this new cadre of saintly soldiers. Kings and sovereigns donated land and money.

But as my college professor pointed out, the vow of poverty merely applied to individual members, and not to the order itself. As the Templar wealth increased, they built and bought their own ships, expanded their bases, and secured strongholds throughout both Europe and the Middle East. And in a series of fascinating circumstances, they invented many of the instruments of modern financial activity. By using their network of fortresses to transfer payments of gold and silver coins, the Templars created the world's first international banking facility. To circumvent church laws against usury, they created the concept of discounted loans. While most investors think the idea of "stripping" the revenue stream of securities was dreamed up on Wall Street, it originated in the Templar practice of making no-interest mortgages which used the revenue of the property until the loan was repaid. The Templars became moneylenders for nations and for popes. Even the check as we know it today had its origins in the Templar practice of accepting money in one location and paying it out in another on production of a written receipt.

By the end of the twelfth century, the Templars had thousands of men under arms, fearless warriors who won battles wherever they might be waged. In addition to their seemingly impregnable fortresses in the Holy Land, new fortresses and chapters were established in England, Germany, Italy, Spain, Portugal, and France. An armada of 242 ships was based in La Rochelle. They had fought and conquered Muslims, Turks, Mongols, and other European armies.

Within a hundred years, they had become the most trusted, most feared, and most powerful organization in the known world.

In another hundred years, they would cease to exist, their leaders executed, their fortresses burned, their knights slaughtered or driven into hiding.

But no trace was ever found of the fabulous Templar treasure: as the bankers of Europe, the brotherhood possessed vast stores of gold and silver bullion. Even more significant were the legendary treasures of the Temple of Solomon, brought back from the Holy Land as part of the historic legacy of the brotherhood. In addition to artifacts of incredible religious as well as monetary value, they claimed possession of ancient documents that contained mystical teachings and suppressed information about the early Christian Church. Only one of these items, a linen burial cloth now known as the Shroud of Turin, ever turned up. While mystical knowledge is said to be part of the secret rituals of the Templars, the physical treasure itself is reputed to remain buried somewhere in the south of France. But eight centuries of searching by everyone from King Philip the Fair to Adolf Hitler's Nazi looters to local hobbyists have proven fruitless. Other reports suggest the treasure was loaded onto the Templar fleet of 200 ships based at La Rochelle, which left port on October 13, 1307, and were never seen or heard from again.

As an impressionable young college student in New York, I found the story of the Templars to be an irresistible tale of medieval chivalry, valor, and mystery.

As a thirty-year-old investigator in Valencia, I wondered if the ancient brotherhood, long considered extinct, was still active, still pursuing its self-assigned responsibilities. One of those responsibilities, as I recalled, was to be the guardians of the Holy Grail, which might, in a certain roundabout way, explain DesRosier's interest in the Convent of the Holy Grail—but of that convent's inhabitants, why was Sister Mariamme alone the object of his attention?

Twenty-Four

INVESTIGATING A NUN without Church approval poses some unusual obstacles, the first of which is gaining access to the subject. Sequestered nuns, in particular, do not move about freely. Their activities are carefully monitored by other nuns, who could be expected to raise an alarm if anyone attempted to intrude on the privacy of one of their members. With the *Guardia* watching me, how could I even approach Sister Mariamme, much less conduct the extensive interviews my investigation would require?

The Basques dropped me off in Valencia before sunrise, when the empty streets belonged to stray cats and sanitation workers. They let me out of the car a few blocks from my hotel, to avoid being seen by whoever was running surveillance on me. I was exhausted, having gone the entire night without sleep. What I really wanted was to get back to the hotel and crawl into bed. But this was the first time in days that I wasn't being followed or otherwise observed, and I was determined to take advantage of it.

Somehow, I knew, I would have to gain access to Sister Mariamme inside the *convento*. While that assignment might not be as difficult as breaking into CIA headquarters, a quick reconnaissance revealed there were some similarities.

First, there was the perimeter security to deal with. This was provided by the *Guardia's* surveillance teams, which apparently were in position 24 hours a day. Even at 5:30 in the morning, as I soon discovered, there was a man standing in a doorway across the street from the *convento*, waiting to follow Sister Mariamme if she left the building. I strolled slowly up the street, offering him a smiling *"Buenos días,"* and memorizing his face for future reference as I walked by. I passed the delivery van with the blacked-out windows, but was unable to see anything inside.

The second barrier was posed by the building itself. It looked like a massive prison, with all the street-floor windows heavily barred. The exterior was faced with some indeterminate smooth stone whose original color had long ago disappeared under a dark patina laid down by generations of pollution and neglect. Except for the four turrets that softened the corners, it was devoid of any architectural ornamentation that might provide handholds for any human fly who attempted to scale its heights. Entry to the *convento* appeared to be severely restricted. Cut into the exact center of the building was a set of arched double doors wide enough to accommodate a team of draft horses pulling an oversize load, or its modern equivalent, an eighteen-wheeled semi-trailer. The timbers were heavy enough to make the protective iron gate seem superfluous. Close by, also guarded by an iron gate, was a standard-sized door used by the nuns and their visitors. A small peephole allowed the doorkeeper to ascertain the identity of any who dared attempt entry.

There were no fire escapes, ladders, or other forms of emergency exit. In the effort to protect the nuns from any intruders, all access was funneled through the two entrances. That made surveillance a simple matter. And entry without permission an utter impossibility.

I headed up the street and ducked into an alley two blocks away, where I could watch without being observed.

At precisely six A.M., the small door opened, the metal gate was unlocked, and six nuns filed out of the *convento*. They walked quickly, two abreast, in a tight formation. The man in the doorway, apparently satisfied Sister Mariamme was not among the six nuns, remained at his post. At the end of the block, the nuns turned north on *Avenida Baron de Carcer*, in the direction of the cathedral. I slipped out of the alleyway and followed them at a discreet distance.

Once inside the cathedral, the nuns quickly dispersed, each performing a series of tasks to prepare for the day's crowds. They moved with wordless and well-rehearsed precision. Kneelers were raised, envelopes and missals neatly arranged, informational pamphlets restocked, burned-out votive candles replaced. The first Mass was scheduled for 6:30 A.M. A few locals, almost all of them women, were already in place. An old man was lighting a votive candle in front of a side altar. A young penitent was slowly moving towards the altar on her knees, beating her chest with one hand and fingering a rosary with the other. This early Mass was for the regular parishioners. The crowds of tourists and pilgrims wouldn't arrive until later.

When the bells for the first Mass sounded, the six nuns put aside their chores and filed into the front pew. Watching these nuns, who bowed their heads so reverently in prayer, I wondered how any of them could possibly be part of a cult that threatened the sanctity of their order. The Mass was a short one. As if to make up for its brevity, when the priest left the sacristy, the nuns remained in their pew. I slipped in next to the oldest of them and blessed myself hurriedly.

"I have to see La Magdalena," I whispered to the startled nun beside me.

She was a stern woman with a narrow face and bushy, almost masculine eyebrows. From the look of horror in her eyes, you'd think I had made some sort of indecent proposal.

"Please Sister," I begged. "*Por favor, Hermana.* I must talk to La Magdalena. It's very important."

The other nuns looked up from their prayers to see what was causing the disturbance. They didn't realize they were blocking the escape route their colleague so desperately wanted to use. She was trapped between me on one side and five of her fellow religious women on the other.

"She gave me a letter," I tried to explain. "She wanted me to deliver it to Padre Serrano."

I thought the name triggered a flicker of recognition in the nun's eyes.

"The letter was stolen from me," I said.

Her eyes grew wider.

"And now Padre Serrano is dead."

"*Dios mío!*" the nun exclaimed, and hurriedly blessed herself.

She turned to the nuns beside her and repeated in Spanish what I had told her.

The other nuns seemed devastated by the report of Serrano's death. They began to murmur prayers which included frequent repetitions of his name.

"So you are the one," the nun said when she turned back to me. "You are the one La Magdalena was waiting for."

Now it was my turn to be startled.

"I don't understand."

"She recognized you at once."

"But how could that be . . .?"

"Tell me of Padre Serrano," she interrupted. "How did he meet his death?"

"The bombing," I said. "He was killed in the bombing."

As I watched her struggle to understand, I realized she knew nothing of what went on in the secular world. TV and newspapers were undoubtedly banned in the convent.

"Four days ago, there was a bombing in a small juice bar near the *Estación del Norte*," I explained. "Padre Serrano and I were there. We were talking about La Magdalena. He was going to show me some documents. I spilled a drink and went to wash my hands. While I was away from the table, a bomb exploded. Padre Serrano and the attendant were killed."

A lifetime of learning to suppress her emotions automatically kicked in. When her jaw began to tremble, she bit down hard against her lower lip. To keep her hands from rising in shock to her face, she squeezed one palm against the other, locking them in an embrace so tight, the knuckles and joints turned white. Despite the protective camouflage of the loose habit, I could sense that her entire body had stiffened, as she struggled to maintain control of herself. If she hadn't been a nun, if we hadn't been in the front pew of the great cathedral in full view of the local parishioners, I would have tried to comfort her by taking her hands in mine. But constrained by respect for the rules by which she and the other nuns lived, I could only wait until the storm passed.

"I'm sure he didn't suffer," I said lamely. "It all happened in an instant."

She took a deep breath and let it all out in a long, sad sigh.

"It is part of God's plan," she said at last. "The Lord works in mysterious ways. He took the padre. And sent you in his place." The part about being sent by God was the same thing Serrano had said moments before he died. But the padre had sounded enthusiastic about what he saw as divine intervention. The nun regarded me with a look of disappointment.

I wanted to correct her, to tell her that I wasn't sent by God, that I wasn't some heavenly messenger here to fulfill whatever prophecy the nuns might think I was part of. But what was I to say? That I was an investigator here on a perfectly earthly mission? That my primary goal was finding Serrano's killer? That I accepted ten thousand dollars from a patron of the convent to determine La Magdalena's true identity?

Or should I tell the truth? The truth I was afraid to admit even to myself: that some unknown force was drawing me to the beautiful young nun; that her image, her voice, the soft weight of her breast on the back of my hand made me yearn to see her again. It was a truth I was afraid to admit because such thoughts were forbidden by my Greek Orthodox upbringing. Romantic fantasies about nuns bordered on sacrilege. Taking the thoughts any further into the sexual fantasies that were normal for a healthy young man my age violated my own principles of self-respect. It was the only religious taboo I still observed.

"Can you arrange a meeting with La Magdalena?" I asked.

"The *convento* is being watched."

"I know."

"There is a man who takes pictures of everyone who enters or leaves."

The man I saw had no camera. I wondered how many other groups were running surveillance on the building.

"Perhaps you could speak to her on the telephone," one of the other nuns suggested. "We're not permitted to use the telephone, but we might be able to arrange it."

"No good," I said. "They're probably monitoring the telephone lines. I have to see her in person. And privately."

"That may be impossible," the first nun said. "They follow her wherever she goes."

"They follow me, too. But I was able to escape them this morning."

"Such tactics may work for you. For a nun, it is not so easy. We are not trained to avoid detection."

She was right, of course. I couldn't picture one of these black-robed nuns darting into doorways or commandeering a taxi and ordering the driver to "Lose that car!" And I hadn't come up with any way of getting into the convent myself. My investigation seemed doomed to failure at the outset.

"There must be a way," the nun murmured.

"I will talk to La Magdalena," she said. "Together we will pray for an answer."

I was never one of those psychologists who dismissed prayer as a form of wishful thinking. Beyond my personal beliefs, I had seen enough research that documented the medical and life benefits that could be derived from a concentrated appeal to a higher power. The Harvard and Duke University Prayer Studies, in particular, validated the healing power of prayer. The data proved the age-old belief that cures can be accomplished and the human body favorably affected even when the prayers are directed over long distances by total strangers. To the best of my knowledge, however, no research had ever proven the efficacy of prayer in avoiding surveillance.

"I don't have much time," I said.

"Come back tonight," she told me. "Before the evening Mass. I will have an answer by then."

She made it sound so simple, so routine, as if she was going to send some sort of e-mail to God, and fully expected Him to respond with a solution to our problem. Of course, she had much more experience in such matters than I. And maybe that was the way prayer worked.

I hoped so.

After they filed out of the cathedral, I waited a reasonable time and exited through the side door. I went into a café across the street, ducked out through the rear entrance, and circled back around to a doorway halfway up the block, where I waited to see who was following me. I knew it wouldn't be the *Guardia,* who were probably still watching my hotel, waiting for my return. And I wasn't mistaken. The slender man who followed me was an expert. He had waited on the steps of the cathedral until he saw me enter the café. Only then did he proceed, strolling slowly up the street, blue jacket slung over his narrow shoulders as if he didn't have a care in the world. No furtive moves for Tito. He blended in by being open.

Some unexplainable intuition caused me to look up the street, in the direction I would have to travel. I could barely make out a bulky figure partially hidden behind a newspaper kiosk. It was Manolo, ready to take over if I spotted Tito. Sure enough, when I looked back, Tito had disappeared from view.

Twenty-Five

I KNEW THEY weren't there to harm me.

It was probably DesRosier's way of protecting his investment, making sure I didn't take his initial ten thousand dollars and leave the country. But the idea that he would have me followed irritated me.

I opened up the Nokia cell phone and pressed the one-touch button that was supposed to connect me with DesRosier wherever he was. A woman answered almost instantly.

"*Hola?*" At first, I thought I had the wrong number. Her voice was soft and whispery, as if she didn't wish to be overheard. She didn't identify herself, the way a corporate secretary normally would.

"I was calling Mr. DesRosier. Jean-Claude DesRosier."

"One moment, please." She reverted to English. Still the intimate tone of voice, but a bit more efficient now. I heard a rustle of paper, a clicking sound, followed by the electronic crackling as my call was patched through to another location.

"Are you making progress already, Mr. Nikonos?" It was the familiar languid voice of my new employer.

"How did you know it was me?"

"The wonders of modern telecommunications," he said. "Your phone sent a signal to my secretary's phone. I believe in your country it's called Caller ID. Now what is the reason for your call?"

"It's the Basques. They're following me."

"You saw them?"

"I'm standing in a doorway near the cathedral. I can see Manolo, or at least where he's hiding. But Tito seems to have disappeared."

"I'm surprised," DesRosier said. "Usually they're much more discreet."

"Why are they following me?"

"It's for your own protection. There's no need to be upset. I asked them to assist you. Consider them your . . . bodyguards."

More likely his spies, I thought. They would have already observed my conversation with the nun and reported it back to DesRosier.

"Call them off. I don't want them around."

"This is a very dangerous game," DesRosier said. "You should not be going about it alone."

"Call them off," I repeated.

"Very well." His words were followed by a click and a dial tone.

I waited in the doorway. After a few moments, Tito stepped out into the open, holding a cell phone to his ear. The call was brief. When it was over, he slipped on his jacket and, before turning back to the cathedral, smiled and arrogantly waved to me. It was his signal that I hadn't managed to elude him after all. At the far end of the block, I could see Manolo's bulkier silhouette emerge from a portal, cross the street, and disappear. Whether they were ordered to end the surveillance or simply drop into deeper cover, I didn't know.

I went back into the café for breakfast: *churros* and *chocolate*. Sitting by the window, I watched the neighborhood slowly come alive. Sidewalks were swept, dogs were walked, sanitation crews opened hydrants to clear the gutters of debris. In Spain, as in France and Italy, a single cup of coffee or chocolate entitles the buyer to sit all day if desired. My people watching continued, as the sidewalks and street gradually filled with Valencianos. Stunning young women in shockingly short skirts hurried across my field of vision, most likely receptionists on their way to open up offices, answer the phones and greet the day's first callers. The briefcase crowd followed, a line formed at the café's takeout counter, taxis were hailed, the rush hour peaked and finally ended with the emergence of the more leisurely senior executives who didn't have to worry about being on time at the office. The workday had started.

The first shops to open had been the bakeries, followed by the pharmacies, the food stores, and finally the specialty shops. That was what I had been waiting for. I headed out to the commercial section in search of an optical supply store. I found what I wanted in the third store I visited. A quick visit to an audio and electronics store completed my shopping. My next stop was an Internet Café, where I settled down to a computer to find out more about my new employer. The Spanish "People Finder" links turned up no Jean-Claude Flamel DesRosier. But when I went to the traditional search engines, the first one I opened turned up 1,627 web pages that contained references to Flamel and 18,471 for DesRosier. The Flamel pages referred to everything from a French Biotechnology company to individuals searching for their family history.

The pages related to the DesRosier name covered everything from diamond mines to container ships, banks and farms to resorts and minority holdings in dozens of major European corporations. He was a patron of the opera, the ballet, the symphony, and a long list of charities. He was mentioned in every listing of Spanish political and economic power brokers. In 1999, he made the Forbes listing of the world's wealthiest men, with assets estimated at 1.2 billion U.S. dollars. The slide in the foreign exchange rates had reduced the dollar value of his holdings, but in round figures, he was still worth at least a billion dollars. A thousand million dollars. It was an unbelievable figure, one that would have left me paralyzed in his presence if I had known it at the time. There were thousands of other pages, too, references to his father René and his grandfather Louis, and some obscure references to his Templar ancestors, but most of them were related to Jean-Claude and his business activities. I found it puzzling that a billionaire, a man with so many important corporate and social activities, would take the time to talk me into investigating the claims of a nineteen-year-old nun. Even if I accepted his explanation that he was a patron of the *convento,* hiring someone like me seemed such a minor matter, the kind of thing he would normally ask one of his employees to handle. Why would a billionaire take the time to talk to me?

The answer wouldn't be found on the Internet, I knew, and after a few hours I gave up the cyber search and headed back to my room.

The morning desk clerk at my *pensión* was a young man with pink hair and a ring through his lower lip. With his red-rimmed eyes and occasional bruises, he usually looked as if he had been thrown out of some heavy-metal club just before coming to work. When I asked for my key, he glanced towards my room.

Allí tiene visitantes," he warned me in a quiet voice.

I hesitated.

"Policía?" I asked.

He nodded, with an expression of distaste that suggested his own previous unpleasant encounters with the authorities.

I handed him the shopping bags containing my optical and electronic purchases. Wordlessly, he hid them under the counter. On a leap of faith that the young clerk saw me as a fellow victim, I also handed over my jacket, which contained the cell phone, car keys, and cash envelope. I wasn't sure I'd ever see any of it again, but it was better than having the police question me about them.

The door to my room was unlocked. Inside, I found *Coronel* Velarde and two of his men.

"Buenos días, Coronel," I greeted him.

The contents of my traveling bag were spread across the bed. One of the *Coronel's* men had turned my bag inside out and was meticulously examining the seams.

"Good morning to you, too, Mr. Nikonos," he said with a smile.

"I didn't expect visitors this early." I tried to keep it friendly. It was never a good idea to antagonize the police.

"We were in the neighborhood and thought we'd stop by," Velarde said, continuing the pretense of civility.

"Did you find what you were looking for?" I asked.

The *Coronel* said something in Spanish too rapid for me to understand. The men started to carefully repack my bag.

"You travel without much baggage," Velarde said.

"I've got some laundry drying in the bathroom," I said. "But I'm sure you checked that. Did you look under the bed, too?"

"Now you are being, *como se dice* . . . sarcastic. You did not sleep here last night, Mr. Nikonos. We were worried about you. May I ask where you were?"

"I was up the coast," I said. In fact, it was true. But I wasn't about to mention DesRosier's name, even though they might be Templar comrades. "I went to Sagunto to see the Roman ruins. It's an important site from the historic point of view. I especially liked the Roman columns in the middle of the town."

Velarde had been watching me carefully, giving me the police stare that's supposed to intimidate suspects into telling the truth.

"The columns in the middle of the town," he repeated. "The ones in front of the fountain."

"You're mistaken," I said, carefully avoiding his trap. "I didn't see any fountain near the Roman columns."

"Ah yes, I must have confused it with another town," he said. "And where did you sleep when you were in Sagunto?" he asked.

Another trap.

"Frankly, by the time I finished sightseeing, it was late at night," I said. "I had a couple of drinks. One of the locals took me to his cousin's place, where they have a room they rent out to tourists. I'd probably never be able to find the place again."

It wasn't a very elaborate lie. Just enough to get the job done.

The two uniformed officers finished repacking my bag. Velarde waved them to the door.

"You will let me know, please, if you are planning any more overnight trips," he said to me.

"I'll try. But my travel plans are pretty unstructured. I usually don't know where I'll be from one day to the next."

"You should remember that you are not in your own country," he said. "Travel outside the city can sometimes be dangerous." And just before leaving, he added, "You should get some rest. You look like you had no sleep at all last night."

I watched from the window until I saw all three of them leave the building. Velarde and one of the officers drove off in a black *Guardia* vehicle. The other officer, the shorter one, went into the building across the street.

The desk clerk was more talkative now that the police were gone.

"They come here every day," he said. "Always when you are out. I think this time they wanted you to find them." He showed me a locker behind the counter where he had stowed my jacket and my shopping bags. "Anything you don't want them to find, you can keep in here," he said. "Except no drugs or guns. They will blame it on me."

A huge smile lit up his face when I rewarded him with a U.S. hundred-dollar bill. "My name is Alfredo," he said. "Anything you want, just call me."

Before going to sleep, I made one last check of the building across the street. The grid pattern I had established had revealed more than one window being used for surveillance. Two were on the floor directly across from me, and two were on the floor above them. The windows were open in the midday heat, as they had been for the past few days. But at night, no lights were ever visible, not even a table lamp. I assumed the *Guardia* had a surveillance team in one of the rooms. The Basques were possibly occupying another.

But who was watching me from the other two rooms?

It was time to find out.

Twenty-Six

FIRST, I HAD to make myself invisible.

One of the fascinating aspects of modern technology is the ease with which even the most sophisticated systems can be circumvented or defeated.

My visit to the optical supply store was to learn whatever I could about the kind of equipment unfriendly eyes might be using to spy on me. It was apparently a request the bored salesclerk had heard before. He treated me no differently than he treated paranoids with delusions of being watched, or voyeurs looking for new ways to peep into their neighbors' bedrooms.

Which is to say he was interested only in selling me as much of his stock as he could.

Playing on what he assumed were either my fantasies or my fears, he happily explained that the traditional protections of darkness could no longer protect anyone from prying eyes. He explained that today's see-through technologies could turn night into day, shadow into light, and penetrate barriers that once provided privacy. The current fad in visual surveillance, he explained, was far more sophisticated than the "night scopes" used by the U.S. military in the Gulf War, which produced ghost-ly figures without much detail. He demonstrated a pair of Russian-made "Nighthawk" binoculars which used battery-powered electronic circuitry to produce an image of incredible detail, even in total darkness. Playing me for both a voyeur and a paranoid, he assured me the Russian binocu-lars were better than anything the Guardia might use. And he sold me a way to make myself invisible from any watchers.

He called it "Stealth Sheeting," presumably to justify the price. But it was strictly low-tech, nothing more than a thin sheet of reflective plastic with a two-way capability. The optically impenetrable sheeting had other benefits. The installation was bound to create confusion in the rooms across the street. As the surveillance team tried in vain to recalibrate their equipment, their activities would give me an opportunity to observe them. The clerk demonstrated the two-way capability of the mirrored plastic sheeting before I left the store, which gave me the ability to stand, unde-tected behind the window, and peer into the rooms where I thought the surveillance teams were located.

When I trained the Russian binoculars on the first room marked on my grid, the one directly across from me, I saw only a small single bed that hadn't been slept in. The doors of a wooden armoire were open, reveal-ing a half-dozen empty plastic hangers. There was no indication that any-one was occupying the room, either on a regular or transient basis. I could only assume the window was opened each day to prevent the buildup of mildewed air.

The second room marked on my grid was on the same floor as the first, two windows away. In the middle of the room, far enough back not to reflect any sunlight, was a tripod-mounted telescope with a lens the size of a grapefruit. I recognized it as a larger version of the nightscope I had seen at the optical shop. It was aimed directly at my room. Happily for me, the way the man behind the scope was fumbling with the controls indicated my countermeasures were successful. There was a second man in the room. He was using binoculars similar to mine, but having no more success than his comrade. I could see their lips moving, and I could imagine their frustration. The man at the nightscope turned away to use a cell phone. His partner shook his head in frustration, but kept his binoculars trained on my window. Both men wore their hair cropped short, military style. They operated in shirtsleeves that bore no insignia. A slight adjustment on the light-amplifying capability allowed me to peer further into the room, where one of their jackets hung over the back of a chair.

It was a dark blue officer's jacket with a narrow gold braid on one sleeve. The lapel insignia identified him as a member of the *Guardia Civil*.

That was pretty much what I expected. I assumed the scope operator was on the phone to *Coronel* Velarde, who would probably be paying me another visit.

I had two more rooms to check. The next window was on the floor above. My binoculars displayed a middle-aged woman with long blonde hair and oversized stomach and breasts. She was wearing a black bra and red bikini panties which looked to be a size too small for her ample hips. She was sprinkling the space between her breasts with white powder, probably talc. She was obviously not a member of any stakeout team.

No nightscopes or cameras or binoculars were visible in the fourth window. The room was small and simple. Atop the dresser were the remnants of a take-out meal: a few scraps of a hamburger bun, a crumpled napkin, and a plastic coffee cup with the golden arches of MacDonald's emblazoned on its side. There was only one occupant in the room. He sat deep in the shadows, as far back from the window as he could get. I had to push the light-amplification control to its maximum level to bring his features into clearer view. He was a young man, with sandy hair, gaunt cheeks and the undernourished look of a student. He was staring at my window with an intensity I found unnerving, as if he could by sheer willpower see through the reflective plastic and watch what I was doing.

What I saw was enough to make me wish I hadn't chased the Basques away.

The young man staring back at me was the backpacker who left the *Naranjas* just before the bomb exploded.

I dropped the binoculars and rushed out of my room.

I had no plan. I wasn't armed. I didn't know if he had a weapon. But I wasn't going to let him get away.

His room was on the fifth floor, third from the end, according to the grid I had drawn. I ran across the street, ignored the shouts of the lobby guard and dashed up the stairs.

Halfway up, I thought of getting assistance from the *Guardia* surveillance team, but I was afraid they'd delay me too long with irrelevant questions.

Just before opening the fire door on the fifth floor, I slowed down. If he was in the hallway, I didn't want to spook him. I turned the knob slowly, opened the door without a sound, and slipped into the hallway. It was empty. But was this the right floor? I wanted the fifth floor, and all the door numbers here started with 4. I did a quick bit of double-counting in my mind before remembering the quirk of the European floor numbering system. What we in America considered the second floor, the Europeans counted as the first. With that resolved, as quietly as possible, I approached the third door from the end. Room 420.

There was no sound from inside.

I knocked. Softly, so as not to alarm my prey.

No response.

"Señor?" I called out in my best Spanish accent.

Still no response.

"Señor? *Está usted aquí?*"

I tried the door. It was unlocked.

I threw the door open and stepped aside, expecting him to jump out at me.

Still no response.

Cautiously, I peered into the room. It looked empty.

I checked behind the door. Under the bed. Inside the closet. In the bathroom.

No one.

The dresser drawers were empty. Except for the remains of the take-out meal on the dresser, there was no indication anyone had occupied the room. The bed didn't appear slept in, although the housekeeper could have already made her daily rounds.

This was another of those Spanish hotels that occupied a few floors in a larger building. The desk was down one flight, the same floor as the *Guardia*'s room. I asked the clerk who was registered in room 420. He checked his registration book.

"*No ocupado,*" he said. When I started to argue, he swung the book around to show me room 420 was vacant.

"*Usted quieres?*" He asked.

No, I didn't want the room, I told him. How long since it was last occupied?

"*Una semana,*" he said. One week.

What I thought had been a clever way of turning the tables on my pursuers suddenly seemed like a futile, if not foolish, gesture.

While I had been worrying about the *Guardia,* trying to find a way to outwit them, a more ominous figure had been watching me without my knowledge. It was only by chance I had seen the mysterious backpacker. How had he learned where I was staying? And why was he following me?

Twenty-Seven

SERRANO'S KILLER WAS back, his attention this time focused on me.

If he was carrying a bomb, it could be planted outside my hotel room door just as easily as it had been left at the *Naranjas.* Like other NDEers, I had little fear of death. But when it came, I wanted it to be after I brought Serrano's killer to justice. More important, I didn't want any more innocents to die in another indiscriminate bomb blast.

I moved my clothing and the night-vision binoculars to the hotel room upstairs where I kept Serrano's books. I paid the upstairs clerk two weeks', rent in advance, more than enough time, I thought, than I would need to complete my investigation of La Magdalena. I sealed the room key and $500 in an envelope and asked Alfredo to hold it for me. He had proven mildly trustworthy so far, and if I needed an ally, the money would ensure his help.

What I needed now was a safe place to get some sleep until later that evening, when I was due to meet the nuns at the cathedral. I knew I'd be followed wherever I went, probably by the Basques, definitely by the *Guardia,* and most ominously by the backpacker. Where could I go, a foreigner in a strange city? Where did I dare close my eyes without fear of some violent attack being launched against me?

In a country with such powerful religious traditions, one place beckoned. It was the traditional refuge of fugitives and the oppressed, a setting whose peace had never been shattered by gunshots or bombings. The concept of sanctuary was still respected in modern Spain, and the great cathedral offered the safe haven I sought.

I selected a pew right down front, in the second row from the altar, in plain view of the priests and all the tourists. It was too exposed a location for anyone to try to do me harm. And I knew the nuns would gather there later for their vesper prayers.

Twice during the afternoon, I was nudged awake by the ushers, who complained about my snoring. The ringing of the Angelus bells roused me at six o'clock, but my eyes remained open for only a few minutes. The evening Mass came and went, the sounds of the Roman Catholic ritual barely making an impression on me. What finally raised me from my torpor was the rhythmic chanting of five nuns in the pew behind me saying the rosary with what seemed to be more vigor than normal.

I looked back to see the linen-framed face of the elderly nun who had spoken to me that morning.

She frowned and chastised me for sleeping in church, keeping her words enveloped within the rhythm of the prayers her colleagues were chanting in unison.

I turned back to face the altar, afraid the watchers might detect our communication.

"Do you still wish to see La Magdalena?" she asked.

"Yes, but I'm being followed."

"I know. But we have found a way to get you into the *convento*. . ."

She stopped speaking each time the nuns completed their response. She waited while the group leader solemnly intoned the beginning of the next Hail Mary, and spoke to me again when her voice was once more camouflaged by the group's response.

"We can get you into the *convento* tonight without the watchers' knowledge. But you must follow my instructions without question. First go to the back of the cathedral . . ."

She paused while the group leader said the first part of the prayer.

"Just outside the Chapel of the Holy Grail is a hallway which will lead you to the comfort rooms reserved for members of the religious orders. Go to the end of the hallway . . ."

I waited for her to continue during the next response.

"At the end of the hallway is the door to the chapel's sacristy. Sister Mary Serafina will be waiting inside for you. Do as she says. And do it quickly, before anyone else enters the room."

I waited for the next response.

"What are you waiting for?" she hissed angrily. "Go now. And hurry. Otherwise we are all in danger."

I rose from my sleeping position, made a show of stretching, looked around the cathedral, and headed up the aisle.

It was late evening. The back of the cathedral was poorly illuminated. I found the door she described. The hallway was dark. Darkness was my friend, I thought, as I felt along the wall for the comfort room doors, moved past them, and kept going until I saw the crack of light from beneath the sacristy door. Cautiously, I opened it. Inside was a plump, middle-aged nun. Sister Serafina smiled conspiratorially and hurried me in with a frenzied waving of her hand.

"*Viene aquí!*" she whispered. "Hurry."

I closed the door.

"Take off your clothes," she said.

"Excuse me?"

She produced a bundle of dark clothing in a clear plastic bag.

"Take off your clothes and put these on."

"This is nun's clothing," I protested.

"*Idioto!* Of course it's nun's clothing. How else do you expect to get into the *convento?*"

I started to roll up my pants legs, assuming they wouldn't be seen under the long habit.

"You must take off everything," she insisted. "In case we are stopped."

"You mean they'd look up a nun's robe?"

"*Por favor, señor,* it is the mother superior's requirement, not mine."

She turned her back and I, modestly, also turned mine. It was bad enough that I was shedding my pants behind a Bride of Christ, but when I looked up, I saw that I was disrobing in front of a large crucifix.

"Do I really have to wear this pantyhose?" I asked.

"Yes, señor," she giggled. "Unless you choose to paint your legs black."

I struggled into the black cotton pantyhose.

"It's too tight," I muttered.

"It is the largest size we had, señor. This clothing all belongs to the mother superior, who is as tall as you."

As I struggled with the pantyhose, I thought of the transvestites who dressed up in nun's clothing for San Francisco's Gay Pride Parade. Did they feel as strange as I did, the first time they wore women's clothing? It was an unsettling feeling, made more so when the nun insisted, her back still turned, that I not forget the ample bra, which she had thoughtfully stuffed with cotton.

"Otherwise, the front of the habit will not appear feminine."

Cross-dressing is described in the psychology textbooks as a harmless form of gender experimentation indulged in by a surprisingly large thirty percent of the population. While it is not necessarily an indicator of homosexual or lesbian tendencies, it does appear to have a strong libidinous component. This can probably be traced back to the psychological excitement induced by breaking sexual taboos. It was this aspect which I found myself struggling to resist.

My body, covered with a dark robe, no longer resembled that of the lean young man who had stumbled down the hallway. My chest had taken on the dimensions of a modest bosom. A crucifix was draped around my neck. A white cord was wrapped around my waist. An oversized rosary hung from the cord. My feet were encased in tight but modest shoes that lifted my heels an inch off the floor. As the nun who assisted me carefully fitted the white linen wimple around my neck and the sides of my face, the last visible markers of masculinity disappeared. No one could see my Adam's apple. My short haircut was hidden under the starched headdress. When I was fully dressed, the only flesh that remained visible to anyone accosting me was the front of my face and my hands, which could be hidden within the baggy sleeves. I had taken on the persona of a Sister of the Holy Grail.

"They can still recognize my face," I said.

"I doubt it. People look at nun's robes, not their faces."

"It's still a man's face."

"Not as much as you think it is. You have soft, gentle features. You must be a kind person."

"They'll see my beard."

"Many nuns have facial hair," she laughed. "We have nuns in the *convento* who look much more masculine than you do."

The door suddenly opened and two nuns entered, excited.

"They have started searching the tourist rest rooms," one nun said. "They'll be here soon."

"It is time to go," the plump nun told me.

"Wait a minute," I said. "What'll I do with this stuff?" I was holding my wallet, DesRosier's cell phone and car keys, and the two small electronic devices I bought at the audio store. "I need to bring these things, but there aren't any pockets in this outfit."

"Stuff them in your brassiere," the plump nun said. "Nobody'll search in there."

The other two nuns giggled.

"Hurry," the plump nun said as she watched me struggle with the ungainly robe. I divided the items up, fitting the wallet and cell phone into the left side of the bra, and the small electronic units into the right side. They fit comfortably in with the tissue, and the weight felt evenly balanced. Probably close to the weight of real breasts, I thought.

"It'll be all right," the nun said. "Just follow me. Keep your head lowered and take small steps. Be ladylike."

I groaned with embarrassment. Dressing up in women's clothing was something I never thought I would experience. It was just a change of wardrobe, I tried to tell myself. Nothing more than garments that fit differently and elastic understructures that produced a change in my silhouette. Yet I couldn't avoid a strange sense of what I can only describe as borderline demasculinization. If dressing as a woman was unnerving, what troubled me even more was wearing the habiliments of a nun. It seemed almost sacrilegious to be standing there with my head encased in starched white linen, talking with three nuns who wore the same garb, and almost unbelievably, feeling a common bond with them. The psychologist in me marveled at the transformation a change of clothing could induce.

But wearing a nun's clothing in the privacy of the sacristy was one thing. Stepping out in public was an entirely different matter. There were men out there looking for me. As embarrassed as I might have felt when I first pulled on the black pantyhose, how much more embarrassed would I feel if the *Guardia* discovered me in this outfit? I could imagine my humiliation if I were dragged before *Coronel* Velarde in my nun's robes.

"Hurry," Sister Serafina tugged at my sleeve.

I followed her out into the hallway, which was now illuminated by a single bare bulb in the narrow ceiling. Two burly men, whom I didn't recognize, were coming out of the men's rest room. My first instinct was to run. But I knew I wouldn't get far in my robe and heels. As any nun would do, I modestly lowered my head, avoiding eye contact.

"*Buenas noches, Hermanas,*" they murmured as they flattened themselves against the wall to allow us to pass. Their voices were polite and gentle, respectful even.

"*Buenas noches,*" Sister Serafina said as we walked by.

Just when I thought I had successfully passed my first test, one of the men called after us.

"*Un momento, por favor!*"

We both stopped. The nun turned to face them, while I turned only partially.

"*Cual es el?*" she asked.

"*Un Americano . . . estamos buscando. Usted lo vió un Americano aquí?*"

"*No hay hombre aquí. Solamente dos mas Hermanas en el sacristy.*"

With perfect timing, the other two nuns came out of the sacristy. The men greeted them and stepped aside to allow the nuns to pass. As our procession continued up the hallway, I could hear the voices of the two men as they searched the sacristy.

"There is a second door in that room," the lead nun whispered. "They'll think you escaped out the back."

"Thank you, Sister," I said, surprised at the humility in my voice. I was in the hands of the *Hermanas del Sangreal,* and for the time being, I felt perfectly content to follow orders.

The cathedral was almost empty. A few latecomers were standing near the main entrance, silently mouthing their prayers. Following the lead of the other nuns, I dipped my index finger in the holy water font, knelt on both knees facing the altar, and blessed myself slowly. As we were leaving the cathedral, I noticed someone watching from the shadows. It was the old priest who had helped me up when I was accosted on the steps four days ago. He was smiling at me. Not with surprise or amusement, I thought, but with what seemed to be approval. He nodded his head ever so slightly, as if he didn't want the gesture of recognition to be noticed by anyone but me.

Outside the cathedral, we formed up into pairs, which seemed to be the traditional way the nuns processed through the streets of Valencia. The market stalls outside the cathedral were mostly closed for the night, but a string of bare light bulbs illuminated the stands selling roast corn, peanuts, *cuchifritos,* deep-fried shrimp, and other *tapas.* Sister Serafina set the pace, taking us quickly down *Calle la Paz.* The streets were filled with *Valencianos* on their evening *paseo,* the traditional Spanish promenade that starts after dusk every day. It was a ritual that had fascinated me since my arrival in Spain. As if by some invisible cue, much of the population of Spain emerges from their homes and apartments every evening to stroll and talk and meet their friends and show off their latest finery before the incredibly late dinner hour. Everyone on the streets, from the youngest children in elaborate strollers to *ancianos* leaning on their canes, was immaculately groomed. The men wore suits or expensive sport shirts, the women were often clad in silk, and even the teenagers dressed as if they were on their way to visit a wealthy uncle. Colorful fans and *mantillas* vied for attention with low necklines and short skirts. Everyone seemed happy to be out and about.

As our black-robed quartet made its way down the street, the crowds courteously parted for us. Those men who wore hats, tipped them. The women smiled. Little children looked at us with curiosity. I had never in my life experienced such an outpouring of affection and respect from complete strangers. At first I felt a bit of a fraud, knowing the public was reacting to what my religious habit represented, and not to me. After a while, however, I found myself enjoying the deference I now commanded.

With a rustle of robes and rosary beads, we made the right turn on *Calle Don Bosco.*

Halfway up the block was the entrance to the convent. Across the street, I could see the guard who kept watch for La Magdalena or anyone who attempted to see her. By now, however, I no longer had any fear that I would be recognized as anything but another nun, returning with her colleagues from evening vespers.

A knock on the door, an eye at the security peephole, and we were admitted to the *convento*. We entered a small waiting room, bare except for two chairs. An opening in the wall was fitted with a turnstile used by the nuns to sell their bread, which was promoted in all the tourist litera-ture. The nun who admitted us opened another door which revealed the main reception area of the *convento*.

It was a sterile room, with polished wood floors, a painting of the Crucifixion on one wall, a large black Crucifix on the other, and age-darkened portraits of two nuns whom I imagined to be the founders of the order, on the third wall. A half-dozen straight-backed chairs were arranged on two sides of a heavy wooden conference table. This was the reception area, Sister Serafina explained, accessible only to visitors with important business to discuss with the mother superior. The heavy door which led to the inner reaches of the *convento* was kept locked to prevent outsiders, particularly men, from gaining even a glimpse into the areas where the nuns lived, worked, and prayed.

The nun who greeted us carried a large ring of keys. She was appar-ently in charge of gatekeeping and security for the night. She stared at me with more than idle curiosity, until Sister Serafina stepped between us and instructed her to unlock the door. A long, narrow hallway led into the nonpublic areas of the convent. Was I the first man to look down this hall-way? It was a stunning thought, one which made me wonder whether I should turn and leave before seeing something not meant for secular eyes. I was nothing less than an intruder, about to set foot in the private quar-ters of the *Hermanas del Sangreal,* who had for centuries walked these corridors secure in the knowledge that their activities were safe from out-side view. As I hesitated, I could feel the other nun watching me. Suspi-cious.

Sister Serafina waved for me to follow.

I entered the corridor. Behind me, I heard the heavy door close, the lock slide into place.

Ahead of us, a side door opened and a nun emerged with what looked like a laundry bag. She smiled a greeting at us and disappeared down a flight of stairs. An eerie silence pervaded the place. I didn't expect to hear the sounds of TV's, radios, or CD players, all of which must be forbidden, but in a building that housed dozens of residents, I would have expected to hear one or more voices. I hoped I wouldn't see any of the residents in a state of *deshabille,* or any form of even partial undress that would unknowingly violate their vows. I could only trust that Sister Serafina was aware of the risk she was taking by bringing me here.

At the end of the hallway was a set of double doors. Sister Serafina knocked once.

"Pase!" came a firm voice from inside.

I was ushered into a warmly lit office filled with furniture that might have been purchased sometime in the seventeenth century. Across the room, with her back to the window, a scowling nun sat behind an enormous desk. The requisite crucifix hung on the wall beside her. In front of the desk was a single chair. The nun looked up as Sister Serafina entered the room and closed the door behind us.

"Buenas noches, Mother Dominica," said Sister Serafina. "I have brought the man we talked about."

Mother Dominica was a tall woman, about my height, heavy in the shoulders for a woman. The part of her face that was visible in its white linen frame was angular, with a narrow nose and thin lips; a serious woman, who in a Chanel jacket would have fit the image of a female executive. Any meeting with La Magdalena hinged on her approval.

"Be seated," she told me.

I had no choice but to follow her instructions. I sat where she indicated, a backless stool three feet in front of her desk, an uncomfortable seat which I assumed was reserved for recalcitrant novices.

"Your name?"

"Theophanes Nikonos."

"You are American?"

"Greek-American."

"All right, Mr. Nikonos. Let me explain your situation. You are now in the private living quarters of the *Convento de las Hermanas del Sangreal.* We are a sequestered order, with minimal contact with the public. Outsiders are not permitted to enter the convent. Obviously, our private living quarters are considered sacrosanct. To have a man in here, at this hour of the night, violates our most basic rules, and is a threat to the chastity of our nuns. If I call the police, you can be arrested as an intruder and charged with trespassing and breaking and entering. Your very presence here would suggest the more serious charge of intent to commit sexual harm to members of our religious community. And since you are dressed in clothing that I recognize as belonging to me, you can also be charged with theft, not to mention deviate sexual behavior. Such affronts committed against a religious order are treated very seriously by the police." She paused to let the chilling words sink in. "I would prefer not to call the police, but that decision will depend entirely on your behavior. Do you fully understand your position, Mr. Nikonos?"

"Yes, I understand," I said, my voice probably sounding as meek as that of the nuns over whom the autocratic woman ruled. What I had thought was a brilliant way of gaining unobserved entrée to the premises now revealed itself also as a way for the nuns to exercise complete control over my activities once inside. If I ever thought nuns were naïve servants of the male Catholic hierarchy, I now realized just how mistaken I had been.

"Good," Mother Dominica said. "Now I assume you will answer all my questions honestly. Why did you come to Valencia?"

"To try the oranges, eat some paella, and see the Holy Grail. Or at least your version of the Holy Grail. I'm just an ordinary tourist."

"Ordinary tourists do not normally pursue our nuns."

"Pursue is the wrong word," I corrected her. "I just want to talk to the nun you call La Magdalena."

"*I* do not call her La Magdalena. The name *I* know her by is Sister Mariamme. What is your interest in her?"

There was no lie, I realized, no matter how believable or preposterous it might be, that would get me past Mother Dominica. I wasn't sure if the truth would, either. I decided to give it a try, anyway. Maybe not the complete truth, but hopefully enough to gain access to La Magdalena.

"With your permission, I'd like to continue Padre Serrano's work," I said.

"His work was suspended by the Cardinal's office."

"Yes. He told me that, just before he was killed," I responded. "I think the two events might be connected."

An American nun would undoubtedly be shocked at the suggestion of so perfidious a conspiracy, particularly one that might involve the church. As I was learning, however, Spanish nuns were a different breed, more cynical in their attitudes about the world outside the convent walls.

"Sister Serafina told us about it. But so far, we have only your word that Padre Serrano is dead," she pointed out.

"He was killed three days ago, in a bomb explosion."

"I was not informed of his death."

"It happened in a small juice bar near the *Plaza de Toros*. I was with him when it happened."

"Yet you survived," she said in a dry tone.

"I was lucky," I said. "The bomb exploded when I was in the washroom. Padre Serrano died instantly. So did the counter attendant."

The expression on her face remained fixed, her voice flat and neutral.

"I heard about a bombing," she said. "Such things are no longer unusual in Spain. But *Dios mío,* I was not informed by the diocese that Padre Serrano was one of the victims."

"That's because the *Guardia* refuses to confirm his identity. They claim it wasn't Padre Serrano who was killed in the explosion, that he was on vacation somewhere in South America."

"The *Guardia* has been known to lie," she said.

"The rector at the Jesuit *Residencia* told me the same story."

"Did that surprise you?"

"Well, I would have expected the truth from a priest."

"Priests and policemen say what their superiors tell them to say," Mother Dominica shrugged. "It might be the influence of the Cardinal's office," she said. "They are probably afraid the media might start asking embarrassing questions about the padre's activities."

"You mean about his investigation of La Magdalena?"

"As I told you, there is no longer any investigation."

"Serrano was upset about that," I recalled. "He seemed frightened, too. He talked about powerful people being interested in her. Why was the investigation suspended?"

"No official reason was ever given," she said.

"You mean the subject was too sensitive for anyone to go on record." Her silence indicated agreement, so I continued. "My guess is the church hierarchy must have felt threatened in some way by the direction the psychological evaluation was taking."

"Very perceptive, Mr. Nikonos. At first, they treated Sister Mariamme as a mentally disturbed individual. I think they expected the padre to confirm that opinion, which would give them the legal justification required for committing her to a mental institution."

"As a mental patient, anything she said would be considered the illogical ravings of a lunatic."

"Exactly."

"It sounds to me like pretty severe punishment for a belief in reincarnation."

"I do not think they are so much troubled about her belief in reincarnation. It is what she claims to remember from her past life that worries them."

"Such as?"

"It would be best if you heard it in her own words." All this time, Mother Dominica maintained her stern demeanor. "If it were up to me, I would never permit you to speak to Sister Mariamme. The only reason we are even having this discussion is because Sister Mariamme told me she wanted to see you. As opposed as I was to your request, I could not find it in my heart to refuse her.

"After all," Mother Dominica continued. "She said she has been waiting two thousand years to see you again."

Twenty-Eight

I TURNED AT the sound of a door opening behind me.

Into that opening, after a pause that seemed interminable, and with hesitant, bashful steps, came the young nun even I myself now referred to as La Magdalena.

She entered the room and paused, just inside the doorway. She tilted her head slightly, those heartbreakingly sad eyes searching the room for a familiar face. At first, she didn't seem to recognize me. Mother Dominica watched in silence; I waited expectantly, hoping for some sign of recognition. As impossible as it must sound, having seen her for only the briefest of moments, I was convinced some bond already existed between us. The red mark on the back of my hand began to throb. I thought I smelled the faintest hint of some delicate flowers or perfume, lavender, perhaps, or was it spikenard, though I knew Mother Dominica would never have allowed such aromatic ornamentation to be worn by any of her nuns. Perhaps it was fatigue or the stress of the past few days, but gazing at her, I suddenly felt light-headed.

The rest of the room seemed to melt away from my consciousness as our eyes met. Her smile drew me up from my chair. Not so much as an act of etiquette, but a force of magnetism which I was powerless to resist. I stood transfixed before her, wanting to reach out, to draw nearer. But an unseen barrier remained between us, warning me to approach no further. She was after all, a nun, a bride of Christ. And as such, rendered untouchable by taboos that even atheists respected. I was loath to violate those taboos, particularly in the presence of Mother Dominica. Instead, I settled for the mildly salacious memory of the way her breast had pressed itself against the back of my hand in the cathedral. I was convinced that gentle pressure of flesh against flesh had continued too long to be accidental. She had, for some reason, chosen to bestow this forbidden intimacy upon me. But why me, a stranger? I had known women who used such incidental bodily contact not as part of the mating ritual, but as a way of subtly inveigling men into doing their bidding. But sexual stratagems of that sort required a level of life experiences well beyond those of a young nun who had been sheltered from all but the most basic contact with the outside world, not to mention men in general. It was impossible to believe this innocent-looking young creature could have been so manipulative.

Was it possible that inside her virginal body resided the soul of another, more worldly woman who had walked the earth in the presence of Jesus Christ? If that was so, what remarkable secrets were buried in her memory? If she truly was the reborn Magdalene, what could she tell us of the man whom the bible said she accompanied to Jerusalem?

On the other hand, the skeptic within me warned there was a very real possibility that a fraud was being perpetrated. And I, for some reason, was being drawn into it. Reincarnation hoaxes often start out quite innocently, usually the result of false memories derived from the exposure to long-forgotten books or stories. This one, with its promise of secret teachings and feminist overtones, had built-in appeal for today's media. Properly hyped by a sophisticated promoter, the young nun could easily become an international celebrity, spinning off huge profits for her handlers. Those handlers wouldn't want anyone interfering with their plans. If that was the case, my life, like Padre Serrano's, was a fungible commodity. If he was murdered because he was getting too close to some forbidden truth, the same fate might well be waiting for me.

My reverie was interrupted when La Magdalena started to giggle. She raised a slender hand to her mouth to suppress her laughter.

"You're very tall for a nun," she said between giggles.

I had completely forgotten that I was still wearing the nun's clothing that had enabled me to enter the convent undetected.

"It's a disguise . . . ," I murmured. "They made me change at the cathedral."

"I'm sorry," Mother Dominica said. "I forgot to tell you to remove the headdress." She stepped forward to remove the black cowl and helped me unwrap the linen wimple from around my face. "Your clothes are being laundered," she said. "They'll be returned to you in the morning."

I kicked off the shoes that had been cramping my toes, and ran my fingers through my hair, happy to be rid of the bulky covering. I was still wearing the heavy black habit, but I felt a lot more comfortable now. All I needed now was some privacy to take off the pantyhose and get rid of the heavily padded bra. But I didn't want to let La Magdalena out of my sight.

"She knows about Padre Serrano," Mother Dominica said in a soft voice. "I told her about it as soon as I heard it from Sister Serafina."

The sadness returned to La Magdalena's eyes.

"You were there?" she asked.

I nodded, unable for a moment to find my voice.

"Did he suffer?"

I shook my head.

"Why do they kill everyone I love?" she moaned. She closed her eyes and began rocking her body back and forth in a movement familiar to anyone who has seen images of the mourners at Palestinian funerals. I half-expected her to begin the traditional tongue-rolling wail of grief. It was a strange scene for a Roman Catholic convent. I wanted to comfort her, to take her hand or put my arm around her or do something to help ease her pain. But of course, touching her would be a violation of the religious norms, a transgression that I assumed would bring the wrath of Mother Dominica down upon me.

"Before he was killed, the padre asked me to continue his work with you," I said.

"But the Cardinal's office . . ." she dutifully started to object.

"The Cardinal's office ordered Padre Serrano to have no further contact with you," I said. "As I understand it, the order applied only to Padre Serrano. Therefore, any interview I conduct with you would not be in violation of the Cardinal's edict."

La Magdalena glanced nervously towards Mother Dominica, who silently nodded her agreement.

"All right," the young nun finally agreed. "But I should like us to pray first. For the soul of our dear friend, Javier Serrano."

I expected her to drop to her knees, lower her head and bless herself, as the nuns had done in Church. Instead, she turned in my direction and smiled. A gleaming, radiant smile full of a love no woman had ever bestowed on me. I smiled back, before realizing she was looking beyond me. Her eyes were fixed at a point in infinity somewhere above my head. I turned to see what merited such rapt attention, half-expecting someone to have silently entered the room behind me. All I could see was a blank wall. There was not even a picture to attract her attention.

"My darling Jesus my Christ," she said to the empty space. "My dear friend Javier is with you now. I know it isn't permitted for me to speak with him yet, but please tell him how much I enjoyed the time we spent together. I'm so very, very glad you sent him to me."

While her cheerful voice and blissful smile might not fit the traditional somber attitude associated with prayer, it certainly correlated with the behavior of mystics such as Padre Pio when he was experiencing visions; or of Maria, Jacinto, and Lucia when they were in communication with the Marian apparitions at Fatima. And as with the witnesses at such events, I could see no external sign of any otherwordly presence. No glow on the wall, no image of Christ in the paint, no unexplained supraphysical activity at all. The only evidence of anything unearthly transpiring was La Magdalena herself.

"He must have been a good person in his previous life," she continued. "Because he seemed so happy in his vocation in this life."

It flowed from her lips so easily, I almost missed its significance. But there it was, a clear summation of the most widely held version of reincarnation theory, that the way one life is lived determines the quality of the next life. I hadn't expected to hear it enunciated so openly, in front of the mother superior.

"When we meet again in another life, I hope he remembers me favorably."

As the padre had warned me, she wasn't bashful about expressing her beliefs. The references to past and future lives would have been perfectly acceptable as part of a prayer for the dead in a Buddhist temple or an Islamic mosque. But these were heretical ideas for a Roman Catholic nun to voice. I could understand why the Cardinal's office was upset with her.

I glanced at Mother Dominica, but she was lost in her own silent prayers and hadn't seemed to notice.

"As for me, my darling," La Magdalena went on with her prayer. "My dreams at night are more and more of you." Her voice dropped into a lower register. It became warm and intimate, not so much the voice of a nun in prayer, but more the voice of a woman speaking to her lover. "I know your plan for me is still unfolding, but it is hard to be patient, now that my memories are returning."

Suddenly, with such effortless ease that I didn't notice the exact transition, she shifted into a language that was totally incomprehensible to me. I wasn't a completely monolingual American, having grown up with Greek-speaking parents. I studied Latin and French in high school, had a nodding acquaintance with Italian and German opera, and had already picked up a little Spanish, yet I didn't recognize a single word she was saying. Padre Serrano told me she spoke dead languages. He claimed, as Professor Stevenson certainly would, that such linguistic ability was valid evidence of reincarnation. But I couldn't tell whether she was speaking an authentic language she had spoken in an earlier life, or simply babbling the meaningless gibberish of *glossalalia*. If it hadn't happened so swiftly, I would have been able to record the strange tongue for later interpretation by linguistic experts. Unfortunately, the video camcorder I bought at the audio store was hidden underneath the folds of the habit, and reaching for it would have been too disruptive of the moment. I could only listen and marvel at the change that came over her when she slipped into the mysterious language.

Beyond the words she spoke, which were peculiar enough, I felt something unusual was occurring. Whatever it was that she thought she saw at that strange point in infinity wrought an amazing change in her. The sadness had left her upraised face, replaced by what I can only call a truly beatific expression. The pupils of her eyes, so dark and withdrawn before, seemed to sparkle with highlights from the reflection of a bright image that existed nowhere in the room. An excited pink blush rose in her cheeks. Her lips, which had been thin and dry and determined, were transformed before my eyes into moist and nubile labia. She had blossomed in moments from a lovely, though bashful young nun into a sensual woman with an animal magnetism that would affect any man. As a psychologist, I was fascinated by the physical transformation I was witnessing. As a man, I found myself responding with emotions I had thought were dead.

I turned once again to see Mother Dominica's reaction. She was still on her knees, head bowed, absorbed in her own more traditional form of prayer. She was apparently accustomed to such behavior

Padre Serrano hadn't mentioned witnessing anything similar during his work with La Magdalena. Perhaps he hadn't seen her at prayer, or perhaps he was afraid I might interpret any such description as suggestive of multiple personality disorder. Having witnessed it myself, however, I did not think her behavior fit the clinical criteria of a dissociative personality. If anything, it came closer to a hallucinatory episode.

Her eyes, for example, remained fixed and unblinking from the moment she began her "prayer." She would speak and then stop, as if listening to words that were beyond my capacity to hear. There was an element of detachment from her surroundings. Yet she wasn't in a completely trance-like state, since her voice fluctuated in tone, and she exhibited facial movements that appeared consistent with the emotions reflected in the tone of the words she spoke.

At some point during this episode, she acknowledged my presence and reached out for my hand. At first, remembering how the back of my hand was inflamed from that initial contact, I was afraid to touch her. But if I hoped to gain her confidence, I knew any demonstration of fear or resistance would be counterproductive. When I finally took her slender hand in mine, her flesh felt smooth and cool and strangely familiar. Her fingers wrapped themselves around mine like those of a trusting child. For some unknown reason, she raised my hand to her mouth. With infinite tenderness, she kissed the red mark on the back of my hand and began to stroke it.

"I waited so long for you to come," she whispered to me in English.

I had no idea what she meant by that comment. There was no way she could have been waiting for me. But my hand felt so natural in hers, that for a moment, I forgot where I was. For a moment, I had an image of us standing on an empty beach in the evening. Behind us flowed a vast river. The air was warm and salty. Alone on the beach, we were about to embrace when a voice came from what seemed like a great distance.

Suddenly, I was back in the convent.

"That's enough for tonight," Mother Dominica said, a hint of anger in her voice. Using the back of a chair for support, she lifted herself from her knees. "You can talk further tomorrow."

A chastened La Magdalena let go of my hand. She nodded obediently to Mother Dominica, and withdrew from the room without another word.

"Physical contact with our nuns is forbidden," Mother Dominica admonished me.

I was about to protest, to point out that it was La Magdalena herself who initiated the contact, but she waved off any explanation.

"You are dealing with a young woman who has no experience in the outside world," she said. "She is naïve and very vulnerable. You must be careful not to allow her to become infatuated with you . . . what you psychologists call transference."

She led me from her office to the first room in the hallway. Inside the door was a barren cell, whose only furnishings were a narrow bed and a small dresser, upon which rested a pitcher and washbasin. A covered chamber pot was slipped discreetly under the bed. A hook on the back of the door held two wooden hangers, which apparently served as a substitute closet. A weak overhead bulb provided the only illumination. On the wall above the head of the bed was a black crucifix with a silver Jesus Christ.

"No man has ever spent the night in our *convento*," Mother Dominica said.

"I'll behave," I tried to make a joke of it.

"I'm sure you will." Her voiced was humorless. "Your door will be locked from the outside. You will not be permitted to leave your room except for your meetings with Sister Mariamme. Two nuns will accompany you to those meetings."

"Psychological examinations are always conducted in private," I protested.

"This is not your office," she pointed out. "I cannot permit you to be alone in a room with any of our nuns."

"But I must have privacy," I insisted.

"Impossible. Our nuns go nowhere without a chaperone."

"What about the confessional?" I countered. "Surely no chaperone listens while they confess their sins?"

Mother Dominica hesitated.

"You are not a priest," she said. "You are not here to listen to her confession."

"There may be things she doesn't want the other nuns to hear," I continued. "Very personal thoughts and feelings. The dialogue between a psychologist and a patient is as confidential as that of the confessional. Even the Vatican has recognized the sanctity of the doctor-patient relationship."

I wasn't a doctor, not even of the Ph.D. variety. But I felt that was just a technicality, and the Vatican reference seemed to be working.

"I could conduct the interview in a room with an open door," I suggested. "That way, your chaperones can watch from the doorway, but not hear what we are saying."

Mother Dominica seemed to be wavering. She had already shown me she could be an imperious woman, but the very fact that she was allowing me to stay here overnight signaled an ambivalence when it came to La Magdalena.

"You don't have to decide right now," I said. "All I ask is that you think about it. Think about what's best for her. Will you do that?"

"I'll think about it," she said. She closed the door and slid the outside deadbolt into place, locking me in for the night.

Sleep didn't come easily on the hard bed. I was restless and uncomfortable at first. I dreamt as usual about Laura Duquesne and that tragic night in New York. But later, surprisingly, images of La Magdalena intruded, some of them, I shamefully admit, of an erotic nature. Sometime during the night, I was awakened by what I thought was the scent of lavender. Although the windows were closed, the delicate fragrance seemed to fill the room. In the hypnagogic state, that vague mental twilight between wakefulness and sleep, I imagined the source of the aroma to be my right hand, the one La Magdalena had taken in hers. I raised the back of the hand to my mouth, pressing my lips in a celibate kiss against the very place where her lips had left their invisible imprint.

After that, I slept peacefully.

Twenty-Nine

THE FIRST INTERVIEW with La Magdalena started at 7:52 the following morning.

I had been awakened at sunrise by the singing of matins, the nuns' morning prayers. Shortly afterward, two nuns appeared at my door. One handed me my clothing, freshly laundered and still warm from the dryer. The second carried a breakfast tray containing a large bowl of oatmeal, a small glass of orange juice, and a cup of hot water with a teabag but no sugar. After allowing me time to eat and dress and complete my morning ablutions, they returned to accompany me to the *convento* dining hall. It was a large room, with plain tables that contained no condiments or table-cloths. I was directed to a square table in the farthest corner of the room. The two nuns, who apparently were the chaperones, took seats on the other side of the room. They had an unobstructed view, but were far enough away to make hearing difficult. Mother Dominica had acceded to my request for at least partial privacy.

While I waited, I carefully set out the electronic tools of the modern investigative trade, the two small devices I bought in the audio store the previous morning. The first, a miniature Sony camcorder would provide a permanent record of the interview. The second device was a voice-stress analyzer, which would serve as a crude polygraph. Its real-time readings were certainly not definitive by any means, but were suitable enough for my purposes.

After a short wait, La Magdalena entered the room.

I rose immediately and pulled out a chair for her. Gathering her robes demurely, she smiled and sat down. I could sense the chaperones watching for any false move on my part.

"You don't mind if I record this interview, do you?" I asked.

Seeing the puzzled expression on her face, I realized she had little knowledge of modern technology. I proceeded to demonstrate the camcorder by taping a few seconds of her image. "It's what they call a videotape camera," I explained. "It records your voice and picture, so that it can be viewed later."

When I played back the demonstration footage on the tiny screen, she gasped, and then giggled.

"Sisters, come here!" she called out. "See what he brought."

I had to go through the ritual once more for the chaperones, recording and playing back their images as well. What I found unusual was that, although they marveled at the demonstration, they asked no questions about the nature of the technology. Was it a demonstration of faith? Or lack of curiosity?

When the nuns returned to their stations across the room, the interview began.

"This interview is being conducted in the *Convento de las Hermanas del Sangreal* in Valencia, Spain on Tuesday, May 8, 2001. The local time is 7:52 A.M. My name is Theophanes Nikonos. This interview is part of an investigation into a possible case of reincarnation."

Normally I would begin an investigative interview in a relaxed, casual manner, hoping to put the subject at ease. The Stevenson protocols recognize the human propensity for falsehood and emphasize the need to separate outright fabrication from inadvertent exaggeration. Given the nature of this particular case, I decided to force the issue of truthfulness.

"Do you believe in God?" I asked.

"Yes, I love God."

"Do you believe in Jesus Christ?"

"Yes, I loved Jesus my Christ."

I noticed she used the past tense. Was it intentional, or a slip of the tongue? I let it pass for the time being.

"Do you swear by Almighty God and his son, Jesus Christ, that you will tell the truth in this and all further interviews?"

"You forgot the Holy Spirit," she said with a smile. "People always forget to mention her." She placed her right hand over her heart. "But yes, I swear to speak the truth in everything I say."

"For the record, would you please state your real name?"

"I am Sister Mariamme."

"And what is your family name?"

"I have no family name."

"Some of the nuns call you La Magdalena."

"Yes," she nodded. "Because I once lived in Magdala."

"And where is that?" I asked, trying to keep the excitement out of my voice. I hadn't expected the issue to be joined this quickly.

"Magdala is a small fishing town on the shores of the Sea of Galilee. It is about four Roman miles north of Tiberius. It is about a day's journey from Jerusalem. Of course, that was a long time ago, when we traveled on foot or on mules. Today, it is probably a trip of only a few hours."

"You once lived in Magdala?" I deliberately challenged her. It wasn't my usual interview technique, but I was hoping an aggressive approach might produce quick results on the voice-stress analyzer. "How can that be? I was told that you were brought to the *convento* when you were still an infant, that you spent your entire life here."

"That is also true," she said.

"But I don't understand," I argued. "If you lived your whole life here in Valencia, why do you say you lived in Magdala?"

"I lived in Magdala at a different time."

Behind me, I could hear whispers and the rustle of beads. The two chaperones, unable to hear us, were praying the rosary.

"I don't understand," I said. "Can you explain that for me?"

"We are talking of two different lives. When I lived in Magdala, in my father's house, that was in an earlier life."

I almost smiled. It was the answer I hoped for, a clear and concise declaration of a claim that on its face seemed impossible. She might have deceived Padre Serrano and some naïve nuns with similar words, but I was confident she wouldn't deceive the voice-stress analyzer. I watched the indicator needle, waiting for it to jump. The needle, however, remained steady. I tapped the unit to be sure it was working. The needle wavered in response. Disappointed that my initial attempt at disproving her story had failed, I settled back and reverted to a more relaxed interview technique.

"Tell me about this earlier life of yours." I said. "How long ago was that?"

"According to the current calendar, about two thousand years ago. It was during the period of the Second Temple, in the time of Caesar Augustus . . . I told all this to Padre Serrano."

The stress needle quivered on the last few words, perfectly matching the hint of irritation in her voice. It was my first proof that the device was actually working.

"He even recorded my voice on a machine like yours, but his machine had no picture."

"I know," I said. "But the padre's records are missing. They must have been destroyed in the explosion."

I didn't believe that, of course. I was certain Serrano's notes and tapes were in the hands of the police or those responsible for the bombing.

"Why does that arrow move when we talk?" she asked, pointing to the indicator on the stress analyzer.

I realized with a start that it had detected what I thought was my innocent lie about the notes being destroyed.

"It's just a volume indicator," I lied again, and watched the needle jump, more dramatically this time. I would have to be more careful, I realized. For some reason, it hadn't occurred to me that the voice-stress analyzer would detect my falsehoods as well as hers.

"In any event, since I don't have the padre's notes, we have to start at the very beginning." Even if I had Serrano's notes, I wouldn't have used them except to check for inconsistencies between the two sets of interviews. In preparing myself intellectually for my investigation, I decided I would follow the Stevenson protocols, which started with a careful documentation of the subject's past-life recollections, with particular interest in material that could later be verified by independent sources. The method would be time-consuming, but would be more acceptable to any future peer review. "Let's go back to Magdala and your earlier life there," I said.

"Actually, it wasn't called Magdala by those of us who lived there. For us, it was el Mejdel, named for the tower which stood on the highest ground."

That was an interesting bit of history, but as an authenticating fact, it proved nothing. She could have acquired the knowledge in some obscure book about the region.

"Where do you want me to start?" she asked. "With my childhood?"

"Whatever you feel comfortable talking about."

"All right, we'll begin at the beginning. I was born in the third month of the ninth year of the time of Herod Antipas, as I said, during the reign of Caesar Augustus."

That made sense from a biblical time-line, but it was a completely impossible claim for me to document.

"I was the only child of my parents."

And so, almost immediately, she was parting company with those scholars who claimed that Lazarus, whom Christ raised from the dead, was the brother of Mary Magdalene, and Martha of Bethany was her sister.

"My father was Syrus, descended from Jair. He was the chief priest at the synagogue in Capernaum."

If she was making this up, she wasn't following the usual script. Although Mary Magdalene's father was never identified in the bible, he was most often described by scholars as a "wealthy merchant." It seemed a convenient fiction invented by medieval academics who, if pressed, would have had to admit the wealth they claimed for the father was based on unspecified dealings in unknown commodities with unidentified partners. In fact, as with much of the Magdalenean myth, the truth of the matter had thus far proven impossible to establish, if not actually suppressed by early Church historians.

"Your father was a priest?" I asked, not because I hadn't heard it properly, but because I wanted to underline the claim for DesRosier or anyone else who might study the videotape in the future.

"He was the chief priest in Capernaum," she repeated. "It was a post that was held by his father and his father's father and all the descendants of Jair since the time of David. I remember going to the synagogue for the first time as a little girl. It was a magnificent structure of white marble. I was very proud of my father."

I had come here expecting to hear generalities, rehashed versions of the old legends, and instead was being given details that might challenge the conventional wisdom. I was delighted at the specificity, since it meant I could check at least part of her story against the historic record. The existence of a white marble synagogue at Capernaum would be easy to establish, even if it had long ago been demolished. And as far as Syrus the Jairite and his predecessors were concerned, the names of Jewish religious leaders were recorded in ancient Roman documents. Whether there was any record of Syrus having a daughter was quite another matter, however.

And that was the frustrating pattern that continued through the first interview. She would describe people and places and events in astonishing detail, providing me with names and facts that sounded authentic, but which only archeologists and historians might be able to corroborate. I listened patiently to the stories of her childhood, hoping that eventually I'd be able to determine how much, if any, of it was true.

"We lived in a large house, built around an open courtyard. That was how most of the houses of the wealthier people in Magdala were built, around a courtyard. We were one of only two families in the village with our own cistern, which was quite a luxury in those days. The other family was that of Joshua, the wine merchant. Our house had two floors, and I used to like to play on the roof, which was flat, and there was a small arbor where I could sit in the shade during the afternoon sun. I liked being up there, because I wasn't allowed in the street, but I could watch all the activity in the streets from up there. Some of my earliest memories were seeing the enormous camel caravans in the distance. Our town was at the intersection of the overland trade routes that came east from Babylon through Sydon and Tyre, and south from Egypt through Gaza. You could see it all from our roof. It was a wonderful place for a little girl. In the evening, I could watch the sun setting over Mount Arbel, and after dark, I could see the oil lamps of the fishing boats on the Sea of Galilee. There were always people on the nearby roofs. The rooftops were gathering places, where neighbors exchanged gossip, and the servants dried flax and reeds and fish.

"Fish!" she laughed. "Our village always smelled of fish. The Greeks called it *Tarichea,* a word that means "dried fish." My mother was a wonderful woman. My father was very stern, as a priest was expected to be. But we always had music and singing and dancing in the house. Our people believed music had the power to drive away evil spirits."

It was possible, of course, that what I was hearing was nothing more than *recitative cryptomnesia,* a trick of memory in which an individual recites a litany of facts or information that might have been subconsciously acquired from some long-forgotten book. The most celebrated example of *cryptomnesia* was the famous "Countess Maud" case in England in 1906. Subjected to hypnotic regression, a young woman described her life as a fourteenth-century countess in exquisite detail. Every fact— from what she ate, to the clothing she wore, the furniture in her castle, even the hangings on the wall—was subsequently proven to be accurate in every detail. Her amazing recollections of a previous life convinced many Britons of the validity of reincarnation—until a researcher for the British Society for Psychical Research discovered that all the amazingly accurate details came from a published article titled "Countess Maud," which the young woman eventually remembered having read.

To guard against that memory trap, I interrupted her from time to time, questioning her in greater detail about specifics. Sooner or later, if she was merely recalling something she had read, she would stumble, contradict herself, or be unable to elaborate on the sorts of things she should otherwise know.

"I'd like to hear one of those songs," I said. "Could you sing it for me?"

"All right," she smiled shyly and made a show of straightening her robe, in preparation for her performance. "This is from 'The Book of the Wars of the Lord.' I don't think any written copy of this song has ever been found, which means you'll be hearing it for the first time in 2,000 years."

How convenient, I thought. Sing me a song whose existence no one can document.

She started out softly, seemingly embarrassed to be performing. Her voice was a lovely soprano, which gradually took on strength as her embarrassment diminished, turning what sounded at first like a form of chant into a haunting plainsong. It came effortlessly to her, as if she had been singing it all her life, this song she claimed hadn't been heard since the first century. Her voice was sweet and pure, whispering in places and soaring in others, playing with my emotions, somehow making the song sound familiar despite the fact that I understood not a word of it. And when it was over, the walls seemed to reverberate with silent echoes of what they heard.

"That was in Aramaic," she said. "It tells the story of a great battle, the deaths of many Jews, and the eventual victory brought about through faith in Yahweh."

What sort of woman was this, I began to wonder? She was providing me with detail after detail about a life she claimed she lived as Mary Magdalene, even singing what she called one of Mary's favorite songs for me, and the voice-stress analyzer refused to accuse her of even the slightest hint of deception.

I stopped asking questions, and just sat back and allowed her to tell whatever she remembered of her early life. It was an astounding outpouring of information, little of which I could confirm as fact or refute as fantasy without seeking scholarly assistance.

She knew the name of the architect, the methods of construction, and the floor plan of the Second Temple of Solomon, for example. She could name the sons and daughters of Herod, the members of the Sanhedrin, the concubine of the Roman tax collector in Jerusalem. She seemed to know the most intimate details of life in the Jewish communities during the early part of the first century: how women cooked and bathed and perfumed themselves; what utensils were used in the home; the relationships between man and woman; and the ways of dealing with both the Roman bureaucracy and the religious authorities.

She explained that not all writing was done on papyrus, that many brief notes and letters and commercial receipts were written on pieces of broken pottery. That the color purple was the most highly sought-after dye, and was made by collecting the secretion of a shellfish caught off the coast of Tyre. She described the sealskin shoes her mother treasured, how the workers used olive oil to heal sunburn and herbal lotions to ward off the flies, how the plague and skin disease and eye troubles were the most common illnesses. She explained how the month begins at the new moon, and was able to name not just *Abib*, "the month of the ears," and *Zib*, "the month of bright flowers," but also all the other months, whose names she said scholars no longer knew. She taught me the various forms of measurement: the *omers* and *ephahs* and *homers* to measure wheat, the *hins* and *baths* and *kors* to measure wine, the *palms* and *spans* and *cubits* of linear measurement. She even demonstrated how those measurements were determined: the *span* being the distance from the tip of the small finger to the tip of the thumb on a man's extended hand; a *cubit* being measured from the end of the second finger to the end of the elbow. It was an encyclopedic outpouring of names and dates (which would have to be transcribed from the Hebrew calendar), places and customs. In its scope, depth and breadth, it was an absolutely stunning dissertation to come from a young nun who had spent her entire life in a convent in Spain. I let her talk unhindered, ranging over topics as mundane as the weather and as intricate as the dietary laws.

She seemed delighted to talk about those times, and I was enthralled by the ease with which she described events. She went on for hours, pausing only for water that was brought to her to by one of the chaperones, or when the ninety-minute videotapes had to be changed. If she was faking it in some way, inventing the history or delivering a previously memorized discourse, it was a virtuoso performance. The only time the voice-stress analyzer registered any significant response was when she spoke of tragic events, such as the death of her mother, the debilitating illness that crippled a childhood friend, or other painful subjects.

By mid-morning, we both needed a respite.

La Magdalena left the room, followed by the two chaperoning nuns. They carefully locked the door behind themselves, which I thought was overdoing the whole privacy bit. I stretched and walked around, finally stopping by one of the barred windows that looked out on the street. Down below, I could make out at least two, possibly three men who seemed to have no reason for being there except for surveillance.

Although I could walk out of the convent any time I chose, I was, in reality, a prisoner of my own investigation. Leaving the convent would immediately alert the watchers to my interest in La Magdalena. It would bring the *Guardia* down upon the *convento*, expose La Magdalena to further repercussions from the Church, and perhaps even place her in physical danger. The person responsible for the bombing that killed Serrano was still on the loose, and it was impossible to know if La Magdalena was his ultimate target.

I had Jean-Claude DesRosier's cell phone on my belt. If I called for a limo to be sent to the front door in the middle of the night, I might be able to exit unrecognized. But that would reveal DesRosier's involvement, which he had already warned me against. It was also possible that the *Guardia's* van outside might contain the usual electronic monitoring equipment which would pick up and record any wireless phone calls. They'd not only identify both of us, they'd learn exactly how and when I planned to make my getaway.

The chaperones returned with tea and crackers for me, and inquired solicitously whether I had to use the comfort facilities. La Magdalena would be delayed a few minutes, they explained. Apparently Mother Dominica had something to discuss with her.

There'd be plenty of time to plan my exit strategy later, I decided. As I sipped my tea, I turned my thoughts to a different dilemma.

I now had three videotapes filled with either a priceless eyewitness account of pre-Christian life in the Holy Land, or a worthless assemblage of fictions from the overworked imagination of a repressed nun.

A Hebrew scholar could probably determine quickly enough whether a thread of truth ran through her ruminations. But the panorama of life she painted could take years of study and comparison with ancient texts and artifacts to finally establish its authenticity.

I was already in over my head, I realized. I was a psychologist and an investigator, and yes, I was fascinated by ancient history and religious traditions. On Mount Athos, I delved deeply into the esoteric traditions of Christianity. And Padre Serrano's library had provided me with a crash course in the Magdalenean legends and resurrection theory. But what I had on tape went far beyond whatever I knew about the Holy Land. I was impatient to hear about the secret teachings of Christ and the missing portions of the Gospel of Mary. But we were moving in chronological order, the standard way of probing memory. The "secrets," if they existed, would come later, along with more definitive examples of ancient language skills. Nevertheless, if even half of what she told me so far proved to be true, the tapes I already had would be a gold mine for biblical archeologists, genealogists, and anthropologists.

As far as proof was concerned, hard, factual proof that she was indeed the reincarnated Magdalene, I hadn't heard any so far.

Part of it, of course, was the paucity of information about this controversial figure. Mary Magadalene's importance to Jesus Christ was demonstrated when he chose her as the first person to whom he revealed himself after his resurrection. Yet there are only a few scattered and ambiguous references to her in the New Testament. The Gospel of Thomas offers an explanation for this neglect, but the fact remains that there is almost no record extant with which I could cross-check any of the personal information she supplied.

The more I heard, the less I believed I was listening to invented memories. The facts seemed to tumble out in a natural manner. She never contradicted herself, although occasionally she corrected a date, or searched for a name, as we all sometimes do.

The Stevenson Protocols postulated a number of alternative explanations, all of which had to be dismissed before reincarnation could be taken seriously. I had questioned Serrano about many of these, and after personal observation, now agreed with his evalutions. She clearly wasn't suffering from dissociative identity disorder. She exhibited absolutely no change of personality during the entire interview. I saw no sign of any of the rapid blinking, facial alterations, changes of voice pattern, or disruption of chain of thought that were the standard signals for individuals switching from one identity to another. She remained entirely within the persona of Sister Mariamme, even while she was recalling events of two thousand years ago. Schizophrenia and other psychological explanations also didn't seem to fit with her apparently normal and rational recollections of past-life memories.

There were any number of paranormal explanations for such behavior, but I could dismiss each of them for basically the same reasons. *Channeling, spirit walking, shamanism, scrying,* and other forms of communicating with the dead all involve some form of mediumistic trance, either self-induced or achieved through artificial means. At no point did the young nun appear to be in a trance-like state.

Serrano had rejected the idea of *spirit possession,* and from my personal observation, I concurred. In such cases, the invading "spirit" takes complete control of the host body. It would have been easy to detect, if it had happened in Serrano's presence.

I also dismissed the possibility that she had found some way of tapping into the *collective unconscious,* that primordial collection of stories and images described by Jung as residing in all our psyches. Her recollections were far too detailed to fit the Jungian archetypes.

Yet in spite of the extraordinary session I had just conducted, my training would not permit me to accept that I was truly dealing with a case of reincarnation. Not as long as there was still one alternative explanation.

The alternative explanation I was considering was a particularly disturbing scenario, one that caused great controversy within the psychiatric community and was currently playing out in courtrooms across America.

It would explain why Padre Serrano, an otherwise sensible psychiatrist, had become La Magdalena's strongest advocate.

It might also explain why he was removed from the case.

It was an awful thing to believe about a dead man whose last request I was fulfilling.

But from a diagnostic standpoint, it was much more acceptable than believing in reincarnation.

Thirty

MEMORY IS A far more fallible mechanism than most people have been led to believe.

Not only do we forget things we should remember, but controlled experiments have demonstrated that we also remember events that never happened. In the still not completely understood process of storage and retrieval, memories of events adapt themselves to fit preconceived notions, imaginings metamorphose into fact, and non-existent events are as vividly recalled as yesterday's thunderstorm. Bartlett's memory distortion experiments also demonstrated how elements at odds with the subject's conceptual framework are distorted or omitted from memory, while elements that are absent, but would be typically expected in the situation, are unconsciously added to memory. This "fill-in" effect is well-known to police investigators and defense attorneys, who consider it the primary reason eyewitness testimony can be so unreliable.

The fluid nature of memory also leaves it vulnerable to source confusion, in which the subject wrongly identifies the origin of the information; and memory reconstruction, in which the subject unconsciously fills in the gaps of partially recalled data; and other forms of contamination.

With such built-in vulnerabilities, it isn't unusual for "false" memories to surface.

It was possible that a lifetime of religious training would provide the schematic framework into which an intelligent and malleable young mind could pour its fevered imaginings, creating a memory pattern that was as real to her as mine was to me. That would explain why the voice-stress analyzer detected no indication of falsification: La Magdalena *believed* her story.

However, it wouldn't explain the incredible torrent of detail she supplied about life in pre-Christian times, much of which I was convinced was beyond the knowledge of any but the most dedicated scholars.

It wouldn't explain the maturity and confidence she displayed when talking about the activities of a woman who was far more worldly than she.

It wouldn't explain the apparent xenoglossic episode she displayed when she sang. I knew it wasn't Greek or Latin, but had no idea whether it was Aramaic, one of the "dead" languages Serrano claimed she spoke and wrote fluently. I was going to have to find a way to test her on the language issue.

And it wouldn't explain apparently heretical behavior in the convent chapel. While such activity might be symptomatic of a repressed personality rebelling against a lifetime of detention, the timing seemed uncannily coincidental.

There was, however, one scientifically acceptable explanation for all that I had seen and heard.

It had nothing to do with reincarnation.

And it pointed directly at Padre Serrano. Her psychotherapist. The person who spent months exploring the deepest penetralia of her psyche. Like any skilled psychiatrist, he probed her dreams and fears and fantasies. He would have learned the structure and limits of her intellect. And as privy to her deepest and most intimate secrets, he might, as psychiatrists sometimes do, have developed a romantic attachment her. Or to the person he imagined her to be.

Serrano was a highly educated man, a Jesuit, a member of the most intellectually disciplined order of the priesthood. As his library indicated, he was a biblical scholar. He would have studied and been intimately familiar with the details of life in the pre-Christian era. He seemed to have an inordinate interest in the Magdalenean legends. He probably knew as much about all matters related to Mary Magdalene as anyone else did.

Had he, consciously or unconsciously, provided her with artificial recollections?

Given the foibles of the memory mechanism, it isn't a difficult task. Especially under the guise of therapy. Guided interviews, repetitive focused questioning, peripheral conversation in which facts are disseminated, verbal cues when the patient responds appropriately on a given topic, and suggested reading are only a few of the ways in which the subject can be led toward discovering the specific memories the psychotherapist intends to find.

Such "recovered" memories have been one of the great scandals of American psychotherapy, particularly in cases of supposed child molestation.

I wasn't prepared to conclude that Serrano might have intentionally reconstructed La Magdalena's recollections. He was, after all, called into the case after she was already claiming to be the reincarnated Magdalene. Perhaps he made a premature analysis, perhaps something about her behavior convinced him of her claim. Whatever the initial reason, his apparent belief in her reincarnation could have become a self-fulfilling analysis, leading to a mutually supportive relationship that made her claims even more credible.

The only problem with my hypothesis, I thought, was that it would be difficult to prove. Padre Serrano was dead. And the vagaries of memory storage and retrieval would make it impossible to convince La Magdalena that her "memories" might possibly be counterfeit.

My musings were interrupted by a sudden flurry of rosary beads and excited whispering at the doorway. I turned to find a distraught chaperone hurrying towards me.

"Come quickly," she urged. "It's La Magdalena. Something terrible has happened."

Thirty-One

I HURRIED AFTER her, the second chaperone falling in behind us. A cluster of nuns was gathered outside the door to Mother Dominica's office. More nuns were inside, some of them angry, others apparently confused. Mother Dominica sat at her desk, shaking her head as if in disbelief.

La Magdalena looked up at me. Her eyes were red, her lashes wet with tears. Her chin was trembling. Almost childlike in her misery, she was biting her lip in an apparent effort to prevent any further outburst. She sat on the backless chair, surrounded by otherwise compassionate nuns, none of whom seemed to know what to do.

As a therapist, my first instinct was to reach out to her, touch her, show her that someone cared. Restrained by Mother's earlier proscription against contact, however, I could only question the reason for her anguish.

"What's wrong?" I asked in a voice that must have sounded foolishly helpless.

No one spoke. La Magdalena offered no explanation for her misery, her eyes turning instead to Mother Dominica. At first, the older nun didn't even acknowledge my presence. She seemed oblivious to the circle of younger nuns around her. Her right hand clutched the crucifix that hung from her neck, squeezing it so tightly, her knuckles were white. I couldn't tell whether it was a display of anger, or whether she was trying somehow to gain strength from the symbol of her faith. The nuns all watched their mother superior, apparently waiting for some sort of decision. I waited in silence with the others until finally she turned to me and spoke.

"The Cardinal has returned from Rome," she said. "I have been informed that an ambulance will arrive here this evening to take Sister Mariamme away."

"No!" shouted one of the nuns. Others murmured their disapproval. The nun beside me began to pray.

"An ambulance?" I asked. "But why?"

"They tell me that, after reviewing all the evidence, it is the considered opinion of the Vatican psychiatrists that Sister Mariamme requires immediate hospitalization. She will be taken to *El Hospital de Santa Dymphna*."

I assumed without being told that Santa Dymphna wasn't an ordinary hospital. Dymphna was the Belgian girl who became the patron saint of mental patients and mental-health workers.

The assembled nuns began to protest. I recognized the words *loco* and *imposible,* and one nun speaking through clenched teeth confirmed my suspicions by muttering, "She's not crazy!" I had never seen a gathering of nuns become so emotional as they wailed and shook their fists and shouted imprecations. One of the chaperones, the younger one with thick glasses and a pronounced overbite, translated much of the outcry for my benefit.

"They are saying the priests are still afraid of the women in their church. They say the priests are out to destroy La Magdalena. They were afraid of her two thousand years ago, and they are afraid of her again. No one sent to Santa Dymphna has ever returned. We must do something."

Mother Dominica held up her arms for quiet. When the uproar subsided, she asked me,

"And what do you think, Mr. Nikonos? You are a psychologist. Do you think our little sister is insane?"

In the charged atmosphere, with all eyes now upon me, it was no time for me to equivocate.

"No," I said. "No, I don't."

It was an honest answer. Even if she was a victim of false memory syndrome, and even if it did affect her behavior and personal interactions, there was no way the diagnosis could possibly be stretched to fit the definition of insanity. In fact, insanity is a legal rather than psychological term, used by the courts in determining whether an individual should not be held accountable for his or her actions.

"Then you believe she is the reincarnated Magdalene?" Mother Dominica asked.

I was unsure whether she was trying to trick me, or whether it was an honest inquiry. I had to be careful.

"My investigation is still in the early stages," I responded. "But so far, I've found nothing to suggest that Sister Mariamme suffers from any severe psychosis. She seems quite normal, and in fact, is extremely knowledgeable about biblical history."

The object of my remarks smiled wanly, her cheeks tear-stained.

"Did they actually use the word 'insane'?" I asked. "It seems to be a particularly harsh word."

"Harsh words from harsh people," one of the English-speaking nuns muttered.

"It offended me, too," Mother Dominica said softly. "I might not agree with Sister Mariamme's claim of reincarnation, but I do believe she has been touched with a special grace." She offered La Magdalena a warm, supportive smile. "And much, not all, but much of what she says has the resonance of truth about it."

"How did the Vatican psychiatrists reach this conclusion?" I asked. "Did any of them come here to interview Sister Mariamme?"

"Not personally, no. They used Padre Serrano's notes, which were turned over to the cardinal, and the results of an extensive physical examination, no part of which was made available to me."

Although it probably wouldn't have altered the outcome, I knew the Vatican psychiatrists didn't have all of Serrano's notes. Someone else had the contents of his missing briefcase, someone who was willing to kill to get his hands on the information those notes and tapes contained.

"She's supposed to take these pills." Mother Dominica offered a small plastic container for my inspection. "I was told they're tranquilizers, but I have no idea what kind. She's supposed to take two every four hours."

The medication wasn't identified on the label, which I thought was unusual. I opened the container and examined the pills inside. No surprise. Anyone with a background in the mental health field would recognize the round, orange-coated tablets as Thorazine. It was one of the most commonly used psychotropic drugs, normally prescribed for acutely agitated, manic or disturbed patients. The black letters SKF identified the manufacturer as Smith Kline & French. Below that was the dosage code, T79, which revealed that each tablet contained 200 milligrams of the active ingredient, chlorpromazine hydrochloride.

"Has she ever taken these pills before?" I asked.

"No," Mother Dominica said. "To my knowledge, she has never taken any medication. Is there a problem?"

Whoever prescribed the medication was taking La Magdalena's case very seriously indeed. The normal initial dosage for Thorazine starts out at 25 milligrams, with an additional 25 to 50 milligrams recommended for severe symptoms. Two of the pills Mother Superior showed me would put La Magdalena at 400 milligrams, a dosage level that should be reached only gradually, over a period of a week. If she took a second dose within four hours, she would already be close to the maximum efficacious daily dosage of 1,000 milligrams. Administering that much Thorazine on the first day was a chemical shock treatment that could render her comatose. If they were starting her out with such extreme measures, I hated to imagine what awaited her. During my college fieldwork at Willowbrook Hospital, I had seen patients who, even after their medications were reduced, were nothing more than zombies. They were victims of chemical lobotomies; their ability to communicate, to eat, to do anything more than stare at the walls of their prison had been wiped out. But those were some of the most depraved members of society, patients judged by the courts to be criminally insane: murderers and rapists who inflicted unspeakable acts of horror upon the bodies of their victims. They were far beyond the ability of any human to rehabilitate them. Permanent sedation, as ethically questionable as it might be, was the only way to calm the evil storms that raged in their minds.

Did a young nun who claimed to have lived in a previous life deserve the same fate?

Four centuries ago, heretics were burned at the stake. Apparently the modern punishment was a chemical fire that left the flesh intact while burning away memory. I wasn't sure which punishment was more cruel.

"It's a medication used for neuropsychiatric conditions," I said. "I don't think she needs these."

I put the drugs in my pocket.

"That solves nothing," Mother Dominica said in a sour voice. "They'll bring more drugs when they come for her."

"You can't let them take her," I protested. "You've got to find a way to stop them."

"What do you think I've been doing?" she snapped. "I've been on the telephone all morning trying to put a stop to this. I've talked to the cardinal's office twice. I contacted my superiors in Madrid, I even called Rome and spoke to Mother General Rittinger, who advises the pope on all matters related to orders of religious women."

"And . . .?"

"Nothing," she admitted. "They were all aware of the case, but they all concurred in the decision of the psychiatrists. They ordered me not to interfere."

"Doesn't it strike you as odd?" I asked.

"The Church bureaucracy can be very rigid," she said.

"I mean weren't you surprised that they all knew about Sister Mariamme? Isn't it odd that the case of a simple nun in Valencia would attract so much attention at the highest levels?"

"Yes . . . I thought of that, too. But there's nothing further I can do about it. The ambulance has already left Madrid. As much as I'd like to help, I'm constrained by my vows of obedience not to interfere."

"Then perhaps you should leave the room," I said.

"What?" And then, "How dare you?"

I could sense the assembled nuns stirring, almost as if they were preparing to attack me for challenging their leader.

"I mean no disrespect, Mother Dominica," I quickly explained. "But I'm not bound by the same vows as you. I plan to interfere. I'll find a way to stop them. And if you don't know what I'm doing, you won't be breaking your vows."

She started to smile, and then suddenly stopped.

"What about the other sisters?" she asked. "They are bound by the same vows as mine."

"Technically, you're the only person here who was ordered not to interfere. If you don't tell them otherwise, they're free to follow their consciences."

"Technically, yes. But . . ." she started to argue, but seeing the expressions on her subordinates' faces, she paused. "You have a very devious mind, Mr. Nikonos. If anyone can help Sister Mariamme, I think it will be you. Perhaps I will go to the chapel to pray for you." She smiled at the other sisters and added, "For all of you."

As soon as she left, I turned back to La Magdalena. "How much longer will it take the ambulance to get here from Madrid?"

"Three more hours, perhaps four at the most."

"We've got to get you out of here."

"How? The entrance is being watched. I am followed wherever I go. The ambulance driver will be told where to find me."

"What about the back door?"

"It was sealed fifty years ago, to keep the priests out."

"Windows?"

"All barred."

"What about the basement? Don't some of these old buildings have tunnels under the sidewalk?"

"Our laundry is down there, and some storage rooms, but any old tunnels were bricked over long ago."

"This place is like a prison." My bravado was turning to desperation. "Isn't there any other way to get out?"

"The only way out is through the front door."

"Where the surveillance teams are waiting for you," I reminded her.

"You managed to get past them last night," La Magdalena said. "They were looking for you in the cathedral, they knew your face, but you managed to walk right past them without being discovered. And I think they still don't know you're here."

I stared at her, feeling like a complete fool that I hadn't thought of it myself.

"If it worked for you, why can't it work for me?" she asked.

It wasn't that simple, of course. My face wasn't all that familiar to the men assigned to follow me. But La Magdalena was well known to the surveillance crews. They had been following her for weeks. They knew her face, the way she walked, the way she turned her head to look for oncoming traffic when crossing the street. The variety of memory cues accumulated during weeks of careful observation enabled them to recognize her from a distance, separating her from the other nuns even when her face was barely visible.

And yet, I thought, there was a way to deceive even the most skilled member of the surveillance team. It would take time to set up. And it would be complicated.

But as Mother Dominica noted, I had a devious mind.

Thirty-Two

DRESSED ONCE AGAIN in my nun's garb, I soon headed out to the *Jardine de Turio* to meet with the desk clerk from the Adriatico Hotel. I was growing comfortable with the black robes that draped my body, the starched linen wimple that encased my head, and the oversized rosary beads that rustled whenever I moved. Fortunately for my toes, a nun with unusually large feet volunteered a pair of her commodious shoes, which fit me much better than the ones I wore the previous day. I was also growing comfortable with the deference I was accorded by passing Valencianos. Except for the occasional small child who seemed frightened by my clothing, most people greeted me with a warmth and respect I had never before experienced from strangers. As I walked to the park, I found myself increasingly subsumed into this new identity. I walked with head bowed, my eyes avoiding direct contact with those of men, but offering demure recognition of greetings offered by women. I kept my arms folded in my voluminous sleeves, and moved with smaller, more careful steps. Where yesterday I had been afraid I would be unmasked as an imposter or worse yet, a transvestite of the vilest kind, today I moved with quiet assurance. I had easily passed my first test, which was to exit the convent without attracting the attention of the watchers. They had little interest in anyone who didn't resemble La Magdalena.

Once I was certain I wasn't being followed, I made my telephone call to Alfredo. It was a call I couldn't risk making from the convent, where any wireless or hard-wired telephone was certain to be monitored. My instructions to him were complicated, but the money I offered overcame any confusion he felt. DesRosier's advance was being steadily consumed.

Now I waited for Alfredo in the park, having selected a bench that gave me a good view of the surrounding area. I knew it would take a while to complete the assignment I gave him, but after an hour and a half, I was getting concerned. The ambulance was on its way from Madrid. If Alfredo didn't show up soon, my efforts would be in vain.

A nun sitting alone on a park bench for an hour and a half was bound to invite curious stares and unwanted attention. Mothers pushing strollers didn't seem to mind my presence. Nor did the elderly strollers. But one man, a gardener, made a point of passing in front of my bench every few minutes. Time was running out, and I was getting worried that someone might inquire whether I needed assistance. My clearly male voice would immediately give me away. In defense against any such intrusion, I began to finger the rosary beads that hung from my waist. Unconsciously at first, and then with growing intensity, I found myself using the words that were taught to me in parochial school. With time running out, prayer was all that was left to me.

I must have been the very picture of the devout religious woman, when a pink-haired young man with a ring in his lower lip passed by.

"Alfredo!" I called out.

He stopped and looked around, saw me, looked away, and then looked back as if he didn't believe what he was seeing.

"Where's your friend?" I asked.

At the sound of my voice, his face broke into a conspiratorial grin.

"*Qué bonita, Señor.* You make a beautiful nun."

I felt my face redden with embarrassment, and he immediately took it as an acknowledgment that I was indeed a cross-dresser.

"It's just a disguise," I tried to explain.

"*Sí, señor,* and a very lovely disguise it is."

"Knock it off," I growled. And suddenly realizing that the deep timbre of my voice was attracting the gardener's attention, I patted the bench beside me and softly asked Alfredo to take a seat.

He was still giving me that goofy smile

"It's not what you think," I whispered.

"*Sí, señor,* whatever you say."

"It's part of my plan."

"*Yo comprendo.* It is a different plan, *no?*"

I decided to quit fighting it. Let him think whatever he wanted, as long as he followed my instructions.

"Where's your friend?" I asked again.

"She will join us soon. She had to call her mother."

He must have seen the alarm in my face, because he quickly added, "You can trust her with your secret, señor. She has many friends who are like you."

I ignored the remark and reached for the black satchel he brought. It was surprisingly small.

"Is this all the clothing?" I asked.

"*Sí señor,* but I think the dress will not fit you. My friend, she is shorter and has a . . . different shape than you. Also . . . , " He glanced down at the bottom of my robe. " . . . smaller feet."

"Where is she?" I asked again. "I don't have much time."

"She will be here soon," he assured me, and then teased, "You know how women are."

145

The entire sequence was a stupid exchange with an immature person, I thought. But I had no time for explanations.

"I can't wait any longer." I rose from the bench. "Send her to the convent as soon as she arrives."

"The money, señor. What about the money?"

I gave him an envelope, which he greedily opened.

"Three hundred dollars now," I said. "The rest when she arrives at the convent. But if she isn't there in thirty minutes, she gets nothing. Thirty minutes. Do you understand?"

"*Sí, señor. Yo comprendo.* And do not worry. Your secret is safe with us."

I could feel his eyes on me as I walked away. Any embarrassment I felt disappeared as my mind focused on the next steps in my plan.

The nuns were gathered in the dining room, almost childlike in their eagerness to examine the contents of the satchel. Red high-heeled pumps and black pantyhose, a surprisingly short red leather skirt and frilly undergarments . . . they seemed shockingly out of place within the austere walls of the convent. I expected outrage from these cloistered women. Instead, the older nuns seemed curious, and the younger nuns appeared transported for a few moments into another world as they fondled these reminders of what life might have been like for them. Soft purrs of delight greeted each item as it was passed from one set of hands to another. I wondered if their reaction would have been the same in the stern presence of Mother Dominica.

"We don't have much time," I warned them.

Three of the younger nuns, apparently self-appointed attendants, gathered up the garments and disappeared down the hallway.

"La Magdalena is praying in her room," one of the remaining English-speaking nuns advised me. "She was afraid you might not return."

"She should be praying for herself," I said. "Praying that I can get her out of here."

It was the wrong thing to say. Acting almost as one, the nuns suddenly seemed to realize that La Magdalena would be traveling alone with me, a man of whom they knew nothing.

They began to advance upon me. The group, which a moment ago had shown me the light-hearted and even frivolous side of its nature, now reverted to the menacing black-robed figures whom I had feared so much as a schoolboy.

One of them stepped forward to speak for the others. She was a small woman, but her voice had more gravity than any fire-and-brimstone preacher I had ever heard.

"La Magdalena is an innocent," the little nun said. "Whatever she remembers from her previous existence, in this life she is still pure and undefiled. If any harm comes to her, we will know. If you violate her, or harm her in any manner, we will pray to our dying days that the wrath of God will torment and destroy you, drive you mad and send you to spend eternity burning in the fires of Hell."

I don't necessarily believe in Hell. But my studies had taught me enough about the mystical power of concentrated negative thought to realize it wasn't an idle threat. Anyone who believes, as the Harvard Study established, that the mystical power of prayer can produce beneficial results must also accept the corollary, the equally traditional belief that evil can befall those at whom malevolent thoughts are directed. I certainly would never do anything to cause an entire order of dedicated nuns to begin praying for my perdition.

I didn't hear the door open. All I heard was a series of gasps and startled whispers.

I couldn't see over the black veils, all of which seemed to turn in unison to the source of the disturbance. For a moment, I was forgotten. And then slowly, with a rustling of robes and rosary beads, the crowd parted, opening a path to allow me to see the woman who had entered the room.

At first, I didn't recognize her.

It could have been one of those incredibly sexy young Spanish women who adorn the covers of *HOLA,* the trendy Spanish magazine, come to show the residents of the *convento* what beauty populated the outside world. The nuns gazed at her in awe, this lovely creature with the short blonde hair and the long golden legs.

She stood motionless, staring at me.

She wore clothing that barely covered her body. A low-necked white sweater that was a few sizes too small for the rich promise of her breasts. A red leather skirt whose hem barely covered her buttocks. And in between the sweater and skirt was a wide swath of bare skin, revealing a perfectly formed and highly suggestive oval *umbilicus,* partially concealed by a golden chain. No wonder the first nun who saw her let out so loud a gasp.

She seemed to be asking wordlessly for my approval.

The most amazing part of it all, the part I couldn't quite believe, was her face. It must have been one of the more worldly young nuns, one who had previous experience with cosmetics, who effected the transformation. It was done simply, but expertly. Just a few strokes of lipstick to draw attention to her mouth, a touch of mascara to lift her eyebrows and darken her lashes, and a hint of color added to her cheeks turned the innocent young nun into an elegant seductress. Golden hoop earrings, the kind Salome once wore, completed the image.

A shaft of afternoon sunlight chose that moment to appear from behind the clouds, filtering through a tall window and singling her out with its soft glow. The dark wooden walls behind her provided a moody contrast. The parted rows of black-robed nuns in the foreground added both perspective and mystery to the setting. It was a magical tableau. If the Renaissance masters had been working today, I was convinced this was how they would have portrayed a modern Mary Magdalene.

Was it reality, or some fanciful illusion created by a tired mind?

Would she disappear as I approached, withdrawing into the dream I was convinced I was experiencing?

I have no memory of how I reached her side, no recollection of actually crossing the room. For all I know, I could have floated across in some miraculous act of levitation. Yet there I was, standing inches in front of this golden woman. Allowing myself to be enveloped within her feminine aura. Close enough to hear her gentle breathing. Close enough to smell the scent of lavender that seemed to emanate more strongly than ever from the pores of her skin. When she tilted her head and smiled up at me, close enough for me to see the delicate convolutions at the edges of her lips, I was ready to violate the mother superior's commandment against touching. If I could but press my lips against hers, I thought, I was willing to suffer whatever agonies the protective nuns might wish upon me.

I tried to fight off the impulse. What little of the rational part of my brain was still functioning warned me against being drawn into her spell. But I didn't care. I felt as if I was born for this woman, that my entire life thus far had been but a prelude, a time of preparation for this mystical convergence. Standing this close, feeling her sweet warm breath on my face, it was easy to understand the power she exerted over Serrano, why he might have truly believed she was the Magdalenean reincarnation. She was a woman worthy of obsession, the one, as the Nag Hammadi described her namesake, who could be "loved above all others."

It was she who pulled back, withdrawing ever so slightly in that maddening way women have which always leaves men feeling unfulfilled. With a tiny sideways movement of her eyes, she reminded me where we were. I turned to face the other nuns, expecting an outpouring of hostility from these avowed protectors of their colleague's virtue. What I saw instead were faces filled with silent wonder. Like the audience members at the end of a play, each was lost in her own thoughts. Some, I was sure, projected themselves into the situation. Others might be seeing in Sister

Mariamme's transformation the fulfillment of some deeply repressed fantasy. But even the most hardened of them apparently had a romantic streak. There were no frowns of disapproval at my behavior.

The enchanted moment was shattered by the front doorbell.

"La ambulancia!" one of the nuns cried out.

La Magdalena slipped behind me. I could feel her body quivering with fear.

"Don't let them take me," she pleaded.

Thirty-Three

OUR FEAR TURNED to astonishment when we saw who walked through the dining room doorway.

Instead of the expected ambulance driver, the creature who entered the room could only be described as a doppelgänger of La Magdalena.

At first glance, she was a perfect body double: the same height, the same general weight, the same pale complexion, also blonde, although a lighter shade. She was wearing a mirror image of the midriff-baring sweater, the immodestly short leather skirt, the red pumps, the golden waist chain, and the golden hoop earrings Magdalena now wore. But on closer inspection, the double's long legs were not quite as shapely, her figure not quite as provocative, and her face, although heavily enhanced with cosmetics, nowhere near as enchanting as that of the young woman who cowered behind me.

Still, I felt certain she was a close enough match to deceive the surveillance crews outside.

This was one of Alfredo's many female friends, the one he had selected based on my specifications. It was she who shopped for the clothing La Magdalena wore, purchasing identical garments for herself. The men watching the *convento* would have seen her enter. Hopefully, during the fifteen or twenty seconds they saw her, most of which would have been a rear view while she waited for the door to be answered, the eyes of the surveillance teams would have been aimed at her legs and provocative clothing rather than her face. The men outside had seen La Magdalena dozens of times, followed her to and from the cathedral, knew the way she looked and how she walked. But they had never seen her in anything other than a nun's veil and robes, which covered all but a small portion of her face and hands. When she walked out wearing clothing identical to Alfredo's friend, I was certain none of them would recognize her. The long legs, the tiny leather skirt and exposed navel would occupy their attention.

The only problem was the hair. Alfredo's friend wore her hair plastered up in a spiked punk-style Mohawk.

La Magdalena slowly peered out from behind me, emerging only when I assured her it was safe to do so.

The two women stared at each other in puzzled disbelief.

"What the hell . . .?" Alfredo's friend started to say in a gum-chewing voice. Realizing where she was, she quickly corrected herself. "I mean, like, I'm sorry. What's going on here?"

The nuns looked from one of the women to the other. As they stood so close together, the similarities between the two of them faded further. Alfredo's friend grew suddenly self-conscious, possibly realizing her own shortcomings. The cosmetics, which she had undoubtedly applied with painstaking care, seemed overdone and gaudy next to the minimal coloring added to Magdalena's face. The double's skin looked rough, her cheekbones gaunt, and her posture and mannerisms awkward, although I think the awkwardness might have had something to do with her confusion at the situation in which she found herself.

I handed her an envelope containing the second half of the promised payment. She carefully counted out the three hundred-dollar bills and stuffed them into a leather shoulder bag.

"You didn't buy another bag," I admonished her. "We may need to use yours."

At the sound of my voice, she took a step backwards. "You're not a Sister," she said. "You're that guy. The one Alfredo told me about." Her face broke into a grin as she looked me over. "You look pretty good. You sure fooled me. But isn't it kind of uncomfortable?"

"The bag," I said. "We're going to have to borrow the bag. And maybe you could do something about Sister Mariamme's hairdo."

"She's a nun? I had no idea. Like, if I knew I was buying an outfit for a nun, I would have picked something more . . . conservative, I guess."

"What you bought is fine," I said. "It's probably better for our purposes. Now what about the hair? We don't have much time."

"I'm still waiting to hear what's going on here." Her manner turned adamant. "Alfredo didn't tell me much."

I had purposely not told Alfredo of my plans, asking him only to find a friend of a certain height and hair color, instruct her to buy two identical outfits, and have her show up at the *convento*. Fortunately, Melba, which was her name, turned out to be an ideal choice for what I had in mind. She was an adventurous young woman, and like Alfredo, she had a strong dislike for authority. Playing the decoy in a young nun's escape plot appealed to the rebel in her. With a jar of mousse from her bag, she quickly shaped La Magdalena's hair into a duplicate of her spiky Mohawk.

I was getting nervous. Nearly three hours had elapsed. The ambulance would be arriving at any moment. I was anxious to leave. I quickly packed my civilian clothes and interview materials in the black satchel.

One of the nuns rushed in.

"A representative from the cardinal's office is on the way," she shouted. "Someone who knows La Magdalena."

That was a complication I hadn't expected, one that added more urgency to the task.

"Hurry!" I said. "We've got to get out of here. Now!"

"What about me?" Melba asked. "What happens to me? If I leave in the same clothes as her, the cops will know something's going down. And, like, nobody told me to bring a change."

"The Sisters will take care of you," I said with a smile. "I'm sure you'll make a good-looking nun when you leave."

"Cool," Melba responded.

I tried to hurry La Magdalena to the front door. Unaccustomed to three-inch heels, she was a little wobbly on her feet.

Our way was barred by the sudden reappearance of Mother Dominica. She stood before the door, arms folded, her face set in a hostile frown. I hoped she hadn't changed her mind at the last minute. My plan, which seemed to be going so well, might be about to unravel.

"I didn't agree to this," she said.

"You promised you wouldn't stop us."

"I'm talking about Sister Mariamme's clothing." She looked disapprovingly at the band of flesh visible between skirt and blouse. "It's . . . it's scandalous. How dare you do this to her? And you, Sister Mariamme, how could you agree to display your . . . your body like this?"

"It was the priests who put us in black robes," La Magdalena said. "It was the priests who made us ashamed to show ourselves."

"There you go again," the old nun sighed.

"I was a little shocked, too," I said. "But the more outrageous the outfit, the more likely she won't be recognized."

"I don't like it at all," Mother Dominica shook her head in disapproval. "But perhaps you are right," she finally said. She leaned forward to kiss La Magdalena on the cheek. "*Vaya con Dios, Hermana.* Now you'd better hurry before the Cardinal's representative arrives."

La Magdalena took a deep breath, opened the door, and headed out into the street alone, with her head held high. Mother Dominica laughed and shook her head as she watched her little nun purposely cross the street to allow the surveillance crews a better look at her body.

"Maybe it's for the best," she said, turning serious again. "I don't think she ever really belonged to us."

One of the *Guardia* men let out a low, plaintive whistle as the young woman with the spiked blonde hair and short leather skirt disappeared down the street. When I looked back at Mother Dominica, her eyes were growing moist. The stern nun pulled a handkerchief from one of her voluminous sleeves and turned away. It was a momentary lapse. When she turned back, she was once again in control of her emotions.

"You must take good care of her," she said. "I protected her as long as I could. She is your responsibility now."

Mother Dominica slipped a piece of paper into my hand.

"You may find this helpful," she said.

Before I could examine the paper, the doorbell began to ring, a loud impatient clamor.

"That will be the Cardinal's Representative," Mother Dominica said. She seemed relieved by the interruption. "Don't worry," she said. "He won't recognize you. The only nun he's concerned about is Sister Mariamme."

She hurried me to the door, and as she greeted the middle-aged priest who waited outside, she gave me a gentle shove.

"*Buenos días, Monsignor,*" she said, motioning him inside with her other arm.

"*Buenos días, Madre,*" the priest said. He gave me a piercing gaze. For a moment, I thought I was unmasked. Fortunately, one of the more hirsute nuns had provided me with the razor she occasionally used on her own facial hair, and my face was as smooth as any woman's. His gruff voice acknowledged me with a curt "*Buenos días,*" and he brushed past me. So much for clerical courtesy, I thought as I stood aside to let him enter.

By now, I felt totally secure in my disguise. Having been in and out of the convent twice, I was a familiar entity to the surveillance crews. I had no fear of being stopped. Carrying the black satchel, I made my way slowly down the street, in the direction opposite the one La Magdalena had taken. A short time later we met, as prearranged, in the waiting room of the Estación del Norte. She already had our tickets for the commuter train to Benicasim, where DesRosier's car was supposed to be waiting for me in the municipal parking lot.

We made an odd couple, she in her skin-baring outfit and punk hair-do, and I in my nun's habit. I couldn't wait to shed the heavy robes and tight headdress. La Magdalena, on the other hand, seemed to revel in the formerly forbidden freedom her skimpy outfit promised.

"I feel almost naked," she giggled, looking around to see how many men were staring at her.

"That's because you *are* almost naked," I said reprovingly.

"Do you think I'm pretty? Or are they looking at me because of this outfit?"

I had to smile. Nineteen years in the convent, and she was suddenly as self-conscious and worried about her appearance as any normal young woman.

"You're the most beautiful woman in the station," I assured her. "But it's also the outfit. We'll have to get you some more respectable clothing."

"But I can keep this outfit, though, can't I?" Quickly turning coquettish on me. "Please, Theo?"

"Don't call me Theo," I said nervously. "At least not while I'm still wearing a habit."

"So what should I call you?" she teased. "*Sister* Theo?"

I couldn't help smiling at her playfulness. "Just call me Sister," I said with a laugh. "At least until I get back into my own clothing. And from now on I'll just call you Magdalena. Is that okay with you?"

"Why not? It's my name."

It was refreshing to see how normal she was. If I had any doubts about her mental health, they were completely dispelled by how quickly she was adjusting to secular life. It was quite remarkable. Most people who spent their lives in a cloistered environment would probably have trouble reentering the modern world.

The person who was having the difficult time adjusting was me. As I sat beside Magdalena, my eyes kept wandering to the vast expanse of legs the mini-skirt revealed. She pretended not to notice, but her attitude suggested she was pleased by the attention. Would I have been so fascinated with her flesh if I hadn't known that she was a nun? Perhaps not.

As the train moved north out of Valencia, I worried that I had already crossed an invisible ethical line. Magdalena was the subject of an investigation

I was conducting, and as such should be treated with cool professional detachment. On another level, since I approached her as a psychologist and had already conducted our first interview, I also had to consider her my patient. The codes of practice for psychologists proscribe not only romantic relationships with patients, but also social relationships, even those as innocuous as taking tea with a patient. And here I was, heading unchaperoned toward unknown destinations with her, and desperately trying to suppress what I was feeling.

Hanging over my head, and outweighing even the professional considerations, was my loyalty to the memory of Laura Duquesne, the only woman I had ever truly loved.

As the train rolled on, I closed my eyes and thought of Laura. The love I felt for her was unrequited and unresolved, at least in this life. I never had the chance to tell her of my feelings while she was alive, never even touched her, except for therapeutic ministrations during her detoxification sequence. Yet she had made the supreme sacrifice, giving up her life to save mine. If that was not an expression of love, I don't know what else could possibly qualify.

We went into the afterlife together, she as my ethereally lovely guide. I wanted to remain there with her forever, but it was she who sent me back, telling me my work was not yet done. It was she who promised that when the time came for my final journey into the Light, she would be there to greet me, and we would remain together throughout eternity.

My life since then had been guided by the heavenly bond between Laura and myself. I remained celibate, feeling no need for any further female companionship, avoiding even innocent friendships. In many ways, my attitude resembled that of a medieval monk, happy in my solitude, finding joy in my contemplation of the life that awaited me after death. My first thought every morning, and my last thought every night, was of Laura.

At least until last night. With both guilt and confusion, I remembered how last night, after hours of restlessness, before I finally went to sleep, my last thoughts were of La Magdalena and the mysterious aroma of lavender that seemed to hover about her. And how I couldn't sleep until I pressed my lips to the mark on the back of my hand, where I thought I could still taste the sweetness of her kiss.

I wondered if such thoughts violated some celestial contract, that my feelings for Magdalena might compromise my chance of spending eternity with my beloved Laura.

Was I in danger of trading earthly pleasure for the joys of Paradise? It was a metaphysical question for which I had no answer.

I was deeply, eternally in love with a dead woman who promised to wait for me, and now I was in danger of falling in love with a woman who claimed to have lived before.

I was beginning to think I was a candidate for psychoanalysis myself.

Thirty-Four

"THIS REMINDS ME of the time we fled Caesarea." Magdalena was staring out the window as she spoke, watching as the last daylight disappeared. "It was about this same hour when we went to the boat. Do you remember?"

"You didn't tell me about that yet," I said. "When did that happen?"

"After the Resurrection. You really don't remember?"

It was an odd comment, I thought. Made odder still when she lapsed into a string of words so completely indecipherable to me that I'm unable even now to approximate them on the written page. She was employing some unknown language for the second time since I met her. But was it a true case of what Stevenson called xenoglossia, the unexplained ability to speak languages that could not have been learned in this life? Or was it simply the nonsensical babble of glossalalia, as most such cases turn out to be? A finding that it was nonsense would undercut any reincarnation claim. But if it turned out to be Aramaic or one of those other "dead tongues" Padre Serrano insisted she spoke . . . well then, I thought, that would certainly be interesting.

Finding someone to corroborate her possible knowledge of ancient languages wouldn't be easy. The logical place to search was in a Spanish university or a museum, especially one with a Middle Eastern department. But I was afraid to expose Magdalena to some independent thinker with his own agenda who might trace her back to the convent, and in the process alert the Diocesan authorities. A far better approach, even though he was in Lebanon, would be to find a way to contact the linguistics professor Padre Serrano had mentioned. Professor Naghib Abramakian was already familiar with the case, and according to Serrano, intensely interested in talking to Magdalena. I had no address or phone number. But I should be able to contact him through Lebanon University's website. Fortunately, there seemed to be Internet Cafés all over Spain. I'd stop in at the next one I found.

The sixty-four-kilometer trip to Benicasim took less than an hour. A parking garage that far outside Valencia might seem a long way to go to pick up a car. But DesRosier had chosen the site well. For someone trying to elude any possible pursuers, the remote location was far enough beyond the metropolitan perimeter to neutralize any surveillance advantages the *Guardia* enjoyed in crowded Valencia.

Eighteen commuters got off the train with us at Benicasim, mostly men. I remember the exact number because I tried to fix their features in my mind, even the wrinkled face of the old woman with the taped-up cardboard suitcase. If I saw any of them again in the next few days, I would know we had to take evasive action. As a further precaution, I led Magdalena on a long circular route, doubling back twice before deciding it was safe to pick up the car. The garage was only two blocks from the train station, on a street with little traffic. The car was parked exactly where the map indicated. It was a remarkably ordinary-looking grey Opel Corsa, a small four-door car that was hard to distinguish from a dozen other models. Exactly the sort of nondescript vehicle that could easily lose itself in traffic. There wasn't enough room in the back seat to change clothing. I had to find a dark corner of the garage where I could shed my disguise without embarrassing myself or Magdalena. I had worn the confining wimple and heavy robes for only parts of two days. Nevertheless, taking them off and slipping into my comfortable jeans was a remarkably liberating experience. I could imagine the psychological impact the similar transition must have had on Magdalena, who had worn the nun's garb all her adult life.

"Where are we going now?" she asked when I returned to the car.

I searched the narrow glove compartment. DesRosier had thoughtfully stocked it with a map of Spain, some tourist guidebooks, and the original registration papers, in case we were stopped by the *policía*.

"I don't know," I admitted as I studied the map.

We certainly didn't want to head south, back in the direction of Valencia. To the east was the Mediterranean. Mountains and barren plains awaited us on the west. The north, with its numerous coastal cities, seemed the logical route. The most famous of those cities, Barcelona, would probably offer the greatest opportunity to go into hiding. If I had any doubts that Fate intended us to head north, they were dispelled when I unfolded the note Mother Superior had handed me.

Carefully typed in the center were four brief lines:

Hermana Maria Generosa
Casa Dolorosa
1007 Via Rampala
Barcelona

Puzzled, I read the name and address out loud.

"Does this mean anything to you?" I asked. "Do you recognize the name?"

Magdalena stared at it with sleepy eyes.

"I think so . . . ," she said. "Yes, it's been a long time, but I remember her. *Hermana Vinagrosa.*"

I looked at the name again. "It says *Hermana Generosa*, not *Vinagrosa.*"

"Yes, but when I was a little girl, I used to call her *Hermana Vinagrosa*, which translates roughly as 'Sister Vinegar' in English. I called her that because she usually had a sour look on her face, as if she had just tasted vinegar." Magdalena smiled at the memory. "But she was a wonderful person, a very devout nun, and she always treated me well."

Did I hear her right, I wondered? I was suddenly alert.

"You knew this nun when you were a little girl?"

"Oh, I knew Sister Vinagrosa as long as I can remember. She was sort of a nanny to me, if you could ever call a nun a nanny. They tell me she was the one who took care of me when I was an infant. Later all the nuns kind of adopted me, but 'Sister Vinegar' was always my favorite."

"Sort of a mother-daughter bond?"

"I guess so, although I know she wasn't my mother. She couldn't have been. She was almost sixty years old when I was left at the *convento.*"

My mind was jumping ahead.

"But she might have known your mother," I said. "She might have met her, maybe even talked with her."

"I doubt it. That was the kind of thing she would have told me. We talked a lot, about a lot of things. We were very close. She wouldn't have kept that from me."

"In the best of all possible worlds, you're probably right," I said. What I didn't say was that in the secretive world of traditional convent life, where nuns are expected to renounce all ties to the outside world, it would have been common practice for "Sister Vinagrosa" to conceal such information. That was especially true for a lonely nun who found herself serving as a surrogate mother to an abandoned child. Human nature being what it is, she would be loath to do anything that might disrupt whatever form of mother-daughter bond developed. Perhaps now, in the twilight of her life, she might be convinced to reveal what she knew.

"I always wanted to see Barcelona," I said as I put the car in gear.

According to the map, the capital of the autonomous region of Catalunya was a 235-kilometer drive up the coast. During the day, it was probably a spectacularly scenic drive. At night, it was a boring trip through long patches of total darkness on an unlit and poorly marked road. We stopped once to eat, in a coastal town lit up with the ghastly yellowish glow of mercury-vapor lamps. The small restaurant, which catered to truckers, had an outdoor grill set up. I ordered a combination plate of *gambas* and *sardinas,* which turned out to be heavily seasoned with sea salt and nearly blackened by the charcoal. Magdalena ordered a more modest dish, the ubiquitous Spanish potato omelet. We ate outdoors, sitting on a rough wooden bench where we drank *Fanta* and *limonada* and watched the moonlight sparkling on the sea. Under other circumstances, sitting near the shore with a lovely young woman might have been a romantic interlude. But I was "wired" and had us on the road again as soon as we finished our food.

Whatever fatigue or uncertainty I should have felt were gone, replaced by the adrenaline rush investigators enjoy when they uncover a new lead. I couldn't wait to get to Barcelona and discover what secrets *Hermana Generosa* might be willing to share. I didn't have too much hope that she knew the identity of Magdalena's parents. Despite DesRosier's interest in her genealogy, I felt that type of information was really peripheral to my investigation. What I hoped to learn was how Magdalena had been raised, what she had been taught, how she might have acquired her unusual knowledge, and whether she might have been influenced by others in forming her reincarnative beliefs.

We reached the outer industrial edges of Barcelona some time around 1 A.M. My earlier rush of energy had subsided, ground down by hours of staring into the beams of oncoming headlights. Nothing further could be accomplished until the city awoke, so I pulled off the road into a parking area where we could get some rest. By the time dawn broke over Barcelona, we were fast asleep.

It was still early in the morning when the heat of the Spanish sun made any further rest impossible. Magdalena was already out of the car, strolling in a nearby field. I sat there, watching her enjoy the freedom of her first morning outside the convent. A slight haze hung over the field, and the sun's rays were soft. Photographers call this time "the magic hour," a precious interlude when the combination of morning sun and lingering evening mist imparts a sometimes dreamlike quality to photographic images. Later, when the harsh Spanish sun burned away the youth of the day, this same field would revert to the barren patch of nameless weeds it really was. But for now, it was a scene with an almost other-worldly quality. In my mind's eye, I saw my companion walking through endless fields of lavender, a gentle breeze brushing long flowing hair against her face, laughing and calling out for me to join her as she stopped to scoop up a purple flower. It was a dream image, an illusion created by a mind that was still half-asleep, seen with eyes that were only partially open. Yet I didn't want to let it go, preferring its soft, slightly out-of-focus sweetness to the reality of a weed-infested field beside a tire factory.

The sound of the car door closing snapped me out of my reverie.

"Is something wrong?" she asked.

"I guess I'm still waking up," I said, unwilling to admit I might have been hallucinating.

I looked out at the field where she had been walking. It was nothing more than a large expanse of weeds at the edge of an industrial park. A plastic shopping bag, caught on a dead thistle bush, fluttered frantically in the wind. It was time to move on.

Our route into Barcelona fed us onto the *Cinturo Litoral,* the Coastal Beltway. It skirted the hump-backed mountain known as *Montjuic,* from whose heights the defense of the city was once organized. We drove past the port area. The city rose on the sloping plain to our left. On our right was the sea. I made a left turn on *Via Layetana* and found a public parking facility right where the guidebook said it would be. We left the car and crossed the street to enter the *Barri Gotic,* the oldest part of the city. The narrow, winding pedestrian streets were as confusing and crowded as those of Venice. It would be a simple matter for us to disappear into the marvelous mélange of tourists and students and shoppers, although after driving all night, those we most resembled were the young vagrants who gathered around the fountain near the cathedral. Magdalena insisted we couldn't call on Sister Generosa until we looked more presentable.

Fortunately, the *Barri Gotic* was loaded with little shops selling every-thing from women's shoes to camping supplies. She led me from shop to shop, studying the contents of each window, examining what other women were wearing, and quizzing me about what was appropriate. At nineteen years of age, she was still a virgin when it came to shopping. She learned quickly, however, and within two hours, we were loaded down with purchases and ready to find a place to stay.

After a few unsatisfactory starts, we settled on two rooms in a walkup *pensión* on a side street near the *Ramblas.* The grimy exterior of the build-ing looked as if it hadn't been cleaned since the sixteenth century. Inside, however, the owners had somehow managed to circumvent the landmark preservation codes and created a series of modernistic rooms that owed more to Picasso than Cervantes. I would have preferred something more in keeping with the character of this old part of town. But Magdalena had the opposite view. She was tired of old furnishings and dark rooms, she said. And she liked the oversized bed. On that point, I had to agree. I rented two separate rooms, next to each other. We cleaned up, changed, had a quick snack of *leche flan* at a nearby café and headed out to find *Hermana Generosa*.

Via Rampala was in the northern part of the city. The nearest Metro stop was *Sagrada Familia*, which let us off in front of the most famous sight in Barcelona, Antonio Gaudi's spectacularly unfinished Holy Family Church of the Atonement. Magdalena, who had spent her entire life in the environs of the severely gothic Valencia Cathedral, seemed staggered at her first sight of the immense and fanciful towers. She stopped at the top of the Metro stairs and stood motionless for long minutes, breathing in the almost absurd beauty of the edifice.

With barely a glance at me, she crossed the plaza and entered the gates. She stood smiling up, like the dozens of other tourists, at the storytelling sculptures of Christ's birth that adorned the *Naixement* entrance. Unlike the other tourists, however, when she saw the carvings over the west doorway depicting the Passion, she grew agitated. As a psychologist, I had previously witnessed the personality changes triggered by bipolar disorders. What was happening before me appeared to be quite different. It seemed to be a genuine anger, an outlet of some long-suppressed fury. Soon she was spewing forth a stream of unintelligible outrage. Not in Spanish, but once again in a language I didn't understand. The nearby tourists drew back, probably out of fear that her apparently irrational rage might give way to violence. Perhaps I should have intervened earlier, but I was fascinated by this third display of xenoglossia. I wished I had brought along my camcorder, so that I could have recorded the outburst.

Magdalena didn't resist when I finally pulled her away.

"What was that all about?" I asked.

"You don't know? You were there. You saw it all, just like I did."

"I saw you lose control of yourself. And what were you shouting?"

Calmed down now, she looked at me quizzically. "You don't remember anything, do you?"

She was talking in riddles now, and I didn't attempt to unravel them.

Casa Dolorosa was a few blocks further north. On a street filled with exuberant examples of the Catalan *modernisme* style of architecture, it was a flat-faced, stolid structure. It stood almost defiantly plain and unadorned among the swirling concrete balconies and wrought-iron decorations of its neighbors. The nun who answered the doorbell was as plain as the building, and almost as old.

By prearrangement, Magdalena did the talking. Although the nun greeted her in Spanish, Magdalena quickly changed to English, keeping the words slow and simple so the nun could understand her and I could follow along.

"We would like to talk to *Hermana Generosa*."

"*Qué?*"

"*Hermana Generosa.* Can we see her?"

"She is no longer here."

"Where can we find her?"

"*En el cementerio.*"

"*Muerta?*"

"*Sí. Muerta.*"

I didn't need a translator to understand what that meant. Magdalena's face told me everything I needed to know.

I had coached her carefully in how to talk to Sister Generosa. We had gone over the various ways to convince the "nanny-nun" to reveal whatever she knew about Magdalena's background. As thorough as I believed I had been, the one thing I hadn't prepared Magdalena for was the fact that her beloved "Sister Vinegar" might be dead. And yet, considering this was a retirement home for nuns, it was probably the most predictable outcome.

For a moment, neither of us knew what to say. The nun at the door seemed as saddened by the event as we were. Although in my case, not knowing Sister Generosa, I was more saddened by the loss of my most promising lead to Magdalena's past.

"*Requiscat in pace,*" Magdalena finally murmured in Latin.

"*Amen,*" the nun replied as they bowed their heads in unison.

"When did it happen?" I asked in English.

"Almost a year ago," the nun replied, switching to heavily accented English. "She died peacefully, in her sleep."

"I should have been told," Magdalena suddenly demanded in an angry voice. "Why wasn't I informed?"

Her outburst startled the nun, who took a step back and reassessed her visitors. I thought she was going to slam the door on us. If Magdalena hadn't abandoned her punk hairdo and changed from the miniskirt to a conservative long-sleeved flowered dress, I'm sure that would have been the case.

"What is your interest in Sister Generosa?" the nun asked.

"I loved her," Magdalena said. "She was like a mother to me."

"Yes, many young people felt that way about Sister. We all will miss her."

"You don't understand. She took care of me when I was a child. Sister Generosa was the only mother I ever knew."

"There was a child . . . , " the nun said, her voice taking on a suspicious tone, " . . . but it can't be you. That child was raised in a convent in Valencia, and that's where she remains today."

"*El Convento de las Hermanas del Sangreal,*" Magdalena said. "That's the *convento* where I was brought as a child. My name is Mariamme. I'm sure Sister Generosa spoke of me."

"But . . . your clothing. And this man . . ."

"He is a detective," Magdalena said. "He's helping me to find out where I came from. Who my parents were. Can you help us?"

"*Perdón, señorita.* I don't believe you. I don't know what it is you're after, but I am certain you're not the Mariamme who was cared for by Sister Generosa."

"Why?" Magdalena challenged her. "Is it just because I'm not wearing my religious habit? Do you think clothing is the only way to identify a religious person?"

"No, señorita. Give me credit for more intelligence than that."

"Then why?" Magdalena persisted. "Why are you so ready to dismiss me?"

"Because if you really were Mariamme, you would already have Sister Generosa's letter."

"What letter?" I interrupted.

"In anticipation of her death, Sister Generosa wrote a letter to Sister Mariamme."

"I never received any letter," Magdalena said.

"Sister Generosa said the letter was to be held here after her death. If Sister Mariamme came here to inquire about her parents, only then were we to turn over the letter to her. She said it would explain everything to the dear child."

"And where is the letter now?"

"Why, I turned it over to a representative of the real Sister Mariamme."

"You gave the letter to an imposter," I said.

"Don't take me for a fool, Señor. He verified his identity by telling me things only Sister Mariamme would know."

"Such as?"

"Well, for example, he knew Mariamme's nickname for Sister Generosa."

"Sister Vinagrosa," Magdalena said.

The nun's arrogant demeanor evaporated.

"How did you know that?"

"When did the man show up?" I asked.

"No more than an hour ago."

"Can you describe him?"

"He was shorter than you are, Señor. A heavier man. Spanish, unlike you. He had a mustache," With a stricken look on her face, she turned to Magdalena. "Are you really Mariamme, the child she raised? Are you really the one?"

"It's a little late for that question now," Magdalena said.

"But why would anyone go to all that trouble to get Sister Generosa's letter?" the nun asked.

Why, indeed, I wondered. And even more important, how did he find out about it?

Thirty-Five

THE GAME HAD suddenly changed.

Whoever was following us had somehow managed to jump ahead, as if anticipating our moves. But how?

Someone else was obviously in pursuit of the same answers as I was. But why?

The mystery man had beaten us to Sister Generosa's letter by a mere two hours, which made me feel foolish. What kind of investigator was I? If we had gone directly to *Casa Dolorosa* instead of wasting all that time looking for a room, shopping and showering and stopping for a *merienda,* Sister Generosa's letter would be in our hands. Now the letter that "would explain everything to the dear child" was irretrievably lost. Taken by a mystery man who used Magdalena's nickname for the retired nun to establish his legitimacy. Who was he, I wondered? The description given by the nun would probably fit one of every five adult males in Spain. Logic dictated it had to be someone who knew of the relationship between Sister Generosa and Magdalena. That narrowed it down to perhaps a thousand people in the Diocese of Valencia, which included male relatives and friends of the Holy Grail Sisters. If I looked at it from a different perspective, from the point of view that the mystery man's visit was prompted by someone with a special interest in Magdalena, I'd have to widen the circle of suspects to include psychiatrists and other officials in Rome, as well those responsible for Serrano's death. Not to mention the heavy-set man who knocked me over in front of the cathedral and ran off with Magdalena's note to Serrano.

I gave up in despair. The list of suspects was not only long, but all on it were unknown to me.

"Why are you so disappointed?" Magdalena asked. We were on the Metro, making our way back to the *Barri Gotic*. "It was only a letter."

"It was a clue to your past."

"I know all about my past."

"I mean your recent past, not what you claim happened to you 2,000 years ago. If Sister Generosa took the trouble to write a letter that she said would explain everything, why didn't she just mail it to you? Why would she instruct the other nun to hold it on the chance that you might come asking for it?"

"I don't know. Do you?"

"Maybe it was something she didn't want you to know until you were ready for it."

"Like what?"

"Something important, obviously. Maybe about the reason you were brought to the *convento*. Maybe about the identity of your parents." Now I was beginning to wonder if DesRosier might have been right, that Magdalena's ancestry might be worth investigating.

"Do you think that's important?"

"Well, haven't you ever wondered about it? Who your mother was? Or your father?"

"I think about it sometimes, yes. But I had different parents in different lives. If I don't know one set of parents, at least I have fond memories of my life with Syrus and Martha."

She spoke in an emotionless, almost casual way about what is normally the deepest and most emotional of human bonds. The journals of psychologists are filled with tales of patients driven to analysis in desperate attempts to work through the way their lives were affected by their parents. The pull of the parent-child relationship is so strong that people-search firms are hard-pressed to keep up with the demands of adopted children searching for birth parents they never knew. Yet Magdalena showed no interest in the subject. Even the death of the nun who performed the role of substitute mother seemed to have minimal effect on her. She had been more concerned about the fact that she wasn't informed about Sister Generosa's death than she was about the larger issue, which was the death of the woman who had raised her from childhood.

Anyone jumping to the conclusion that her behavior was indicative of Borderline Personality Disorder would be making a serious mistake. Even though emotional detachment is one of the diagnostic criteria for BPD, Magdalena's apparently indifferent attitude towards death was eerily similar to that of NDE survivors.

It was a mind-set with which I was all too familiar. After having seen what waits on the Other Side, those of us who have returned to life no longer share the universal fear of death that haunts the rest of mankind. The prospect of our own final demise stirs no anxiety; the deaths of others, including those closest to us, are no cause for grief. Which was why I didn't view Magdalena's calm acceptance of death as an aberration. By definition, any person who claimed to have lived before must also have experienced death's journey into the afterlife. The fact that Magdalena's indifferent attitude towards death so closely mirrored that of NDE survivors was actually evidence supportive of reincarnation.

We left the Metro at the *Plaza de Catalunya,* a broad open area where I slowly circled the fountain, pretending to study the ornate water spouts while actually watching for anyone who might be showing unusual interest in us. It was a futile gesture, but a precaution I was convinced had to become a matter of routine. Only when I was certain we weren't being followed did I walk Magdalena back to the hotel. When she was safe in her room, with instructions to allow no one but me to enter, I set out in search of an Internet café.

In Europe, where home computers don't have the widespread penetration they do in America, Internet cafés are more abundant. I found three within a few blocks of the hotel. They were wonderful examples of the incongruities that exemplify modern Spain: tiny outposts of twenty-first-century technology in prefabricated modules shoehorned into the bottom floors of buildings that were older than the United States. The first two Internet cafés were jammed with young people waiting to get on the computers. Probably because of higher prices, the third Internet café actually had two computer terminals available. I logged on, using a filter that allowed me to run my search in English.

Finding the website for the University of Lebanon took less than a minute. Unfortunately, the site was poorly constructed. It consisted mostly of self-congratulatory prose more suitable to a PR brochure than a university portal. Although there were listings for the various departments, including the Department of Linguistic Studies, it was impossible to access further information on each department. I tried searching the course catalog, but again, it dealt in generalities. There was plenty of general information about the "distinguished faculty." The university president was handsomely profiled. Individual professors such as Abramakian were ignored. The only information I was able to get was the university's central telephone number in Beirut.

I punched the number into the cell phone DesRosier had given me. It was busy. I redialed again and again. Busy and busy. It took a half hour to get through to the university switchboard. By that time, I was back at the hotel. The first university operator who answered didn't speak English, and hung up rather than deal with me. It took another ten minutes to get through again.

When I finally reached Professor Abramakian, the connection seemed to deteriorate. I had to shout into the telephone to be heard. His voice was scratchy and faded in and out, like an old short-wave broadcast.

"Hall-llo! Yes, this is Professor Abramakian!"

"My name is Theophanes Nikonos. I was given your name by Padre Javier Serrano."

"Padre Serrano?" In spite of the bad connection, I could sense a change in his voice, as if this was a call he had been waiting for. "Yes! Very good! And how is Serrano?"

"Not good," I said. "The padre is dead."

"Oh no, no! I don't believe it! How can that be? I spoke to him only two weeks ago! What happened?"

"It was a bombing. They say it was terrorists." I didn't see any point in alarming him with my suspicions. "In any event, before he died, Padre Serrano asked me to continue his work."

The distant voice on the telephone brightened up again. "You are also a psychiatrist?"

"A psychologist, actually."

"Close enough!" In the typical professorial fashion heard in the lecture halls of colleges around the world, Abramakian carefully enunciated each word and spoke as if there exclamation points at the end of every sentence. "The Padre was telling me about a young nun who aroused his professional curiosity!"

"Sister Mariamme," I said.

"Yes! Sister Mariamme! I was very interested in her case, also!"

"There is the question of languages she claims to know," I said.

"Quite! One of the languages she claimed to speak was ancient Aramaic, which no one in modern times has heard in its original spoken form!"

"Do you think . . . is it possible that she really speaks those languages?"

"Well! That is the same question Serrano asked! But I never heard her speak! All Serrano sent me was a short note which he said the nun had written!"

"I thought he sent you a tape."

"No! It was only a note he said was written by the nun! The note seemed legitimate! The grammar was correct, the spelling correct, even the accent marks and the penmanship were consistent with first-century writing! But I have no idea of the circumstances in which the note was written! She could have copied it from an old text! I told him I couldn't give him more than an educated guess at that time!"

So Serrano had stretched the truth when he told me Abramakian had verified her knowledge of dead languages.

"This is not a matter to be taken lightly!" Professor Abramakian bellowed. I had to hold the phone away from my ear. His voice, honed over years of making himself heard by the last student in the last row, was at least twice the decibel level of the normal human voice. It easily overpowered the electronic interference on the phone. "Finding someone who could speak these languages the way they were spoken 2,000 years ago, including the knowledge of idiomatic expressions and slang that Serrano claimed for this woman, would be the linguistic equivalent of opening Tutankhamen's tomb! Reputations can be made or broken with such discoveries! I was not prepared to risk my reputation with a long-distance analysis! I offered to fly to Valencia at my own expense to meet with her in person! For some reason, however, Serrano did not want me to meet with the young woman!"

"Would you be willing to come to Barcelona?"

"The young woman is there?"

"Yes, she's with me."

"And I can meet with her in person? Talk to her and test her abilities?"

"Whatever it takes. I need to find out whether she's really speaking in dead languages or just faking it."

For a moment, all I heard was the ever-present static. I could imagine the professor pacing back and forth behind his desk as he considered his response.

"Do you have reason to believe she might be . . . as you say, 'faking it?'"

"I just don't know," I admitted. "That's why I need an expert opinion."

"Yes! Very wise of you! But before I invest my time and money in this affair, I have a few questions for you!" His stentorian voice turned cagey. "Have you contacted anyone else regarding this person? Any other linguistic scholars?"

"No. You're the only language expert I know."

"And what about Padre Serrano? Did he contact other people in my field?"

"Not as far as I know."

"Very good! In that case, I will fly to Barcelona and examine this young nun's abilities! Since I will be recording everything she says, I will require a quiet room, without interference from street noise or other extraneous sounds!"

"I understand." It was the same type of setting I preferred for recording my own interviews.

"All recordings I make will remain my property!"

"Agreed." I was beginning to feel like an agent, negotiating legal terms on behalf of my client.

"I also reserve the right to publish my findings, including any photographs I take during our sessions!"

"That could be a problem," I objected.

"It's standard practice for researchers to publish their findings, Mr. Nikonos! The young woman's language skills, if genuine, would be of enormous interest to linguistic scholars!"

"It wouldn't hurt your reputation, either," I pointed out.

"Yes! Of course! I'm sure you've heard the phrase 'publish or perish'! Well! The community of linguistic scientists may be very small, but it is also very competitive! In any event, I believe it's an eminently fair quid pro quo! You get the expert opinion you need, and I get the prestige of publishing that opinion!"

"I just don't think we want any publicity about Sister Mariamme. At least not right now."

I heard a short laugh through another burst of static.

"We are talking about *The Journal of Linguistics,* not *The New York Times!*" he proclaimed. "Any article I write will have to pass the challenges of a peer-review board before it would even be considered for publication!

Now certainly the popular press might pick up the story, but even if I submitted an article today, it would take at least four months before it was in print! I hope that time frame is acceptable, because without the possibility of publishing my findings, there is little benefit for me in flying to Barcelona!"

"All right," I finally agreed. "It's just that I didn't expect it to be this complicated."

"I'm just being honest with you! What you Americans call being up-front!"

I had never identified myself as an American, but then it probably only took a few words for a linguistics expert to pinpoint not only my nationality, but also the region, the state, and possibly even the city where I was raised.

"I simply didn't want to take you by surprise when I show up with my recording equipment, releases, and legal forms!" he explained. "Now! Let me write down your telephone number, please! I will make my airline reservations and call you back with my arrival time! I'm sure this will be a fascinating experience for all of us!"

My ear hurt from listening to him, and I was grateful when he hung up. He called back in less than fifteen minutes, loudly announcing that no airline served the Beirut-Barcelona route with direct flights. In any event, he was able to get a seat on Middle East Airlines Flight 213 out of Beirut at 8:30 the next morning, changing at Geneva to Iberia Flight 4493, and arriving at Barcelona International at 3:10 P.M. local time. Once again, he repeated his eagerness to get started. The electronic interference was just as bad as before, making me wonder whether there might be something wrong with DesRosier's cell phone.

For supper I took Magdalena down the *Ramblas* to the *Barceloneta* area. It was a warm evening, and she selected a café where we could sit outdoors and watch the pleasure boats moving in and out of the marina. We ordered bouillabaisse, the seafood stew that is as much a specialty of Barcelona as it is of Marseilles. Magdalena was in an ebullient mood. She was wearing a short flower-print dress that showed off her stunning legs. The mousse had been shampooed out of her hair, which now revealed a slight natural curl. She put her elbows on the table, chin in her hands and, flashing a smile, suggested we share a bottle of wine. Red wine.

"You sure you can handle it?" I asked. "The wine they serve here isn't communion wine."

"In Marseilles, we always had red wine when we ate. Goodness, we drank red wine all the time."

"When were you in Marseilles?" I innocently asked.

"The year after the death of Jesus my Christ," she said.

"Oh."

"Don't you remember?"

She was giving me that strange sort of smile again, as if she knew something I didn't. While I hesitated, she broke off a piece of bread and buttered it.

"I think I read something about it," I said.

In fact, I knew a lot more about it than I was willing to admit. Some of France's most revered oral traditions describe Mary Magdalene's ministry in Marseilles and the South of France, where she took up residence after the Crucifixion. I first learned of those legends during my stay on Mount Athos, but having no interest at the time in Magdalenean mythology, I paid little attention to them. Now, however, sitting across the table from a woman who claimed to have lived that life, those legends offered a wonderful opportunity. One of the Stevenson Protocols involved returning with the subject to the locations of significant past-life events. Taking Magdalena back to some of the places her namesake visited would give me the chance to evaluate the accuracy of her recollections. Would she be able to identify the cave at Ste. Baume, the landing site at *les Saintes-Marie-de la-Mer*? Until I took her there, I didn't want to offer any hints of that part of my investigation.

The waiter brought us a bottle of *Sangre de Toro,* which he explained was one of Catalunya's finest wines, from the Penedes region south of Barcelona, and also *"más económico, señor."* Apparently trying to impress my beautiful partner, he went through the entire prescribed ritual of removing the cork, offering it for me to smell, pouring a small amount in my glass to be swirled and tasted, and then, following my nod, filling both our glasses to the customary halfway mark.

We touched glasses wordlessly. The wine was worthy of the ritual. It was a full-bodied red, with a rich and flowery bouquet, the perfect complement to the heavily flavored meal we were about to enjoy.

Our waiter brought us a platter on which was displayed the seafood that would go into our bouillabaise, which he explained in his broken English should more properly be called *sopa de mariscos.* Carefully arranged on the platter were fat shrimp, tiny reddish-brown baby octopi, clams, mussels, a small red snapper, a filet of skate, some *langostines,* and two medium-sized crabs. I doubt that Magdalena ever saw so elaborate a display of seafood at the *convento.*

"All for us?" she asked in disbelief.

"It's not as much as it looks," I assured her. "When they get rid of the bones and shells, there'll be a lot less to see."

It might seem that I should have been attending to business, questioning Magdalena in front of my camcorder, watching the needle on the voice-stress unit to determine if she was lying. After all, I did have a client who was anxious to find out the truth about this young woman. I was anxious, too, and worried about the mystery man who managed to reach *Casa Dolorosa* two hours before we did.

Nevertheless, I knew the importance of maintaining a calm outward appearance in front of Magdalena. If she was to have confidence in me as her analyst, I would have to act as if I was in control of the situation, however confusing it might be to me. A pleasant dinner beside the harbor was the ideal prescription, I thought.

By the time we finished our first glasses of wine, the waiter returned with a large bowl. He set up a serving tray beside our table, and removed the seafood from the bowl. An assistant, wielding nothing more than a tablespoon and a fork, skillfully removed shells and bones while we watched, amazed at his dexterity. Once again the edible portions were displayed for our approval. Two soup bowls appeared. Portions of fish, shrimp, octopi, clams and the rest were artfully arranged in the two bowls. With a flourish, the waiter produced a large ladle and filled the bowls with steaming red liquid.

I couldn't have asked for a more elegant service.

"*Bon appetit,*" he said, slipping incongruously into French.

Magdalena was dazzled. She stared at her dish for long moments, studying the chunks of seafood that rose like tiny mountains above the broth.

"This is so wonderful," she said. "We never ate like this in the *convento*. Thank you, Theo. Thank you."

I took another sip of wine and smiled sadly.

She was so beautiful, and yet so untouchable.

It wasn't professional ethics that held me back. Rules promulgated by some obscure board of mental-health administrators couldn't compete with the feelings this young woman aroused in me. I was certainly no Pygmalion, responding to some idealized creature of my own making. I was nevertheless responsible for the metamorphosis taking place before me. Twenty-four hours ago, she was an anonymous young nun, sequestered from the world, everything but her hands and face protected from prying eyes by black robes and white linen. Now she was sitting across the table from me, her hair and face aglow in the last golden rays of the evening sun, her arms bare, her legs exposed, her breasts barely covered by a low neckline. She was drinking wine and eating bouillabaisse and laughing, and yes, probably teasing me. If she had been anyone else than herself, if this had been any other time than now, I would have let myself fall madly in love with her.

Perhaps I already had, but was afraid to admit it.

"You're not eating your food," she said. "It's so-o-o good. Do you want some of mine?"

She playfully offered me a spoonful of broth.

Had I gone too far with her, I wondered? She was, I had to remind myself, a Bride of Christ, committed by her vows to a lifetime of purity. I had removed her from the sanctity of the *convento,* from the protection of her sisters, and brought her here to drink wine and expose her beauty to every man who passed by.

As I reached out to take the spoon, so playfully proffered, it suddenly began to tremble in her hand. A few drops of the red broth spilled on the tablecloth. She was staring at the red mark on the back of my hand.

"What's wrong?" I asked.

"Nothing . . . I'm . . . I'm sorry."

"You're shaking."

"I . . . I feel cold."

I offered her my blazer. She wrapped it tightly around her shoulders.

"Do you want to eat inside?"

"No . . . no," she said, her jaw quivering. "I think I'd like to go now. Do you mind?"

I put my arm around her and she leaned against me and held on for support. I could feel her body trembling.

"Me siento enfermo," she managed to mumble to the waiter, who seemed disappointed that we had barely touched the elaborate meal.

We took a cab back to the hotel.

"Do you want me to find a doctor?"

"No. I'll be all right. I think I'm just exhausted."

The explanation made sense at the time. Neither of us had had much sleep in the last twenty-four hours. I helped her up the stairs to our rooms on the second floor. She leaned against the wall while I unlocked the door for her.

"You're sure you don't need a doctor?"

"A good night's rest is all I need," she said in a weak voice.

Despite my misgivings, I had no reason to disbelieve her.

Thirty-Six

MY SECOND INTERVIEW with Magdalena took place immediately after breakfast the following morning. She was bright and cheerful. Except for some dark rings under her eyes, indicating a restless night, she seemed fully recovered from whatever malady had affected her during dinner. I closed the windows and hung a blanket over them to further deaden the street sounds. Although Barri Gotic was a pedestrian zone, motorized deliveries were permitted in the morning. I didn't want the noise of motor scooters and the occasional shouts of merchants to obliterate any significant part of the recording.

After a simple lighting, focus, and sound-level test, I was ready to begin.

"This is interview number two with Sister Mariamme, a nun from the *Convento de las Hermanas del Sangreal*. The interview is being conducted in Room 17 of the Hotel Luna in Barcelona, Spain. Today is Wednesday, May 9, 2001. The local time is 8:45 A.M. My name is Theophanes Nikonos."

Only my voice was being recorded. The camcorder, which I set up on the table between us, was focused on Magdalena. The image in the viewfinder was wider than the standard head shot. I wanted to record any significant body language she exhibited, which might later be examined for signs of nervousness or other indicators of possible deception.

"Do you remember where you left off in our first session, Sister?"

She seemed perfectly at ease, no longer curious about the camera or voice-stress analyzer.

"I was talking about my childhood in Magdala," she said.

I made a minor volume adjustment as she spoke.

"I was telling you about my parents and how we lived and about our neighbors," she said. "It was a very ordinary and uneventful life. I think I was a well-behaved child. Did I tell you about the professional storytellers?"

"No, but I'd like to hear about them."

"Well, my father was always busy with the temple, and later with his commercial interests. In those days, it wasn't unusual for priests to supplement their income with outside activities. And my father was very successful in everything he pursued. He acquired a small fleet of fishing boats, and was soon shipping dried fish to Cana and other communities."

A priest/merchant? That was an interesting modification of her earlier portrayal of Syrus, but one that put it at least halfway in agreement with the tradition. If she was making this up, however, claiming dual roles for a priest was an unnecessary complication, and one that just might be open to verification.

"With all his duties, he was so busy, he had little time for Mother and me, so he hired a storyteller to come to our house twice every seven days. It was a form of entertainment and education that was very common at the time. My favorite storyteller was named Achan. He was an old man, and he told us stories about the Roman heroes, and about Caesar and how the legions conquered the provinces, and about the Roman gods. But he also told us about the creation, and how the Jews were a glorious people, the chosen people of God, and about the kings of Israel and the prophets."

Rather than looking at her, I watched her image in the viewfinder. It gave me, I thought, the professional separation I needed.

"My mother was responsible for my education. If I had been a boy, my father would have taken over my instruction. But the education of girls was always left to our mothers. We were supposed to be taught domestic chores such as weaving and cooking, but my mother was an educated woman, and she wanted me to learn more than just household chores. She taught me to read and write, and how to speak not only Latin, but also Greek, two languages which were used almost as often as Aramaic in our region. Would you like me to say something in those languages?"

"No. I think it would be best if we saved that for Professor Abramakian. He'll be here sometime around 4 o'clock." I explained the reason for his visit before we continued.

"All right," she said. She didn't seem concerned about having an expert listen to her Aramaic. "Whenever my father was away, I would sleep with my mother in her bed. And then one evening . . . ," She paused, taking a deep breath. " . . . It was so strange. I remember the servants wouldn't let me enter her room. I could hear her inside, coughing, and I knew she was sick, but they wouldn't let me in. They were very frightened. That night, two of the servants left our house. They fled. I never saw them again. When I tried to enter my mother's room, she shouted out for me to stay away. I sat outside her door that night, crying.

"In the morning, my father took me in his arms and explained to me that the reason I couldn't go in the room was because my mother didn't want me to get sick, too. But he let me look at her and talk to her from the doorway. She was sick for almost a week. I set up a chair outside her door, and would sit there for hours, watching her. Sometimes she would sing to me in a weak voice. By the second or third day, I could see she was vomiting. What came out was foamy and red, like raspberries. And she complained to my father about a swelling in her neck. I could see the swelling from where I sat. I could see one of her arms was turning black."

The needle on the voice-stress analyzer was bouncing wildly against the rubber bumper at the maximum edge of its range. Although she was keeping her voice relatively calm, the needle was registering powerful stresses that weren't obviously apparent to me. There were two possible ways for me to interpret the stress-analyzer's response. The first and most obvious was as an indicator of deception, that she was lying. But there had been no previous indication of falsehood during her entire description of childhood in Magdala, which suggested the analyzer might actually be validating her story! The Holmes-Rahe scale of life stress factors lists changes in health of a family member as one the twelve most powerful stressors. Recollection of a mother's serious illness, however distant, would certainly account for the wild behavior of the analyzer.

"On the fourth day, my father burned five golden mice in a sacrifice. I knew what that meant, because I heard from one of my friends that his father died after five golden mice were sacrificed. And sure enough, before seven days were gone, my mother passed away."

The stress-analyzer needle remained firmly lodged against its maximum reading. Death of a mother would be near the top of the Holmes-Rahe scale.

"I watched from the doorway as they wrapped her. The bed sheets were drenched in blood from hemorrhaging. Much of her body was already blackened. I later learned this is common with the plague, which had struck our village that summer."

From the symptoms she described, the "plague" Magdalena referred to was bubonic plague, the dreaded "black death" which earns its macabre nickname from the blackening of flesh and limbs, the result of tissue necrosis due to intravascular clotting and other interruptions to the blood supply. Plague death comes painfully and swiftly, usually in a matter of days, just as Magdalena described. Watching a mother suffer the agony of the black death and seeing the resulting discolored corpse would be a terribly traumatic event for any child. Unfortunately, it was the most common cause of death in those times.

"She was buried the next day. Her room was cleaned and washed and her clothing was burned, which was the normal ritual following a plague death. There was nothing left of her in the house for me to remember her by. No scarf, no robe, no sandals. Everything was burned. All that was left was an empty room in which no one would be allowed to sleep for two months. The only reminder I had of my mother was her grave, which I visited every day."

Except for an occasional quiver in her voice, Magdalena displayed little outward sign of emotion as she related the story.

She did, however, ask for a drink of mineral water before continuing.

"I visited her grave every day for months after . . . maybe even years. I don't exactly remember. Something happened to me after her death. Much of it is hazy. I do remember praying to the gods, the Roman gods, the Greek gods, to Moses and Yahweh and every god I could think of . . . praying for them to send my mother back to me. Every time I would go to the cemetery, I would hope with all my heart that she would be alive again, sitting there on the stones, waiting for me with open arms. I used to talk to her at home, as if she were still alive."

What she was describing, a refusal to accept the finality of death, was a normal part of the grieving process. For an adult, such behavior during bereavement might seem a bit excessive. In the case of an only child losing a mother, it was probably not all that unusual.

"This went on for many, many months," she continued. "I stopped seeing my friends. I barely ate. I grew very thin. I could feel I was growing weaker, but I didn't care. I didn't talk to the servants. I barely spoke to my father. And then one day, when I was praying at my mother's grave, I began to bleed."

She took another drink of water. The voice-stress needle once more started to swing violently.

"I thought the bleeding was a sign from the gods that I would be taken to be with my mother. I was so happy! I watched the blood stain grow on my robe. I stayed by her grave all afternoon and into the evening, slowly bleeding. My father came out with two servants. I told him I was dying, that I was so happy that I was at last going to be with my mother. He put a cloth between my legs and lifted me in his arms. Oh, how I fought him. I didn't want to leave my mother's grave. I screamed and cried all the way home. One of the female servants took me to my room and explained that I wasn't going to die, that it was perfectly normal for girls of my age to begin bleeding at certain times of the month. But I didn't believe her. I knew they were lying to me. They were trying to stop me from going to my mother."

As a psychologist, I was both fascinated and horrified by her account. A child linking a mother's hemorrhagic death with the sudden onset of her own first menstruation could suffer devastating psychological consequences.

"They said I was unclean, and locked me in a darkened room for five days. I cried and cried, but they said it was the Jewish law."

Such attitudes towards menstruating women were not only part of the old Jewish laws, I knew, but typical of many cultures, and practiced even today among cultures as diverse as the primitive tribes of New Guinea and the Amazon rain forest.

"Strange things began to happen to me in that room," she continued. "I saw my arms and legs turning black, just like my mother's. I heard voices telling me I was being punished. At night, I heard Satan laughing at me. I couldn't sleep. Voices told me it was my fault my mother died, that I didn't love her enough. There was a hideous creature sitting in one corner of my room . . . I couldn't tell if it was human or animal because of the shadows, but it watched every move I made."

What Magdalena was describing was almost a textbook case of the progression from ordinary depression, whose etiology was rooted in her mother's death, to a major depressive episode (MDE) with mood-congruent psychotic features. The time of onset, with the arrival of puberty, was particularly significant. Depressive episodes occur twice as often in women as in men, with the highest risk factor being the time frame around the initial menses. Without the presence of a mother to explain what was happening, the event simply overwhelmed the adolescent girl's already fragile coping mechanisms.

"I tried to kill myself," she said in a quiet voice.

Suicidal ideation was the ninth and final symptom of MDE.

"Killing myself was a way to be reunited with my mother."

My own throat had gone dry. Without averting my eyes from my recording equipment, I took a drink of mineral water.

"I found death to be a very appealing idea," she continued. "Death would provide me with an escape from a life that had become unbearable. I thought about it every day, and even tried to discuss it with my father. I remember once asking him to help me kill myself. He was very upset. Not angry, mind you, but worried about what was happening to me. He brought in physicians, some from as far away as Jerusalem. At first, they said it was a problem 'of the heart,' that I was just a young woman who couldn't get over the loss of her mother. They said it would pass."

The voice-stress needle had settled back into the "normal" position.

"I don't remember many specific events about the following years. It all seems to be a foggy distant blur, as if my actions belonged to someone else. I slept very little, and when I did, I woke up exhausted. They tell me I used to walk the streets of Magdala at night, sometimes crying, sometimes wailing for my mother. I do remember that I heard whispered voices all the time, like a running commentary that I couldn't turn off. The voices were talking about me, sometimes arguing about me. I have no idea what they were saying, but when I would turn around, I would see no one. At other times, I would see strange creatures, frightening creatures, lurking in the shadows. I was afraid to be outside, but I was too frightened to remain in my room, where I could easily be trapped. My mind seemed to be enveloped in a black fog. I think the servants used to dress me, and sometimes even feed me against my will."

What Magdalena was describing was nothing less than a descent into madness. Yet there were no histrionics accompanying her chilling account; no feigned emotions or dramatic attempts that a charlatan might use to convince others of the fear felt when seeing those awful creatures in the night. It was a simple, straightforward exposition of events that, as she said, could have been happening to someone else. This "depersonalization effect" was a fairly common protective screen for recovered depressives, shielding them from the horrors of their past.

"The people of Magdala told me I was possessed. The physicians told my father I had seven devils within me."

At last, we had reached familiar ground. The "seven devils" were the infamous words of the New Testament which had been twisted over the ages to tarnish Mary Magdalene's reputation. I waited to see if the young nun would now transition into the familiar story of Mary Magdalene as a sinner and prostitute, perhaps using her tale of grief as an excuse for the wicked behavior. Though it was immortalized in centuries of art and religious literature, I knew the story was a lie, and any attempt at retelling it now would immediately brand her as a poseur.

"Years later, my father explained that he brought in healers, magicians, priests, astrologers . . . anyone he thought could help me," she said. "They all failed. He told me of his agony as he watched my condition grow worse. People in the village shunned me. Children threw rocks at me. My father assigned a servant to follow me to be certain I came to no harm."

She was fortunate, I thought, to have such a loving parent. In biblical times, those with mental disorders were feared by their own families for the physical harm they might inflict, as well as the shame they brought. Those suffering from mental disorders were often disavowed by their relatives, left to wander homelessly until drifting off into the desert to die. Not totally dissimilar from the way some of the mentally ill are treated by their families today.

"There were days when my body itched and I thought I was being consumed by insects. I would scratch at myself and tear off my clothing. Other times I would carefully wrap my arms and legs to prevent them from rotting away. In the daytime, I was afraid the sun would fall down from the sky and burn me. At night, I thought the sun would never rise again. I lived in constant fear that the villagers were plotting to kill me. I could hear their whispers, even when I was alone in my room. I was even afraid that my father's actions were part of a plot to harm me, that he was the one who had killed my mother, and all the healers and magicians he hired would one day kill me, too."

Left untreated, severe depression generally leads to premature death, whether through fulfillment of suicidal ideation or as a result of medical conditions that arise from an inability to maintain minimal standards of health.

"Eventually my fears drove me out of my own home. I left my father and took up residence in a cave outside town. The servants came each day to set food outside my door, but I thought they were trying to poison me. I lived on berries and food I stole from gardens. I think some village women who took pity must have left extra vegetables for me in their gardens; otherwise, I don't know how I could have survived."

It was a lifestyle not very different from today's homeless, a rather large number of whom also suffer various mental disorders.

"And then one day, my father arrived with a new healer."

Her eyes focused at a point in space beyond me. Her lips parted in a luminous smile. I waited, already anticipating what she was going to say.

"His name was Jesus."

Thirty-Seven

"HE STOOD AT the mouth of the cave and extended his arms to me. At first, I was afraid. He was a stranger, not of our village. I thought he was there to do me harm. I drew away from him, deeper into the cave. Then he called my name." Her eyes grew wide, as if she was still amazed at the memory. "He called my name and the whispers in my head suddenly stopped. He called my name again, and I was no longer afraid. I went to him then. I went to him and saw his face and in his eyes I could see I was cured. Do you understand, Theo? He didn't say anything except my name and I was cured! I was no longer afraid. The seven devils had gone out."

I sat back, strangely relieved that she had avoided the trap that had been laid for her by long-dead religious leaders.

The Gospel of Luke had, innocently enough, described several of Christ's followers as . . . *some women who had been cured; Mary called the Magdalene, from whom seven devils had gone out* . . . In and of itself, the reference to "seven devils" was of little significance, being nothing more than a first-century description of a specific mental condition.

But in the sixth century, at the Basilica of San Clemente in Rome, Pope Gregory the Great committed one of the greatest libels in Christian history, when he declared that Mary Magdalene was the sinful woman Luke described elsewhere, that the "seven devils" signified "all the vices," and that the Magdalene "used the unguent to perfume her flesh in forbidden acts."

From that point on, theologians and church authorities relentlessly used the "seven devils" phrase to vilify the Magdalene's early life, portraying her as a whore, a woman of the streets whose sins were forgiven by Christ. It was a characterization so thoroughly accepted that she became the patron saint of prostitutes, and homes for reformed prostitutes were known in England as "Magdalen houses."

Yet when Magdalena recounted her past-life memories, she never once even hinted at any interest in prurient activities, much less sins of any nature. Instead, she described a tortured descent into depression from which Jesus rescued her.

It wasn't until recently that scholars concluded, and the Catholic Church agreed, that the "seven devils" of Luke referred to mental problems related to severe depression. It was certainly possible Magdalena was aware of this, and was using this more truthful interpretation to impress me. But even if she was, that didn't explain her chillingly detailed, and clinically accurate account of not only the etiology and indicators of a major depressive episode, but the accompanying descent into psychotic behavior. Her description of the way the people of Judea reacted to such cases also corresponded to what psychologists know about the treatment of the mentally disturbed in ancient times. And of course, there was the mechanical testimony of the voice-stress analyzer, which reacted at all the appropriate moments. If she was a fraud, she was proving to be an impossibly clever one. Clever enough for me to want to hear more of her "memories."

We had now reached a critical point in our interviews. Everything she had said thus far had been prelude, interesting but relatively dull background material that could later be submitted to experts for verification. What I really wanted to hear was what she had to say about the relationship with Jesus. That was the central mystery of Mary Magdalene: the one many people felt had been suppressed since the death of Christ.

As eager as I was, however, further revelations would have to wait.

Magdalena was emotionally exhausted. We had gone without a break for three hours. We were both hungry. And we still had the session scheduled for that afternoon with Professor Abramakian. As much as I wanted to continue, I realized it was time to terminate the session.

I threw open the windows, allowing the hot summer sunlight to flood the room. Outside, the narrow streets of the Barri Gotic were already filling with tourists and shoppers. We joined the lunchtime crowds, making our way through the flower market on the *Ramblas,* stopping to laugh at the mimes in their outlandish silver-and-gold-painted costumes. We went through the *Bocqueria,* Barcelona's oldest market hall, and found a loud little restaurant in the back where we settled down to a leisurely lunch of *fritura mixta* and *vino blanco.* She was dressed in black today. Not anything like the modest black robes nuns wear, but a body-hugging black sweater and black slacks and black flats. Her clothing was made of a stretch fabric that clung to her flesh so tightly, it revealed every dimple and crease of her anatomy. The vaguely erotic outfit drew admiring stares, some quite brazen, from the men we passed. Their reactions seemed to please her. Frankly, I took a guilty pleasure in accompanying a woman other men found so attractive.

After lunch, we were taking a leisurely stroll down the *Ramblas* when I noticed a familiar face staring back at me from the front page of *El Periodica,* a Barcelona newspaper. The face was mine; the photograph was one taken by the *Guardia Civil* during my interrogation. I bought a copy and quickly walked away, hoping the vendor didn't make the connection. Back at the hotel, I unfolded the newspaper. *Deseado!* read the headline above my photo.

"It means 'Wanted,'" Magdalena translated. Beneath the photo was a subhead in a bold typeface: *Busqueda del fugitivo para bombardeo del terrorista y de la monja que secuestran.* The most ominous of the words were recognizable even before Magdalena's translation. "It says 'Fugitive sought for terrorist bombing and . . .' she paused, before continuing in a puzzled voice, ' . . . and nun's kidnapping.'"

She silently read the rest of the story. "They mean me," she said. "They don't identify me by name, but they mean me. The *Guardia* thinks you kidnapped me! What a terrible mistake!"

"I had nothing to do with that bombing."

"Of course you didn't. And you didn't kidnap me, either. I'm here of my own free will. We should contact them. I have to tell them I wasn't kidnapped."

"And then what?" I asked. "You think they'd believe you? They'd either assume I was forcing you to lie, or that you were a victim of 'Stockholm Syndrome.'"

"But I'm not from Stockholm."

I had forgotten how far removed she was from cultural markers of the modern world.

"What Stockholm Syndrome refers to is the sympathetic bonding that often develops between a hostage and captor. If you try to defend me, they'll assume you fell victim to that syndrome. Even if they did believe you, they'd arrest me for the bombing and send you off to spend the rest of your life in a padded cell at Saint Dymphna's. Let's just hope nobody recognizes me and calls the *Guardia*."

I had planned to enjoy the traditional midday *siesta* after lunch. The newspaper story made that impossible. After Magdalena returned to her room, I lay down in bed, eyes wide open, considering my plight. So now I was a fugitive. The photograph had probably been released to newspapers all over the country, scanned and digitized and distributed instantaneously from *Guardia Civil* computers. Policemen, security guards, and the paranoid population would be watching for me, searching the face of any suspicious stranger for features that resembled mine. The accompanying story detailed exactly how dangerous I was. The Valencia terrorist bombing, which suggested I might have links to the Basque ETA organization, had resulted in two fatalities. One of the two dead men, according to the news article, remained unidentified. Not content with the murder of innocents, the newspaper reported, I had gone on to commit the sacrilegious act of kidnapping an unnamed nun from the *Convento de las Hermanas del Sangreal*. It was possible, I thought, that the kidnapping of a nun might stir more indignation among Spaniards than the bombing. Which was probably why Velarde added that charge to the other.

The sound of heavy footsteps on the stairs sent me into a state of fearful alert. I listened as the footsteps stopped outside my door. The thin door shook under my visitor's knuckles. I padded quietly across the room to peer through the security peephole.

The man outside was shorter than I expected, his head barely reaching the level of the peephole. He was a thin, fidgety man wearing a brown suit, white shirt and slender black tie. His tan leather luggage rested on the floor beside him.

He knocked on the door again, more impatiently this time.

"Mr. Nikonos?" he called out. "I am Professor Abramakian."

Relieved, I opened the door. "Welcome to Barcelona," I said. His hand felt weak and clammy when I shook it. "How was your flight?"

"Tiring. Very tiring." He looked past me into the room, his eyes searching to see who else might be there with me. "I am very fatigued by my long trip. I had to change planes in Geneva, you know."

"Yes, you mentioned you would on the phone. How was the weather?" I hoped he hadn't looked at the Barcelona newspapers at the airport.

"It was raining as usual in Geneva, which caused some delay. I am thinking I have the beginnings of a cold."

That would explain why his voice sounded different. He still pronounced his words precisely, as he did on the phone, but the emphatic professorial delivery had weakened.

"Carrying your bags through the *Barri Gotic* didn't help," I said as I lifted his two leather bags. One was more like an oversized briefcase. The other was a two-suiter, with the airline baggage tags still intact. "I should have told you this was a pedestrian quarter."

"It's all right," he sighed. "I just have to catch my breath. Do you mind if I sit?" He slumped into one of the two chairs in the room before I could answer. "Do you have some water?"

I offered him a bottle of mineral water. His hands trembled as he struggled to open it. He seemed nervous, for some reason.

"I am truly exhausted," he repeated when he noticed me watching his movements. "But I would like to get started. Where is this young woman you told me about?"

I knocked on the wall. It was my prearranged signal for Magdalena to come to my room.

When the introductions were concluded, he propped open the smaller bag on his lap, and began to shuffle through the contents. He removed a battered Polaroid camera, a well-worn tape recorder, and a large yellow legal pad. He examined each of them carefully, as if he had never seen them before. I had to smile. They were the actions of the stereotypical absent-minded professor. After a bit of fumbling, he managed to take a photo of Magdalena. Having never been exposed to television or the mass media, she was unaware of the many consumer toys the public takes for granted. For a woman who had never seen a photograph of herself, the concept of instant photography seemed almost miraculous.

"Can I keep it?" she asked. She jumped up and, like a delighted child, compared the photographic image to her image in a mirror.

Professor Abramakian chuckled at her response and agreed. He had her pose for a few more photos, close-ups and side views and full-length shots, and even took a few photos of me.

His initial nervousness soon disappeared. As he grew more comfortable with us, he settled down and began to take control of the situation. He laid out the tape recorder, inserted a cassette, and tested for volume. When I started to set up my camcorder and voice-stress analyzer, he protested.

"No videotape," he said. "No recording or electronic equipment of any kind except mine. That was our agreement on the phone."

"I don't remember that part," I said.

"It's standard procedure," he said. "This is my session, and we will proceed according to my rules. And now, you may please leave the room."

Magdalena looked up at me, surprised and a bit frightened. Being alone in a room with anyone other than me was apparently a prospect she didn't relish. I didn't like the idea either.

"No," I said. "I'm staying."

I moved to a place in a corner behind the professor, where I could observe his interviewing technique without being too intrusive.

"Mr. Nikonos," he objected. "As a professional, surely you understand the need for privacy in a session like this."

"You're not a doctor. You're not a psychiatrist or a lawyer. As far as I know, professors of linguistics aren't covered by the rules of professional privacy. This interview doesn't happen without me in the room."

"You put me in a difficult position," he said. "I traveled all the way from Lebanon to meet with this young woman."

"My rules," I said. "I stay."

"I am guessing I have no choice," he said. He turned back to Magdalena. "All right, miss, will you please give me your name."

"My name is Sister Mariamme."

"*Sister* Mariamme? But you don't look like a nun . . . I mean, you're not wearing . . . "

"It's a long story," I interrupted. "Just get on with it, Professor."

"All right. Would you please give me your date and place of birth, Sister?"

"I am told I was born on July 22, 1982 . . ."

Part of the myth, I thought. July 22 was the feast day of Mary Magdalene.

" . . . As far as where I was born, I don't know," she said. "I am told I was brought to the *convento* when I was two months old."

"The name of your mother?"

"I never knew my mother."

"What about your father?"

"I never knew him, either."

"Do you have any aunts, uncles, any living relatives that you know about?"

"No. I already told you, I was brought to the *convento* when I was two months old."

I could tell she was getting upset. The voice-stress analyzer, if it was on, would be at the maximum reading.

"Do you have any idea where you were born? Was it in Spain? Or was it France?"

"I don't know." She looked up at me again. "Why is he asking me all these questions, Theo? Is all this really necessary?"

Before I could answer, Professor Abramakian supplied the explanation.

"Before testing your language abilities, we must document your linguistic history. Where you were born and the languages your parents spoke are fundamental to any analysis I might make."

It sounded logical to me. With a nod of my head, I signaled to Magdalena that she should proceed.

"I don't know where I was born," she said. "I don't know where my parents were born. I don't know if they're alive or dead or why I was left at the *convento*."

"You don't know anything about your birth, yet you're certain you are the reincarnation of Mary Magdalene?"

"Now wait a minute," I interrupted. "That question is out of line. It has nothing to do with the reason you're here."

"I'm sorry," the professor hastily apologized to Magdalena. "Your friend is right. I shouldn't have asked you that question."

"You shouldn't even know about it," I said, suddenly suspicious. "I never discussed the subject with you."

"It must have been Padre Serrano who told me," he responded without turning to look at me. "We had earlier conversations, you know."

"In that case, you must have already known she was a nun. Why did you seem surprised when I told you that?"

"I was simply trying to be polite," he shrugged. "I thought I was paying her a compliment by remarking on her beauty. You see, these distractions are precisely why I wanted to conduct this interview in private. Now with your permission, may I proceed?"

185

"Go right ahead."

"Who was responsible for your care at the convent?"

"Many nuns helped, but the one who was like a mother to me was Sister Generosa. I was always at her side. She was my nanny, my teacher, my friend, even my playmate."

"She taught you to read and write?"

"Yes."

"And what languages did Sister Generosa speak?"

"Spanish. Only Spanish."

"You're sure of that?"

"She spoke pure *Castellano*. She said it was the language of the great Queen Isabella the Catholic, and she refused to speak any other language or dialect. She was from Toledo, and it was a matter of pride with her."

"What about the other nuns who were in the convent when you were growing up? What languages did they speak?"

It was an interesting line of inquiry, I thought. It covered much of the same ground I had covered with Padre Serrano, but the professor was probing in greater detail, and I was able to hear the answers directly from Magdalena.

"They spoke Spanish, of course, in all the dialects. Plus Catalan, Portuguese, Euskadi, which is the language of the Basques. Also Italian, French, and one or two spoke German. Oh, and English, too. Definitely English was the second most common language."

"And what about Hebrew?"

"No. For five hundred years, ever since the Jews were expelled from Spain, no one in the *convento* spoke Hebrew."

"Except you," the professor said. "You claim you can speak the Hebrew language."

"Yes, but I don't use it in the *convento,* because no one understands it except me."

"Would you please say something for us in the Hebrew language?"

"What do you want me to say?"

"Anything that comes to mind. I'll be recording whatever you say, so would you please continue talking in Hebrew for at least two minutes?" He checked his wristwatch. "Starting . . . now!"

She began to speak, slowly at first and then more rapidly, in a language softened with sibilant sounds. I understood not a word of it. Without a videotape to review, I cannot provide even an approximation. Nevertheless, it went on for two minutes until the professor cut her off in what sounded like midsentence. He then handed her a pad of unlined white paper and asked her to write down what she said. She carefully printed out two pages of letters that reminded me of Jewish newspapers I had seen.

"Would you like me to say the same thing in Aramaic?" she asked in a surprisingly cooperative tone.

Professor Abramakian quickly agreed. The same procedure ensued, first verbal, then written.

"Of course, those languages are quite similar," he said. A little too dismissively, I thought.

"In some ways, yes," Magdalena said. "They are both Jewish tongues, but Aramaic was the language of the Essenes, and was the language spoken by Jesus my Christ."

Frantically, I signaled her with my eyes not to take that particular subject any further.

"Do you want to test me on any other languages?" she asked in what I recognized now was her playful tone.

"I am told you also speak Latin."

Her answer was given in Latin, a language I had studied in prep school. Some of the words were vaguely familiar, the ones that explained that she could speak and write Latin. But it all went by too fast for me, spoken with the assurance of someone who learned the language as a child. As she went on to give Abramakian his requested two minutes of recorded language, I thought I could detect a bit of laughter in her voice, as if she considered all this some sort of joke. At his request, she again wrote out what she had said, writing it all as quickly and with as little apparent thought as someone jotting down a quick memo to a friend.

Abramakian looked at the note, nodded, and placed it in his briefcase along with the others.

He quizzed her on Greek, a language which, thanks to my parents, was more familiar to me. As with the Latin, however, she spoke it so rapidly, and with so different an accent that I found it hard to follow. Many of the words I had never heard before. Were they archaic words? Part of the language that lay dormant since biblical times? I wished that Abramakian would use his knowledge of these languages to explore that possibility. His preliminary questioning had been skillful, but now he seemed to have slipped into a neutral mode, neither challenging her nor seeking elaboration of anything she said. It wasn't the sort of linguistics testing I expected from him. I could only assume he was getting enough input from the two-minute speeches and written statements to make his analysis.

He asked her to repeat the exercise in Proto-Provençal, which seemed an oversight on his part. That name, as Serrano had explained, was a modern label applied to the dialect which was a precursor to Old Provençal. Magdalena had no idea what he meant by "Proto-Provençal," until I explained that he wanted her to speak in the local dialect used in Gaul during the Roman times.

By this time, I was getting impatient with Abramakian's behavior. I couldn't understand why he wasn't testing or challenging her at all. I guess I was expecting him to at least try to engage her in a spontaneous conversation in one or more of the languages. As any language teacher knows, conversation is the surest way of determining proficiency in a foreign tongue. The two-minute statement was a short recitation that could have been memorized in advance. I wasn't sure what it really proved. And I would have also been interested in historic vocabulary analysis. Abramakian made no attempt to determine if her knowledge of those languages was confined to only those words that would have been in use during biblical times. For a man who was described by Serrano as being fluent in a variety of Semitic languages, the Professor seemed remarkably unwilling to engage her in any direct conversation, much less even demonstrate his linguistic ability with at least a few words of Hebrew.

When I saw him snap his briefcase closed, I could restrain myself no longer. I took him into the hallway, out of Magdalena's hearing, and confronted him with my concerns.

He smiled and explained why he didn't feel there was any need to question her in the manner I described.

"Such questions would be useless," he explained. "As a matter of fact, this entire trip has turned into a waste of my time and money. I don't need to analyze my tapes to give you my expert opinion."

It was exactly the wrong time for the cell phone on my belt to start ringing. The professor seemed startled by the disturbance. He checked his watch impatiently, as if he wanted to make sure he didn't waste any more of his precious time. I turned off the phone, not wishing to upset him any further.

"I'm sorry, Mr. Nikonos," he said, edging away from me. "I am not knowing why your little nun is doing it, but she is playing a game on you. It appears she has only a rudimentary knowledge of those languages. She knows a few words, particularly in Greek and Latin, which can easily be acquired with a bit of study."

He already had his bags in hand and was heading for the stairs.

"She is a fake," he called over his shoulder. "She is a total fraud."

Thirty-Eight

THAT WAS THE end of it, I thought.

If Magdalena's claim to speak those languages was false, how many of her other statements were fabrications? How could I now believe anything she said? Those stories about ancient Judea? All fiction. Her description of the "seven devils," which I in my hubris immediately diagnosed as a major depressive episode with psychotic features? An elaborate invention. What I was dealing with was at best a delusional young woman operating in a fantasy world. Although the Church authorities might be guilty of overreaction in their decision to commit her to a mental institution, it was obvious that they had already come to the same conclusion. What a fool I was for interfering with their efforts.

Having disillusioned me with his pronouncement, our visitor wasted no time in taking his leave. I watched him quickly disappear down the steps. It might have been impolite of him not to bid Magdalena good-bye, but under the circumstances, it was perfectly understandable.

I remained in the hallway for long moments, trying to think it through. One of the most troubling aspects was the involvement of Padre Serrano. A psychiatrist with far more experience with mental disorders than I possessed, he should have been able to see her delusions for what they were. I took no solace in the fact that he was apparently misled as easily as I was.

The worst-case scenario, the one I didn't want to believe, was that I was the victim of a deliberate and elaborate hoax, perpetrated by both of them. A hoax in which I was called upon to play a specific role. After all, what was the initial contact between her breast and my hand, if not a method of selecting me from among the many tourists in the cathedral? Seen from that viewpoint, the letter addressed to Padre Serrano was a brazen way to deliver me into his hands, where he would beguile me with his story of church intrigue. But to what end, I wondered? What was the motive? And what role did they intend me to play?

By now, I was not only disillusioned, but totally confused.

Through the half-opened doorway, I could hear Magdalena humming an unfamiliar, but strangely haunting tune. When I entered the room, her chair was facing the window, casting part of her face in shadow. Her smile faded when she saw my expression.

"What's wrong, Theo?" she asked.

At first, I didn't know what to say. I didn't want to lie and pretend everything was just fine. I also didn't want to accuse her of lying to me, which I was certain would lead to an ugly scene.

"Is something bothering you?" she asked. And then quickly, "Is it something that man said to you?"

Still confused, I studied her face, looking for some sign of dissimulation.

"I didn't like that man," she said. "I don't trust him."

Was that a clue? Attacking the messenger was the time-honored method of diverting attention from an unpleasant truth.

I couldn't detect the slightest hint of guile in her expression. She stared at me with the same naïve, vulnerable expression she had worn during our first encounter. Unfortunately, some of the most innocent smiles often mask the most disturbing disorders.

"What were you talking about out there?" she asked in a worried voice. "Were you talking about me?"

"Wait just a second," I said. The cell phone had interrupted me in the hallway. Now I used it as an excuse to avoid giving her an immediate answer. "I have to return a phone call."

The number displayed on the LCD screen was a local one. I punched it in and got an almost immediate response from someone who had apparently been impatiently waiting for me to return his call.

"Hello!" The voice sounded familiar.

"This is Theo Nikonos. I'm returning your call."

"Theo! At last I am able to talk to you! A terrible thing has happened!"

He didn't have to tell me who he was. The professorial tone of voice was the same one I heard barking into a bad telephone connection yesterday. There was no mistaking his identity. It was Professor Naghib Abramakian.

The *real* Professor Naghib Abramakian.

Thirty-Nine

"I WANT THAT stupid driver of yours arrested!" Abramakian shouted. "Do you hear me? Arrested!"

"I'm sorry, professor, but I don't know what you're talking about."

"I am in a hospital bed with a broken leg, a fractured kneecap, and a mild concussion! That stupid driver you sent . . ."

"I didn't send any driver."

"Of course you did! He met me at the gate! He had my name on a sign! He said his name was Abelito, and he was sent by you to bring me directly to your hotel!"

"Professor, I didn't send any driver to pick you up," I repeated. My denials didn't seem to register on him. By now he was screaming into the phone.

"He took my bags, Mr. Nikonos! Do you imagine? The bastard hit me with his car and then sped off with my bags! He stole my bags and left me lying in the street like a dog! Even in Beirut, during the worst of times, no one acted like this! A man like this must be arrested! He must be jailed!"

"Listen to me, professor," I said in a patient and firm voice. "I didn't send anyone to pick you up. Do you understand? I did not send anyone to the airport."

There was a pause on the end of the line.

"Then who was this man?" he demanded.

"I have no idea."

"But he knew my name! He was waiting as I got off the plane! He told me how anxious you were to meet me! And what about my bags? Are you saying you have not seen my bags?"

I was ashamed to admit that I did see his bags, and upon seeing them, assumed the man carrying them was their owner. It was an inexcusable error on my part; not the first error I ever made, but certainly one of the stupidest. The clues had been there all along, in every word the imposter spoke. The accent was close, but the intonation and speech pattern were all wrong. Worse yet, I was aware of the differences, but had accepted the excuse that he was suffering from a cold. That was the brilliance of the imposter's bringing along the professor's baggage. How could I doubt his identity, when I saw the professor's name tags and Beirut University letterheads? Never mind that a cold might change the nasal quality of a voice, yet never change the basic speech pattern. In what was the ultimate irony, I had allowed this mountebank to function in the role of a linguistics expert. What a double fool the imposter must think I was.

"What did the man who met you look like?" I asked.

"He was a short man, ugly and fat! Well, not really fat but heavy! He wore a chauffeur's hat, so I couldn't see his hair! But he had a day's growth of beard, I could see that!"

His description didn't fit the man who interviewed Magdalena. There must have been two of them, I thought. One for the rough work, and the other, more skilled, for the imposture.

"Tell me exactly what happened."

Abramakian calmed down a bit as he recounted the earlier events.

"Well! As I said! He met me as I was coming out of the jetway! He had a white card with my name on it! The spelling was wrong, but when I approached him, he said he was sent by you!

"By Theophanes Nikonos! I tell you, he knew your name, also! Why else would I go with him?"

"Was anyone with him?" I asked. "Did you see him talking to anyone else?"

"No! He was talking only to me! He led me to the baggage claim area, where we waited for my suitcase! He said his name was Abelito! He said you were staying in a hotel in an area called the Barceloneta!"

It was a lie, of course, an inconsequential one, considering that Abramakian had my cell phone number and could locate me easily. But the too-coincidental mention of the Barceloneta made me wonder if I had been followed last night.

"Actually, I'm in the Barri Gotic," I said.

"What matter is it? I don't know Barcelona! Anyway! He was kind enough to carry my bags for me! We had to cross the street to reach his car!"

"What kind of car was it?"

"A small one! I thought that was strange! Normally when a driver meets me, he is driving a bigger car! This one was not like a chauffeur's car! It was a small black car!"

"Do you remember the make? The name of the car?"

"I don't know! Maybe a Spanish car! Or Italian! It all happened too quickly after that! The driver put the bags down in back of the car! He said he had to open the trunk from inside! I waited in back with my bags, so they wouldn't be stolen! That happened to me once before, you know! In Italy, at Fumicino Airport! I lost a suitcase to a thief there! But nothing like this!"

"Calm down, Professor. Calm down."

"Calm down! I was almost killed and you tell me to calm down!"

"You were telling me what happened."

"Yes! I am telling you he opened the trunk, just as he said he would! I put my bags inside and closed the trunk lid and then, boom! I was hit by the car! He backed the car into me! I was knocked to the street! My head hit the pavement! My leg was broken! Just before I lost consciousness, I saw him speed off! He didn't even wait to see how badly I was hurt!"

"Was there anyone in the car with him?"

"For the love of Allah, how would I know? I am lying in the street in agony! I am not looking to see who is in the car!"

"I'm sorry, Professor. I really am. But I assure you, I had nothing to do with what happened at the airport. I didn't send anyone to meet you. Maybe I should have gone myself. Maybe then none of this would have happened."

"The world is full of thieves! But there is nothing of value to a thief in my bags! I am thinking the bags themselves are more valuable than their contents!"

"Where are you now, professor?"

"They have brought me to the *Hospital de la Santa Creu i de Sant Pau!* I am scheduled for a CT scan in a few hours! They say it is just a safety precaution!"

"I'm sure it is, professor."

I consulted my tourist guide. According to the map, the hospital was about three kilometers northwest of us, in the *Camp del Arta* section.

"I'll be there in half an hour, professor."

"What about the nun? Sister Mariamme! Is she with you?"

"Yes, she's here."

"Can I talk to her?"

"I'll bring her with me."

"I've come all the way from Beirut, and I am lying in a hospital bed and you will not let me talk to her for only a moment on the telephone? I ask you again, Mr. Nikonos! Please let me talk to her!"

I handed the phone to Magdalena. She had apparently never handled a telephone before, and held it an awkward distance from her ear.

"*Hola,*" she said, instinctively reverting to Spanish.

She jumped when she heard Abramakian's powerful voice booming through the tiny earpiece. It was loud enough for me to hear from three feet away, although I couldn't understand his rapid-fire Spanish.

She replied in Spanish, smiling at the novelty of talking to someone she couldn't see.

The conversation moved on into other languages, short bursts of each, as she responded to questions he was asking. She seemed much more cheerful and relaxed speaking to Abramakian than she had to the imposter.

"I like him," she whispered when she returned the phone to me.

"Well! I'm impressed!" the professor said. "I am now more anxious than before to meet this young woman! But please do be careful! This Barcelona! I am thinking it might be a dangerous town!"

He was right about that, I thought. Especially dangerous for anyone associated with Magdalena. There were at least two men out there who knew where we were staying. Two men who had already rammed a car into Abramakian and left him unconscious in the street. It seemed a particularly brutal way of relieving him of his bags so that they could accomplish their impersonation. I had no idea whether they were also connected with the bombing in Valencia, but I had no doubt they would use whatever tactics were necessary to achieve their goals.

"What happened to this professor?" Magdalena asked. "Why is he in the hospital?"

"Someone tried to kill him."

"*Dios mío!* Was it the man who came here?"

"There was another man, too. A driver."

The question now was how to get to the hospital without being followed. I didn't wish to visit any more trouble on Professor Abramakian by leading his assailants once again to him.

"Are you ready for more shopping?" I asked her.

"I thought we were going to the hospital."

"We are," I explained. "But first we have to make sure the men who tried to kill Abramakian don't follow us."

Fortunately, the only clothing we had was what we had purchased the previous day in the nearby stores. I loaded everything, including my recording equipment, into two shopping bags. I paid the hotel bill, and we headed out into the streets to visit the stores whose names were emblazoned on the two bags. We exchanged one item in each store, making a show of the process for anyone watching us. Magdalena thought it was all a lark. She was accustomed to being watched and followed in Valencia, and enjoyed the "game" we were playing. We bought a few more clothing items; she tried on some shoes; I bought a short-sleeved knit shirt. We strolled the streets like two carefree shoppers, pretending that we were still unaware of the deception that had been played on us. We stopped in a few more stores, gradually making our way toward *Via Layetana*, where the Opel was parked. Just before crossing *Layetana*, we stopped in one last shop, a heavily mirrored, modernistic shoe store.

While Magdalena tried on pair after pair of sandals, I searched the mirrors for a glimpse of any surveillance. I was looking for anyone loitering in doorways across the street, anyone who gave more than a passing glance at the interior of the store, or anyone who passed by outside more than once. I was interested, in particular, in anyone who fit Abramakian's sketchy description of the bearded man who ran him down. This being

Spain, however, men with facial hair were quite common. After identifying at least fifteen men who looked suspicious, I finally gave up. Magdalena bought a pair of yellow sandals and we continued our pretense of shopping while we crossed the street. I had the car keys at the ready. We strolled nonchalantly up the street, until we were abreast of my car in the outdoor parking lot. I unfolded my tourist map and pretended to ask the parking lot attendant for directions. With a profusion of pointing to hide our true intentions, I slipped the attendant a 5,000-*peseta* bill, more than enough to cover the two-day charge. There was only light traffic on *Via Layetana* at this hour. Although internationalization and the move to the European Union had eroded the traditional Spanish *siesta,* the hours after lunch remained a lethargic time of day. When I was sure there were no taxicabs in sight, Magdalena and I jumped into the nearby Opel. The engine turned over immediately, and I pulled into the nearly empty street.

I gunned the motor and watched in the rear view mirror as a bearded man ran into the street, frantically searching for a taxicab. For once, my timing was exquisite. I reached the next traffic light just before it turned red, and with the safety of the synchronized traffic lights holding back any pursuers, raced ahead to make a right turn on *Fontanella,* left on *Carrer Girona,* right on the *Gran Via,* and after a little more than a kilometer, lost myself in the confusion of the enormous traffic circle at *Placa de los Glories Catalanes.* From there, it was a short drive north to the hospital.

"The man who visited us, the one who took pictures of me, I knew he wasn't who he claimed to be," Magdalena said. "I told you I didn't trust him, but you didn't believe me."

"I apologize," I said.

"There are many things about me you don't believe."

"I'm an investigator. Being skeptical is part of my job."

"And who sent you to investigate me?"

"Padre Serrano," I answered. "It was his last request. I already told you that."

"Yes, I know Padre sent you to me. And I know why he did. But I think there is someone else you are working for, also." She was staring ahead, almost as if she already knew the answer.

"Who is it that is so interested in me?"

"Who?" I laughed. "There seems to be a long list." I tried to make light of it. "Let's see, there are the people who were watching you in Valencia, there are the psychiatrists and some anonymous officials at the Vatican, there's the Cardinal in Valencia . . . plus whoever killed Serrano, the men who almost killed Professor Abramakian, the imposter who showed up at our hotel, the man behind us who tried to flag down a taxi-cab to follow us here . . . do you want me to go on?"

"I mean the person who is paying you," she said. "The person who is paying you to investigate me."

Her words were the verbal equivalent of a slap in the face.

"Is that what you think of me?" I asked. "You think I'm doing all this just for the money?"

I realized, too late, that I had inadvertently admitted the truth of her charge.

Glancing at her, I could see a surprising sadness in her eyes.

"I would like to think not," she said softly. "But now it is *me* who is not so sure I should believe *you*."

I drove the next few blocks in silence, unsure how to phrase my response. This was not the time to be evasive, and she was not a person whom I wished to deceive. A partial truth would be better than a complete lie, I decided.

"The truth is, I am continuing Padre Serrano's work," I said. "I was hired by Serrano, but my expenses are being paid by a certain man . . . a well-intentioned man, I think . . . who is a friend and patron of the convent. I promised him I would not reveal his name, but I am sure he has your best interests at heart. If it was not for him hiring me, you would already be at *Santa Dymphna*, from which you would probably never be released."

"No. I think if it was not for *you*, I would be at *Santa Dymphna*," she corrected me. "I think perhaps you were right when you said you were not doing this just for the money. You have already taken grave risks to help me, Theo. You do not seem the kind of man who would put his life at risk for money. So if I may ask, why are you doing this for me?"

Somewhere along the line, the great thinkers of the western world decided it would be a bad idea for psychologists and private investigators to have romantic relationships with their clients. How right they were! Mere mortals like me ignore those rules of professional conduct at our own peril. Recurring unresolved nightmares were the penalty I was still paying for having fallen in love with the subject of my investigation on my last case. Now here I was, on another case, with another woman, finding myself responding in an all-too-familiar manner. What treason was this? Was I forgetting my vow to the woman who gave her life to save mine? Was I so lonely and vulnerable and yes, despicable a creature that I would take advantage of a young nun who had been remanded into my care? I was ashamed to admit harboring such feelings.

"I've been wondering about that myself," I finally said. It was only half an answer, but it was as truthful a response as I dared give.

Forty

I HAVE NEVER seen a medical facility that could compare in any aspect with the *Hospital de la Santa Creu i de Sant Pau.* In terms of sheer size, it dwarfed any hospital complex I had seen in the United States, including the Rockefeller Institute and the Cornell University Medical Center combined. The site was breathtaking. It was situated in the northwest part of Barcelona, with the Collserola foothills rising in the hazy background. Almost three dozen separate medical buildings, each devoted to a different medical specialty, were widely spaced on a beautifully landscaped campus the size of Central Park. In any other country, the buildings would have been functional structures of steel and glass. But in an exuberant expression of Spanish *modernisme,* the architect employed colorful ceramics and brick and variegated stone to line the facades, added turrets and domes and undulating curves, borrowed freely from Baroque and Moorish influences, and created a fairyland of imaginative structures that brought a smile to my face.

This was the unique Catalan style of creativity pioneered by Barcelona natives Gaudi and Miro. While more conservative hospital administrators might frown at such joyful architectural excess, an accumulating body of evidence suggests that it may well serve a therapeutic purpose as well. Medical schools, spurred on by the findings of hundreds of research projects, are now grudgingly beginning to accept the importance of the link between the psyche and the soma in patient outcomes. A better bedside manner, more comfortable and ego-supportive hospital environments, and even the acceptance of the healing powers of prayer are now becoming part of mainstream medical thinking.

The architects of *Santa Creu* were at least a century ahead of their time, I thought.

It took us a half-hour to find the building where Professor Abramakian was recuperating.

When we entered the room, he barely glanced at me. His eyes immediately went to Magdalena. The frown on his face disappeared. His eyes lit up.

"Buenos días, señorita!" he said. He couldn't hide the resonant lecture-hall tone of voice, but he managed to soften it for her.

"Buenos días, profesor," she smiled, and immediately went to his side.

She seemed a child next to the huge man. Although his flesh was flaccid with age, Naghib Abramakian's physical proportions matched the grand scale of his voice. His hands were twice the size of mine. He had an enormous forehead, huge bags under his eyes, and a long, narrow face that ended in a turkey-like wattle of loose flesh under his chin. The bed was barely wide enough to accommodate his shoulders and not quite long enough to contain his legs; the one in the cast projecting eight inches beyond the edge. I judged him to be in his late fifties.

He reached out to take her hand in greeting, and she gladly gave it to him.

"Ah, qué linda, qué bonita," he said in a breathy voice. He placed his other hand atop hers, trapping it and holding it as gently as if it were a tiny bird. For a moment, I almost thought he was going to raise her hand to his mouth and kiss it. "Now I understand why Padre Serrano was hiding you from me. You are more beautiful than he led me to believe."

"Gracias, Señor Profesor," Magdalena responded with a nervous giggle.

"I am so glad to finally be meeting you." The stentorian tone had disappeared from his voice, replaced by a warm intimacy.

Was it possible? I stared in amazement. Was he actually stroking her hand? Was he trying to seduce her right in front of me? Had I delivered her into the hands of an old lecher? He might be accustomed to playing Svengali with his young female students, but I certainly wasn't going to let him do so with Magdalena.

What I really wanted to do was "accidentally" bump against his injured leg, but I decided that would be too obvious. Instead I focused the camcorder on him, pretending to catch this particular moment of tenderness for posterity. He quickly withdrew his hands, as I knew he would, and adopted a more professional attitude for the videotape.

"We'll talk later," he assured her. "After the interview."

In your dreams, professor, I couldn't help thinking. If I hadn't needed his linguistic expertise, I would have quickly steered Magdalena out of there.

"How do we know you're really Professor Naghib Abramakian?" I asked.

The dreamy romantic expression disappeared from his face.

"Because I tell you so!" The sharply punctuated lecturing tone was back in his voice. "I am talking to you on the telephone yesterday! Who else would I be?"

I noticed Magdalena had slowly backed away from him.

"Do you have any identification? Your passport or anything else with a photo?"

"You are being outrageous! Of course I am Professor Abramakian!"

"We were visited a few hours ago by a man claiming to be Professor Abramakian. He gave us a business card identifying him as Abramakian. The name and address matched the ID tags on his luggage. Inside his briefcase was Abramakian's personal stationery from Lebanon University. He turned out to be an imposter, and I don't intend to be fooled again. Now I repeat, do you have a passport or anything else with a photo that would confirm your identity?"

"You are stupid! The man who visited you was the thief who stole my bags!" he shouted. "You should have called the police!"

"If you don't produce any ID within the next thirty seconds, we're leaving," I said. Magdalena slipped her hand into mine to show her agreement. "You can spend the next couple of days shouting at the walls for all I care."

I had little doubt he was the real Naghib Abramakian. What I was doing was playing a little mind game, my way of diverting his attention from Magdalena's charms and getting him to focus on the seriousness of the situation we were all in.

With a loud groan, he rolled his large frame just far enough to reach over to the nightstand beside the bed. From the top drawer, he extracted a green Lebanese passport and tossed it disdainfully to the foot of the bed. I made a show of matching the picture to his face, and turning to Magdalena for her concurrence. When I was finished with my charade, I replaced the passport in the drawer.

"He was carrying your bags," I said. "But I don't think he was the thief. He didn't fit your description of the driver."

"So there must have been two of them!" he said.

"That's right," I said, glad that I finally had his full attention.

"But why would they come to you?"

"Because they wanted access to Sister Mariamme," I said, reverting to the name by which he knew her. "That's why they stole your bags. It wasn't a random act of thievery. They planned all along to impersonate you. The man's voice didn't sound right, but when he showed up with your bags and your name tags and your documents and recording equipment, I assumed it was really you."

"Yes! Now I understand! That explains why the driver ran the car into me!"

"They wanted you out of the way. They didn't want to take a chance on having you suddenly show up while the imposter was still with us. And frankly, Professor, you were very lucky."

"Lucky? You call a broken leg and fractured kneecap lucky?"

"They probably intended to kill you."

"*Qué?*"

"Consider what happened to Padre Serrano."

"You think they were the same men who killed him?"

"I don't know," I said. "It's possible."

"But why? Why would anyone go to such lengths to meet this . . . this innocent young nun?"

I held back a smile at the way he now tried to verbally distance himself from her. From a beautiful young woman whose hand he had been stroking, she was suddenly transformed into an "innocent young nun." His ardor had apparently cooled at the first suggestion that any liaison with Magdalena might prove fatal. He regarded her now with a curiosity that seemed a bit more apprehensive than amorous.

"I don't know that, either," I said. "All I know for certain is that we're being followed. And whoever is following us sometimes seems to know where we're going even before we get there."

"Now I am not understanding you! How can that be?"

I told him about the visit to *Casa Dolorosa* and the mystery man who arrived there two hours before us.

"But how do you know it was the same man?"

"I don't. And that's the problem. If I knew who was after us, or how many were involved, I might be able to deal with it. All we can do now is try to stay ahead of them."

"Were you followed here?"

"An attempt was made, but I think we lost them."

"You think! Here I am bedridden and you only *think* you weren't followed? What if they come here tonight, while I am sleeping? Whose fault is it then? I should have stayed in Beirut! At least there I know who my enemies are!"

"I'm sorry," I said. "When I called you, I never imagined you'd come to any harm."

"It is too late for regrets! But now I am here! So let us get on with it! Since my recording equipment was stolen, you will please be kind enough to videotape the session for me! Do you have sufficient tape?"

"I just loaded a fresh ninety-minute cassette. I'll alert you when I have to reload."

"Good! Now what I want is nothing fancy, please! This is a research tape," he said, and in a few quick commands, demonstrated his familiarity with the language of visual media. "You can start with a close-up of me, then move to a tight two-shot of both of us, and then mostly close-ups of Sister Mariamme! I assume that is how you would like me to address her on the tape!"

He motioned for me to help him out of bed. The leg cast made the transfer clumsy and painful, but I finally got him settled in a chair near the window, facing Magdalena. He asked for his blue blazer and a mirror, and after donning the jacket and brushing back his receding hairline, asked to borrow a red scarf he saw in Magdalena's shopping bag. In a display of professional vanity, he wrapped the scarf around his neck foulard-style, completing his transformation from a patient in hospital pajamas to a rather stylish older gent. At least from the waist up, because if I photographed any lower, I would reveal one spindly leg and a large white cast.

"You look good," I had to admit.

"Very well!" he ordered. "Roll tape!"

He slated the videotape much as I had been doing, with his name, the date, the location, and the identity of his interview subject. He quickly moved into a long conversation with Magdalena in Spanish, asked her questions, and apparently challenged some of her answers. I kept the camera mostly on Magdalena, who was relaxed and comfortable speaking with him. I wasn't quite as relaxed, because what little I knew of Spanish suggested he was asking about her background. I stopped the tape.

"Please, professor. I have to ask you not to inquire about her religious beliefs or any unusual memories she may have."

"But I have to establish where she might have learned the languages she claims to know!"

"You wanted permission to publish your findings about her knowledge of lost languages. That's all we agreed to. Anything about her life history or problems with the church or any other subject is strictly off-limits. It's a question of personal privacy."

He turned back to Magdalena and asked her a long, complicated question in Spanish. I assumed he was trying to convince her of his viewpoint. Rather than answering him, she spoke to me instead.

"Don't worry, Theo," Magdalena said. "I will not say anything about the subjects you and I have been discussing."

Having established her facility in Spanish, Abramakian now shifted to Greek.

I listened carefully, trying to understand what they were saying. But this was not the Greek I heard spoken by my parents, nor the tongue used by the monks on Mount Athos. This was Greek as spoken two thousand years ago, delivered with intonations and expressions that made it difficult for me to comprehend, particularly the version Magdalena spoke, which was Hellenic Greek as spoken by the Palestinians. When the impediments of mixed accents, archaic construction, and antiquated idioms were added to a language in which I wasn't really fluent, I was in a position comparable to a Swede trying to understand Old English as spoken by an American with a heavy Brooklyn accent.

Nevertheless, Magdalena seemed to be having no problem. In fact, she was enjoying herself. If what Serrano had told me was true, that no one in the convent had any knowledge of ancient Greek, this was the first time in her life she was able to carry on a conversation with someone who understood her. Which once again raised the haunting question: where did she acquire the facility with which she now spoke?

Following Abramakian's directions, I kept the camcorder focused on a close-up of Magdalena. She seemed relaxed and comfortable with the language. The only time she hesitated was once, when she was apparently searching for a more precise word. It wasn't the desperate search of a foreign-language student trying to remember something she memorized, because when she found that word, it was immediately followed by a torrent of Greek spoken with a speed and complexity of construction that left both Abramakian and me dazzled.

I cut away to his face occasionally, to record expressions that ranged from delight to surprise to jaw-dropping awe.

They moved seamlessly on to another language, which I later learned was Hebrew. Although it sounded strangely familiar, I understood nothing of the language. Unlike the Romance languages, it contained few cognates or otherwise familiar words. Like any New Yorker, I knew some Yiddish expressions. But words like *gonif* and *meshugenah* and *chutzpah* never came up in the dialogue. At least not in pronunciations that I could understand.

I had no idea whether they were speaking a pure form or with acquired accents, although there did seem to be a difference between Abramakian's delivery, which seemed a bit stiffer, and Magdalena's, which seemed more fluid, perhaps even slurring certain words. Since I really didn't understand any of it, I couldn't tell whether I was reading something into the delivery that didn't in fact exist.

After a half-hour that seemed like ten minutes, we all took a break.

Magdalena accompanied me out into the hallway in search of a soda machine.

"I hope he's not asking you about past lives or reincarnation," I said to her.

"No. And I wouldn't tell him if he did. That's only between you and me. At least for the time being."

We found a soda machine at the end of the hallway, near the back stairway. The selection included Fanta, Orangina, the inevitable Coca-Cola, and apricot nectar.

"You seem to be enjoying yourself," I said.

"At first I was nervous," she said. "Especially when he was stroking my hand. But once we started talking, he was fine. Not like that other *idioto*, who didn't even understand what I was saying."

"You mean the imposter? I had that same feeling, even though I wasn't able to understand what you were saying either."

She picked the apricot nectar. I settled for an Orangina, and assumed Coca-Cola would be the safest choice for the professor.

"What I was telling the imposter was that I didn't think he knew what he was doing," she laughed. "I said that he had the brains of a flea, and the breath of a camel, and that his true vocation in life should be cleaning stables. He didn't understand a word of it, no matter what language I spoke. I wrote the same thing on the papers he handed me."

"That's not exactly the kind of language I'd expect from a nun."

"Do you think it was cruel of me?"

"Not as cruel as what's going to happen to him when his employer has the notes and recordings translated."

Back in the room, Abramakian accepted his Coke with a grudging nod. He seemed to have grown more irritable, if that was possible, while we were gone.

"I had copies of some very complicated ancient texts in my briefcase!" he grumbled. "I wanted to have her read them aloud and translate them! It would have been an interesting test! But now they're gone, and so I won't be able to make that determination!"

I wasn't about to apologize to him again.

"Also my briefcase contained writing materials, so that I could test her ability with the written language!"

"Is that really necessary?" I asked, recalling the simplistic approach of the imposter. "I mean, you're hearing her speak, and I'm going to give you the recording. It would be the same words, wouldn't it?"

"To answer your second question first, no! It would not be the same words! As for the necessity, there are important variations between the spoken and written forms of any language! Written text involves the use of more complex structures, the kind that can be ignored in casual conversation! I will be seeking constructions that can be found only in writing! These are grammatical and lexical differences resulting from more formalized thought processes! Not to mention details such as punctuation, capitalization, accent marks and so on! And despite how highly you may value your videotapes, Mr. Nikonos, the academic world still relies heavily on the written word!"

Publishing academic papers is the way scholars build their scholarly reputations. If Abramakian was considering writing a paper on this session, copies of Magdalena's handwriting would be far more useful than a tape transcription.

"Would you be so kind as to get me some writing materials from the nurse's station?" he asked.

I didn't trust this sudden politeness on his part. Broken leg or not, there was no way I was going to leave him alone with Magdalena for even a few moments. A man like him could work too much intellectual mischief in that time. I summoned the nurse with the call button beside his bed, and kept my eyes fixed on Abramakian until she returned. He was a crafty man, I thought. I wondered whether I could trust him to keep quiet about Magdalena.

The professor now engaged her in Latin. Abramakian's Latin sounded stiff and formal, like that of my teachers in parochial school. Unrestrained by tediously studied rules, however, Magdalena's Latin was the language of the Roman colonizers, flowing and fast and with the first melodic hints of the Italian tongue that would succeed it. In the middle of the conversation, Abramakian suddenly switched back to Hebrew. It caught Magdalena only slightly by surprise, but she managed the switch easily. I marveled at the wonderfully changing palette of sounds that filled the room as they moved from one language to another.

Even in the camcorder's tiny viewing screen, I could detect a growing sense of awe in Abramakian's face. The professor's demeanor was becoming more like that of a student. His speech pattern was often stilted. Magdalena would occasionally correct him, a process that irritated him at first, but which he soon accepted with equanimity. Magdalena appeared to be in complete control of the situation. The *Apostola Apostolurum*, they had called the original Mary Magdalene: the "Apostle to the Apostles." It was easy to see Magdalena in that role as she patiently spoke in ancient tongues to this learned man, slowly converting him into a follower.

I could tell when they switched to Aramaic, because the communication became more difficult. Abramakian's modern Syriac was less well understood by Magdalena, and her ancient Aramaic was causing even more difficulty for Abramakian. They stumbled along verbally, each struggling to completely understand the other. This was high-wire linguistics, with no safety net of dictionaries or interpreters. I watched, understanding absolutely nothing of what I was hearing, but knowing this was probably the single most important exchange of the afternoon.

He switched abruptly back to Latin, then Hebrew, then Greek. This time around she seemed puzzled by some of his words. He pressed on, as if giving her a vocabulary test. One which, it seemed to me, she was suddenly failing. I felt some of my confidence in her slipping, particularly when Abramakian appeared pleased by her non-responsiveness.

"And now we come at last to Proto-Provençal!" he said. He turned to me and explained in his professorial way, "Proto-Provençal was the language spoken in the South of France when it was known as Gaul! That language was subsumed by the influx of Romans and Palestinians around the beginning of the Common Era! It was a totally different language from the later Provençal dialect, which was popular in the ninth century and is occasionally spoken today! Therefore, I cannot determine the authenticity of her words! However! As a researcher! I very much want samples of the language for future study!"

Turning back to Magdalena, he said, "I must confess I know very little about this language! Therefore, I will ask you questions in Latin, and you will please respond in the language spoken in the South of France during the Roman times . . . if you know that language!"

"Of course I do."

"Very well! Following your response, I will ask you to translate your reply, word for word, into Latin! That will allow me to understand your answers."

It sounded reasonable to me. At least he was finally admitting that he had some limitations, an admission that surprised me. Had he met his match in Magdalena? She was smiling, apparently convinced she had won him over.

The dual-language approach worked well. Instead of a one-sided discourse, as the imposter had requested, Abramakian was fully engaged with her. He questioned her at length, and her answers were long and sounded detailed. The Provençal portions were phonetically more sonorous than the Latin, although they sounded little like modern French. The session was taking much longer than I had expected. I had already changed the ninety-minute tape once, and the counter indicated we were halfway through the second tape. With at least two pursuers presumably searching for us, I was also getting nervous about being in one place for so long a time. Would they be smart enough to check the hospitals and search for Abramakian? I thought not. It was a fairly safe assumption that they had probably left him for dead.

At last, Abramakian fell silent. He gave me the traditional hand-across-the-throat gesture to stop the tape. When I complied, he turned back to Magdalena and clapped his hands enthusiastically.

"Estupendo! Maravilloso!" he exclaimed. With the camcorder off, he felt free to express his delight. "You were superb! You have opened a por-tal into antiquity that scholars will study for years to come! All we have left to do now is the written portion, señorita*!"*

He removed a slim packet of papers from the inside pocket of his blazer.

"I selected some brief texts and had them typed up before I left Beirut!" he explained. "Fortunately, I was studying them on the plane and didn't put them back into my briefcase!"

While he unfolded his papers, I drifted over to the window. The scale of the hospital grounds was immense. Patches of carefully tended shrub-bery were sprinkled across the broad grassy areas. Wooden benches sat in the shade of the largest trees. Pedestrian paths were lined with flowers. Small roadways wound through the pastoral setting. From the window, I had an unobstructed view of a few dozen acres. I could see no suspicious vehicles. I looked for the man who had dashed out into the street behind us earlier, but saw no one who resembled him. Nevertheless, I was getting nervous.

"Mr. Nikonos!" Abramakian interrupted my reverie. "I would like you to please record this procedure! You may start with a wide shot to identify the writer, and then move in as close as you can to the actual writ-ing! It would be useful to see the individual letters as she forms them!"

I turned on the camcorder, focusing on the professor as he handed the first sheet to Magdalena and gave his instructions.

"And now, señorita," he said in a surprisingly deferential voice. "Would you please translate this text into Greek? In block letters, please!"

I turned the camcorder to focus on Magdalena, taping her image as she took the pad, read his text, nodded, and quickly began to translate it. The telephoto setting allowed me to sit with Abramakian on our side of the bed and still see the individual characters which she was carefully printing.

"This is the final test!" he whispered to me. "As I explained to you, the written language is more complex. Errors which might be ignored in casual speech cannot be concealed on paper."

"What is she translating?" I asked. "What text did you give her?"

"I carefully avoided anything biblical! Otherwise a peer-review committee could attack the translations on the basis that she might have studied them in the convent!"

It sounded reasonable to me.

"For this first text, I selected the standard English translation of the inscription on the Rosetta Stone. One of the three texts on the stone was in Hellenistic Greek, inscribed in the second century before Christ. I will be able to compare her version of Hellenistic Greek with that on the stone."

When Magdalena finished, he handed her another text. While she worked on that one, he explained it to me. "She will be working from Hebrew this time. I gave her a Jewish translation of a Roman real-estate transaction from the first century after Christ. Her Latin translation can be compared with the original. You see, these assignments are all in languages once-removed from the original. So in effect, I am confronting her with a double barrier, requiring the greatest possible precision in her answers."

I adjusted the camera to compensate for a slight shift in her writing position. While she wrote, Abramakian studied the first completed sample, and I kept watch on the street outside.

The third text he gave her was a Latin translation of a biographical obituary notice announcing the death of Herod Antipas, the Tetrarch of Galilee and Petraea, published 39 A.D.

"Get her facial reaction when she first reads this text!" Abramakian whispered.

I widened the shot, just in time to catch a sad smile as she read the news of the death of the man who ordered the beheading of John the Baptist and refused to intervene in the sentencing of Jesus Christ, leaving the decision to Pontius Pilate.

"He died in Gaul," she murmured. I zoomed in on her face as she said, "Jesus my Christ forgave him and so did I."

Effortlessly, she translated the Latin announcement of Herod's death back into Jewish Palestinian Aramaic, the language in which it was originally written.

Each text she finished was eagerly examined by Abramakian, who handled the sheets of paper as if they were treasures.

The fourth text was in Greek. It was a description of the destruction of a Jewish settlement by Alexander the Great, which she translated back into its original Hebrew.

The fifth and final text was to be the translation into Proto-Provençal.

"There are no surviving texts in this language!" Abramakian said. "I have given her a simple Latin text describing Gaul and its geography and inhabitants. I will have no idea whether she translates it correctly or not, but whatever she writes can be a useful tool in reconstructing the language."

When she was done, the professor carefully folded the papers and returned them to his jacket pocket. He turned to me and said, "I must thank you for giving me this opportunity! It was worth the broken leg! Now may I have the tapes, please?"

"You were supposed to give me an evaluation," I reminded him. "The only reason this session took place was for you to evaluate her language skills and give me your opinion."

"I thought I already did!" he said. "I said she opened a portal into antiquity that scholars will study for years to come."

"Beautiful words," I said. "But not precise enough for my needs. I want to know whether she really speaks those languages the way they were spoken two thousand years ago."

After listening first to Serrano and now, interminably it seemed, to Abramakian, I knew a little about the science of language-dating—enough to realize that the way Magdalena spoke could turn out to be the single most important clue to her claim of reincarnation. After having observed Abramakian's responses during the session, I was convinced she wasn't spouting the meaningless babble of *glossolalia*. However, if she spoke tongues that could be dated to a later period, then she wasn't speaking the languages Mary Magdalene would have spoken. It was that simple. There might be other mysteries worth pursuing, such as the circumstances of her birth, how she learned those languages, or why she was so carefully watched by so many people; but it would be the end of my investigation into this purported case of reincarnation. And it would take an expert of Abramakian's stature to give me the final word.

"You ask too much!" Abramakian said. "It is hard to be precise! Languages change! We have no voice recordings of that time period! Therefore no one knows for sure exactly how people spoke or pronounced their words in biblical times!"

"You have written records."

"But as anyone who has ever studied languages knows, there can be a vast difference between the written and spoken word! In China, for example, there is a single written language, expressed in ideograms and used by everyone! But when that language is read aloud in northern China, it is enunciated as Mandarin, which is completely incomprehensible to a resident of southern China, who speaks the Cantonese dialect! Yet the ideograms have identical meanings! Thus we have many Jewish scholars who can read ancient Aramaic, but almost none who can, with absolute certainty, speak the language as it was spoken during the time of Christ!"

He shifted in his chair and reached out his hands for us to help him back into bed.

"I don't need a lecture," I complained. "All I want is an answer. A definitive answer."

"I am trying to explain how difficult it is to answer your question!" He straightened up with his weight on his good leg, and with a loud grunt of pain shifted himself onto the bed. "Even in the English language, for example, we can read *Beauwolf* in its Old English form and understand it! But the Great Vowel Shift of the 1400's dramatically changed the way the narrative would be spoken! Spoken English in the thirteenth century was dramatically different from that spoken just three hundred years later! Considering all the changes that take place over the course of time, you must agree that determining the authenticity of any language as it was spoken 2,000 years ago is an imprecise art at best!"

"You didn't sound very imprecise on the telephone," I reminded him. "You were so sure of yourself you insisted on permission to publish your findings in an academic journal."

A crafty look came into his eye. "But only if a more careful examination of the tapes and written text warrants it! And of course it would have to be approved by a peer review panel."

After carefully placing the written texts under his pillow, he removed his blazer. Magdalena hung it in the closet.

"Well, we can't wait for peer reviews and academic journals." I glanced out the window again. "There are people following us, probably the same people who killed Serrano and tried to kill you. I need an answer now."

"You are putting me in a difficult position!"

"Why is this suddenly turning into such a problem?" I asked. "You came all the way from Beirut to give me an opinion, and now you're refusing to do it."

"Patience, Mr. Nikonos! Have patience! These matters do not lend themselves to instant analysis! Whatever conclusions I may reach will most properly be revealed in an academic forum, where scholars may evaluate the results for themselves! It would be foolhardy for me to permit premature discussion, or what you Americans call 'leaks,' to occur before publication."

"What makes you think I would 'leak' your opinion?"

"Come now, Mr. Nikonos! You're a writer yourself! You think I don't know about the book you wrote? Perhaps you may already be working on another book! About this very matter!"

I was losing patience. "Without these videotapes, you won't be able to publish much of anything," I said, waving the tapes in front him. "Now if you want the tapes, just answer my question. If you were writing your paper today, based on today's session only, what would the conclusion of your paper be?"

"Well!" He eyed the cassettes greedily. "There would be disclaimers, of course!" He swallowed nervously. "Footnotes and transcripts and copies of her written texts to compare with the originals!" He turned to Magdalena and addressed the rest of his response to her. "I would write, based on my knowledge of the Semitic languages and years of study of their predecessor dialects, that I am completely convinced that she has the extraordinary ability to speak at least five languages exactly the way they were spoken in Judea and in Gaul during the early part of the first century!"

Magdalena glanced up at me, her lips forming a cryptic smile.

"That is my considered opinion!" Abramakian said. "Based upon what I heard and saw in this room today! Now I am having the tapes, if you please?"

I handed them over without any further argument.

Forty-One

ABRAMAKIAN'S OPINION, WHEN it was finally delivered, surprised me.

I was expecting a verdict less conclusive; perhaps a hit on one or two of the languages, a miss on the others. It would at least have given the skeptic in me the opportunity to argue that somewhere along the line Magdalena had been coached or had the opportunity for independent study. That line of thinking was completely demolished by the unequivocal nature of the professor's opinion.

It still didn't prove her claim of reincarnation. But it was a big step in that direction.

I didn't have much more time to think about it. From my perch near the window, I saw a familiar black vehicle on the roadway, moving in our direction. There must have been hundreds of vehicles like it in Spain, each with the by-now-familiar *Guardia Civil* logo emblazoned in red on its side. We were a long way from Valencia. To the best of my knowledge, no one had followed us from downtown Barcelona. There was no logical reason for me to assume the passengers of the vehicle were any threat to me. Yet I watched, fascinated, as the vehicle snaked along the winding roadway and came to a stop in the courtyard directly below us. The first man out of the vehicle was in full *Guardia* uniform, with a white cord that led from his shoulder epaulet to his holstered pistol. He opened the rear door and stood aside to allow a man in a grey suit to step out of the car.

I stared in disbelief at the man as he stretched his shoulders. The man in the grey suit was *Coronel* Velarde, the neatly groomed officer who interrogated me in Valencia. He stood beside the car for a moment, smoothing out his jacket and adjusting his tie. With my attention focused on him, I hadn't noticed two more uniformed officers get out of the other side of the car. Now there were four of them. A search-and-arrest team. I drew back from the window.

"The *Guardia* is here," I said. "They've come for us."

Magdalena jumped up and came to my side. I held her back from the window so she couldn't be seen.

"How many are there?" she asked.

"Four. Three in uniform; one in plainclothes."

"What makes you think they came for us?"

"They're not local. They're from Valencia. I recognize the one in plainclothes. He interrogated me after the bombing."

"Who is this *Guardia?*" Abramakian asked.

"The civil police."

"And what do they want with you?"

"To arrest me, probably. They think I'm a terrorist. They think I had something to do with the bombing in Valencia. The one that killed Padre Serrano." Seeing the look of alarm in Abramakian's eyes, I decided not to mention anything about the kidnapping charge. "I had nothing to do with the bombing," I explained. "Whoever did it almost killed me, too." I quickly packed the camcorder and started for the door, "We've got to get going."

"The back stairs," Magdalena suggested.

"Wait!" Abramakian asked. "What about me? If they are thinking you are a terrorist, what about me? I am here from Beirut! They will suspect me, too!"

I hesitated.

"The videotapes," I said. "You'd better give them to me."

"Why?"

"You've got Magdalena talking on the videotapes . . . that's going to automatically implicate you in her disappearance. And the languages she uses on the tapes and the written texts are going to be unknown to the *Guardia*. They'll probably confiscate them to get them translated, and then hold them for evidence."

Abramakian hesitated.

"I'll mail them to your address in Beirut," I said.

He still wouldn't surrender them.

"I promise I'll mail them to you," I said. "Either give them to me, or the *Guardia* will confiscate them. God only knows when you'll get them back."

Abramakian turned to Magdalena and spoke to her in what sounded like Hebrew. Whatever she said to him in response brought a smile to his face. He handed her the tapes and papers. She bent over to kiss him on the cheek.

"Don't worry about me!" he said. "I've dealt with the Israeli police! These Spanish can't be any worse!"

"You can tell them we're going to Madrid," I said as we headed out the door.

"I understand!" he called out. "Good luck to you!"

There were two nurses assisting a patient at the far end of the hallway. A male nurse was approaching us with a tray. I could feel Magdalena pulling at me to hurry.

"Walk slowly," I said, holding her back. "Pretend we're going to the soda machine."

"But the *Guardia* . . ."

I tightened my grip on her arm. "Don't run unless you hear them coming after us."

The soda machine was five doorways away. The back stairway was just beyond and around the corner. It was as excruciating for me as it must have been for Magdalena to walk slowly, each step taken as silently as possible, and all the time listening, listening for the sound of the elevator ready to discharge its passengers.

When the elevator bell rang, we both stiffened. We were still two steps from the corner. Don't panic, I told myself. Just place one foot in front of the other. I could hear the elevator doors opening behind us. By that time, we had just managed to get safely out of sight around the corner. I raised my finger to my lips as we headed for the stairway door. I didn't hear Velarde's voice. Another elevator bell rang. I heard voices this time, but couldn't tell if any of them was Velarde's. My heart pounding, I wondered if the stairway door had an alarm, as many fire-exit doors do. Too late to worry about that, I thought, and slowly turned the doorknob.

Hopefully the professor would stall the *Guardia* for the time we needed to get down the stairs. We hurried down four flights of concrete steps, listening all the way for the sound of a door opening above us. When we reached the ground floor, the final door bore large red letters reading:

Salida de emergencia

And below it, in smaller letters:

Alarma sonidos cuando se abre la puerto

It didn't take a genius to figure out that meant an alarm would sound if we opened the emergency exit. Freedom was on the other side of the door; the alarm suddenly put it beyond reach. What now?

"We'll have to go out through the lobby," Magdalena said.

"Velarde might have left one of his men there."

"I'll go out and check," she said, suddenly taking control of the situation. "They're looking for you, not me."

"They might be looking for both of us by this time."

"They won't recognize me," she said. "Not without my nun's habit. You wait here. I'll let you know if it's safe."

There were no alarm bells on the door that led to the lobby. She opened the door, glanced around, and strode out into the lobby with her chin up, shoulders back, as if going to her execution. I, who had been the leader up until now, was left to hide in the stairway shadows. I strained to hear any sounds that would indicate the presence of the *Guardia*. After what seemed a long time, but probably took only a few seconds, the door was carefully opened.

"*Nada,*" she said with a smile. "There is no guard in the lobby. Maybe out by the car, but not in the lobby."

We found the side door. "Perhaps we should split up," Magdalena said. "They'll be looking for two people, not one." I smiled at how quickly she was learning the way of the fugitive. She waited for me to go through the revolving doors first, and once outside, followed, not directly behind me, but off to one side, as if she was a visitor strolling through the grounds. I headed west, then after a few hundred yards, did a circle around a fountain, sat on a bench to be sure we weren't being followed, and finally set out north, in the direction of the sports stadium to the indoor parking garage where I had left the Opel.

When she joined me in the car, I headed north to the *Cinturo de Ronda*, the Barcelona beltway.

"Where are we going now?" Magdalena asked. She seemed exhilarated by our narrow escape. "Not to Madrid, I don't think."

"No," I smiled. "That was just a cheap trick. I'm not even sure Velarde will fall for it. If he's as smart as I think he is, he'll figure out where we're going. I just hope Abramakian stalls him long enough to give us a good head start."

After a few miles, I took the exit that led us onto the N11, heading further north.

"We're going to France, aren't we?" she asked.

"It's our best shot. We're not that far from the border. And once we get into France, we won't have to worry about the *Guardia Civil*."

We headed up the N11 towards the *Costa Brava*. The initial stretch of road from Barcelona was fairly flat and not especially scenic, although it paralleled the coast. Much of our view of the Mediterranean was blocked by industrial buildings and apartment houses. Once past Mataro, the road took on a more photogenic character. Sweeping vistas of wide sandy beaches appeared on our right. Apartment buildings gave way to hotels and beach houses. Rooms for tourists were advertised in four different languages. Campgrounds were filled with rows of silver trailers, many with colorful awnings that identified their owners as vacationing Germans, who found the prices in Spain more agreeable than in nearby France. I drove at a steady pace, about 20 kph over the speed limit, slowing down only as we moved through the dozens of small resort towns along the way. It was a relatively straight road, but the heavy tourist traffic made it difficult to detect whether anyone was following us.

I wouldn't feel safe until we were out of Spain and beyond the reach of the *Guardia*. Her adrenaline rush having worn off, Magdalena soon fell asleep. Her cheek rested on her shoulder, a faint smile on her lips. In an idle thought, I wondered if dream analysis techniques might help in getting to the truth about her. But of course, if her story about reincarnation was a fiction, there was nothing to prevent her subconscious from inventing the kinds of dreams that would support that story.

North of Blanes, the road took on a serpentine character as it made its way along more mountainous roads. This was the beginning of the *Costa Brava*, the "Rugged Coast" where piney cliffs, strange boulder formations, and wind-sculptured rocks rose precipitously above sheltered beaches. I was glad there were still a few hours of daylight left. Not so much to enjoy the scenery, spectacular as it was, but because the cliffs and curves would make it a dangerous road to drive at night. The road signs marked our progress through Tossa de Mar, with its whitewashed houses, the Hermitage of Sant Elm, and Palamos with its fishing fleet. The mountains on our right were topped with deserted castles and crumbling battlements.

As I drove, I couldn't help wondering about the mysterious forces that seemed to have placed me on this particular route. Oh, I could explain each leg of our journey on purely rational grounds: we left Valencia because I didn't want Magdalena to spend the rest of her life in a psychiatric hospital; I brought her Barcelona to find the "nanny nun" who raised her and might have information about her past; and now I was taking her even further north, because the nearby border would put us beyond the reach of the *Guardia Civil.*

Given the circumstances, no other destinations would have made sense. And yet, I wondered if other unexplained factors were at work in charting our route. Was it fate? Karma? Predestination? Whatever theory of divine determinism applied, we were being inexorably drawn, as if by some unseen hand, in this northerly direction. Because of what seemed too serendipitous to be entirely coincidental events, we were heading toward the south of France, the one place in Europe, if not in the entire world, that might hold the key to proving or disproving Magdalena's claims.

Any police investigation invariably includes a visit to the "scene of the crime." Reincarnation investigations follow a similar pattern. Rather than a crime scene, however, investigators visit the actual locations of the subject's previous life. There, with the testimony of eyewitnesses, the historical records, and the commonplace artifacts of everyday life, reincarnation claims can be either confirmed or discredited.

Early on, I had dismissed the idea of taking Magdalena back to the Holy Land in search of such verifiable evidence. The Romans had methodically destroyed Jewish records after the revolt of 70 A.D., obliterating any hope of finding written documentation of her life. Centuries of effort by church leaders to obfuscate and rewrite the Magdalene's life history had tainted whatever oral traditions or legends might still be uncovered in Palestine or Rome. The Holy Land contained no known relics of Mary Magdalene, no buildings in which she once lived. And Arab-Israeli tensions made even the land on which she once walked difficult, if not dangerous, to visit.

The only site that offered anything approximating reliable evidence of the Magdalene's activities was the South of France, where she had reputedly spent the last thirty years of her life. There, among the physical relics and actual locations of her ministry, I might find clues that would unravel the mystery of this young nun who claimed to have once walked with Jesus Christ. It was truly the land of the Magdalene to which we were headed.

Little did I know what surprises awaited me.

Forty-Two

THANKS TO THE European Union's open-borders policy, there were no immigration officers to stop us from fleeing Spain. No one to check my passport against the list of fugitives from the law. No one to question why Magdalena didn't even possess a passport.

Once we crossed the border, *Coronel* Velarde was no longer a threat. If he was serious about the charges reported in the newspaper, he could certainly begin the paperwork for extradition. But given the slow-moving bureaucracies in both countries, that would take months. And he would have to find us first. That wouldn't be an easy matter, because Spanish authorities had few friends in this part of France. We were following the route taken by thousands of refugees who fled over the border during the Spanish Civil War, probably close to where we had crossed. No matter what the philosophy of succeeding governments, descendants of refugees who lose their homes and members of their families seldom forgive the country they fled.

The road took us on a long downhill slope into the Languedoc-Roussillon region. Although we had left Velarde and DesRosier behind, reminders of the ancient brotherhood that united them abounded. In addition to its Magdalenean traditions, this part of France was once the stronghold of the legendary defenders of the Holy Grail. Remnants of Templar castles once thought impregnable occupied the mountain crests to our west. They served as tombstones for the men, women, and children who were slaughtered within their walls during the fourteenth century Albigensian Crusade. Thousands of Templars, like their religious allies the Cathars, went willingly to the stake rather than renounce their vows . . . or reveal the secret knowledge they were reputed to possess. For many years the Knights Templar were considered extinct. In reality, they were merely hiding in the shadows of history, their treasure and secret knowledge still intact and passed down through the generations until centuries later their descendants reemerged, calling themselves the Freemasons, the Rosicrucians, and eventually, once again the Knights Templar. The apparent wealth of Jean-Claude DesRosier and the influence of *Coronel* Fulgencio Velarde suggested that they were still a powerful force in Europe.

I was eager to press on to *les Saintes-Maries-de-la-Mer,* where Mary Magdalene was reputed to have first set foot in France. I wanted to see what reaction the landing site might evoke from Magdalena. But I was getting tired, and I knew we'd never make it before dark. I turned off the A9 and headed for the small fishing villages that dotted the coastline, driving through Cerbere near the French border and working my way north through Port Vendres and Banyuls. It was only by chance that I settled on Collioure, a village that was distinguishable from the others by a large castle that overlooked its harbor. In a wonderful illustration of the cultural *mélange* that still thrived in this region, my guidebook explained that although we were in France, the red- and yellow-striped flag flying above the castle was actually Catalan; the castle itself had been built in the thirteenth century by the Templars, and there were some excellent Basque restaurants in town.

Magdalena woke up as I drove down the hill into the *centre-ville.* The massive *Chateau Royal* occupied the top of an enormous rock outcropping that stood between two beautiful crescent beaches, cutting off the view of one beach from the other, and similarly dividing the center of town into two sections. The castle was visible from every part of Collioure, including the narrowest streets and alleys. Just as important to its defenders, every activity on the streets below could be viewed from the castle's battlements.

Its remote location made Collioure the perfect hideaway for vacationers seeking privacy, which also made it ideal for fugitives like us. I avoided the parking lots near the *Chateau Royal* as being too exposed. Instead, I circled back up the hill and left the car in a quiet residential area, where it wouldn't be noticed by anyone searching for us. From there, we walked back down the hill to find a hotel.

I ignored the obvious choices: the *Hotel Les Templiers* or its neighbors along the canal, or the hotels that faced the crescent beaches. Instead, we passed through the arched entryway into the old *Moure* quarter, a pedestrian zone without sidewalks. The narrow streets were blessedly devoid of not only cars, but also the motor scooters that were so annoyingly prevalent in southern Europe. The neatly laid stones on which we walked sloped gently upward to the center of the street, forming a natural drainage system for storm water. The buildings were made of stone, most of them washed with a facing of rough concrete.

"This reminds me of Jerusalem," she said, and then laughed self-consciously. "Of course, they didn't have electric lights when I was there. And at this time of day, when the evening meal was being prepared, there was always a dense layer of wood smoke in the air. On calm days, when there was no breeze to move the air, the smoke would burn the eyes and make it difficult to see very far. The old people and the children would have a difficult time breathing."

The picture she painted was easy to visualize in the old quarter. Put the tourists in robes and sandals, ignore the souvenir shops and *gelatto* stands, and we could have been walking through any of dozens of towns in ancient Judea.

To supplement their income during the tourist season, many of the local residents rented out spare *chambres* in their homes or apartments. After examining a few that had problems with privacy or plumbing, we finally settled on adjoining rooms in a narrow building a short distance from the arch. They were tiny rooms, carved out of a single larger room on the third floor. What I liked was the location. Our rooms each had a window looking out on the street, with an unobstructed view all the way down to the entry arch. During my more paranoid moments, I could glance out the window and examine anyone coming up the street. And if paranoia turned to panic, the roof garden one flight up provided an escape route across the tops of the attached buildings.

"She says this used to be her son's bedroom," Magdalena translated the words of the building's owner, Madame Ernestine Gramont. "He was killed fifty years ago during the war in Algeria, and she couldn't bear to see the room remain empty."

Madame Gramont was in the seventh decade of a life whose accumulated miseries had extracted a terrible physical toll. The left side of her body was partially paralyzed. She moved awkwardly, a stiffened leg forcing her to climb the stairs one at a time. Her left arm was frozen at an odd angle, the fingers forever clenched in a distorted fist. The paralysis, which resembled the remnants of some long-ago stroke, also affected the left side of her face, immobilizing part of her mouth and forcing her to speak with only a minimal movement of her lips. As with many old people, however, she seemed intent on sharing the memories that haunted her most. We listened courteously, Magdalena continuing to translate, as the old woman shuffled around the room, adjusting the window shades, smoothing the bedspread, straightening the lampshade, and giving us the steady stream of patter that she delivered to everyone who rented her son's room. I wondered how many people had been driven away by her morbid reminiscences. At some point in our lives, we all occupy rooms whose former occupants are dead. We often sleep innocently in hotel and hospital beds in which some soul spent his or her last few moments on Earth, gasping in futility for that final breath. Fortunately, those unsettling facts are never revealed to us. The law doesn't require a landlord to list the occupants who died there; no plaque hangs over a hospital bed honoring the dozens who expired on its sterilized surface.

Madame Gramont, *née* Ernestine Malvoir, was born in Collioure, in a smaller house up on the hill. She married young, when she was sixteen, to a *"très beau, très merveilleux"* older man named Henri Gramont, from whose family they inherited this narrow, three-story house. Like many of his generation before tourism became the main industry in Collioure, Henri was an anchovy fisherman. Each night, he and the others would head out to sea with lights to attract the schools of fish. The couple had one child, Charles, named after DeGaulle. When Charles was ten years old, Henri was lost at sea. His body was never found. But Ernestine Gramont compensated by giving all her love to Charles. She took in boarders, and as Charles grew older, he worked at various jobs. But she would never, she waved her good hand and repeated the word *jamais,* never allow him to become a fisherman. He was eventually conscripted into the French Army and sent to Algiera, where he was captured and presumably executed by the rebels. His body was never returned.

There is no grief as deep as that of a mother who loses her only child. Husbands, no matter how deeply loved, are merely visitors in a woman's life. A child, however, is the ultimate expression of her womanhood, as much a part of her body as a hand or a leg or, as any mother will attest, her very heart. Time helps most women deal with the loss of a child. It was clear to me that Madame Gramont was not one of those women. Although she spoke freely about the tragic event, her stricken body and the melancholia that lingered in her voice suggested she was still blocking the pain. It was a fairly common psychological defense mechanism erected by those unwilling or unable to face up to unpleasant realities. The result is a deadening of feeling, social isolation, and the adoption of what Wilhelm Reich labeled as *character armor,* all designed to protect the individual from any further pain the world might choose to inflict. Ernestine

Gramont, I decided, was an extreme example of Reich's thesis. Fifty years of mourning had left deep lines of sorrow in that side of her face that was not frozen with paralysis. Her eyes had retreated into dark caves from which they looked out on a world that no longer interested her. Her voice, when she spoke, was a croak of despair. And by her own admission, she had cut herself off from contact with former friends, preferring to sit in the darkened room where she once took meals with Henri and Charles.

To wipe away fifty years of such sorrow would take a miracle.

For Magdalena, it took but an instant.

I watched spellbound as she put one arm around the old woman's shoulders and drew her close. She pressed the palm of her other hand against the old woman's paralyzed cheek and spoke to her in a voice so filled with compassion, it brought tears to the old woman's eyes. Gently, tenderly, like a mother kissing her child, this unaffected nineteen-year-old pressed her lips to the wrinkled forehead of a widow who was more than fifty years her senior.

Ernestine Gramont seemed to shudder for a moment, much like someone shaking off the lingering effects of a long sleep. As impossible as it sounds, I could almost see the grief departing her body. Her chin rose. Her shoulders drew back. The frozen frown melted; the left side of her face seeming first to relax and then resume a normal configuration, her lips turning up in a full smile that could only be described as relieved. The deep lines in her brow didn't disappear, but they softened, changing from the sharp lines of anger into the dignified lines of age. She raised her left hand, staring in disbelief as she opened her fist and was able to move and flex her fingers for the first time in decades. Her eyes were filled with wonder as she tested her leg, raising it first, and then rotating the ankle to see if it worked, and finally putting her full weight on it.

The wonder was replaced with tears of joy as Ernestine Gramont dropped to her knees and kissed Magdalena's shoes.

"*Merci, merci, madame,*" the old woman sobbed. "*Je remercie de votre bénédiction. Vous êtes vraiment une Sainte.*"

Magdalena placed her hands on the woman's head.

"*Je vous aime,*" she said. "*Le bon Dieu vous aime.*"

She raised the kneeling woman to her feet.

"*Allez et rendez grâces à Dieu.*"

Tears streaming unhindered down her cheeks, the old woman bowed her head and backed away from us, beating her breast and whispering prayers all the way to the door.

Throughout this extraordinary episode, I was speechless, stunned by what I was witnessing. It was not until Madame Gramont was gone that I regained my ability to speak.

"What happened to her?" I asked. "I mean, what did you do to her?"

"Nothing. I just gave her a *bénédiction*. A blessing."

"A blessing?" I was still trying to understand what I had seen. "You gave her a blessing?"

"Why are you so surprised? Do you think only priests can give a blessing?"

"I don't know much French, but I think she called you a saint."

"Why do you find that so unusual? The Catholic Church long ago elevated Mary Magdalene to sainthood."

"But . . . what did you say to her?" I persisted.

"I told her I love her. I told her God loves her."

"That's it? That's all you said?"

"What more does anyone need to hear?"

I could see I was getting nowhere. She had effected a cure—I had to call it a cure, even though psychologists rarely use the word—and it was a cure that defied everything I knew about medicine and psychotherapy. Medical science has not yet been able to reverse the effects of a stroke.

Pop psychologists and faith healers, New Age holistic practitioners, and the trendy philosophers who regularly appear on *Oprah* preach unashamedly about the healing power of love. A believer in it myself, I had always envisioned it as a gradual inner response that increases self-esteem and provides an injured ego with a reason to recover. Medical researchers, as they usually do, have subjected the entire issue to examination with their electron microscopes, brain scans, magnetic resonance imaging, protein regression factors, and dozens of other tests with laboratory animals and humans, and finally reduced the entire process to a chemical function in which the brain releases endorphins that flood the bloodstream and activate proteins that perform therapeutic functions. Whatever the explanation, I had never seen so immediate and dramatic a transformation.

All Magdalena did was touch the woman and speak a few gentle words in a quiet voice. There was no question-and-answer, no interplay of dialogue, nothing but those few words.

I refused to believe that a few words about God and love, however well-intentioned, could have produced such results. The only explanation was that my initial diagnosis was wrong; perhaps the old woman wasn't a stroke victim, but simply a hysteric, or suffering from the emotional roller-coaster of bipolar disorder. In that case, what I had witnessed was a catharsis: the emotional breakthrough that occurs when a patient's deepest subconscious fears and anxieties are suddenly purged by bringing them to a conscious level. But catharsis is a dramatic moment usually reserved for motion pictures about psychiatrists. The reality usually is a gradual improvement over years of sessions. Even a program of short-term psychotherapy normally requires twenty-six sessions. This "cure" had been accomplished in a matter of seconds.

But was it really a cure?

Perhaps it was simply some momentary aberration, a hypnotic phenomenon that would evaporate in the absence of the hypnotist.

I'd have to see how Madame Gramont behaved tomorrow before I ascribed any miraculous healing powers to Magdalena.

Forty-Three

WE ATE SUPPER in a tiny restaurant nearby, where the specialty of the house was a simple fish soup known locally as *bullinada*. Served in small earthenware pots, the reddish stew was a peasant version of bouillabaisse, made with smaller fish and more intensely flavored.

While I was breaking off a piece of baguette, Magdalena began to talk about Jesus.

"He wasn't at all like most people think," she started to say.

I thought about interrupting her, asking her to reserve her comments until we were back in my room at the hotel, where I could record what she said. But she seemed in a pensive mood, perhaps because of the encounter with Madame Gramont, and it felt like an opportunity to explore her more personal impressions of Christ. I could always cover the same ground later, in front of the camcorder.

"For one thing," she said. "He didn't have a powerful voice, like John the Baptist or the priests in today's churches who speak with such authority. He spoke very normally, just like I'm speaking to you. When he cast the devils out of me, he didn't shout or rave. He simply took my hand and looked into my eyes and very quietly said, "You are healed." That was all. But when he said those words, I felt a warmth; not like the warmth of the sun or the desert, but a warmth that grew from some place deep inside my body. He smiled at me, as if he knew what was happening, as if he could feel what was happening to me. It was the most wonderful moment of my life, and yet, I don't think anyone around us even heard what he said to me."

Her eyes were looking past me, out the window and towards the ocean.

"That was when I fell in love with him," she murmured. "The very first moment I saw him."

The words hung between us for a long moment.

The bullinada was temporarily forgotten.

It was a moment whose intimacy I chose not to interrupt.

If she was a fraud, if this was all information that had been acquired from secondary sources or fed to her by a co-conspirator, it was the most stunning performance possible. Her eyes remained focused on the distant horizon, as if she was truly looking back in time.

When her eyes finally returned to me, and she realized where she was, she gave a self-conscious smile and occupied herself once again with the soup.

"Of course, all of us were in love with him," she said. "How could anyone not love a man who had the ability to touch your soul? But then, you know that. You loved him, too."

I wasn't exactly sure what she meant. Not wanting to distract her, I let it pass.

"I don't think I ever saw him lose his temper," she continued. "I know those men who wrote the Gospels claimed he was angry when he chased the merchants and moneylenders out of the temple. But they weren't there. I was. And what I saw was a man who was disappointed by what he found at the temple and was determined to restore the sanctity of a place of worship. He didn't shout or raise his voice or beat them with a whip."

This was a direct contradiction of John's version of the cleansing of the Temple. It was one of those unnecessary divergences from tradition that added credibility to her accounts. A charlatan would never attempt to dispute Gospel teaching.

"He wasn't the type to lose his temper," she said. "That wasn't his way. And it would have been foolish. The moneylenders had guards who would have attacked him for disrupting their business. What he did instead was make them feel ashamed. They left grudgingly, but willingly." She smiled. "And all they did was to move their stands just outside the temple, where they continued to conduct their business. It wasn't at all as dramatic as what you read in the bible, although the result was the same."

"What did he look like?" I couldn't resist asking.

It was a trick question; another attempt of mine to see if I could catch her in a mistake, or force her to overreach.

One thing I learned from the Orthodox icon painters on Mount Athos was that the physical appearance of Jesus Christ is as open to speculation as his famous "missing years."

Images that some scholars once claimed were of Christ have been discovered on ampullae, sarcophagi, and the walls of catacombs under the Vatican. Most of those images, however, bear strong resemblance to Roman Emperors and to Greek and Roman gods. This visual camouflage was a common practice in those early centuries, when a fish was used as a symbol for Christ, and the cross was often disguised as an anchor. As a result, those early images of Christ cannot be considered any more reliable than the one in DaVinci's famously inaccurate portrait of the Last Supper, which portrays the Apostles sitting at a table, rather than reclining at low platforms, as meals were typically served in those days.

The icon painters believe there are only three images of Christ that can have any claim to being accurate representations of his appearance. Two of them have disappeared into the mists of history, and one is the subject of continuing scientific investigation and controversy. The legendary Edessa Portrait was a painting of Jesus Christ which he himself sent, along with a letter, to Agbar V of Edessa. The correspondence between the two was documented by Eusebeus, the father of ecclesiastical history, in his writings during the third century. The letter was seen by the Aquitaine pilgrim Aetheria on her trip to the Holy Land in 383, and the existence of the portrait was further confirmed in the sixth century by Evagrius Scholasticus. The portrait appeared and disappeared through the centuries, making its way from Edessa to Constantinople, when that city was the center of the Christian faith, and then once again disappearing. The second image is that of Veronica's veil. According to the legends, the image miraculously transferred to cloth when Veronica wiped the face of Jesus during his carrying of the cross. Although there is no mention of the incident anywhere in the New Testament, *Veronica Wiping the Face of Jesus* was enshrined by the Roman Catholic Church as the sixth Station of the Cross. After almost a thousand years of the faithful praying before it, Pope Paul II replaced the sixth station in 1991, raising doubts about the legend's validity. Nevertheless, the veil, with its faint image, is still occasionally placed on public display.

The third, the most controversial, and probably the most legitimate image of Christ exists on the Shroud of Turin. This was the purported burial shroud that was wrapped around Jesus when he was placed in the tomb. It is an anatomically correct image, one of the few in existence that accurately places the spike marks in Christ's wrists, where the carpal bones provide support, rather than the palms of his hands, where the flesh between the metacarpal bones would have torn away under the weight of his body. The image appears to be three-dimensional when viewed in the negative, and offers an extremely detailed representation of his face. A number of scientists claim that a well-publicized carbon-dating experiment "proved" that the Shroud was created no earlier than the fourteenth century, although they have no explanation for how it was created, or why pollen from first-century Judea is embedded in the weave. Those claims were refuted by scholars who offered historical records proving the Shroud had been exhibited and written about as early as the sixth century. The methodology of the carbon-dating experiment was later discredited. But the skeptics continue their attacks.

With so much confusion and so little factual information, artists and sculptors have been creating their own interpretations of Jesus Christ for centuries. My question, which on the surface might appear very simple, was actually a trap, an invitation for her to overreach and make some sophomoric mistake of invention.

"He was a little less than two meters tall," she started out rather tentatively. "About your height. A bit heavier than you, although he wasn't very powerfully built. Oh, he was strong, just not as muscular as you'd expect a carpenter's son to be."

That description could have fit half the men of Galilee, I thought.

"He didn't look at all like Joseph, which you'd expect, since Joseph wasn't his father. It was his brother James who looked like Joseph."

I wasn't surprised by the reference to James. Despite the common belief that Jesus was an only child, the bible itself reveals that James was in fact the brother of Jesus . . . and in fact, was not his only sibling. What I found intriguing, however, was the theological escape clause she constructed with her comment about the physical resemblance between Joseph and James. Establishing Joseph as the father of James preserved the concept of the singular divinity of Christ's birth.

"Actually, Joseph and James were the handsome ones in the family. Jesus took after Mary, who was really quite plain."

It wasn't exactly a sparkling assessment of the Savior's appearance, particularly coming from a woman who claimed she loved him. Maybe she thought that a little criticism would help establish her credibility.

"He had a long, narrow face, just like his mother."

At last, she was getting specific.

"He had a long nose, a really long nose, and it was a little misshapen at the left nostril."

"How do you mean?" I asked.

"You know how nobody's nose is perfect? Well, I remember his left nostril was smaller than the right." She gave a nervous laugh. "Maybe it sounds silly to you, remembering a little detail like that."

"It's not silly at all," I said. "The more details you can remember, the better."

"He didn't have fair skin, like you see in all those paintings. Nobody who lived in that region had fair skin except the Roman women, who stayed out of the sun."

So the Savior was suntanned, like millions of other Palestinians. Not a particularly dramatic observation, I thought.

"He had a deep crease across his forehead," she went on. "As if he spent too much time squinting into the sun, maybe when he was in the desert."

We had forgotten our food, which remained half-eaten on the table as she continued to draw a word-picture of a man she claimed to have known 2,000 years ago.

"He had black hair . . ."

As did ninety-five percent of the Hebrews at that time.

" . . .which he wore long, down to his shoulders."

The standard style.

"His beard wasn't full. It didn't meet under his nose. You could see the skin and an indentation between his nose and his upper lip. You know, right here." She pointed to the small valley above the center of her upper lip. "And the beard didn't grow under his lower lip. There was a line there, too. It looked almost as if he shaved the area below his mouth."

As she continued to add details, some of them as superficially inconsequential as the way his beard forked in an inverted V beneath his chin, I grew more intrigued.

"He had deep, brown eyes," she continued. "There was something about his eyes that I never saw in another human being. Not then. And not now. They seemed larger than normal, almost owlish in nature. They were set deep, with heavy eyelids, and he always looked at things with a deep intensity. When he looked at you, it was hard to look away. It was as if he had the ability to see into your soul."

So far, this was the only part of her description that even seemed to approach what anyone might call mystical. The preternatural gaze was a description that was traditionally applied to those endowed with mystical powers, such as Padre Pio and Katherine Neumann, as well as more sinister practitioners of mind control such as Charles Manson. As a psychologist, I knew such interpersonal evaluations tended to be purely subjective and often overstated by those most susceptible to the influence of charismatic personalities.

And then . . . I saw those haunting eyes in my mind: the way they probed and seemed to have an intelligence of their own; how sad they looked when they saw pain and suffering, even in those for whom the rest of us have no pity. I shook my head to clear it of the sudden image.

"He had high cheekbones. When he was fasting, they became even more prominent."

Despite my efforts to shake it off, the image persisted. I had heard of mental projection, the ability of one person to plant an image in another's mind. However, none of those experiments produced an image as vivid as the one I was now receiving.

"Another peculiar thing," she said. "His left eyebrow was higher than his right."

That was a common occurrence, also. Both sides of a face are seldom identical, unless they've been exposed to the ministrations of cosmetic surgery.

If she had claimed to remember a beatific face like those painted by the old masters, or a holy light shining in the Savior's eyes, it would have been much easier to dismiss her word picture. What she described, in far greater detail than I expected, was a variety of individual facial characteristics that could have been shared in greater or lesser degree by a majority of the male population of Judea. A higher right eyebrow, a deep line across the forehead, a large nose with a misshapen left nostril: they were details so specific, and yet so general, that they seemed to neither prove nor disprove anything. The word-picture she painted was that of an ordinary, not-so-handsome man with haunting eyes and a long nose. And yet, I found myself responding in a strange way to her verbal portrait.

I was starting to believe I had seen the man she was describing.

But where?

Where had I encountered that face?

I tried to remember. I usually had a very good memory for faces, yet it was failing me now. The beard should have made him easier to identify. Yet I couldn't quite make the mnemonic connection. Was it someone I met on my travels? One of the bearded Orthodox monks on Mount Athos? A face in the crowd glimpsed fleetingly in some airport or railway station?

Or someone from so far in the dim past that I couldn't dredge up any memory other than his face?

"And he had two short locks of hair that hung loosely over the center of his forehead," she concluded.

I knew the man!

The more she described him, the more convinced I was that I knew that face from somewhere!

"Do you take American dollars?" I suddenly asked the waiter.

"Mais oui, monsieur."

Pushing aside my unfinished meal, I counted out more than enough to cover the bill and a tip. The amount I left on the table brought a smile to the waiter's face.

"Merci. Merci beaucoup, monsieur. Vous êtes très gentil."

"Where are we going?" Magdalena asked as I rose from the table.

"You'll see," I said.

Forty-Four

I HURRIED MAGDALENA out of the Moorish quarter and down to the beachwalk. It was a warm night, and the beach walk and its open-air restaurants were busy with hungry tourists. The small beach itself was deserted, except for a few barefoot lovers strolling along the water's edge. A mime dressed as a Roman gladiator was working the crowd. Above it all, illuminated with floodlights, the massive *Chateau Royal* stood guard over the town.

Just as I did in Valencia, I went looking for an artist who could draw a credible likeness from a word-portrait. There isn't a tourist town in the world that doesn't have a sidewalk artist sketching instant portraits. This part of Collioure had three. I picked the one beneath the tree near the Tourist Information Office, a jovial charcoal artist who worked more quickly than the other two. He eagerly offered Magdalena the chair reserved for customers, thinking I wanted him to sketch her portrait. Fortunately, he understood English, so I was able to explain what I wanted with a minimum of confusion. Magdalena joined me behind him, where we could both watch while he sketched the face she described.

He started, as most artists do, with the shape of the head: a large oval representing the long face, resting on two lines that formed the neck. The next most important part of the face, as far as he was concerned, was the position of the eyes. He was very precise in the way he approached the project, asking Magdalena for details in a specific sequence, and sketching them in outline form, to be filled in after her corrections and his erasures ensured the accuracy of his work. The eyes, for example: there was the question of the positioning of the eyes within the head, the distance between the eyes, the size and shape of the eyes themselves, the eyelids, whether there were bags under the eyes, creases, shadows or wrinkles. Only when she was satisfied with what she saw did he move on to the eyebrows, the nose, the mouth, the shading of the cheeks, the line across the forehead, the beard, the hair.

I watched, fascinated, as his hands darted over the paper, expertly rendering facial characteristics with a few strokes of his pencil. Under Magdalena's guidance, the face began to take on a familiar quality.

The portrait was still in outline form when he filled in the two locks of hair hanging down over the forehead.

"Stop!" I said.

"But *monsieur,* I am not yet done."

"No. That's fine." I turned to Magdalena. "Is this what he looked like?"

"Yes. Exactly as I remember him."

"This is just an outline, *monsieur,*" the artist protested. "I can finish it in only a few more minutes. All it needs is some shading, the addition of some dimension."

I stared at his work. There was a familiarity to the pencil strokes, the rough outline style of the sketch that finally triggered my memory. What I thought I remembered was the face Magdalena had been describing, when it reality, what I really remembered was an outline sketch almost identical to this one.

In a wonderful example of Tulving's encoding specificity hypothesis, the outline sketch provided the specific visual cues that brought back not only the place I had seen the image, but a flood of additional related information as well.

In the monastery library on Mount Athos was an old book documenting the work of Paul Vignon, a scholarly Frenchman who devoted much of his adult life to the scientific study of the Shroud of Turin. Vignon performed an exhaustive analysis comparing the image of Christ on the Shroud with other early portrayals of the Savior. Until the sixth century, most of those sacred images were of a young, unbearded idealized Christ who more closely resembled Roman or Greek gods, and could easily be dismissed as fictions. The first portraits of the bearded Christ whom we know today were not rendered until around 565 A.D. Few relics of that period survive, but the ones that Vignon studied, including the Emessa vase, the silver paten of Riha, and the icon of Christ in the Church of St. Catherine in Sinai, all bear an amazing resemblance to the man of the Shroud.

Excited by the discovery, Vignon began a comparative analysis of sixth- and seventh-century Byzantine icons, coins, and other images, and compared them with the Shroud. He was able to identify twenty distinguishing facial characteristics, many of them as minute as a U-shaped feature on the forehead, which tied all these images together. He published his work in 1938, complete with an outline sketch identifying those features. That sketch, in that book, was almost identical to the charcoal sketch I was looking at in Collioure.

Now that my memory was refreshed, I could clearly remember my excitement when I first saw the illustration in Vignon's book. His documentation had convinced me then that I was looking at the real face of Jesus. Was there any reason for me to doubt it now?

"That's what he looked like," Magdalena said, as if in answer to my unasked question.

"A fascinating face," the artist said. He stood back from his easel to better appraise his work. "He is a friend of yours?"

"From a long time ago," Magdalena said, her voice barely a whisper.

A small group of people began to gather behind us.

"This man, I think he is a good man," the artist said. "I draw many faces, sometimes fifteen, twenty a day. But never do I see a face like this. So kind. So gentle. So sad."

Murmurs of agreement came from the onlookers. None of them seemed to recognize the subject of the portrait.

"You captured him perfectly, "Magdalena said. "You have a great talent."

The crowd continued to grow.

"No, it was not me," the artist said. "It was you. My hand was moved by your words."

I was beginning to think this was some sort of ploy, an attempt to flatter us before charging some exorbitant price for the sketch. But when I tried to pay the artist, he refused to accept any money.

"He is yours, *monsieur*. He belongs to you and the pretty lady. Please. *S'il vous plaît*."

The onlookers applauded his generosity as he carefully rolled up the sketch and slipped it into a cardboard tube before handing it to me.

"*Merci,*" I said. "*Merci beaucoup.*"

"*Il n'y a pas de quoi,*" he replied. "I am honored to be of service to you." He turned to Magdalena and bowed with a Gallic flourish. "And also to you, *madame. Enchanté.*"

As we walked away, I realized we had become objects of curiosity. The flurry of activity at the artist's stand had attracted the attention of the people watchers who were dining and drinking at the outdoor cafes. Their eyes followed us until we passed through the gates of the old Moorish quarter.

I could only hope none of them had seen today's Barcelona newspapers, with my photograph and a description of my crimes on the front page.

Forty-Five

IN THE MORNING, I was awakened by what sounded like the voice of an angel, a sweet and gentle voice singing the praises of the Lord. For a moment, I thought I was back on the Other Side, where I remembered hearing such seraphic sounds in the mysterious distance. I lay still for a while, afraid that if I moved, the heavenly melody would stop. Gradually, I recognized the verse as one of the morning *matins* I had heard at the *convento.* The voice belonged to Magdalena; she was singing her morning prayers.

The first tentative rays of sunlight were already filtering through the wooden shutters. It seemed odd that I heard no other sounds, none of the usual discordant noises that signal a village awakening from slumber. When I opened the shutters, I saw the reason why. Instead of going about their morning activities, a small crowd of villagers was standing in the street, staring up at Magdalena's window. They were enthralled, as I was, by the loveliness of her song. Her voice floated effortlessly and free, a natural soprano unburdened with technique. It moved through the upper registers with a shimmering ease that Sarah Brightman would have envied. The song ended when the church bells rang for the morning Mass. Not until then did the normal morning activities of the neighborhood resume.

A knock at my door announced the arrival of a jovial Madame Gramont with a breakfast I had not ordered. The old woman was smiling and cheerful, and she moved about with an easy mobility she hadn't known in years. All signs of her disabilities were gone. Whatever magic Magdalena worked on her had apparently lasted through the night. She brought in a tray containing a pot of coffee, a plate of cheese, two large croissants, jam and butter. The croissants were fresh from the baker's, their warm scent mingling wonderfully with the rich aroma of the freshly brewed coffee. Madame Gramont placed the tray on a table near the window, where I could enjoy a view of the Mediterranean with my breakfast.

She looked around the room until her eyes finally settled on the charcoal sketch, which I had pinned to the back of the door last night. That must have been what she was searching for, because she hurried across the room to examine it more closely.

"This is the drawing done by Eduard last night?" she asked. "When you were strolling with the lady?"

"Yes. But how did you know?" In the excitement last night, the artist had neglected to sign his name.

"They were talking about it this morning."

"Who was talking? Where?"

"The baker and his wife. They were saying it is the face of Jesus."

"How did the baker know about it?"

"He heard it from his brother, who talked to Eduard. By now, many people know. To make a picture so beautiful, just from her words, Eduard says he doesn't understand how he did it."

"He must have been inspired," I said. It was a casual remark, the kind of throwaway compliment not meant to be taken too seriously.

"That is what Eduard said. He was going to give up his art, you know. He never made much money from it. But now, after creating the most beautiful drawing of his life, he told his brother he is inspired to go to Paris and study at the *École*. He worked through the night sketching dozens of copies of this portrait, which have already been sold. Everyone at the bakery is talking about this young lady of yours, and how she has touched Eduard's life for the better."

"I'm glad for him," I said. As far as I was concerned, it was an example of an affair getting overblown by small-town gossips who had nothing more exciting to talk about.

"She has a gift from God, this young lady of yours."

"I'm not so sure about that," I demurred. I left her staring at the portrait while I busied myself with breakfast. The croissants, although now cold, were wonderfully crisp on the outside and soft on the inside. The coffee was thick and dark; I mixed it with fresh cream at a 1:1 ratio. "My life is changed, too," Madame Gramont continued. "The great sadness has been lifted from my heart. I went out last night, for the first time since my son died. I joined some old friends at the café along the canal, and we peeled *crevettes* and drank wine until after midnight. Everyone in the bakery knew about my cure this morning. I told them it is all because of the young lady. She is truly a saint."

"And I suppose you told them she's staying here, in your house."

"But of course," Madame Gramont said. "I am proud to have her here."

That would explain the people in the street this morning, and why they listened so attentively to Magdalena's morning song.

"She's not a saint," I said.

"Isn't it true she told Eduard she knew the man in the picture?"

"Yes," I said. There was no point in denying what she told the artist; I was sure she would repeat it to anyone who asked.

"Then if she knows Jesus, she is a saint."

"She's just an ordinary human being," I said. "Like you and me."

"Ordinary people don't cure the sick."

"Doctors do."

"Doctors don't sing to the Lord in the morning. Not the way she does."

"Maybe they should," I murmured. I didn't dare reveal Magdalena was really a nun, singing her morning *matins*. The old lady would surely take it as further proof of sainthood.

Madame Gramont seemed in no hurry to leave.

"Is there anything else?" I asked as I started on my second croissant.

"There is a woman . . . ," she said. "Marguerite Diderot . . . a cousin of my cousin . . . she has a son, Philippe . . ."

I waited while she tried to find the right words to express what she wanted.

"The boy does not speak . . . he is what we call in French a *muet*."

"A mute?"

"*Oui.* The child is only four years old." The words came out faster now. "It is heartbreaking. Such a beautiful little boy, and he is unable to even call his mother."

"I'm sorry for him," I said. I had an idea where this was leading, and it was making me uncomfortable.

"Do you think the young lady could . . . help him to speak?" she asked.

"You're asking for a miracle."

"Yes. A miracle. She has the gift, does she not?"

Her voice reflected the innocent faith of one who had been cured herself. If I attempted to deny Magdalena's "gift," did I risk undermining Madame Gramont's sudden recovery from decades of depression? I was convinced whatever "cure" had taken place occurred at some subconscious level in the mind of this old woman, and I knew it could be reversed as easily as it first happened.

"What worked for you might not work with the boy," I cautioned her. I didn't want her faith to be shaken when nothing happened. "Even if she has the gift, she may not be able to produce miracles on demand."

It wasn't the answer Madame Gramont wanted.

"A saint can work miracles anytime," she declared. "And I believe she is a saint."

Resolute in her faith, she left me to finish my breakfast. I could only hope she didn't suffer a relapse when the expected miracle didn't occur.

The reputed "miracle worker" answered her door looking more like a carefree young tourist than a saint. She was wearing a white sleeveless blouse and white slacks and was putting on a pair of silver shell earrings. A pair of white patent sandals waited neatly by her bed, while she padded around the room in her bare feet. For a woman who had never used make-up until three days ago, when Alfredo's female friend had painted her face, she showed an amazing ability with lipstick and eyeliner.

"So!" she said. "You've come to ask me more questions."

"Where would you like to sit?" I asked.

She sat in the middle of the bed and assumed a yoga position, bare feet curled under her thighs. I pinned the charcoal portrait up on the wall, which seemed to please her. Looking at Magdalena through the camcorder's viewfinder, I had to remind myself that this beautiful creature in the form-fitting clothing had just a few days ago been an innocent young nun hidden away in a Spanish convent. What would the other nuns think if they could see her now, sitting barefoot and cross-legged on her bed, alone in a room with a man who was obviously admiring her figure? As if she knew what I must be thinking, she gave me a warm, almost flirtatious smile.

"This is the third interview with Sister Mariamme." I entered the usual formalities at the head of the videotape. "This session is taking place in Collioure, France, in a room on the third floor of the boarding house owned by Madame Ernestine Gramont. Today is Thursday, May 10, 2001. The local time is 8:13 A.M."

Before proceeding any further, I reviewed last night's events to make the videotape record as complete as possible. I had Magdalena repeat her description of Jesus, I described how the sketch was made, and finally recorded a long close-up of the sketch itself. With that out of the way, I refocused the camcorder on Magdalena's face.

"Now," I began. "Tell me about your relationship with Jesus."

Normally, I wouldn't start an interview with so provocative a question, but I was getting impatient with the slow progress of our sessions, and was eager to get into some of the more provocative myths surrounding the exact nature of the friendship between the Magdalene and the Savior.

As I anticipated, the request caught her by surprise.

"What do you mean?" she asked in a suddenly guarded voice.

The needle on the voice-stress analyzer jumped into the red zone. It was only the second time in our sessions that the machine registered so strong a reading.

"What was the nature of your relationship with Jesus?" I repeated.

"I was one of his followers," she said.

The needle remained lodged in the red zone. That didn't suggest she was being untruthful; it simply indicated that, despite the calm demeanor she attempted to display, the unit was detecting a high level of stress in her voice.

"You said you loved him," I reminded her.

"Of course I loved him. We all loved him."

"But he loved you more than the others," I insisted. "That's what is written in the Gospel of Mary. And in the Gospel of Philip, it is written that he kissed you on the lips."

She suddenly seemed unable or unwilling to respond. I watched in amazement as her cheeks turned red, her breathing grew heavier, her facial features grew taut. The vein in her forehead began to throb, suggesting an increase in both heart rate and blood pressure.

I was stunned to see the sudden display of embarrassment.

It was at that moment, with the two of us staring speechlessly at each other, that I first began to admit to myself that I might, just might, be dealing with a genuine, provable case of reincarnation. Everything up until that moment could have been faked. The stories of a childhood in ancient Judea could have been the product of false memories or even careful coaching by persons unknown. Her command of dead languages was more problematic, but so far, I had only Professor Abramakian's testimony to support that claim. And there was a tenuous, though credible, psychological explanation for her "miraculous" cure of Madame Gramont.

What was before me now, however, was a simpler, more basic form of evidence: the embarrassment of a woman suddenly confronted with intimate revelations she would have preferred to keep secret.

The physiological manifestations of shame are produced by the sympathetic branch of the autonomous nervous system. They are instinctive responses that are difficult, if not impossible, for even experienced actors to summon up as quickly as they appeared on Magdalena's features.

Indeed, it would have been much easier, if she was a fraud, to have quickly offered me some delicious and self-serving details about her relationship with Christ.

With narrowed eyes and a voice struggling to maintain its composure, she picked up where we left off at the end of the last session.

"I was twenty-three years old when Jesus my Christ healed me. I had grown into womanhood while I was possessed by the demons. During that time, my childhood friends shunned me. I became a stranger to everyone except my father and his servants. After I was cured, they washed me, bought me new clothing, and brought me a mirror to show me the beautiful woman I had become. I was pleased with what I saw. The men in the village who had shunned me now looked on me with desire. My father was overjoyed to see his daughter return to health again. My life was good.

"But I was drawn to the man who healed me. Jesus my Christ was preaching throughout the Galilee, and with my father's permission, I left home to become one of his followers. Part of what attracted me was his attitude toward women. In those days, Jewish women had no civil or legal rights, were segregated in the synagogues, and were not even permitted to pray aloud in the privacy of our own homes. The rabbis urged women not to appear in public, lest we incite lust. Men were not allowed to speak or even look at women, treating us as if we were some despised species. A woman could be divorced by her husband for speaking with a stranger. A woman found guilty of adultery would be stoned to death, while a man usually escaped with a rebuke. It was a terrible time to be a woman.

"Until Jesus my Christ came along.

"He openly violated many of the prohibitions against associating with women. He talked to women in public places, even women he didn't know . . . any woman who approached him was welcomed. And he challenged those who said it was wrong, including Peter and the other male apostles. Jesus my Christ cured more women than men, and when he did so, he physically touched them, like he did with the woman with the fever; or allowed them to touch him, like the woman with the hemorrhage. He went into Martha's house when there were no men present, and he spoke at length with her sister Mary. Part of the Good News he preached was that women and men were equal in his eyes. It was so radical an idea, that even his disciples had a difficult time accepting it."

She paused for a moment, as if to collect her thoughts.

"There were seven of us women who became disciples. Besides myself, there were Joanna, the wife of Herod's steward, Susanna, Salome, and the three other Marys from Jerusalem and the Galilee. The twelve male disciples didn't like the idea of women being part of the ministry, but they were afraid to complain, because they knew Jesus my Christ treated women as equal to them." She gave a wry smile. "Also, they couldn't complain because we women were the ones who provided the financial support for the ministry, and supported Peter and the male apostles as well. They left their work to follow Jesus my Christ, and we provided for them out of our means. We used the income from our farms, sold property and jewelry, whatever was necessary. But still the men resented our presence."

Certainly there was nothing debatable in that account. Any reading of the New Testament confirms that Jesus welcomed his female disciples and they supported him financially. Yet one has to search for any reference that the women were actually disciples, the Gospel translators and editors reducing their role to "followers.'

"We traveled with Jesus my Christ and bore witness to his miracles. It was a wonderful time, those days before he entered Jerusalem. So many of the sick were cured. In many towns, they laid the sick in marketplaces, where they could touch the tassel of his cloak. Do you remember those miracles, Theo?"

She looked at me with a curious expression.

"I've read about them," I said.

"Do you remember the miracle of the blind man at Jericho?"

"You mean Bartimaeus," I said. "The son of Timeus and Leah." I started to say something more, but stopped, wondering where I came up with the name of the blind man's mother. To the best of my recollection, her name appeared nowhere in the New Testament. It must have come from some other reading, I thought.

"Yes," she smiled knowingly. "That's right. Leah. I'm glad you remember her."

She went on for a while about the many miracles she claimed to have witnessed: the raising of Lazarus, the calming of the storm, walking on water, and many others. The miracles were an essential part of his ministry, she contended. They were the proof of divinity, the signs which the people demanded before they would accept him as a prophet.

"Even his mother Mary and his brothers didn't believe him at first," she said. "They thought Jesus was out of his mind. They tried to intervene and stop his preaching. It was the miracles that eventually convinced them he was fulfilling the prophecy. But of course, you know that, don't you?"

She was quoting almost verbatim from the third chapter of Mark. Because so much of what she said came from both biblical and respected extra-biblical sources, it would be easy to dismiss most of what she said as proof of nothing more than an encyclopedic knowledge of the source material. Of course, it was also just as easy to consider those sources as confirmation of her past-life memories.

Her recital continued for another half-hour, until a little red light on the camcorder signaled that we had reached the end of the 90-minute tape. While I inserted a fresh tape, she stretched her arms and arched her back in a cat-like movement that made me uncomfortably aware of her femininity.

"Can we stop now?" she asked. "It's such a beautiful day. Why don't we go down to the beach?"

Without waiting for an answer, she jumped up and headed for the door.

"Come on, slowpoke," she called from the open doorway.

It was too late to stop her.

I should have warned her they'd be waiting for her at the bottom of the stairs.

Forty-Six

I WAS SO preoccupied with the interview, I had forgotten to tell Magdalena about Madame Gramont's earlier request.

I tried to catch up with her on the stairway, but I was too late. She was already encircled by the crowd that filled the tiny lobby and spilled out into the street.

Madame Gramont's voice could be heard, trying to restore order.

"*Calme! Calme!*" she shouted.

I slowed down, watching as Madame Gramont introduced Magdalena to her cousin Marguerite.

The cousin was a tall, underfed woman with black hair and a prominent French nose. In her bony arms was a small boy, dressed incongruously in a black velvet suit with a white shirt and red tie, the sort of presentation outfit boys his age wore only at weddings or for their First Holy Communion.

He was much better fed than his mother, a sign that she cared more for his well-being than her own. His cheeks were plump, he had shiny brown eyes, pouting lips, and a small dimple in his chin. His hair was wet and freshly combed. He looked as if he had been freshly bathed especially for this occasion.

This, I realized, was Philippe.

The mute.

As I watched Magdalena approach him, I could see the terror in the little boy's eyes. All these other women pressing against each other, jostling for a better view of the encounter, chattering excitedly all the while, frightened the boy. Unable to voice his fears, all little Phillipe could do was clutch his mother tightly with those tiny hands.

I felt sorry for the frightened child.

And I felt sorry for the disappointment his mother was sure to feel when the miracle for which she must be so fervently praying failed to materialize.

The crowd of women suddenly fell silent. Philippe's mother began to explain his condition to Magdalena. I didn't understand her French, but from her anguished facial expressions and the ragged quality of her voice, I knew she was begging for help. In the middle of her plea, she broke down in tears. The sight of his mother crying brought tears to little Philippe's eyes, too. His mother tried to comfort him, stroking his hair and kissing him on the cheeks, wiping away his tears with her lips. Soon half the women in the crowd were crying, too.

Magdalena moved closer to the boy.

She smiled and whispered something to him.

Little Philippe tried to smile.

She whispered something again.

He nodded his head slowly. His fear seemed to have evaporated, replaced with an expression of wonder.

Magdalena whispered something again, and this time, she reached out and touched his throat.

I could feel the electricity that raced through the crowd. Everyone seemed to have stopped breathing, waiting for the little boy to respond.

I knew there would be no response. How could there be? Magdalena was just a simple nun who was carried away by the excitement of the moment. What really worried me was how the crowd would react when the "miracle" they had gathered to witness didn't occur. The psychology of the crowd could shift suddenly, with unpredictably dangerous consequences. When anticipation turned to disappointment, it would take only a single spark, maybe the angry outburst of a single woman, to direct their fury at Magdalena. I had to get her out of there before things turned ugly.

I pushed my way through the crowd.

Philippe was smiling at Magdalena when I reached her side.

"Let's go," I said, perhaps a bit more brusquely than I should have. As I expected, the boy hadn't reacted in any way that would suggest a cure.

"Why are you interrupting me?" Magdalena asked.

She turned back to Philippe and with her hand on his throat, repeated words I had heard before.

"Je t'aime," she said, *"Le bon Dieu t'aime."*

Philippe smiled and reached out to touch her mouth. She kissed his little fingers as lovingly as any mother would.

"All right," she said to me. "We can go to the beach now. I'm done here."

Disappointed at the lack of the miracle she hoped for, Philippe's mother watched sadly as I edged Magdalena through the crowd. The onlookers, now quiet, almost sullen, parted for us.

As we reached the doorway, I heard a strange, anguished outcry from behind us.

The crowd, which had been allowing us through so far, suddenly blocked our way. We couldn't proceed any further.

The strange noise was repeated again. It sounded almost like the bleating of a goat.

I felt a sudden chill go through me.

A low murmur began to fill the lobby. The women who blocked our way began pushing us back inside.

The next time I heard the sound, it seemed to be struggling to take on the characteristics of a human voice. Still almost animal-like, but crying to be heard.

And then at last, finding the voice that eluded him all his life, little Phillipe cried out, *"Maman! Maman!"*

The boy's mother let out a scream.

"Philippe, Philippe, tu parles! C'est un miracle!"

"*Maman! Maman!*" The boy's voice was suddenly clearer, no longer tortured, the light, playful voice of a child. "*Je t'aime, Maman!*"

The little boy was using his first words to tell his mother he loved her.

As mother and son sobbed and hugged each other, the crowd of onlookers dropped to their knees in prayer. I took the opportunity to lead Magdalena away, before the crowd could recover from the shock and surround us again. No one in the street outside knew exactly what had happened, but apparently sensing from the screams and the sound of prayers that something extraordinary had taken place, they stared at Magdalena with the mixture of awe and curiosity usually reserved in our modern world for celebrities.

After what I had witnessed, I have to admit I shared their feelings. Was it possible that I was in the presence of a saint? Restoring the power of speech to a child who was born mute certainly should qualify as a miracle. And most religions accept miracles as proof of saintliness. But was what I had witnessed a genuine miracle? Or was it something more benign, a form of spontaneous remission of a fairly common psychosomatic disorder, triggered by the faith of a devout mother and the loving touch of a stranger?

Of course, given those reductionist criteria, many of the cures performed by Christ, including driving the "seven demons" out of Mary Magdalene, would not rise to the level of miracles. Nor, I thought, would some of the miracles attributed to Mary Magdalene herself.

Yet whatever explanation the cynics might offer, there was an undeniable symmetry between the cure I had just witnessed and the biblical cures of blind men, hemorrhagic women, the halt, and the lame.

As with her earlier "cure" of Madame Gramont, Magdalena was exhibiting a mystical skill which was far beyond the capability of a normal human being. The ability to perform miracles, however, was one of the talents the old French legends attribute to Mary Magdalene. And according to the Stevenson protocols, the exhibition of special skills that the present personality could not be expected to have acquired in its present life was a strong indicator of reincarnation.

Unless there was fraud involved, and I was too flustered and in too much of a hurry to go back right now and investigate the incident further, it appeared that this young nun was in possession of healing skills similar to those attributed to the Magdalene. It was a stunning discovery: a particular kind of proof of reincarnation that Stevenson himself had postulated, had searched for . . . but had seldom found.

What made it especially convincing was that the apparent miracles happened in a town neither of us had visited before, an isolated village selected by me on a whim. No one could have known we were coming to Collioure, much less staying at Madame Gramont's house, which made it unlikely that a fraudulent "cure" could have been arranged.

Forty-Seven

AS I HURRIED her away, Magdalena didn't act as if she had done anything out of the ordinary. To an onlooker, she could have been any of the dozens of beautiful women her age who were here on holiday. Like them, she was attracted to the window displays of beachwear and resort fashions. When we reached the beachwalk, she wrenched her hand out of mine, took off her shoes, and ran out into the sand. I smiled as she pushed her feet deep into the warm sand, and made little-girl sounds of delight at the way the fine grains flowed between her toes. It was one of those simple pleasures most of us experience during childhood. I sat on the low stone wall that bordered the beach and watched, bemused by this nineteen-year-old woman who a few moments ago had performed what seemed like a miracle, and was now happily focused on feeling the sand between her toes.

It was the middle of the morning, and the small beach was getting crowded. Sun-worshippers lounged on their blankets, children splashed with their parents at the water's edge, and farther out, almost dangerously distant from shore, a lone swimmer sought the solitude of the open sea. Magdalena studied the scene with a wistful expression that made me wonder if she was regretting all those years spent in the confines of the convent. Two young women her own age screamed happily as they dashed past her on their way to the water.

"I think I'd like to buy a bathing suit," she said to me. "Would that be possible?"

"As long as you don't tell Mother Dominica I paid for it," I said, remembering my promise to the stern nun.

I gave her what I was sure would be more than enough money and waited on the wall while she went off to shop. I needed the time to think about what I had witnessed at Madame Gramont's. True to my skeptical nature, I still wasn't completely convinced it was a miracle. In theological terms, a miracle is an event that requires the suspension of the physical laws that govern our universe. If the boy's inability to speak was due to some deformity of the larynx, then his "cure" was indeed a miracle. There was another possible explanation, however. Unless there was prior medical evidence of some physical defect in his vocal cords, the boy might have been suffering from a rare form of conversion disorder known as *aphonia.* The disorder is psychological in nature, one of a number of somatoform disorders that mimic acute medical conditions. Patients suffering from *aphonia* can exhibit sudden recovery of their ability to speak, but that normally comes only after long periods of psychotherapy. What Magdalena had done was simply whisper a few words and touch his throat. Did that fit the criteria of a miracle? Not necessarily, I kept telling myself.

And yet, I had to admit, he was cured. Whether it was a miracle or not, Phillipe was cured by Magdalena's touch . . . suddenly and dramatically cured, in front of dozens of witnesses.

It could be the result of some monumentally fortuitous coincidence of timing. Or an extraordinarily sympathetic psychological response to Magdalena's personality. Whatever had happened, it was difficult for me to believe that this woman who was now shopping for a bathing suit was capable of performing miracles.

"Well?" Magdalena asked. "What do you think?"

I looked up to see her exhibiting an unbelievable expanse of exposed skin interrupted by two strategically placed pieces of bright fabric.

She spun around, offering me a 360-degree view of a body that I would never have believed a nun could possess. In spite of the hints provided by her clothing of the past two days, I was unprepared for the almost total nudity that confronted me. She was wearing a yellow-and-blue flower-printed bikini with the skimpiest of tops and a thong bottom, both of which left extremely little to the imagination. She looked absolutely ravishing.

I knew how Philippe must have felt when he couldn't mouth the words that came to his mind. I could only stare in silence as Magdalena smiled and paraded proudly past me out onto the beach. She was barefoot, carrying a beach mat under her arm. Her clothing was stuffed into a colorful straw bag. I followed, spellbound by the transformation.

"Well?" she asked again after she spread out the mat.

I tried to keep my eyes on her face, but in spite of myself, they kept wandering down her body, to areas of flesh I found embarrassing to look at, but impossible to avoid. Her skin, sheltered all her life from the deleterious effects of sun and wind and air pollution by the heavy fabric of her habit, was as smooth and flawless as that of a baby's cheeks.

"You're beautiful," I finally said. "But you're a nun. You took vows. Isn't it wrong to display yourself like this?"

"God made my body," she said. "There's nothing shameful in displaying his work."

It was the rationale used as a refuge by every woman who poses nude for Playboy or takes off her clothes in strip joints.

Slowly, and very deliberately, with her eyes fixed on mine, she put her hands behind her back to unfasten her top. Watching my reaction, she slowly lowered the top, allowing her ample breasts to hang free.

I felt my jaw drop. My cheeks grew hot. I couldn't believe what had just happened. We were less than three feet apart, in the middle of a crowded public beach, and she was revealing her breasts not only to me, but to everyone else who wanted to look upon them. A few men did, but only casually. This was the South of France, after all, and topless sunbathing was common on beaches. Still, what would these men think if they knew this particular topless sunbather was a nun, a creature whose breasts the church hierarchy considered forbidden fruit, the very existence of which St. Augustine insisted had to be hidden beneath black robes, lest they arouse impure thoughts in others.

"Well?" she asked again.

"What do you want me to say?" I responded.

"You think it's a sin, don't you? Letting people see my breasts?"

They were lovely breasts, larger than I imagined when I first saw her in street clothing.

"It just sort of took me by surprise," I said.

"Why should you be surprised? There are plenty of other women going topless on the beach. Why shouldn't I?"

From what I could see, none of the other women had breasts as beautiful as hers. She was at that perfect moment when her bosom was fully developed and yet still unaffected by the ravages of gravity, or age, or suckling infants. They were a virgin's breasts, with small nubby nipples that stood erect in pink, oversized aureoles. I looked away from her, staring out to sea as I tried to shake off the prurient thoughts that were racing through my mind.

"You're a nun," I admonished her. "You shouldn't be exposing yourself like this."

She smiled at my apparent discomfort and reached into her bag.

"They told me I should cover myself with this lotion, or else my skin would get burned by the sun," she said. "That's a problem I never heard about in the *convento*."

I kept my face turned away as she started to apply the lotion. In my mind's eye, I could see her hand spreading the creamy white liquid into the hollow of her chest between her breasts, and from there moving gently down to her navel and then back up to her bosom, stroking and massaging herself unashamedly. Afraid to look, I could imagine her bosoms glistening and moving with pendulous grace as her hands cupped the smooth flesh and worked the lotion first underneath, and then around, and finally into the pebbly protuberances of her nipples.

As a reincarnation investigator, I should have been examining her body for birthmarks, those biological markings inherited from a past life that Stevenson considered to be the most important evidence of reincarnation. But I couldn't overcome my embarrassment.

Instead, I tried to focus my attention on a sailboat moving past the lighthouse at the end of the breakwater. Other men in the vicinity were looking at her, some of them trying not to be obvious, although one middle-aged man in abbreviated bathing trunks had turned completely around on his towel and was staring quite openly at her breasts. I mentally cursed him for daring to look so hungrily at the naked flesh I so puritanically avoided.

"Would you do my back?" she asked.

At first I hesitated. But when I saw the middle-aged man begin to rise in response to her request, I quickly changed my mind. I took the lotion, and averting my eyes, moved around behind her. I poured a white line of the creamy fluid across her slim shoulders and started spreading it down her back. The lotion smelled of coconut oil. It had a lubricious consistency which allowed my hands to glide smoothly over her body. Her flesh felt warm and soft. Just beneath the surface of her skin, I could feel the outlines of her ribs. My hands continued stroking her back, gliding over the surface long after the lotion had been absorbed by her skin. She didn't seem to mind.

"I'm not a whore," she murmured.

"I know."

"I never was a whore."

She leaned back against my hands, as if enjoying the massage.

"All those years, as a little girl growing up in the convent and listening to the priests and nuns, I thought Mary Magdalene was a sinner, a whore, a prostitute who perfumed herself for evil acts. They said she was the adulterous woman who would have been stoned to death for her sins if Jesus hadn't intervened."

"They were wrong," I said.

I could feel her back muscles tightening as the anger welled up inside her.

"As I child, I thought they were talking about some evil woman, someone who fell under Satan's control. Can you imagine how I felt when I realized that the woman they were talking about . . . the whore . . . the prostitute . . . was me in an earlier life?"

She stiffened, and I moved my hands up to her shoulders, working my fingers into the suddenly taut muscles, trying to relieve the stress.

"It was a mistake," I said. "The church admitted its mistake."

"I never heard that," she responded.

"Most people don't know," I agreed. "It was done quietly, by Pope Paul the Sixth."

Her neck muscles softened slightly. By now, the curious gaze of her middle-aged admirer was turned to other women who had arrived and were removing their tops.

"It happened in 1966," I continued. "The Church officially admitted it was wrong about Mary Magdalene. That she wasn't the sinner, and she wasn't the adulterous woman."

"They lied about me," she said. "Why did they do it?"

"The Vatican now says it was an error, a 'wrongful confabulation,' they called it. They said it was a confusion in the early teaching."

"Confusion? I don't think so," she said. "For almost two thousand years, they've been lying about me. Priests and bishops and popes have been telling the world I was a whore, proclaiming loudly that I was guilty of seven sins, that I perfumed my body for sinful acts, and now like thieves whispering in the night, they say they were mistaken?"

I worked harder at my massage, probing my fingers into the rigid band of sterno-mastoid muscles where they meet the trapezius.

"At least they admitted it," I said.

"If it was a mistake, they've kept their admission a secret. I haven't heard a single priest confess to that mistake in a Sunday sermon. All those years at Sunday Mass, they've been filling the minds of the faithful with the image of the sinful Magdalene, and now are they going to start rebuilding my image? I doubt it. And what about all those paintings showing me as a sinner? What about those?"

"There are even more paintings that show you witnessing Christ's death and resurrection," I said, and realizing the mistake I had made, quickly amended my words. "I mean . . . paintings that show Mary Magdalene witnessing Christ's death and resurrection."

All this time, I had been careful to keep Magdalena's identity separate in my own mind from that of the real Mary Magdalene. Now, with a single misplaced pronoun, I had performed my own act of confabulation.

Was it a slip of the tongue?

Or a Freudian slip?

Was it my subconscious sending me a message? Had I, at some subliminal level, already come to believe that Mary Magdalene lived on in this half-naked woman whose warm flesh rippled beneath my fingers?

Forty-Eight

"THEY DID IT on purpose," she said.

"Did what?"

"Ruined my good name. It must have started with Peter. And maybe Andrew. Even when I told them I saw Jesus my Christ was risen from the dead, they didn't believe me. He told me to give them the good news, but they didn't believe me. They never believed women."

It was another of those statements that was taken right out of the Gospels. A few days ago, I would have dismissed it as another factoid she probably read; now it had more of the ring of firsthand truth.

"We were all followers, equal followers. Jesus said there was no difference between man and woman. But Peter always refused to accept us as equals."

I guess I knew what was coming next.

"I told Jesus my Christ that I was afraid of Peter because he hated the female race."

It was almost a direct quote from *Pistis Sophia*.

"Peter complained to Jesus my Christ that 'women are not worthy of life,'" she said.

I remembered reading that stunning statement in the final paragraph of the Gospel of Thomas.

"Jesus my Christ told him that whoever is inspired by the Spirit is divinely ordained to speak, no matter whether it is man or woman."

Again, from *Pistis Sophia*.

I was waiting for her to give me more details, perhaps explain those gospel passages that described how Jesus used to kiss her on the lips. What was the real relationship, I wondered?

"He loved me more than the others," she said, as if hearing my unasked question. "And I loved him."

Her shoulders sagged. The tenseness drained from her muscles without any further help from me, and I was suddenly conscious of a strange sensation. As if I had been here before, performing the same activity. *Déjà vu*, I thought. It was a sensation I had experienced before, sometimes on hearing certain phrases, other times while walking through what should have been unfamiliar places. But this was a sensation more powerful than any I ever felt before. I withdrew my hands from Magdalena's naked back, but the uncanny feeling persisted. What triggered it, I wondered? It could have been the location, with its gently curving coastline reminding me of Orchard Beach in New York. Or a familiar sound or odor. Almost anything, I thought, could have prompted that sudden feeling of familiarity.

Yet it never lasted so long before. I wiped my hands and rose, as if repeating some long-forgotten action, and seemed to know what she was going to say before she said it. To prove to myself this wasn't some distortion of the limbic system or a sudden dislocation of the right-left brain coordination, my lips mouthed her next words quietly to myself before I heard them:

"I knew him in ways that only a woman could know a man."

It was a breathtaking claim, completely unsupported by anything in any of the four canonical gospels or the Pauline epistles.

Of course, the canonical gospels had been heavily edited over the years, with sections that even traditional Vatican scholars acknowledge were added by unknown hands, and other sections eliminated by early church leaders such as Iraneaus and Clement of Alexandria, and perhaps more significantly by the Emperor Constantine. The fact that there was no written record of the Magdalene's relationship with Jesus didn't automatically mean the relationship didn't exist. There was, after all, no written record of the famous "lost years of Christ," yet obviously he lived and traveled somewhere between the ages of 11 and 30. The absence of a reference proved nothing.

And when placed in the context of the distortions promulgated about the moral character of Mary Magdalene, the absence of such documentation takes on a different motive. One which might well be explained in the words Magdalena used next:

"They were jealous of me, I think. Jealous because they thought they could never be as close to him as I was."

This was extremely dangerous theological ground, I realized. If she had made any such statement to Serrano, it would explain the vicar general's decision to terminate the padre's contact with her. It would explain why no other psychiatrist had been assigned to her case. And it would certainly provide a motive for committing her to an institution where she could be kept sedated and prevented from telling her story to others. Even a fictitious story about a nun recalling an affair with Jesus Christ was bound to appeal to the more sensational tabloids and TV talk shows. The church certainly wouldn't want to face such embarrassment.

But was it really heresy? Even Hippolytus of Rome, that great second-century foe of heresy who was martyred for his faith, suggested that Mary Magdalene might have been the wife of Jesus Christ.

I stared at Magdalena's naked back, at the flawless skin, smooth and moist with lotion. I watched as she lifted her arms, as her hands went to pull back her hair. Was it possible that Jesus looked at the flesh of this woman with similar admiration in her earlier life? Did he admire the work of his Father, who had created so perfect a feminine torso, so lovely a flow of surface and curve, a creature worthy of divine love? Did he run his hand down her spine, the way I had done? I fell to my knees, almost giving in to the very human impulse to take her in my arms and hold her close, the way God intended man and woman to be.

What stopped me was the realization that indeed, she might once have been the object of divine love. And if that was so, who was I, a mere mortal, to place my hands on a woman whom the son of God had once possessed?

Helpless to intervene in Magdalena's newfound freedom, I watched as she reclined on the sand, her body on display for any who passed by. I knew she wouldn't listen to my pleadings for modesty. What sort of woman was this, I wondered, who would claim to be a disciple of Christ, who would bemoan her portrayal as a licentious woman, and yet was now willing to expose her flesh for all to see?

There were hints of what might have transpired between Jesus and the Magdalene in the Gnostic gospels, which acknowledged a much deeper relationship between them. But even those records had been excised. No complete version of the Gospel of Mary was known to exist. Most copies had been methodically destroyed by competing sects in the early days of the

Church. And of those fragments that were left, key sections were destroyed in a mysterious fire in Cairo in 1966. Those who intended to keep such matters from public view were apparently still active. Active enough, I wondered, to eliminate anyone who might get close to Magdalena?

Whether her recollections were fictitious or genuine, I wanted to hear more of them. I wanted to compare her story with what I knew from my studies at Mount Athos and what I had read in Serrano's library. And, I'm ashamed to admit, I was as eager for what amounted to sacred gossip as those who seek the latest celebrity gossip. But it was not to be.

She drew away from me.

"I shouldn't have said that," she whispered, looking around to see if anyone other than me might have overheard her. "Those things shouldn't be spoken aloud. Not even between the two of us."

She quickly replaced the top of her bathing suit, and suddenly modest again, reached in the bag for her shirt. Only then did I realize a small crowd had gathered at the edge of the beach, waiting for her. Among them were a few of the women who had witnessed her "cure" of the young boy. In the middle of the crowd was the charcoal artist of the night before. He was making hasty, but fairly accurate copies of the sketch he made last night. Now he had a young assistant, selling them as quickly as he produced them. The crowd parted as Magdalena stepped onto the beach walk. At first, she smiled. But when one of the woman started to bless herself with the Sign of the Cross, Magdalena's smile froze. Much to the shock of the onlookers, she grabbed the woman's hand.

"*Arrêtez!*" She commanded the woman to stop. Frightened at first, the woman dropped back. A murmur ran through the crowd, which seemed in its collective religious wisdom to decide her action was an example of saintly humility and reached out to touch her clothing.

The fervor of the faithful has always intrigued me, with its ability to transform living people, corpses and bones and articles of clothing into objects of veneration. What I find even more fascinating is the evidence that contact with such objects has in many cases healed the sick, cured the incurable, answered prayers, and worked other wonders that are deserving of the word *miracle*. Whether the saintly relics possess such thaumaturgical powers themselves or whether the supernatural results are a function of the power of concentrated belief has never been properly documented. Now here I was, with the opportunity to study the phenomenon firsthand. I ducked into a small souvenir shop and purchased a crucifix without Magdalena's seeing what I bought. The clerk obligingly boxed and gift-wrapped it for me.

Catching up with Magdalena, I followed along a few steps behind her, constantly jostled by the crowd. Just before we entered the Moorish Quarter, I broke free to pick up that day's Barcelona newspaper from a newsstand. I wanted to see whether they had yet correctly identified Padre Serrano as the victim of the bomb blast.

Instead, I found myself trying to translate a story about another dead man. This one in Barcelona. A citizen of Lebanon, who was suffocated in his hospital bed. The photograph accompanying the article was the same one I had seen in his passport.

The murder victim was Professor Naghib Abramakian.

And once again, I was named as the prime suspect.

The only good thing about the story was that it didn't include my photograph. Still, I looked around nervously, to see if anyone was following me. Between the normal midday jam of tourists on the beach walk and the crowd that was trailing Magdalena, it was impossible to sort out anyone who looked suspicious.

Except for one man. Technically, he wasn't following me. He was stationed on the walkway at the top of the Chateau Royal. From that position, he could see everything that happened in Collioure. Which meant he had watched Magdalena strip off the top of her bathing suit, watched me massage her back, and was watching me right now reading about myself in the newspaper.

When he saw me looking up at him, he drew back from the edge, back into the hard midday shadows. But not before I recognized him.

It was the old priest who helped me up in front of the cathedral.

Forty-Nine

"BUT HE WAS alive when we left him at the hospital," Magdalena said.

We were in my room, where she had just translated the story for me. Quoting *Coronel* Velarde, the newspaper article explained that the *Guardia* arrived only moments after Abramakian was murdered. Hospital attendants had seen a man and a woman fitting the description of two fugitives sought in a terrorist bombing in Valencia. One of the fugitives, a woman, was believed to be a nun who had been abducted from her convent, and was probably an unwilling accomplice. The male fugitive,

Theophanes Nikonos, had been arrested previously in New York City on charges of murder, embezzlement, and fraud. The fugitives were believed to have crossed the border into France. Interpol had been notified, and French authorities promised their cooperation.

"We should call the police," Magdalena said.

"And tell them what?" I countered. "That we're here in Collioure, so they can come and arrest us? They'll find us quickly enough on their own, I think."

"We could tell them the Professor was alive when we left him."

"And two minutes later he was dead? Who would believe us?"

"They'd believe me. I'm a nun."

"A nun who thinks she's Mary Magdalene," I pointedly reminded her. "I'm sure the Cardinal's office told the *Guardia* all about you, about the Vatican psychiatrists and how they were going to have you committed to a mental institution. The *Guardia* is not going to believe anything you say."

"We could play them the professor's tapes. You haven't mailed the tapes yet, have you?"

"All that would prove was that Abramakian was alive when we were there. They'd use the time-code on the videotapes to prove there wasn't enough time for anyone else to enter Abramakian's room before the *Guardia* arrived."

She sat down on the bed and covered her face with her hands.

"Maybe I should just give myself up," she sighed. "Let them do with me what they will."

"Hey, come on, what happened to your fighting spirit?" I asked. "A little while ago you were angry about the way Mary Magdalene's reputation was destroyed. You sounded like you wanted to do something about it. Now it's happening all over again. Except this time, the accusation is murder. That's a lot more serious than being called a prostitute."

"But how can they believe such a thing about me?"

"It's easy," I said. "I've been through this kind of situation before, so I know how it works. The police look for patterns of behavior, just like a psychologist does. And in your case. . . I should say, in *our* case . . . the pattern suggests deviant behavior."

"Deviant?"

"Well, for starters, there's your disruptive behavior in the chapel and at the convent, tearing up the bibles and arguing with the priests at Mass."

"But that was all about religion and the mistakes in the Gospels."

"Law-enforcement officials aren't concerned with matters of theology. They'll see your actions as violent behavior, outbursts against authority, criminal destruction of property."

"But . . . nobody called the police in those matters."

"Of course not. The Cardinal's office will say it was an internal affair, that they decided you might be mentally unstable, so they called in a psychiatrist. That was Padre Serrano. And after working with you for a while, Serrano was killed in a bomb blast."

"They can't think I had anything to do with the bombing."

"At the time, they didn't. I was the primary suspect. But the police will be looking at what happened next. An ambulance was sent to take you to a mental institution. Automatically, they've got you labeled as a psychotic, possibly dangerous."

"I'm not crazy," she protested. "You know I'm not crazy."

"Look at it from the police point of view. Just before the ambulance shows up to take you to the mental hospital, you disappear from the convent. Last seen in the company of the man they believe killed Serrano."

"But you didn't . . ."

"Of course not, but suddenly, we're linked. Two fugitives, one running from the police, the other from a mental institution."

"You make it sound so awful," she moaned.

"It gets worse. We head to Barcelona, where we visit Abramakian in his hospital room. By the time the *Guardia* shows up, Abramakian is dead, and we're headed for the French border."

"*O, Dios mío!*" she moaned. "What can we do now?"

"Keep going," I said as I began to pack my meager belongings in a shopping bag. I removed the charcoal sketch of Jesus from the back of the door. "The only thing we can do is keep going and hope that nobody recognizes us."

The street artist in Valencia, the one who drew the likeness of the backpacker, had provided me with a tube in which to carry his sketch. Magdalena watched as I removed that first portrait from the tube and spread it out on the bed, where I intended to roll both sketches together.

"Who is that man?" she asked when she saw the drawing of the backpacker.

"Someone I saw in Valencia."

"He looks familiar," she said. She rose from the bed and studied the drawing.

"You've seen him before?" I asked.

"Yes, I think so. Yes, I'm sure of it. I recognize him. But usually he carries a blue backpack."

A blue backpack! I held my breath while I waited for her to continue.

"I've seen him at the cathedral," she said slowly, reaching back into her memory. "He's usually in the company of an old priest. A very old priest . . . and very tall. He walks with his head bent, and this young man is often with him. Who is this young man?"

"I think he's the man who killed Padre Serrano."

"I don't believe you," she said. "He seemed like such a nice man. He always smiled at me. Both of them did."

"Even killers enjoy their work," I said.

Fifty

THE TRUTH IS, I didn't really think they were here to kill Magdalena. I was convinced it was me they were after.

Padre Serrano had warned me our fate was already sealed by the mysterious "watchers" who noted everyone who came in contact with Magdalena. She herself was safe from harm, he had said cryptically. But he and I were both doomed, he warned. At the time, I shrugged off the comment. After all, what harm was there in talking to an innocent young nun?

Moments after telling me about Magdalena, Serrano was dead. And moments after interviewing Magdalena, Professor Abramakian was dead, too. Now the "watchers," whoever they were, had somehow managed to trace us to Collioure. I had no illusions why they were here.

While Magdalena went to her room to shower, I tried to concoct an escape plan. After twenty minutes of desperate concentration, I had come up with absolutely nothing that made any sense. Wherever we went, we could be seen from the Chateau Royal. By the time she returned to my room, I decided my only hope was to try to get to the car and lose them on the open road. But to get to the car, I needed help.

Magdalena watched as I pressed the preprogrammed number on the cell phone DesRosier had supplied me. The familiar operator's voice answered almost immediately and asked me to please hold for a moment.

"Who are you calling?" Magdalena asked.

"The man who hired me. He's the only one who can help us."

I waited a few seconds longer while the electronic switching system connected me to the man who was paying the bills. He wasted no time on niceties.

"You are in trouble, Mr. Nikonos," DesRosier said. "I have been reading about you in the newspapers."

"It's all a mistake."

"I'm sure it is. I must say, the way you extricated Sister Mariamme from the convent was brilliant. And the way you avoided the police in Barcelona, superb. I assume you are now somewhere in France. Are you making progress with your investigation?"

"I'm having a bit of a problem right now," I said.

"You mean the watchers are after you?" I could swear I almost heard him smiling, as if he didn't take the danger seriously. "The old priest and the young one?"

"They followed us here. They know where we're staying."

"That was very careless of you," DesRosier said. "Is Sister Mariamme with you right now?"

"Yes. She's fine."

"I mean literally, Mr. Nikonos. Is she in the same room with you?"

"Yes, she is."

"I trust you're not getting . . . how shall I put this . . . emotionally involved with her?"

His voice had taken on a harder tone.

"Of course not," I lied.

"Good. Very good. Because I would be very, very disappointed if anything happened between the two of you. If you understand what I'm saying."

"I understand," I said, momentarily puzzled by the direction of the conversation. "But that's not what I called about. I need some help getting her out of town."

"As a patron of the convent, I'm very concerned about the well-being of our nuns," he went on, as if he hadn't heard me. There was a hint of irritation in his voice, a reminder that he considered me not only his employee, but also his inferior. "I wouldn't want anything . . . unexpected . . . to happen to Sister Mariamme. The repercussions could be quite serious."

"You're not listening to me," I said impatiently. "I said I need help getting us out of town."

"Don't snap at me, Mr. Nikonos. I am well aware of the gravity of the situation. You are calling from your hotel in, where is it, Collioure?"

"How did you know?"

"Come, come. You don't think I would let you out there on your own, do you? Collioure is Basque country. I have men there who can help you."

"Tito and Manolo?" I asked. "You sent them here?"

"Fortunately for you, yes."

"How did they know we were here? I never saw them following us."

"Tito and Manolo are very good at what they do," DesRosier said. "Wait twenty minutes. Then you can leave Madame Gramont's house. By that time, the problem will be solved."

I hadn't mentioned Madame Gramont's name. Was that information supplied by the Basques . . . or did my billionaire employer have other sources?

"Now, if you please, I wish to speak with Sister Mariamme," he said.

It seemed a reasonable request, so I handed her the phone. Magdalena at first seemed puzzled, but gradually warmed up and soon was smiling and having what looked and sounded like a delightful conversation with my employer. Unfortunately, I understood very little of what she was saying, the conversation taking place entirely in rapid bursts of French.

"He seems like a very nice man," she said, still smiling after she hung up. "He's very easy to talk to."

"A bit glib," I muttered.

"What is this 'glib?' I don't know that word."

"A fast talker," I replied.

"Ah yes," she said, not understanding the true meaning of the idiom. "We always speak more rapidly in French than in English."

"We have twenty minutes before we can leave," I said. I set up my interview equipment. "We might as well use the time to continue our work."

In fact, an incident on the beachwalk had reminded me of a question that had been troubling me.

"When we were coming back from the beach, a woman started to make the Sign of the Cross. You stopped her. The way you did it, I thought was very rude."

"Yes, I guess it was." She bowed her head. "I'm sorry if I offended her."

"Padre Serrano said you were caught destroying crucifixes in the chapel, and that you had to be restrained from doing the same thing in the cathedral. Is that true?"

"Yes," she murmured. I glanced at the voice-stress analyzer. Her one-word answer had the indicator needle going wild. It was curious that the mere mention of the crucifix seemed to elicit so powerful a response. Why was the subject so sensitive?

"I have a gift for you," I said. I offered her the small package I bought in the souvenir shop. Her eyes lit up.

"What is it?"

"Open it and see."

With childish delight, she tore at the wrapper. I kept the camera carefully trained on her face to record her response. In retrospect, it was probably one of the most cold-hearted tricks I could have played on her. But I was getting tired of these question-and-answer sessions, and wanted to witness for myself her reaction to a crucifix.

She hesitated before opening the box.

"Thank you," she said. "Thank you, Theo."

The smile on her face froze when she opened the box.

Staring up at her was the crucified Christ, nailed to his cross, the most sacred icon of the Christian faith.

She dropped it on the bed, recoiling as if her fingers had been burnt by the contact. She turned on me, those lovely eyes flaring with anger, that beautiful mouth frozen in an angry scowl.

"How could you do this to me, Theo?" Tears flooded into her eyes. "I thought you knew better than to confront me with this! It's awful! Take it away!"

She lunged for the camcorder, which had been automatically recording her reaction for posterity, but I managed to pull it out of her reach.

"Why, Theo? Why?" she moaned. "Why hurt me like this?"

Fifty-One

MORE CHASTENED THAN shocked, I gathered up the crucifix, replaced it in its box, and put the box in a drawer. I waited in silence until she recovered and dried her eyes. It was an awful thing to do, I realized. I feared I had jeopardized our relationship, and with it, the opportunity for any further interviews.

But when she recovered, she offered me a wan smile and began to explain. Unexpectedly, she asked me to turn on the video cam, so that her explanation would be recorded.

"I'm sorry," she said. "But I can't bear to look at a crucifix."

"Why?"

"Because it's a terrible thing. You have to understand . . . I was there. I saw him standing there when he was condemned. His garments were bloodied and torn from the terrible scourging the night before. They didn't even have the decency . . ." She struggled to maintain control of herself. "They didn't even have the decency to hide his wounds." She closed her eyes, as if that would help blot out the memory. "I followed him when he carried the cross through the streets of Jerusalem. His mother and the other women were there. You can't imagine how we felt, watching him stumble, watching him bleed. There were some people jeering him, cursing him for having claimed he was the Son of God. They turned on him because they didn't believe God would allow his Son to be humiliated like this. And to be very honest, even I wondered about that.

"They taunted him with the crown of thorns, but except for that, they treated him like any other criminal who was sentenced to death. The scourging at the pillar was common practice. And the cross, that evil monstrosity, I'll never forget what it looked like." She closed her eyes. "When the memories of my past life started coming back, that was the first memory I had. The cross on which he died was made of two heavy sections of pine tree. The vertical section was dragged by horses to Golgotha, where a hole had been dug to receive it. That section was at least five meters long. The horizontal section was about two and a half meters long. That was the section they made him carry through Jerusalem."

"He didn't carry the whole cross?" I asked. This was another obscure fact that could be checked, I thought.

"It would have been too heavy," she said. "The condemned usually carried only the horizontal crossbar. But the one they chose for him must have weighed over a hundred kilos. They lashed it to his shoulders so that he couldn't drop it or even drag it. Do you know, they didn't even take the bark off when they tied the sections together? They wanted to make it as painful as possible for him. The bark bit into his shoulders, gouging out deep wounds in his flesh. It was too horrible to watch, yet how could I turn away? It seemed impossible that he would survive the journey. He fell, I don't know how many times, but it was definitely more than three. He was losing blood. We tried to give him water, to wipe his face, but the guards pushed us away. When it looked like he might die before he reached Golgotha, the guards let Simon the Cyrenean help him for a while. That was a very brave thing Simon did. Because he revealed his devotion like that, I thought the guards might kill him, too. I didn't see Peter or any of the others. They must have been hiding.

"When we reached Golgotha, two crosses were already in place. The other men to be crucified were tied to the cross, rather than nailed. That final torture was reserved for Jesus my Christ."

She wasn't looking at me as she talked. She was staring out the window, her gaze focused on some point where the sea met the sky.

"They stripped him of his clothing. All of his clothing," she repeated the words for emphasis. "He was totally naked, not like the man in the loincloth you see in the paintings or on the crucifixes in church, but totally naked. They did it because they knew the sight would be so shocking to us, we would always remember him that way, a humiliation that would stay with us for their rest of our lives." She paused. "He looked so pitiful. This man who had drawn thousands of people, who had preached of love and forgiveness, who had reached out to the lame and the sick, to women and slaves and children, who could have done so much more if he had been allowed to continue his ministry . . . stood before us naked and bleeding, so weak from carrying the heavy beam, he didn't have the strength left to close his mouth. His breath came in gasps. His body was bathed in blood. And when they started to nail him to the cross . . . *Dios mío,* the spikes were so big . . ."

She started to tremble. This time, I put aside all thoughts of religious propriety and took her in my arms to comfort her. Gradually, her trembling stopped. Pulling herself away from me, she continued.

"When they nailed his hands to the crossbeam, he went into convulsions. He screamed, and when he did, blood came out of his mouth and nose. It was the most horrible sight anyone could ever see. His mother, Mary, fainted in my arms. I was accustomed to the brutality of the Romans, but they treated him in those final moments as horribly as they treated those who were convicted of murdering Roman soldiers. And this was a man whose only crime was to preach the word of God. He stole nothing. He killed no one. He broke no Roman law. Yet they seemed intent on making his final moments as excruciating as possible for Jesus my Christ.

"It took four men using ropes to raise the crossbeam into position so that it could be lashed to the main post, with Jesus my Christ hanging in agony as they moved the crossbeam into position. Every movement brought screams of pain. Only after the crossbeam was in place did they finally nail his feet to the bottom platform. The guards laughed and joked then, and sat down to eat their lunches while they waited for him to die.

"When he was carrying the crossbeam, his blood was mixed with sweat and glistened on his face. But hanging there in the hot sun, all that came from his pores was blood, which began to dry and turn to crust. When one of the soldiers finally stuck a lance in his side, there was little blood left to come out. I stood there with his mother, and her sister Mary, the wife of Clopas, and Mary Salome, and a few other women who followed Jesus my Christ from Galilee. None of the twelve male apostles were there. The only men who stood with us were Joseph of Arimethea, John the Evangelist, and Nicodemus, who had defended him in the Sanhedrin." She shook her head and said, sadly, not angrily, "We were the only disciples who witnessed his death. Peter, who had denied him, was in hiding with Andrew and the others. They saw nothing of the horror of the cross, the terrible agonies he suffered on that cursed tree."

Her voice cracked as she turned to me. With tears streaming down her cheeks, and mouth agape, she was the perfect replication of the anguished Magdalene in Grunewald's Isenheim Altarpiece.

"And you dare ask why I can't stand the sight of the instrument of his death?" she moaned. "How can anyone glorify a man by erecting images of his final moments?"

"He died for our sins," I mouthed the words that had been driven into my mind by countless nuns and priests. "He didn't have to die. He gave his life for us."

"That is not what proved him to be divine," she responded, wiping her eyes with a tissue. "Many people die so that others may live. Everyday, there are people who willingly sacrifice their lives for others. That makes them heroes; it doesn't make them divine."

She was right, of course, and my thoughts immediately turned back to Laura Duquesne, who willingly took the bullet that was meant for me.

"He suffered for us," I mouthed another set of words, realizing their inherent philosophical error as soon as I voiced them. As sacrilegious as it would once have seemed to me, I now had to admit history was filled with Christians who had suffered as much, or even more than the founder of the faith. Some of them, like those grilled over hot coals, or slowly cooked in oil during the Inquisition, endured sufferings administered not at the hands of Romans or pagans, but by so-called followers of Christ, with the enthusiastic endorsement of their ecclesiastical leaders.

"But the cross is a symbol," I said, still unwilling to completely give in to her point view. "It helps us remember Christ's mission on Earth."

"If a man was killed by a dagger, would we revere the dagger? If we truly loved a person who died in an auto accident, would we remember her by an image of the car in which she died? Does anyone in America pray to the bullet that killed Kennedy? I saw what the cross did to Jesus my Christ, how he suffered and died on it. To have the instrument of his death become the most sacred symbol of the faith he founded does nothing to honor his memory. To celebrate his death does not honor his life."

"What should we celebrate?" I asked, feeling suddenly like the student that Serrano must have become.

"His resurrection from the dead is what we should celebrate," she responded. "It was his resurrection that proved his divinity to a skeptical world. If not for his resurrection, Peter and the others would have gone back to fishing. If not for his resurrection, there would be no Christian community. It is his resurrection that should be celebrated, not his death."

She looked around, as if she had forgotten for a moment where she was.

"I'm sorry," she said. "I didn't mean to preach to you. It's just that the cross has terrible memories for me. I'd like to take down all the crosses from all the churches in the world and destroy them."

"You'd also have to take down all the paintings of the Crucifixion from all the museums in the world." I said it with a smile, trying to lighten the mood a little. "And all the reproductions of those paintings in all the books in all the homes and libraries in all the world."

"You think it's a hopeless goal, don't you," she said, still serious.

"Too much has happened in the last two thousand years to be undone by one person."

"That depends on the person," she said.

It was a conversation that would have to be continued at another time, I thought as I glanced at my watch. DesRosier had promised we could leave safely in twenty minutes. The time was up. I paid Madame Gramont, and after checking the street, we took our chances.

DesRosier was true to his word. No one bothered us as we headed up the hill to the street where I had left the car. No old priest or young backpacker jumped out from between the buildings to challenge us. No one seemed to be following us. The car was exactly where I had left it.

What I didn't expect was to find Manolo and Tito waiting there for us, too.

Tito's seemingly lifeless body was draped over the hood.

Manolo's larger figure, too heavy for his assailant to lift, had been left sprawled on the ground by the driver's side of the car.

At first glance, they both appeared to be dead.

Fifty-Two

THE ATTACK MUST have occurred only moments earlier, conducted with such speed and silent efficiency, it hadn't attracted the attention of anyone in the immediate vicinity. Except for us, the street was empty. The nearby houses were mostly small white stucco buildings with red-tiled roofs, neatly manicured shrubbery, and low stone walls. As was the summer custom in the South of France, window shutters and doors were closed to keep out the midday heat. Although I was certain we were being watched, I couldn't detect where the attackers might be hiding.

Magdalena froze. She at first seemed too frightened to react. Yet, as if another personality was struggling within her, she quickly started forward to see if she could help.

"They're not dead," I assured her.

A quick examination revealed a single wound on each of the Basques: a blow to the forehead which resulted in minimal bleeding, but left a rather large and ugly contusion that would certainly grow in size over the next few days. The location of the wounds indicated a frontal assault, which meant they had seen their attackers. Yet the assault had been carried out with a speed that left them defenseless. It was hard to believe that the old priest, against whom the Basques were supposed to protect me, was capable of such swift violence.

While Magdalena watched, I checked their breathing and pulse rates, which seemed relatively normal. With her help, I dragged them away from the car and into the shade of an olive tree. Given the circumstances, that was as much of the Good Samaritan as I dared to be. Even that, I feared, might be my undoing. If this was a trap, I was already in it.

Trying to hide my fear from Magdalena, I carefully surveyed the neighborhood. Halfway up the block, an orange-striped cat padded out into the street, stopped to look back at us, and continued on its way.

Other than that, there was no suspicious movement, no activity of any kind to attract my attention. Yet I couldn't ignore the fact that violence and death seemed to be hovering about me. This was no time to take chances. Since no enemy seemed to be lurking in the bushes, my attention turned to the car itself. I didn't know much about car bombs, other than what I read in the newspapers or saw in Bruce Willis movies. Supposedly, sticks of dynamite or dough-like plastic explosive were usually wired to the engine, or attached beneath the car. I dropped to my knees and looked under the frame. I wasn't sure what I should be searching for, but I knew what the underside of a car looked like. All I saw under the Opel was the usual muffler, catalytic converter, frame, brake lines and cables, all coated with a black layer of road grime. Anything that didn't belong there would have been instantly noticeable.

The engine compartment was a different story. It was a confusing tangle of wires, many of them connected to cylindrical objects, any of which could contain a bomb as easily as brake fluid or a/c refrigerant. It made me realize just how mechanically illiterate I was. If I survived long enough to get back to New York, I vowed to spend a little more time looking over the shoulder of the guy at Jiffy Lube. As with the underside, I ended up relying on oil stains and road grime to determine if anything had recently been tampered with, and prayed I was right.

In as calm a voice as I could muster, I suggested to Magdalena that she check the two Basques while I tried to start the engine. She was too innocent of things such as car bombs to suspect that I wanted to keep her far enough away from the vehicle in case my inspection proved inadequate.

My nerves were ready to explode when I turned the key in the ignition.

There was a short click that I hadn't noticed before, followed by a roar and a wild vibration. It took a moment before I realized that the engine was racing madly, the result of a panicky driver unwittingly flooring the gas pedal. I backed off on the gas and let the engine settle down to a steady drone. Just to be on the safe side, I left the engine running and stepped out of the car. I waited a full minute before getting back in. Only then did I motion for Magdalena to join me.

Such behavior might seem ludicrous, my nervousness an overreaction. Having survived one bombing attempt, however, I didn't want to give my enemies a second chance.

My goal now was get us out of there as quickly and as safely as I could.

The car seemed to run fine, which I found surprising. It would have been a simple matter to cut a wire or disconnect the battery or pour some sugar into the gas tank. But everything seemed normal. Nevertheless, I kept watching the gauges and testing the brakes to be certain a more devious form of tampering hadn't been performed on the vehicle. The rear-view mirror revealed an empty road behind us. I didn't relax until we were half-way to Perpignan, speeding past the vast salt-drying flats that lined both sides of the highway. There were no other cars anywhere in sight.

"Did you know those men?" Magdalena asked.

"They were supposed to be our bodyguards."

"Bodyguards?" She was puzzled. "I don't know that word."

"A bodyguard is somebody that protects people from harm."

"Like you're doing with me?"

"Well, sort of."

"Those bodyguards, were they employed by the man I spoke to on the telephone? The one you said was the *patrón* of the *convento?*"

"Yes," I said. "I didn't want the bodyguards at first, but I guess he was worried about our safety."

"And this car, did he supply the car, too?"

"Fortunately, yes," I said. "If we didn't have the car, we'd probably be in *Guardia* custody right now."

"And the telephone, too. Does the telephone also belong to him?"

"It's for emergency use," I said. "He set it up so that we can call each other by pressing a single button. To call him, all I have to do is press the button marked 1. To call me, I think he said he presses the button marked number 5 on his phone. It's what they call speed dialing. It automatically connects us with each other."

"And you can talk to each other wherever you are? Without any wires?"

"That's right," I said. "It's modern technology."

"Amazing," she said. And then added, "He seems to have thought of everything, this *patrón*."

"He's very successful, very wealthy. Men like him always think of everything. That's how they get to be wealthy. They're always thinking two or three steps ahead of everyone else."

"You're very lucky to know someone like him."

"It wasn't very lucky for the bodyguards," I said.

"But still, the *patrón* was trying to help us. And for that, I think we should be grateful to him."

Should we, I wondered?

For a wealthy businessman who must have hundreds of other matters competing for his attention, he seemed to be showing an unusual amount of interest in my investigation. My first impression, that he was an effete and not particularly likable patrician with a strong Machiavellian nature, was proving to be correct. Despite his quick response to my request for help, I was troubled by the fact that he was so closely tracking our movements. He knew exactly where we were staying, and apparently even where the car was parked. Didn't he have better things to do with his time? I was troubled by the fact that he sent the Basques along to protect whatever interest he had in my mission. What troubled me most of all was his apparent change in attitude toward Magdalena. Initially, he said he wanted me to prove her claims were fraudulent. But the distrust he exhibited at our first meeting certainly seemed to have dissolved rather quickly. Their telephone conversation had been unusually warm and friendly.

And his warning to me about any emotional involvement with her certainly was unexpected. Did he have some hidden agenda?

Maybe I was reading too much into the situation.

And maybe, just maybe, I was a little jealous of Magdalena's growing interest in her protector.

Fifty-Three

THE INVISIBLE HAND that seemed to be guiding me was now shepherding us deeper into Magdalenean territory. We were heading north into Provence, where I hoped to make it to Arles by nightfall. From there, the most important part of my investigation would begin.

If I say that I was becoming convinced of Magdalena's story, I should point out that the operative word was *becoming*. Some investigators who boast of having discovered "proof " of reincarnation base their claims on much less credible evidence than I had already accumulated. They might consider the linguistic evidence alone enough to make the case. Certainly the tapes containing Abramakian's lengthy examination of her language skills would create a sensation within the scientific community, forcing many skeptics to consider the rest of her prior-existence testimony with a seriousness they might not otherwise display. The "cures" were perhaps even more dramatic, and if they held up under future medical scrutiny, could create a burst of religious fervor that would go a long way in forcing the church to investigate her claims with similar seriousness.

But as for me, the most important part of my investigation still lay ahead, in the land where Mary Magdalene spent the last years of her life.

Unlike some scholars, I tended to believe the old legends of the Magdalene's arrival in France. My belief was based on a careful analysis of the notes Padre Serrano left in his own copy of the bible, in which he linked particular portions of the New Testament with the Book of Acts and the Epistles of Paul. The Padre's marginal notes pointed out that, with the exception of the Mother of Christ, Mary Magdalene is unquestionably the most important woman named in the four canonical Gospels. Wherever her name appears with that of other women, Serrano highlighted the fact that she is always named first. Large exclamation points added emphasis to each Gospel's depiction of her role: that she and other women provided for the support of Christ and the twelve male Apostles. That she witnessed the Crucifixion and helped carry Christ into the tomb. That alone at night, she wept outside the tomb. And of course, that she was the first person to witness the resurrection, and was instructed by Christ to "spread the good news" to the others. Even the most traditional theologians would concur that she was a central figure in the Christ story. When all the other apostles deserted Christ, she was the one loyal follower who witnessed the passion, the crucifixion, the death, and the resurrection of the Savior.

And yet, as Serrano's notes pointed out, she is missing entirely from Luke's Acts of the Apostles, and from the Letters of Paul, both of which pick up and interpret the Christian story after the Resurrection. It was a fact that I never noticed before. I reread those portions of the bible twice, but Serrano had made no mistake. The woman who followed Christ from his preaching in Galilee to his death and resurrection disappeared completely from the New Testament after she delivered the Good News of the Resurrection to the male apostles!

Why?

After all, Luke's Acts of the Apostles describes the activities of the twelve, describes the work of Paul, the formation of the early church, and the important role of women in that infant church in great detail. Yet he never mentions the Magdalene. It is possible, of course, that any mention of her was purposely eliminated by later editors of Scripture. Theologians acknowledge such things were commonplace when the church was trying to establish its primacy over competing sects. However, that theory falls apart when contrasted with the canonical gospels, in which the Magdalene's central role as the first witness to the divinity of Christ remains untouched. It is inconceivable that those anonymous heavy-handed editors would write her out of Luke's Acts, without performing the same sort of censorship on the four canonical gospels. It is also inconceivable that the woman who played so prominent a role in the most important part of the Christic experience would allow her voice to be stilled. The logical conclusion is that Mary Magdalene is not mentioned in Luke's Book of Acts because the author of Acts had no further contact with her. The Magdalene must have already left Judea for France.

Serrano's theory also is further supported in the Pauline Epistles. Paul didn't begin his preaching and writing until after his conversion on the road to Damascus. The "conversion," according to his own accounts, took place after Christ's death and resurrection, since by Paul's own words, Christ appeared to him *after* appearing to the twelve male apostles and the 500 other unnamed apostles. After his conversion, Paul traveled much of the Mediterranean region, exhorting and describing the growing Christian communities.

Yet as Serrano pointed out, nowhere does Paul mention the woman who carried the news of Christ's resurrection to the apostles. Granted, Paul's writing shows a strong prejudice against women. Yet he describes the work of a number of women in the early Christian communities. So why not mention Mary Magdalene, even if damning her with faint praise? The logical conclusion is that he never met the Magdalene. If she left for France shortly after the crucifixion, as the old legends insist, she would have been absent from Judea at the time Paul was there.

As many bibles do, Serrano's also included a map of Paul's travels, which placed him in almost every country in the Mediterranean Basin. Except, as Serrano noted in the margin, for the Roman province of Gaul, where Mary Magdalene had gone. The most important figure in the Resurrection story is never mentioned by Paul, because he never met her. He never visited Gaul, the one land in which she preached and spread the good news of the Lord.

The fact that Paul never mentions the Magdalene also undercuts the claims of those who, since the sixth century, have promoted the fiction that she was martyred and buried at Ephesus. Although some biblical scholars have raised doubts about the Pauline authorship of *The Epistle to the Ephesians*, it is well documented that he lived in Ephesus for at least three years, devoting his time to building up the Christian community and preaching of Christ's resurrection. It is inconceivable that he would not have been aware of the presence in Ephesus of the first witness to the resurrection, or that Mary would not have taken an active role in that Christian community. Unless, of course, she wasn't there.

It was a brilliant and original piece of biblical detective work, an exegesis worthy of the finest Vatican scholars. That the analysis came from the mind of an otherwise obscure Spanish Jesuit was astonishing; that his only reward for his efforts was to die in a bombing was outrageous; that the two events were somehow connected was indisputable. Which is why I would have eventually come to Provence, in search of answers, even if events in Barcelona and Collioure hadn't forced me north.

Magdalena was silent as we drove up through the mostly flat coastal plains, skirting the eastern edge of the Pyrenees. The highway was smooth and straight and fairly uncrowded. Much of the traffic along the early part of the route was heavy trucks coming up from Spain. We passed quickly through Perpignan, a half-hour later through Narbonne, and in another half-hour passed Montpelier. As we headed north on the A9, we started picking up more tourist traffic. It was late afternoon when we passed into the southern part of Provence. It was as if we entered another country.

Physical scientists have never been able to satisfactorily explain the magical quality of the sunlight that shines on Provence. Some contend the alleged magical quality is an illusion, a harmless myth fostered by local promoters and the French Tourist Office. But anyone looking at the works of Van Gogh, Cézanne, Matisse, Courbet, even Gaugin before he left for the South Pacific, cannot help but marvel at the heightened color and brightness of the work they did in Provence. In fact, the landscape took on a different character as we drove. Magdalena commented that the roadside poppies seemed more brilliant, the colors of the landscape deeper and more intense. It was as if the atmosphere itself had changed. If she was delighted by what they saw, I was equally delighted by the opportunity that lay ahead.

Provence would be the final, most crucial testing ground for her claims. It was one thing to talk about memories and personalities from previous lives in the quiet of a convent or hotel room. It would be another thing entirely to see if she could retrace or recognize, without any prompting from me, landmarks or locations that she had never visited before in this lifetime. Granted, many of the places to which I was taking her might be totally unrecognizable after two millennia. But even that fact, depending on what changes had taken place, could be a form of proof.

About an hour south of Arles, I turned off the A9 and headed toward the sea without any explanation. By now, Magdalena was accustomed to my taking evasive detours to insure we weren't being followed. She didn't question where we were going.

The turnoff led us onto a narrow two-lane asphalt road bordered on both sides by low shrubs and salt grass. It wasn't a very scenic route. The sea was still far out of sight. The land was flat, with no buildings except for an occasional squatter-like structure. Most of the land was planted, surprisingly, with rice. A herd of black cattle rested in one field. A white egret stood on the roof of a small shed. In another field, three goats were tearing at a low shrub. A hand-lettered sign advertising *Promenades a cheval* stood above a stable of sturdy white horses.

Up ahead, on the other side of *Aigues-Mortes*, was *les Saintes-Marie-de-la-Mer*, the site where the boat carrying the Marys and their companions was supposed to have landed. I was waiting to see at what point Magdalena would claim to recognize where we were. I was also keeping a close look-out to be sure she didn't see any signs that might give away the location.

We were on the southern edge of the famous Camargue, the vast marshy delta created by the Rhône where it empties into the sea. Much of the Camargue is a nature preserve, home to herds of wild white horses and the greatest variety of aquatic birds to be found anywhere around the Mediterranean.

We passed through the medieval walled city of *Aigues-Mortes,* which elicited no response from Magdalena. That was understandable. Although the town is known to every schoolboy in France as the place where Louis IX set off for the Crusades, it didn't exist prior to 1241.

I turned off at the first road, another narrow two-lane strip of asphalt, this one lined along one side with rusted barbed-wire fencing. There were still no road signs to tip off Magdalena, but she seemed to have come alert. In spite of the flat and uninteresting terrain outside the car, she was sitting up, as excited as a little girl coming home. She was constantly turning her head, looking from one side of the road to the other, as if she expected to see someone she knew.

Up ahead, a thick pink blanket lifted itself languidly from a swampy area and rose slowly into the sky. I thought my eyes were playing tricks on me until we drew closer to the undulating blanket and saw it was made up of thousands of pink flamingos. The huge flocks of flamingos are the pride of the Camargue, one of only three places in Europe where the exotic birds can be found in the wild.

"Aren't they beautiful?" Magdalena sighed. "I used to love to watch them in the evening. But there were so many more in those days. When they lifted up, it looked like the sun was setting."

I pulled over so we could get out of the car for a better look. The flamingos were headed inland, away from the sea.

"They're looking for taller stands of trees," she said. "Where they can roost safely in the branches."

She closed her eyes and took a deep breath, pulling the thick muddy odor of the marsh into her lungs. I found the smell of the stagnant muck mildly disagreeable, but she seemed to enjoy it.

"It takes me back," she said. "Back to those days so long ago."

The sense of smell is the most primitive of the senses. Once imprinted on the brain, an odor carries with it the power to stimulate not only specific memories but emotions as well. This particular odor triggered memories for me, too, but the only image that came to mind for me was a camping trip in the New Jersey swamps.

Another trademark of the Camargue is the huge swarms of mosquitoes which rise up every evening to attack any living creatures. We dashed back to the safety of the car, with me swatting wildly at the insects that followed us inside.

"I forgot about the mosquitoes," Magdalena laughed. "We used to rub garlic on our arms to keep them away, but even that didn't work very well."

Off to our right, in the direction of the sea, the green marshlands gradually gave way to the salt pans, a spectacular expanse of glassy, shallow-water ponds. The varying stages of evaporation gave each pond its own unique shade of blue, ranging from deep indigo to the palest cerulean. Cut up into a bewildering array of irregular shapes by white salt roadways, the flats resembled nothing less than an enormous stained-glass window.

"Stop the car," Magdalena suddenly said.

"Why?"

"I know this place, Theo." Her voice was filled with wonder, as if she didn't believe what she was seeing. "I was here before. I know this region. I used to come here to bring the Good News to some settlers."

They were the words I was waiting to hear. I pulled to the side of the narrow road and followed her out of the car.

"It's different now," she said. "The salt ponds are much, much bigger than I remember. But other than that, it's still the same."

I studied the glassy ponds, trying to imagine what they would have looked like 2,000 years ago. There wouldn't have been much difference, except, as she said, for the size of the ponds. The process of extracting salt from sea water by evaporation hadn't changed since primitive man discovered the first crusted salt in a tidal pond. The only change since then was the equipment used for harvesting, in which beasts of burden were replaced with specialized mechanical equipment, which allowed for a greater magnitude of scale.

"We're still far from where our boat landed," she said, looking off to the horizon. "But I remember these flats when we came through here on our way to Narbo."

Shielding her eyes from the reflected glare of the sun, she stared out over the salt ponds. She was a time traveler looking for landmarks that might no longer exist. There were few clues in front of us, except for the fact that the salt ponds were laid out on only one side of the road.

"We landed . . . somewhere over there, I think." She pointed across the ponds to the southeast, towards the Gulf of Lyon.

It could have been a lucky guess, I thought. But standing there in front of the barren landscape without glancing at my map, not having seen a road sign since we left the A9, without any discernible sign of civilization, she was pointing in the precise direction of *les Saintes-Maries-de-la-Mer.* The road didn't lead in that direction. I couldn't see any turn-off up ahead.

"We're not far from the road we used to take," she said.

I consulted my road map. In fact, *les Saintes-Maries* was less than 10 kilometers away, exactly where she was pointing. Unfortunately, the only road on the map, the one we were on, headed directly to the sea, where it ended abruptly. According to the map, I had taken the wrong route, turning off prematurely onto a salt-harvester's service road. There was no secondary road linking it with our destination. To reach *les Saintes-Maries,* it looked like we'd have to retrace our route back to Aigues-Mortes, or get back on the A9 and come down from Arles.

I was halfway through a U-turn when she put her hand on the steering wheel.

"Why are you turning around?" she asked.

"Because this road goes nowhere," I said. "According to the map, it's a dead end."

"There used to be another road up ahead."

Those mythical hairs on the back of the neck that are supposed to stand on end at spooky moments started to tingle. This might be one of those proofs every past-life investigator hopes for. In the middle of the most desolate location I had ever encountered, she was not only directing me to a place her predecessor was supposed to have landed, but she claimed to know about a mystery road that didn't exist on my map.

I climbed up on the roof of DesRosier's car. I was sure he wouldn't mind a few scrapes when I explained that I wanted to be certain there wasn't anything ahead, no sign or arrow or marker of any kind that she might have seen with her younger eyes.

"I think it's about two kilometers ahead," she called up to me. "On the left."

The road we were on formed the eastern border of the salt flats. All I could see to the left was sawgrass and marshland. If there was another road up ahead, it was well-hidden.

"The only turnoffs I can see are service roads that go out over the salt flats," I told her. "I can't see any road that turns off to the east."

"It's there. I know it's there."

We were dealing with something stronger than memory now. If I had asked her about the salt flats during one of our interview sessions, she would almost certainly not have remembered the road. But research has shown that recognition is stronger than memory. Anyone visiting a childhood home is familiar with the powerful rush of not only forgotten memories, but emotions that surface as well. I could only imagine what must be running through Magdalena's mind if it was true that we were now approaching the site of her previous life in France.

"You're talking about a road that existed two thousand years ago," I said when I climbed down from the car. "This is a marshy area. Even if there was a road in those days, it might be gone by now."

I was offering her an escape clause, a perfectly rational excuse she could use to explain later why we didn't find the road. But she was adamant.

"It was a Roman road," she said. "And the Romans built their roads to last forever. Some part of it still has to be here."

That was certainly true. All over Provence, there were examples of Roman structures, not just simple affairs like roads, but the Pont du Gard aqueduct at Nimes, the arenas at Arles and Avignon, the amphitheaters and temples and baths that still stand despite, in many cases, the kind of neglect and vandalism that no modern structure could possibly survive. Even the scavengers who descended on those structures in later centuries proved unable to walk off with all the stoneworks.

If the Roman road did exist, however, the problem was going to be finding it. We were right in the middle of the demarcation line between vast salt flats and seemingly impenetrable marshland. On our right, no vegetation was able to survive at the edges of the evaporation ponds.

Even the smallest pathway used by the salt harvesters was clearly visible. On our left, however, where the ancient road was supposed to exist, tidal waters flushed the marshes twice daily, fueling a lush green mat of vines and shrubs and grasses so dense and water-logged that not even the wild horses of the Camargue appeared to have entered it. The endless cycle of growth and decay had built up a layer of soggy humus that rose slightly above the level of the ground where we stood. Which meant the ancient road, if it existed, was covered with a thick layer of mud and vegetation.

"It's just up ahead," Magdalena said. "I'm sure of it."

We left the car and started walking. It was a humid summer evening. I would have thought the heavy presence of salt in the air would serve as some form of insect repellent, but the bugs must have long ago adapted themselves to it. I swatted with little effect at clouds of mosquitoes and black flies. Salt dust dried out my face, and when the dust was picked up by perspiration, the salinated rivulets stung my eyes.

"I think we passed it," Magdalena said.

It felt like we walked about six kilometers, but looking back at the car, I decided it was probably only three or four. We hadn't seen any sign of a turnoff that might have been used by man or vehicle in the last decade. I didn't expect the search to be easy, but I was realizing now just how impossible it might really be. The only breaks in the vegetation on the swampy side of the road were pools of open water, which suggested that much of the marshland might be a floating carpet of vegetation, with no firm ground below. It could probably support a man or a horse for a few steps, but a single misstep would plunge any creature into the water below. That was probably why the wild horses and other large animals who inhabit the Camargue avoid such areas.

"I know it's here," Magdalena insisted. "It was a coastal road that ran from the Rhône River to Montpelier. We used it when we traveled to Narbo."

I went back to the car and double-checked the map again, and looked through the stack of tourist brochures. Narbo checked out. It was apparently the old Roman name for Narbonne, a major port in Caesar's time. The only roads visible on the maps were a few like the one we were on, which stretched finger-like from inland down to the sea. I couldn't find any mention of a coastal road, even an abandoned one, in the brochures.

"It's all marshland," I said. "If there was ever a road here, it might have been eroded by storms."

"It's here," she insisted. "I remember it very clearly. It was built up almost a meter above the high-water mark. And it came out of the marsh right about here."

"If it was that high, it should still be visible." I couldn't see anything in the marsh that resembled the remnants of an elevated roadway. "You're sure this is the right place? Things can change a lot over the course of two thousand years. Especially in a river delta."

Although it might sound as if I was arguing with her, there was nothing I wanted more than to find her mystery road. If there was such a road out there, and it turned out to be a 2,000-year-old Roman coastal route whose existence was known only to her, it would mean that she must have acquired the knowledge in a previous life. And the more difficult it was to find the ancient road, the better it was hidden, the longer it was forgotten, the more valuable it would be as documentation not only of a previous life, but also of the oral legends of Mary Magdalene's migration to France.

"The marsh seems to be higher than I remember," she admitted.

"That could be a function of the buildup of silt coming down the river," I said.

I found myself wanting to believe that her mystery road existed.

It might have been a case of wishful thinking, but I was convinced it was out there.

The question was how to find it.

As I swatted away at the mosquitoes, I felt a kinship with the archeologists and dinosaur hunters, the geologists and historians, with every specialist who must search through the detritus of the ages to locate an object they alone believe might be found.

In my case, the detritus was a morass of swamp and vegetation that was impenetrable to humans. Only the cleverest animals could find their way through. I knew there must be a variety of creatures who thrived on the food available in the swamp. Not just fish and amphibians and flamingos and the other wildfowl who flew in, but the predators and scavengers who fed on them, too. The banquet inside the swamp was too inviting for foxes and feral cats and other hungry carnivores to ignore.

I stood there, transfixed.

"What is it?" Magdalena asked.

I am not a naturalist. I was never a Boy Scout, much less a woodsman. I couldn't tell the difference between the tracks of a wild boar or a wild dog. But I had seen enough nature specials on PBS to know how such four-legged predators roam the night in search of food. They might be very efficient killing machines, but they're basically land-based mammals.

To find food, they need solid footing. If anybody could find a way into the swamp, it would be a hungry animal. If any remnants of an ancient roadway remained above water, the creatures of the night would already be using it as a feeding route. That didn't mean it would be easy for us to find their pathway in. Those same nature programs showed how cunningly those animals hid their haunts.

"Look for any kind of tracks at the edge of the road," I said. "We're looking for a path that animals might be using to go into the marsh."

We soon discovered, however, that there weren't any tracks to be found. The shoulder of the road was covered with a thick glaze of hard-packed salt. Even a blow with a hammer wouldn't have left a visible impression.

The sun was getting low. The shadows were getting long. The mosquitoes were getting worse. There we were on an empty road, miles from the nearest human being, searching for signs of . . . what? A stray dog that might have passed this way? A wandering goat that lived in the marsh? What if one of the Camargue's wild boars came roaring out of the bushes, angry that we dared disturb its lair? I shuddered as I remembered a PBS narrator describing how easily a boar's tusks can eviscerate a human.

Any rational human being would have given up the search. But I had moved beyond rational thought patterns. I was, by that time, operating on a different plane.

Fifty-Four

THE SLIMMEST OF clues have resulted in some of the greatest archeological discoveries of all time. A seemingly insignificant piece of stone in an Egyptian valley, for example, turned out to be the first of twenty-six steps that led Howard Carter down into the long-lost tomb of Tutankhamen. It was a well-worn goat trail on the cliffs at Qumran that led shepherds to the pottery which contained the Dead Sea Scrolls. In our case, a few blades of dead grass led us to a discovery with far greater implications for the future of Christianity than any pharoah's tomb or ancient manuscript.

Magdalena noticed the blades of dead grass first. They were lying on the marsh side of the road. They could have been blown there by the wind, except that they were matted down, as if they had been trampled by some creature. They rested, almost carpet-like, in a small tunneled opening in the sawgrass. The opening was barely wider than my fist. But it was an opening: the single hole in an otherwise solid wall of vegetation. I bent down to examine it more closely. Parting the grass, I saw that the opening continued. It was an animal path! The entrance we had been seeking into the marsh!

What species of animal used the path, I didn't know, and I didn't care. All that mattered was whether the path continued on dry land. Parting the vegetation ahead of me, I followed the grassy tunnel for about a dozen paces. The ground felt spongy beneath my feet, moist though not completely saturated. It was, I hoped, vegetation and humus covering a firmer base. When I tried digging with my hands to see what was underneath, the tangle of roots refused to yield. It was getting too late in the day to drive to the nearest town in search of a shovel. Fortunately, the car trunk contained a lug-wrench, one of those four-pointed flat-tire tools that includes a sharpened edge for removing hubcaps. I used the sharp edge as a probe, thrusting it directly into the animal path.

The point penetrated about four inches before hitting a rock. I moved to the side and once again drove the point into the ground. It hit solid rock again. Excited now, I moved to the other side of the path, where the probe wedged itself between what must have been adjoining rocks. The mosquitoes were forgotten as I continued probing to determine the width of the stones beneath the surface. By the time I hit the soft muck on both sides, I had staked out a section about twelve paces wide. That was the standard width of Roman roads: wide enough for two columns of soldiers. Although the vegetation cover was fairly level, my measurements indicated the underlying stone was crowned six inches higher in the middle than on the sides: the usual form of drainage in the empire's roads. A bit of scraping back and forth revealed the dimensions of the stone blocks. They were rectangles, each measuring roughly two feet long and half as wide.

By now, I was sweating heavily and my hands and knees were covered with mud. Yet I was laughing with delight, calling out to Magdalena to describe each new discovery. Using my probe, I traced the road about thirty feet into the marsh.

"Look along the edge of the road," Magdalena called out. "Look for a narrow stone with a rounded top. There'll be an inscription on it."

"How tall is the stone?"

"About half a meter above the roadway."

An inscription? The search was getting more interesting. With renewed energy, I swung the lug wrench back and forth, machete style, cutting through the grass as I walked back toward her. About eighteen feet from where she stood, the wrench hit what felt and looked like a moss-covered tree stump. It was about a foot higher than the ground on which I walked. I swung at it again, harder this time. It felt as if the wrench was hitting decayed wood. One final thrust rewarded me with the solid feel of metal against stone.

"I found it!" I called out.

"I knew it was there!" she clapped her hands in delight, but made no effort to join me in the weeds.

Chiseling away two centuries of lichen and mossy growth revealed the narrow stone with a rounded top, just as Magdalena had predicted. Organic matter partly obscured the inscription she said I'd find.

"What is it?" I asked.

"It's a Roman milestone. If I remember correctly, the inscription will tell you the distance to the Rhine on one side and to Montpelier on the other."

I rubbed a handful of mud against the rock, bringing the chiseled lines into better contrast. On the side of the milestone facing into the marsh, which would be the direction of the Rhône, was the letter R. On the opposite side of the milestone was the letter M, which I assumed meant Montpelier. Below both markings were some Roman numerals. They were measures of distance, just as she said. There were more markings all around the rock.

"There should be some other inscriptions visible," she called out. "The emperor's initials should be there, too."

"Julius Caesar," I murmured as I stared at the precisely carved J and C. As a sign of respect, Caesar's initials were more deeply chiseled into the stone than the directional information.

"He was emperor of Rome when the road was built," she said. "That was thirty years before we landed. You should also find the initials of Pontius Maximus," she continued. "He was the Roman governor of the province who authorized the construction."

The P was partially chipped, but the M was as readable as the day it was carved.

I have to admit I found the entire episode unnerving.

She was standing fifteen feet away, which meant she was unable to see the markings. Yet she knew exactly what was carved on the stone. She knew about the milestone and where I would find it. She knew in fact, the exact location of an ancient Roman road that wasn't supposed to exist.

"How did you know there'd be a milestone right here?" I asked when I came back to the road. "It could have been farther out in the swamp."

"I remembered that the road turned here," she said with a shrug. "The Romans always put a marker wherever there was a turn in the road."

"It turns?" I looked out over the salt flats. "Then where is the rest of it?"

"We're standing on it," she said.

I looked down. The road we drove in on was about the same width as the mystery road. The residue of centuries of salt harvesting could have obscured the original Roman paving stones long before the end of the first millennium.

"It goes off at this angle towards the Rhône River, where there was a ferry crossing."

"But why build a road through the swamp? There were plenty of roads inland."

"The Camargue was mostly uninhabited, except for the small fishing village of Rastis on the coast. The generals convinced the governor that an enemy force could secretly land in the area and use it as a base for attacking Arles or Narbo or even Marseilles. By building a coastal road, the generals could quickly move troops in to attack any invading force."

It sounded like a typical Roman strategy. I knew from my own history studies that the Romans built their fabled road system primarily for military reasons. That the road would have fallen into disuse after the Romans left Gaul in the fourth century wasn't surprising. A swamp road required upkeep, particularly the wooden bridges that spanned swampy areas. The collapse of a single such section would have rendered the rest of the road impassable. Once that happened, paving stones would have been taken by the locals, just as much of the old aqueducts and forums had been disassembled. Over time, most of the road would disappear.

"You seem really interested in the road," she said. "I could draw you a map of what I remember about it."

"That would be terrific," I said. "I'd really like to have a map."

I took out the camcorder and in the fading light, carefully videotaped the inscription on the milestone, the lug wrench stuck into what seemed to be the middle of the road, and the surrounding location and landmarks, so that I could find the site again. After all, what better way to prove a case of reincarnation than with an archeological discovery as newsworthy as this one would be? Before leaving, I carefully replaced the moss on top of the milestone, obscuring its identity. I didn't want anybody else finding it before I could use it as proof.

Magdalena seemed to have absolutely no idea of the significance of her mystery road. In a country that raised the commercialization of its history to an art form, every Roman arena, wall, bridge, ruin, and rock in France was carefully catalogued, described, marked with appropriate signage and otherwise merchandised to tourists. Finding a long-forgotten Roman road anywhere in France was an extraordinary accomplishment. Finding it in the Camargue could rewrite the history of that region. Finding it at all was possible only because a young Spanish nun claimed to remember it from a previous life.

Had I found the sort of irrefutable evidence of reincarnation that had eluded Stevenson and other researchers?

It certainly seemed so to me.

Fifty-Five

AFTER BECOMING HOPELESSLY lost in the maddening tangle of Arles' ancient streets, I gave up on the map and checked into the first hotel that had a parking spot outside. Although I felt self-conscious about the odor of decay that clung to my muddy clothing, the desk clerk was apparently accustomed to tourists emerging from the Camargue in my condition. He gave me directions to the nearest clothing shop, where I replaced my damaged garments with new ones; and to a nearby pharmacy, where I bought a large tube of the locally manufactured ointment for mosquito bites. After a hot shower and shave, I felt almost normal again. Except for the maddening itch of the dozens of red marks on my face and arms.

We had dinner under the stars that night, at an outdoor café directly across the street from the massive Roman amphitheatre. At the restaurant, I marveled over the fact that Magdalena didn't seem to have suffered a single mosquito bite. The insects that attacked me so viciously had apparently refused to inflict any pain on her.

"I never get mosquito bites," she said. "Not in this life." As if that explained everything.

As usual, she seemed to attract the attention of every man within sight, even those dining with other women. She was wearing white slacks and a red sleeveless blouse whose fabric was so lustrous, it cast a rosy glow on her face. I may be guilty of overidealizing, but she was looking particularly virginal that night. Her hair, still damp from the shower, looked fresh and clean and innocent of any chemical artifice. Her eyes were clear and trusting; her mouth undefiled by any man's lips. It was that air of purity that continued to fascinate me. Yet I was realistic enough to know it was her fully developed woman's body that was attracting every other man's attention.

We were drinking, as a little joke of mine, Chateauneuf du Pape, a red wine from nearby vineyards once owned by the Avignon popes. It was one of the better wines of the Rhône region. I was pleased that she enjoyed it, and I was happy to watch her drink it. I could imagine the red fluid sliding down inside her long, smooth throat. When the pink tip of her tongue slowly emerged to lick the last drop of wine from her lips, I forgot to breathe.

"I think we'd better order," I quickly said.

The waiter recommended we start with *Aigo-boulido,* a traditional Provençal soup made with the pink-skinned sweet garlic from Albi.

"Garlic is good for keeping away the mosquitoes, monsieur," he added in too-obvious reference to the red welts on my face.

Magdalena smiled sympathetically.

"The local garlic is so much more delicate than the garlic in Valencia," she said. "Or Jerusalem. Especially the *Rose D'Albi* variety. I missed it when I was growing up in the convent."

She had this habit of slipping casually between the memories of both of her lives, as if they were part of the same continuum. I had found it disconcerting at first, but I was getting used to it now. It was starting to seem almost normal.

The soup was wonderful, much sweeter than I expected. In addition to the garlic, it was prepared with sage leaves and saffron and chopped greens and sprinkled with grated cheese. When I praised the soup to the waiter, he gave me a disdainful Gallic shrug, as if I was making too much fuss over a simple dish.

"Maybe that's why I lived so long," she said. "Because of all the garlic I ate."

Although I didn't have my camcorder, I couldn't let the opening pass.

"Exactly how long did you live?" I asked. "I mean, you don't have to answer if it's too sensitive a subject."

"There's no need to feel embarrassed," she said. "Padre Serrano asked me the same question." She finished her soup and wiped those beautiful unpainted lips before answering. "I died thirty years after the death of Jesus my Christ. I was sixty years old."

"That was remarkable," I said. "People didn't normally live that long in those days."

"Especially women," she said softly.

We were silent while the waiter removed our soup plates.

"How did you," I hesitated, unable to bring myself to apply the word 'die' to my lovely dinner companion. " . . . how did it happen?"

"It was very ordinary," she said. "I was old. I was tired. I had . . ." She caught herself in the middle of the sentence. That second set of eyes, the ones that seemed to be watching from behind the real eyes, studied me, as if trying to decide how much to tell me. When she spoke again, the tone of her voice was different. I was convinced she had almost revealed something about her life that she wanted to keep secret. "What happened was that I was taken ill with a fever . . . what you now call influenza. It grew worse, and I had trouble breathing. The mistral was blowing and the weather was cold. I remember there was a light covering of snow on the mountains. That last night, I was coughing and coughing until I was gasping for breath. My friends were with me. They boiled water to fill the room with steam, and that seemed to help. But during the night, when everyone was sleeping, my soul passed away from my body." Her voice softened. "It was painless."

"And then what happened?" I persisted.

Our waiter arrived at the table with our main courses just in time to hear her irritated response.

"What does it matter?" she asked. "I died. Isn't that what you wanted to know?"

I looked up at the waiter. He raised his eyebrows, but otherwise pretended to ignore the conversation. He set a plate containing a grilled *loup de mer* on a bed of fennel leaves, carefully turning the plate so that the fish's head faced away from her to the right. The faint fragrance of anise rose from the dish. My *cassoulet* was served in a glazed stoneware crock. After warning me the pot was '*très, très chaud,*' the waiter removed the cover with a flourish, revealing the still-bubbling mixture of beans, lamb, pork, bacon, sausage and vegetables. It was a peasant dish, perfect after a long day of driving and mucking around in the swamp.

"We used to make that in a big pot," she said as she watched the steam rise from the bowl before me. "We'd put in whatever we had, rabbit, lamb, duck, onions . . ."

"Garlic," I joked.

"Yes. Definitely garlic. And whatever vegetables we had. We threw in everything we could find. It was sort of our version of *paella*, except with beans instead of rice."

At the risk of irritating her again, I decided to revisit the subject of her death.

"The reason I wanted to talk about what happened when you . . . passed away . . . was because I wanted to know what you remember about the discarnate state."

"Discarnate?"

"After you were separated from your body . . . the period of time before you were reincarnated. The interval was almost 2,000 years. What was that like?"

After blowing on the spoon, I took my first tentative taste of the *cassoulet*. It was superb. If this was how Provençals prepared "peasant" food, the *haute cuisine* of the region must be absolutely ambrosial, I thought. I held that first taste in my mouth for a long moment, savoring the flavor that I couldn't trace to any single ingredient. The sum was indeed sweeter than its parts.

"Do you remember the tunnel?" I asked when I returned to my senses.

She stopped with her fork poised in mid-air.

"How do you know about the tunnel?" she responded.

It was a question I dared not answer. That I possessed considerable expertise in the field of afterlife journeys was a fact I had purposely withheld from her thus far. The entire case for her reincarnation claims depended, after all, on the delicate vagaries of distant memory. Any details of the afterlife that I provided might easily pollute those memories, or worse yet, cause her to subconsciously alter her responses to fit what she thought I wanted to hear. In my best professional mode, I remained silent, unwilling to reveal anything about myself that could affect the integrity of the interview.

"But of course," she answered her own question. "You would have gone through the tunnel when you died."

I concentrated on my *cassoulet*, pretending not to have heard.

"Don't you remember how you died?" she asked.

What I remembered was being very careful not to have told her anything about the shooting or my Near-Death Experience.

"Don't you remember anything about your previous life, Theo?"

I continued working on my cassoulet, which was really quite delicious.

"You should try to remember," she said. "Everybody should try to remember their previous lives."

It began to occur to me that she wasn't referring to my NDE. The previous life she was talking about was a previous existence. A previous incarnation. I let her continue.

"If you try hard, like I did," she said. "You can remember the most amazing details about a past life, even though it was one you lived two thousand years ago."

I raised the napkin to wipe my mouth before taking a sip of wine.

"You're the one who claims to have lived two thousand years ago, not me," I countered, smiling as I spoke so as not to offend her. "I'm just an investigator. Can we get back to the tunnel?"

"You want me to remember my former life," she pouted. "But you refuse to even try to remember yours."

One of the professional tricks of any good interviewer is to remain silent, even past the point of discomfort, until the subject feels compelled to fill the empty space. I watched as Magdalena poked at the *loup de mer,* working with the fish knife to remove the backbone. I finished my *cassoulet* in silence.

"All right," she finally said. "I'll tell you about the tunnel."

Warily at first, she began to describe her journey into the afterlife. It was much the same story as that reported by the hundreds of Near-Deathers I interviewed for Professor DeBray. Magdalena spoke of the moment of calm, the cessation of pain, the feeling of infinite peace, the buzzing sound, and the separation from the body through the Brahmic aperture. She described how she hovered above her dead body, and of the strange trip through what seemed to be a tunnel. I had heard it all before. From people who had died in accidents, on operating tables, from heart attacks. People who had gone to The Other Side and returned. I wasn't surprised by her description of the moments immediately following her death, because my previous work had convinced me of the universality of that experience. Although death comes in many forms, everyone follows the same path into the afterlife. The great unanswered question is why some souls quickly return to their own bodies, waking up after the doctors have declared them clinically dead; while other souls, some of them still clinging to memories of a previous life, are sent back from the afterlife to inhabit new bodies.

The waiter removed our dishes and returned almost immediately with a platter of Provençal specialties. Magdalena recognized them immediately and began describing their merits to me. Anyone who didn't know her background would think such knowledge was unusual for a nun who had never before traveled outside Valencia.

"The little round cheeses are *Tomme de Camargue*," she explained. "They're made from the milk of both cows and goats and they're wonderfully creamy. The figs are from Marseilles. They're so much sweeter than figs from Italy or Jordan. The small ovals are *Callisones d' Aix*. Under that cream coating is a layer of almond."

The waiter, whose explanatory functions she had taken over, stood listening, ready to interrupt if she got anything wrong.

"*Bravo, mademoiselle*," he said after she had described all twelve specialties. "Are you perhaps from around this area?"

"I used to live here," she said. "A long time ago."

I ordered another bottle of wine, a white Rhône wine to go with the cheese and fruit.

While she peeled figs for me, she told me about the Light, the Guide, the Life Review and a dozen other details familiar to anyone with experience in the field. I didn't challenge her or cross-examine her, because everything she said about the journey to the Other Side fit perfectly with what I already knew. We had a lot more in common than she realized.

"I never told these things to anyone," she interrupted herself.

"Why not?"

"Because it all sounds too . . . unbelievable."

"You think it's more unbelievable than being the reincarnation of Mary Magdalene?"

"Well, no, I guess not. It's just different. In my past life, I was a real person. I was a woman, a human being who walked on the ground, and ate and drank and combed my hair and fell in love and had a real body." As she spoke, I made a mental note to ask her about the falling in love part. "And in this life, I'm a real person again." She reached out her hand and wrapped her slender fingers around mine. "See? I can feel you and you can feel me. We're real. But in between these two lives, I don't know what I was. I don't remember ever eating or drinking or sleeping. And that went on for two thousand years, Theo, except that it felt like a fairly short period of time. How can I expect anyone to believe I existed in that state if I can't even describe it properly?"

I could understand her frustration. Even the most ardent believers in the afterlife, including NDE survivors like myself, have always found it difficult to describe the exact nature of the entity that leaves the body at the moment of death. It has been identified as the soul, the spirit, the astral body, the ethereal being, the *bardo*, the animating force, the spark of life. The form it takes is equally difficult to characterize. Some describe it as an exact duplicate of the corporal body, others describe it as a phantasm, or a shadowy figure, or even a collection of thoughts and memories.

I listened patiently while she talked about the Being of Light and the Elysian Fields and the strange ethereal music and the panoramic vista of every moment of her life that would have been revealed to her. I was surprised that she made no reference to Jesus Christ, whom I assumed would have greeted his faithful disciple as soon as she entered his Kingdom.

"What happened after the Life Review?" I asked.

"It took place by a stream," she said. "The Being of Light, which I assume was God, was standing by a bridge."

We were getting to the part I was most interested in. Only those of us who ventured deepest into the afterlife ever saw the bridge. In Zoroastrian tradition, it was known as the *Chinvato Peretu*, the Bridge of the Separator; in Western vision literature, it generally takes the form of a bridge to a purgatorial experience. No one who returned from an NDE had ever seen what was on the other side of the bridge. It was the point of no return. Crossing it meant leaving your old life forever behind.

"It was a narrow bridge over what seemed at first to be a small stream, but as I crossed it, the river grew wider and wider until it seemed I would never reach the other side, and when I finally did manage to cross over, I could no longer see where I had been."

Some of the esoteric writings describe the bridge as crossing the River Lethe, whose waters wash away all conscious memory to prepare the soul for the next life. No one knows for sure how it happens, because the only documented testimony about the existence of the bridge comes from NDEers like myself, none of whom had ever claimed to have set foot on the structure. During my own journey into the afterlife, I remember approaching the bridge, and having a powerful awareness that once I crossed it, I would never return to my former life. I desperately wanted to cross the bridge, to be united for all eternity with Laura, but was prevented from doing so. And almost immediately, I returned to my body, where the paramedics took credit for reviving me.

"What happened after you crossed the bridge?" I asked. "What did you see?"

"Nothing much. I waited. Somehow I sensed that I was waiting for the right body."

The waiting period between lives is described in the Eastern religions as the *bardo state* or 'interval.' The timing of the interval appears to be extremely elastic, with those whose death is premature or violent returning more quickly, while those who die peacefully remain in the *bardo* state for longer periods of time. Stevenson reports cases in which the rebirth takes place almost instantaneously after the death of the old body, but there are other reports of cases in which the *bardo* state lasts thousands of years. The ancient Egyptians, for example, believed the standard cycle to be 3,000 years. Most reincarnation scholars, however, have set the average length of the intermission between lives at 49 Earth days.

"Can you describe what you did or where you were while you waited?" I asked.

"It's vague, but I remember being near water. Maybe I was near the stream that runs under the bridge. It was kind of foggy, though, and everything seemed indistinct."

The stream again, I thought. The stream or river seems to be an inescapable image in the literature of death and reincarnation. The River Styx was made famous by Dante as the final crossing point between life and death. Plato and Origen spoke of a stream on whose banks discarnate souls wait for re-embodiment. Many of Stevenson's Indian case histories included accounts of a riverbank as a kind of afterlife "staging area," although this might be a cultural phenomenon influenced heavily by the central role of the Ganges River in Indian death rites.

Her eyes took on a distant look, as if she was trying to peer back in time. "How long I was there, I don't know," she said. "Time didn't seem to matter. What was important was to wait for exactly the right body. It seemed like it wasn't just a question of being born again, you know. I had the sense there was a very specific role I had to fulfill in my next life. Which meant I had to be reborn into the right family, if I was going to have the opportunity to fulfill that role."

"You had to be born into the right family," I agreed. Such predetermination seemed to be a basic principle of reincarnation theory. "To the right parents. And yet you never knew who those parents were."

"That's right."

"But weren't you disappointed that you were going back to a new life, back to mortality?"

"How do you mean?"

"Well, you were so close to Jesus in your previous life. Didn't you expect to be reunited with him after you died?"

"I did see him. He was part of the Being of Light."

"But didn't you want to stay with him for all eternity?"

"Yes, of course I did. But the time wasn't right."

"How did you know?"

"I don't know. I just knew. I knew that I had to live at least one more life."

"But why?"

It was a puzzle I wondered if I would ever solve. The deeper I probed into this case, the more mystifying it seemed to get. According to everything I had read about reincarnation, the theories of Karma and Samsara, Tao beliefs and Greek philosophy and even the words of early Christian leaders, the cycle of life and rebirth is a school for the perfection of the soul. The new life offers the opportunity to repent for crimes and evil deeds, to work through unresolved conflicts and unfulfilled desires and other spiritual imperfections that stand in the way of enlightenment. For some, the cycle takes many lives to fulfill.

But the Magdalene was the "woman who knew the All," the "eternal feminine," the "companion of Jesus Christ," the "Apostle to the Apostles." Her assistance made it possible for Jesus and the male Apostles to conduct their ministries. Her spiritual resume included accomplishments no other human being could claim. She was as close to spiritual perfection in her previous life as it was possible to be.

Why was she sent back?

What unfinished business was she expected to accomplish before being reunited with her Savior?

If she knew, she wasn't telling me.

After dinner, she took me for a stroll through the old Roman quarter. I wasn't surprised that she was able to find her way to the sights she wanted to show me. While many original buildings had been demolished or drastically remodeled over the last two millennia, the basic pattern of the narrow streets remained. She said she had visited Arles many times in her previous life, and pointed out houses once owned by friends with whom she stayed. She named many of those friends and told me anecdotes of life in Arles during the first century. I didn't have the camcorder along, and she promised to repeat the names later, so that I could check them against whatever records might still exist. Some of those friends were the children and grandchildren of veterans of the Sixth Legion of the Roman Army, she explained. Those veterans formed the original colony of Romans who populated the town. She told me of the bridge of boats that was built over the Rhône.

A skeptic could easily say everything she told me might have been derived from history books and tourist literature, but my doubts about her were receding. There might still be unanswered mysteries of who she really was, mysteries that I might never solve in this life, but I was beginning to accept her as who she claimed to be.

At the same time, I was finding it increasingly difficult to deny the aphrodisiacal effect of strolling under a starry sky on a warm summer night in one of the most romantic towns in Provence. With only the purest of intentions, I took her hand in mine. Her fingers were small and delicate, fitting comfortably in the embrace of mine. In an era when even sexual favors are bestowed so casually, it might seem ludicrous for two mature adults to derive a guilty pleasure from so apparently innocent an act as holding hands. Yet it was intimacy enough for both of us. We were frightened to go any further, yet delighted we were finally coming together. She smiled at me and we walked the rest of the way back to the hotel in contented silence. I dared not kiss her good night, although I was certain she would not have rejected the attempt.

There was no longer any point in denying that I was slowly, perhaps inevitably, falling in love with Magdalena. Although I could rationalize the growing emotional bond between us as an inevitable product of the shared fears and forced inseparability of two fugitives on the run, I couldn't deny the pleasure I took in having her beside me. I felt enveloped in a warm glow when I returned to my room.

The radiant mood dissipated when I discovered an intruder had been there while I was out.

Fifty-Six

THE DRESSER DRAWERS weren't overturned, and no pillows were slashed. Nevertheless, whoever had searched the room had made no attempt to conceal their activities. The bedcovers and pillows had been removed and replaced, marks on the floor indicated where the dresser had been moved, and my meager toilet articles were rearranged. Because I had so few possessions, it took only a moment to see what was missing. The tube containing the rolled-up sketches of Jesus and the bearded backpacker was gone. More important, so were the ten videotapes containing fifteen hours of interviews with Magdalena, the linguistic examination conducted by Professor Abramakian, and the discovery of the Roman road in the Camargue.

In what could only be construed as a message, the camcorder was left behind. Its loading door hung open to reveal an empty interior. Three unused tapes, still in their plastic wrappers, were also untouched.

Which meant my visitor wasn't some anonymous petty thief looking for anything of value. The tapes would be useful only to someone who was interested in my investigation. Leaving the camera and the unused tapes behind was an act of arrogance, the intruder's not-so-subtle warning that any future recordings would meet the same fate.

I immediately called DesRosier. He seemed more concerned with Magdalena's well-being than the missing tapes.

"Forget the tapes," he told me. "Your testimony will be enough for me. What I'm more concerned about is Sister Mariamme's well-being. Is she safe?"

I hesitated, ashamed that my first thought had been to call my employer rather than to check on Magdalena.

"Is she safe?" he repeated. "With all that's happened, I worry about her."

"Don't worry, she's fine," I said, hoping he'd hang up so I could hurry next door to be sure I was right.

"Good. I'm depending on you to protect her. Please express my concern to her."

"You said you didn't want me to use your name."

"At this point, I think it might be better if you did. You may reveal my identity. And you may also assure her that if anything happens to you, she can come to me for help."

"I'm sure she . . . ," I started to say, but he had already cut off the connection.

His reaction to the news of the break-in puzzled me. I expected disappointment, perhaps even outrage that all the evidence I accumulated was lost. After all, that was why he hired me. In fact, he didn't even ask what was on the tapes, or whether I was getting any closer to completing my assignment. All that seemed to concern him was Magdalena's well-being. Not whether she was the fraud he originally considered her. Suddenly he not only wanted me to reveal his name, but to assure her of his protection if anything happened to me. Was that a display of compassion on his part? Or was it a hint of some hidden agenda?

Magdalena answered my knock at her door in a white floor-length nightgown, one of her purchases in Barcelona. Delicate lace scalloping drew my attention to the neckline, beneath which rose those lovely breasts I had been too embarrassed to look at in Collioure. The sexuality she exuded was unnerving. To avoid upsetting her, I decided to say nothing about the intruder who visited my room.

"I just talked to the man who hired me," I said, dutifully carrying out DesRosier's instructions. "He wanted me to tell you he was concerned about your safety."

"That was very nice of him."

"If anything happens to me . . ."

She raised a hand to my lips.

"Don't speak of such things," she said.

I wanted to kiss her fingertips when they brushed my mouth. Only a superhuman effort of willpower prevented me from doing so.

" . . . he promised me he'd take care of you," I finished my sentence. "Of course, I don't expect anything to happen to me, but just in case, the man you should go to, the man who will help you, is named DesRosier. Jean-Claude DesRosier."

"DesRosier?" she repeated the name in a quizzical tone. "I think I know that name."

"Perhaps from the *convento* or the cathedral."

"Yes, that's probably where I heard it," she said. "I'm sure this DesRosier is a good person, as you told me before. And very thoughtful too, if he's so concerned about me." A flash of jealousy must have shown in my face, because she quickly touched my arm and added, "But as long as you're with me, he has no reason to be concerned."

From anyone else, I would have treated the comment as a common politeness, an effort to assuage any wound to my pride. But the power of the emotions beginning to stir within me magnified every word, every gesture of hers, imbuing it with deeper meaning than she could possibly have intended. She must have sensed the struggle that was going on inside me, because her cheeks colored, and she moved her body coquettishly behind the door, placing herself partially out of sight as well as out of reach. The air seemed suddenly sexually charged. Without having exchanged any of the amorous words that traditionally pass between lovers, without having touched in any romantic way, without having done anything except look into each other's eyes, something had changed between us, and we were both aware of it.

"Is there anything else?" she asked, in a voice that almost invited me to move the conversation to a more intimate level.

"I . . . I just wanted to tell you . . ." Stumbling over the words, I coughed to clear my throat and quickly reverted to my professional voice. "I just wanted to tell you to get a good night's sleep. We'll be doing a lot of driving tomorrow."

Back in my room, I realized I still had the phone in my hand, and in my frustration at myself, felt like throwing it against the wall.

What was wrong with me? I could deal with murderers, lawyers, juries, the *Guardia Civil*. I could survive bullets, bombings, and even death itself. But when it came to dealing with a young woman who had spent most of her life locked up in a convent, I was reduced to the state of a sophomoric suitor who knew exactly what he wanted to say but was too terrified to actually voice the words. Terrified, perhaps, because I didn't know to whom I was really attracted.

Was it Sister Mariamme, the naïve young virgin whose religious life I dared not ruin with any sexual liaison?

Or was it Mary Magdalene, the woman who knew the most intimate secrets of Jesus, a woman of such enormous religious significance that it seemed sinful to think of her in amorous terms?

Fifty-Seven

A BLACK CAR fell in behind us when we left Arles in the morning.

It followed us across the Rhône bridge, through the cloverleaf and onto the road leading down into the Camargue. At first, there seemed nothing unusual about the vehicle behind me. Hundreds of cars follow the same route every morning, the D570 being the only road from Arles to *les Saintes-Maries-de-la-Mer*. What caught my attention about this particular car was the steady pace it maintained behind us. When I slowed down, other cars passed. When I hit the accelerator, other cars dropped behind. All except for the black car, which never varied its distance. As best as I could make out in the rear-view mirror, there appeared to be two men in the vehicle. They were too far back for me to identify them any further. For the moment, they seemed content to follow us.

I said nothing about our pursuers to Magdalena, not wishing to alarm her. She was enjoying the scenery, the rice farms and the vast *étangs*.

The D570 took us right down to the edge of the Mediterranean, where on a narrow strip of sand almost entirely surrounded by water, sits the town of *les Saintes-Maries-de-la-Mer*. On the beach fronting the town, according to the legend, was the site where the boat containing Mary Magdalene and her companions landed. As if anticipating our movements, the black car turned off just before we reached the beach road.

I found a parking spot and led Magdalena out onto the sand. I watched her carefully as she studied the place, looking for some flicker of recognition in her eyes. The empty beach that allegedly greeted the voyagers had been dissected by developers and town planners and environmental activists. What was once an unbroken strand was now cut in half by a stone breakwater which guarded the entrance to a marina. More than a hundred pleasure boats and yachts were moored within its protective embrace. Additional sand-trapping stone jetties further cut the two long stretches of beach into smaller sections. Sitting unexpectedly next to the marina was a huge white-walled bullring, surrounded by parking spaces. The busy beach was separated from the town by a four-lane roadway, only two lanes of which were useable, the other two being occupied by parked vehicles. Hundreds of additional cars filled long parking lots on the Mediterranean side of the road. The other side of the road was fronted with the usual assortment of open-air restaurants, souvenir shops and boutiques, which gave way grudgingly to the white-washed houses and vacation villas that had long ago replaced the simple homes of fishermen.

With all the development, I wouldn't have believed Magdalena if she said she recognized the town. What she did say, however, was stunningly accurate.

"This isn't the place where we landed."

"This is *les Saintes-Maries-de-la-Mer,*" I said. "In Roman times, it was known as *Ratis*. According to the legends, this is where your boat landed."

"No, it's not. This town is not *Ratis*."

"Well, of course it looks different now. Things change over two thousand years."

"We landed at the mouth of the Rhône River," she said. "The *Ratis* I knew was on the shore of the Rhône. You could come right down the Rhône from Arles to *Ratis*. If this is *Ratis*, where is the river?"

The question went right to the heart of her credibility. Once again, she was demonstrating a knowledge that ran contrary to current belief. With astonishing accuracy, she was remembering a landscape that ceased to exist centuries ago. The Camargue is a land of endless change, its very existence dependent on the silt carried downstream by the Rhône. Like the Mississippi delta region, the river's sediment created muddy islands and swamps and sandy beaches that appeared and disappeared as the forces of nature and man caused the river to change its course. During Roman times, one of the main branches of the Rhône in fact did empty into the sea at *Ratis*. It was documented in one of the maps in Serrano's 1912 edition of *A History of Alluvial Sedimentation in the Rhône Delta*. But when I found that volume, it was still in its original shrink-wrap, indicating it had been unopened, unread. Which meant Serrano couldn't have shared this information with Magdalena. She was working from ancient memory.

"The mouth of the river is now about thirty kilometers in that direction," I pointed to the east, in the direction of Port St. Louis. "There's also a smaller branch, the *Petit Rhône*, a few kilometers to the west."

"Then why did you bring me here?"

"Because this is where the Rhône emptied into the sea in the first century," I said. "Or at least one of the three branches of the river that existed in that time."

"Then this *was* Ratis?"

"Well, not quite. The original village was somewhere out there."

I pointed out to sea.

"Maybe two or three kilometers from where we're standing," I said. "Changing erosion patterns and storms altered the shoreline. The beach was eaten away here, and it was built up to the west. It's still being eroded by the ocean . . . that's why they built all those stone jetties along here, to stop the erosion. "

"And the Temple of Artemis, where we took shelter after we landed?"

"Out there, too. Maybe one of these days, some divers will find a few artifacts."

She looked out over the water, shielding her eyes from the sun, in the direction where I said the Temple of Artemis lay drowned.

"That's probably also what happened to the old Roman road," I said. "Most of it is either under water or under sand dunes."

"So I was right about the river," she said.

"Yes, you were right about that."

"You knew this all along."

"Yes, I did."

"You wanted to see if I knew. You were trying to trick me."

"I'm sorry," I said. "It's just an investigative technique. A way to establish credibility."

It was mid-morning, the sky was cloudless, and the sun was growing intense. I led her to a shaded area behind the beachfront Tourist Information Office. There was no sign of the black car or anyone who seemed to be interested in our movements.

"I would have liked to see the actual spot where we landed." Magdalena said. "I would have liked to stand on the same sand where we beached our boat." She turned back to look out to sea again. Her voice grew pensive. "We felt so lonely, so lost when we left the harbor at Ceasaria. It was two months after Jesus my Christ was crucified. The boat was loaded and prepared for the journey by friends, so as not to alert those who would try to stop us. We left after dark. No one spoke as the boat pulled away. We were frightened and sad, knowing that we would never return to our homes."

"Why did you leave?" I asked. "Peter and the others stayed."

"Peter?" She pronounced the name with derision. "Peter who ran away and hid when Jesus my Christ was crucified? Peter who remained in hiding in his room fearing for his life, leaving us to carry the body to the tomb? Peter who didn't believe in the Resurrection until Jesus my Christ appeared in the locked room?" She shook her head at the memory. "Peter was the one who wanted me to leave."

"I thought there was a general persecution of Christ's followers."

"There was tension, but there was no serious persecution, not immediately. If there was, Peter would have been the first to flee. His actions before and after the Crucifixion showed the kind of person he was."

"He died a martyr's death," I pointed out. "He was willing to die for his faith."

"As did many others," she countered. "But that was later in his life, after he attracted a following. Perhaps he changed."

"You didn't like him," I said. "That's not a very Christian attitude."

"It was Peter who didn't like me," she insisted. She spoke without rancor, as befitted the recollection of a distant memory. "He didn't like women, and he especially disliked me because I was . . ." she stopped herself to reformulate what she was about to say. "Because I was closer to Jesus my Christ than the others. Because the secret teachings were revealed to me, and not to him. He refused to believe that Jesus my Christ would reveal those teachings to a woman, and not to him. Fortunately, Levi was there to rebuke him." Now we were into the Gospel of Mary, with its partially obliterated description of the "middle eye" Christ used for prophecy, and the missing portion where he told Mary how he performed his miracles. "Peter was jealous of me. He saw me as a threat, and convinced me to leave."

"If you had the secret teachings, why didn't you stay in Galilee instead of coming to France?"

"In my condition . . . ," she started to say, and then quickly amended her words, " . . . because I was the person closest to Jesus my Christ, both Peter and I worried that it might be dangerous for me to stay there. Also, it was time to begin our missions, spreading the good news, and he wanted to be rid of me. It was my idea to go to Gaul, since it was as far away from Peter as I could get. He immediately agreed. He promised if I went to Gaul to spread the word, he would not follow, nor would he send any of the other disciples to interfere with my mission there. And he kept his word, for which I was very thankful."

One of the factors that I continued to find so convincing about Magdalena's past-life memories was the casual manner in which she mixed familiar material, such as the *Pistis Sophia* account of the quarrels provoked by Peter, with original disclosures, such as the heretofore unknown agreement that sent the Magdalene to France. Peter's attitude toward women was well documented. So was the puzzling fact that although the original Apostles went to preach throughout the Roman and Greek worlds, none of them went to Gaul during Mary Magdalene's lifetime, except for Philip, who accompanied her in the boat. Even Paul, who spoke longingly of someday traveling to Spain, never envisioned a visit to Gaul. Yet the towns of southern Gaul were the most important of the Roman colonies. Arles itself was called the "Rome of Gaul." And the large Jewish population was a ripe target for missionary work. Magdalena's account of a secret treaty with Peter provided the first logical explanation for what I always thought was the surprising neglect of Rome's most important province by both Peter and Paul. It was a stunning notion, one that to my knowledge had never before been advanced by any biblical scholar. In a field of study where reputations are built by studying tiny scraps of ancient papyrus that might yield a single word or date, it is hard to overemphasize the importance of this new insight. Yet as was typical of Magdalena, it was mentioned almost in passing, without any effort to impress me.

A few hundred meters from the beach, a medieval fortress-church towered over the town. The *Église de Saintes-Maries* was reputed to be the final resting place of three of the women who sailed on the boat with the Magdalene. The interior of the church consisted of a single large nave, and for a place of such supposed religious significance, was in a state of remarkable neglect. Inside, we joined a rather sparse complement of tourists: a dozen or so elderly people, three nuns, and two couples who looked like honeymooners. Again, I saw no one who looked suspicious, no one who seemed the slightest bit interested in us. One of the senior citizens had positioned himself in the middle of the center aisle, and appeared to be slowly and methodically videotaping the entire gloomy interior of the church, despite the sign prohibiting photography. His camera focus came to rest high above the altar, where in the rectangular opening of what was once the Guard's Room, rests the reliquary containing bones reputed to be those of the *Saintes-Maries*. They were placed there after being unearthed in 1448 by King René.

"Can we go up there?" Magdalena asked.

"I'm afraid it's locked," I said after reading the tourist booklet. "They lower the reliquary to the church floor on certain feast days, but other than that, it's forbidden to the public."

"Then we shall pray here," she said.

Dutifully, I knelt beside her. These were, after all, her friends whose bones were presumed to rest in the reliquary.

"They were my dearest companions," Magdalena said at the conclusion of her prayers. "Mary Jacob was the wife of Clopas, and the mother of the Apostles Jude and Simon. Mary Salome was the wife of Zebedee and the mother of the Apostles James and John. Some say the only reason they gave up all their wealth and properties to follow Jesus my Christ was because they wanted to be near their sons. But they truly believed in his word, and that was why they followed him. Like me, they should be considered *diakones*." She used the Greek word for deacons, a word which was applied to both men and women of the earlier church, until the second century, when it was decided that all such titles were reserved for men. "They came here to spread the good news, as Jesus my Christ instructed us all."

Contrary to current popular belief, and certainly contrary to the wishes of Peter, the women who followed Christ were considered *diakones*, a Greek word meaning "messengers."

For that reason, scholars agree they had as much authority to preach the word of God as their male brethren. The case is made by many theologians that Mary Magdalene had even greater authority to do so than the male Apostles. This authority, they believe, derives from the Gospels of Matthew and John. In both of those accounts, the first act of the risen Christ was to appear to Mary Magdalene, making her the first witness to his divinity. After being instructed to "go and carry the news to my brothers" it was Mary Magdalene who carried the good news of the Lord's Resurrection to the other Apostles. Through his actions and his words, the scholars contend, Jesus appointed Mary Magdalene as his first and most important messenger to the world. Although the significance of this fact was later to be down-played by the male hierarchy of the medieval church, Hippolytus and other early Christian leaders not only acknowledged the special status of Mary, but honored her as the *Apostola Apostolorum:* The Apostle to the Apostles.

We went downstairs beneath the altar to the crypt, which houses the relics and statue of Saint Sarah, the black Egyptian servant who accompa-nied the Magdalene. The crypt was warm and stuffy, filled with the heat and smoke of nearly two hundred blazing candles. Although a servant, and not one of the *Saintes-Maries* for whom the town and church are named, it is she who draws the greatest crowds. Every year on May 25th , thousands of Gypsies from as far away as Africa and Greece converge on this little church to pay homage to Sarah, whom they consider one of their own, and whom they have adopted as their patron saint.

"My dear, sweet Sarah," Magdalena said softly, as she knelt down before the elaborately costumed effigy of Sarah. Again, I knelt beside her. The stone floor was cold. Before long, my knees ached. I shifted my weight from one leg to the other, but it didn't help. The man with the videotape camera hovered behind us. I didn't like the idea of being pho-tographed for someone else's amusement, but I didn't dare break Mag-dalena's concentration.

A subdued Magdalena told me the details of the voyage over lunch. We were sitting in an outdoor café across the street from the beach, where I could look out over the water and imagine what it was like on that cloudy day when the boat landed in France.

There were twenty-seven of them on the boat, she explained, includ-ing the captain and a crew of four. Some of the names were quite familiar to me. There were the saints before whose reliquaries we had just prayed. Magdalena laughingly described how the trio took refuge in the vestibule of the pagan Temple of Artemis. She told me about Martha of Bethany, and how she went on to found a convent of pious virgins, living the life of a meditative penitent. Martha's brother Lazarus was another passenger: the same Lazarus who was raised from the dead by Christ, and later become the first bishop of Marseilles. Another passenger was the apostle Philip, whose description of Peter's hostility to Mary Magdalene was even-tually incorporated by another writer into the gospel that bore his name. She told me of Maximin, who became the bishop of Aix-en-Provence, and remained her friend and adviser until her death. She explained how Joseph of Arimethea accompanied them on the boat, but went on immediately to what is now Britain, where he founded that nation's first Christian church at Glastonbury. There were other names I didn't know: Marcilla, who was

Martha's maid; Cedon, a blind man who was cured by Christ; Aurelius of Paro, a Greek physician; four veterans of the Roman Army's vaunted Eighth Corps, who volunteered to serve as bodyguards for the women; also Sidonius, Martial, Eutropius, Trophimus, Saturninus, and two other converts who joined the expedition at the last moment. It was a full complement of missionaries who set sail for Gaul, with Mary Magdalene as their leader.

Those who revere the religious history and oral traditions of the French people argue that the true beginning of the Christian faith in Europe can be traced to the arrival of Mary Magdalene in the south of France shortly after the crucifixion of Jesus Christ. That Mary Magdalene arrived in France by boat, and the identity of the vessel's other passengers, has been documented by countless scholars, historians, and church leaders. One of the most significant early studies confirming the factual basis for the oral histories was published by the theologian Raban Maar in the eighth century. When a manuscript of his forensic inquiry was rediscovered in the early 1400's, it was considered so important to European religious history, it inspired the founding of Magdalen College at Oxford University. I first came across a translation of the Maar manuscript during my studies at Mount Athos. The rest of my knowledge of that event and its subsequent impact on French Christian tradition came from Padre Serrano's small but superb collection of books.

At first, the Magdalene's preaching in Provence fell on empty ears. She traveled the countryside, visiting small outposts in the Camargue, until finally arriving in Marseilles. Known as Masillus in those days, it was already a major trading port, the terminus for vessels from Rome, Tyre and Sidon, Alexandria and Athens. The city was a magnet for fortune hunters and traders, sailors and prostitutes, merchants and vagrants. As I ate my lunch, I thought about what Marseilles must have been like when the Magdalene arrived. The scenes had been idealized by Renaissance painters, but unbidden images that suddenly flashed through my mind made me think they had it all wrong. They missed the filth, the garbage in the streets, the smells of fish and open sewers. The images were so powerful, so strangely real that I found myself coughing to clear my nose and lungs.

Although the Magdalene's first attempts at evangelization met with failure. Biblical scholars would say she was lucky to have survived. In a society where Hebrew women were considered the chattels of their husbands, were not allowed to own property of their own, were not educated beyond household duties, were not even allowed to enter the synagogue, the very idea that a woman would attempt to preach in public was certain to bring down upon her the condemnation of the domineering male community. In the first century, that often meant stoning or banishment. For a Hebrew woman to attempt to preach to the Roman occupiers of Marseilles was an act of incredible courage, especially when the subject matter was the divinity of a man recently executed by a Roman governor.

More images flashed through my mind: a beautiful young woman, with features not unlike those of the woman who sat beside me. Her hair was longer, of course. But much the same reddish-blonde color. She stood atop a wagon, calling out to gather a crowd around her. Her words flamed in my mind: words spoken in a language I didn't understand, but sounded remarkably like one of the languages Magdalena had used with Professor Abramakian.

The legends impute Mary Magdalene's eventual success to a fortuitously timed miracle. Accounts differ as to the exact nature of the alleged miracle. Serrano's books included a translation of the thirteenth century *Legenda Aurea,* which identifies the beneficiary of the miracle as Peregrinus, governor of the province of Marseilles. In that version, Peregrinus promised to become a Christian if Mary Magdalene would pray for his wife to bear a child. In response to Mary's prayers, the wife became pregnant. When the wife died during a voyage, Peregrinus left the living child at the dead mother's breast on a small island. After two years in the Holy Land, Peregrinus returned to the island to find his child playing along the shore. The child ran to his dead mother, who promptly was restored to life. The three returned to Marseilles, where they were baptized as Christians.

According to his marginal notes, the only part of the "miracle" Serrano was able to confirm was that Peregrinus really did convert to Christianity, an extraordinary action for a Roman governor. The conversion took place not long after the birth of his first child, at the time the legends placed Mary Magdalene in Marseilles.

How much truth there is to this and other miracle stories attributed to her is irrelevant. What is important is that the people of Provence apparently believed them. The Magdalene soon developed a following. She moved from town to town throughout the region preaching the good news of Jesus Christ and converting Jews and heathens alike. More miracles, not very well documented, were attributed to her. The legends have her eventually retreating to a cave at Sainte Baume, where she lived out the last years of her life in prayer and meditation. She died, according to most of the accounts, in the year 63, at the age of 60. Although some traditions say she was buried in Toulon beside Lazarus, the most credible accounts are those which located her tomb in a crypt constructed by her good friend Maximin, not far from Ste. Baume. The tomb was guarded by Cassianite monks through the fourth century, later hidden from invaders and rediscovered on December 9, 1279 beneath what is now the *Basilique Ste. Marie Madeleine* in the town of *Saint-Maximin-la-Sainte-Baume*. The discovery was authenticated by Pope Boniface VIII. The Magdalene's skull, devoid of flesh but with long strands of hair still attached, was encased in a golden reliquary donated by Charles, the King of Naples. The grim relic remains on display today at the *Basilique*.

The success of Mary Magdalene's ministry is attested by the reverence which her memory still evokes throughout Europe. For centuries, the continent's Kings and Queens and nobles made pilgrimages to her refuge at Sainte Baume. It was a place of prayer for the Crusaders; a sacred site for the Knights Templar, a shrine of the Cathars. Hundreds of French Catholic churches have been dedicated to her memory, including the landmark *La Madelene* in Paris. There are credible sources who claim that even the famous *Notre Dame* cathedrals in Paris and Chartres, built by the Templars, were secretly dedicated to her. At the latest count, 1,100 hymns have been written to her in France alone, and many more in Germany, Belgium, and Italy. As a demonstration of the influence this remarkable woman continues to exert on the French, the people of Provence still celebrate her feast day every year with parades, fiestas, and prayer. Thousands of her followers gather on that day in St. Maximin, to line the streets and cheer as her skull is paraded through town.

There will always be skeptics, I know. After all, I was one myself. And even I am willing to admit that whatever objectivity I had brought to this investigation had been compromised by my feelings for Magdalena. But I am convinced that what I heard that day was nothing less than an eyewitness account of the difficulties the group faced during those early days in Provence. As a psychologist, I had a good deal of experience in clinical settings with delusional patients, with individuals lost in their own complicated fantasy worlds, and with pathological liars. Even the most convincing of them were unable to maintain the linear cohesiveness of structure and detail that Magdalena had demonstrated since our first conversation. Given the vast amount of often obscure information she was providing and the conversational ease with which she responded to my questions, I didn't understand how anyone could doubt her.

And yet, the more she talked, the more I became convinced that she wasn't telling me the whole story. She was willing to talk almost endlessly about what all her companions did during those first few months in

Gaul. But she seemed very secretive about her own activities. What was she hiding?

Perhaps when confronted with the reality of her own tomb, she might finally reveal her secret.

When we left *les Saintes-Maries-de-la-Mer,* the black car fell in behind us once again.

Fifty-Eight

MY ORIGINAL PLAN was to head for Marseilles, where Mary Magdalene preached extensively and made some of her most important converts. Although many of Marseilles's ancient buildings and historic sections had been devastated by wars, misguided building booms, and the pressures of population growth, there were still a number of sites, such as the *vieux port,* that might resonate with her memory. The ancient seaport was now the second largest city in France, overcrowded and tumultuous and, according to the gentle souls who write the guidebooks, a sometimes dangerous city. It sounded like a great place for two fugitives to hide out. But first I had two other sites to visit, and along the way I hoped to lose the black car that had been following us all morning.

The Opel Corsa didn't have the power to outdistance them, either on the D570 or the expressways ahead. Instead, I headed back to Arles, driving at a leisurely pace to lull them into thinking that we were returning to our hotel. The historic section of Arles, where our hotel was located, is a bewildering labyrinth of narrow lanes, some only three blocks long, designed for the horse-drawn traffic of ancient times. The tangled streets that so frustrated me when I was searching for a hotel now became my allies. I drove aimlessly up and down the tight one-way streets, circling back and around with no goal except to wait for that one golden moment when the driver of the black car finally fell far enough behind for me to make an unseen turn and disappear from his sight. It happened near the river, when someone on a motor scooter suddenly pulled out behind me. After a few evasive turns, I managed to make my way out onto Avenue Victor Hugo, the route that led north towards Tarascon and St. Remy.

From St. Remy, I headed back down to Aix-en-Provence. It was a circuitous route, one that gave me ample opportunity to be certain I had lost our pursuers. The scenery along the way changed from low scrub bushes and salty marshes to the mountainous views beloved by Cézanne. From Aix-en-Provence, I headed east and south to the tiny town of St. Zacharie.

I was purposely taking the back route to our next destination, hoping to once again test her distant memory.

On the Michelin map, the D480 appears to be a pleasant road through a forest preserve. In reality, it was a single-lane dirt road that wound almost a thousand meters uphill in a series of hairpin turns to the top of Grande Bastide. We encountered only one vehicle during the long drive, a van parked by a stream while the passengers enjoyed a snack of sausage and cheese. At the top of Grande Bastide, I had a good view of the road below. No one was following us.

There were also no signs to alert Magdalena where we were headed. But as soon as we rounded the final bend leading into Plan d'Aups, she suddenly straightened up.

"Sainte Baume," she murmured.

The brilliant white limestone cliffs of the *Massif* were visible from miles away. It was an enormous vertical wall that formed the entire eastern side of the valley. Somewhere up on those cliffs was a cave which Mary Magdalene used as her hermitage, and where some of the most improbable events of her life were reputed to have taken place. By now, I was accustomed to Magdalena's ability to recognize places associated with the Magdalene. Of course, I have to admit I recognized this particular location myself, from the photographs in Serrano's books.

"We used to come here on horseback," she said in an excited voice. "There was no road, just a narrow trail. It took two days to get here from Marseilles. We brought along donkeys loaded with food, and canvas for shelter. There weren't any houses or places to stop. This whole area was really wilderness."

"It's still wild, at least by modern standards," I said. "The legends say Mary Magdalene spent the last thirty years of her life in the grotto of Sainte Baume."

"The legends are wrong," she replied. "I came to the grotto only for retreats, usually forty days, the way Jesus my Christ went into the desert."

Her explanation sounded reasonable. The idea that a woman would travel to France to spend thirty years in a cave always seemed to me rather pointless; she could have done the same thing back in Judea, closer to the place where her Savior once preached.

"But you *did* come here," I said. My use of the personal pronoun wasn't a mistake this time. It felt so right when I said it, that I decided to drop the unnatural references to Mary Magdalene, and treat both their lives as the continuation of a single spirit. "You know, in spite of the legends, some of the local priests claim you never visited the grotto."

The denial by the local priests seemed equally implausible to me; how could they be so certain about events for which there was no written record?

"Many people came here," she said. "There was a time when the pagans came here to pray to Isis, the Goddess of Wisdom. You'll see why when we reach the grotto."

"In that case, I guess those stories about you being naked except for your hair weren't true, either," I teased.

That brought an embarrassed grin to her face. "The most anybody ever saw of my body in France was on the beach at Collioure, when you were ashamed to look at me."

We parked in the lot beside the old *Hostellerie la Ste. Baume* and made our way across the open fields, following the path taken by kings and popes on their way to pay homage to the earlier incarnation of the woman who was accompanying me. The pathway turned steep, leading through stands of northern hardwoods, maples, and beech trees, with a scattering of firs. The weather was more comfortable, not really much cooler, but certainly less humid. A few other pilgrims were ahead of us. They were better prepared for the hike, with rugged jeans and heavy walking shoes. Magdalena was wearing thin-soled slip-ons, and my shoes had leather soles that tended to slide on the smooth rock surfaces. It took us a half-hour to make our way up to the Dominican monastery that guarded the mouth of the cave. We paused there to look back. We were hundreds of meters above the floor of the Heuvaune valley, high enough to look down and see an eagle soaring on the thermal currents below us. Magdalena led me into the grotto. The interior was much larger than it looked from down below. I would guess it could hold a hundred people. Magdalena made a face at the crucifixes that had been installed on the sides of the cave and on the white marble high altar. I squeezed her hand as a warning not to make a scene. She frowned and bit her lip, but remained quiet. The marble altar was flanked by two marble staircases that led to the rear of the cave.

"The last time I was here, there was nothing in the cave except a few rocks on which to sit," Magdalena said. "My favorite rock was way in the back of the cave, where I could sit completely surrounded by darkness, and stare out at the countryside, as if I was looking out from the bottom of a well. That was part of what made this so wonderful a place for meditation, but now with the altar blocking the view, I think you can't do that anymore."

She led me toward the back of the cave in search of the rock, which had long ago been removed. If the people who removed it knew it was the rock on which Mary Magdalene once meditated, it probably ended up in a church somewhere, or had been chipped into hundreds of pieces for the private collections of priests and parish benefactors.

"They've polished the floor," she commented. "It's so smooth now. It used to be rough and painful for kneeling."

"It's not polished," I told her. "It's been worn smooth by the footsteps of all the pilgrims who came here over the centuries."

She shook her head in amazement.

"And the walls," she ran her fingers over some large hollowed-out areas. "What happened to the walls?"

"Souvenir hunters, I expect. Wherever the rock was soft enough, they'd break off a piece to take home."

"Amazing," she murmured.

In the farthest end of the cave, illuminated by hundreds of devotional candles and surrounded by bouquets of fresh flowers, was a statue of Mary Magdalene being raised up by angels.

"What about the angels?" I asked.

"Which angels?"

"There's a story that two angels visited you before you died. Supposedly, they lifted you up and carried you to Maximin, who gave you Communion before you passed away."

She smiled. "You don't really believe that, do you?"

"That's one of the stories," I said. "When you think about it, it's no more incredible than the concept of reincarnation."

"Well, in the first place, I didn't die up here. I passed away in a small house in Aix-en-Provence. And the only angels who were with me at the time were the two women who were ministering to me."

"No levitation, either?" I probed.

"No levitation," she said. "I was just an ordinary woman who was lucky enough to become . . ." Once again, as she had done a few times before, she stopped and corrected what she was about to say. " . . . Lucky enough to be a participant in some truly extraordinary events."

Fifty-Nine

ONE OF THE most gruesome traditions of the Catholic faith has been the dismemberment of the cadavers of its holiest members. From the earliest days of the Church, the faithful have treasured relics of those they consider saints. Although some relics, such as bits of fabric cut from garments worn by the venerated personage are benign reminders of a holy life, the most treasured relics are actual body parts. These grim mementos are normally removed when the body is disinterred as part of the process of elevation to sainthood. In many cases, such as that of Francis Xavier or Catherine Labouré or dozens of other saints, the corpses are discovered to have defied the normal laws of decomposition. Independent observers, often non-Catholic and confirmed skeptics, describe flesh that remains pink and life-like, eyes that are still clear and liquid, blood that remains fluid and uncongealed, and often a sweet perfumed smell emanating from the figure. This has been true not only with corpses entombed in airtight lead coffins, but as in the cases of Charbel Markouf and Francis Xavier, it was also true of corpses thrown into lime-filled pits or dumped in swampy graves.

Yet instead of venerating such apparently miraculous discoveries, the traditional practice has been to dismember the body and distribute fingers, bones, hearts, even tongues to various churches and convents, where they are enshrined in golden reliquaries of often shameful excess. The fame of a church or cathedral was often directly related to the importance of the relics it displayed. But not all relics are genuine. The number of saints is limited. And as with all other commodities in scarce supply this led to spurious claims and even outright counterfeiting. In the case of Mary Magdalene, for example, six different churches claim to be the final resting place for her remains, and there are enough bones on display in other churches to complete three additional skeletons.

Of all those various claims, however, only the relics at the Basilica of Sainte Marie Madeleine at *Saint-Maximin-la-Sainte-Baume* bear the official imprimatur of the Catholic Church.

The remains were found on December 9, 1279, hidden beneath a crypt in the Church of St. Maximin. In a grim testament to the importance of the cadaver, relic hunters had already removed one leg at the time of burial. Sixteen years later, Pope Boniface VIII officially declared the remains to be those of Mary Magdalene. The skull, with patches of hair still attached, was removed and set into a golden reliquary for public display.

It was with great trepidation that I led Magdalena down the stairs into the narrow crypt.

How would she react upon seeing the skull of the woman she once was?

I was about to subject her to a test that even Professor Stevenson never contemplated.

In the literature of reincarnation, there were dozens of cases where the reborn were taken to visit the graves of their former selves. While some experienced nausea or panic attacks, most were simply depressed. Some, like Howard Darden of Britain, made annual pilgrimages to the grave of the man he once was. But in all those cases, the physical evidence of their dead predecessors was covered with earth or locked away in a mausoleum.

None, to my knowledge, had ever viewed the actual corpse of their former self, much less their former skull with its vacant eye sockets and bared teeth. It was a sight I was not looking forward to myself.

We descended into the crypt, the same space where the body had been found eight hundred years earlier. The roof of the crypt was blackened by centuries of candle smoke. The air was damp and smelled of mildew. It was cooler down here; Magdalena wrapped her arms around herself to stay warm.

In front of us, at eye level, was an alcove shielded with bulletproof glass and further protected by a gate of black metal bars. Behind the bars, gleaming in the cone of a single spotlight, was the golden reliquary. It was fashioned in the likeness of a woman's head and shoulders, supported by two golden angels. Set into the polished metal, where the face should have been, was an age-blackened skull. Bits of leathery skin stuck to it in places. Strands of yellowish hair were visible between the skull and the silver.

Beside me, Magdalena had an oddly impassive reaction. There was a curious expression on her face. She moved closer, right up to the metal bars to examine it more carefully.

"That's not me," she said in a calm voice.

"What?"

"I'm sure it's not me," she said. "If it was me, I would have felt something. Like I did in the grotto, or at the old Roman road. But I don't feel anything."

"That's a pretty subjective reaction," I said.

"That's not my skull," she insisted.

"Do you know the history of this relic?" I asked. "It's been authenticated by popes, and venerated by the Kings and Queens of France since the thirteenth century. Thousands of believers come from all over the world to see it paraded through the streets every year on Mary Magdalene's feast day. This is probably the single most celebrated religious relic in France."

"I don't know whose skull it is, but it's not mine," she insisted. "It's not the skull of Mary Magdalene."

I didn't really know how to respond. We had come all this way, to arrive at what I thought would be an emotional confrontation with her past, only to have her deny the very reason for the existence of this enormous basilica.

"I tend to be a skeptic about such things myself," I said. "But when it comes to traditions as old as this one, I don't think you should dismiss it so lightly."

"Theo, this is not my skull," she continued to insist. "I know what I looked like, and even though this is only a skull, it doesn't look like me. To begin with, the teeth are all wrong. These front teeth are wide and flat and they're lined up straight across. My teeth were rounded, and not as thick as these, and they curved more naturally. And the cheekbones . . . I had higher cheekbones. And this hair is yellowish. By the time I died, my hair was almost completely white. This is somebody else's skull, not mine."

Before I could protest any further, someone behind me started to clap.

"*Bravo!* You have seen through their deception," said a familiar voice.

I turned to see a smiling Jean-Claude DesRosier, who had descended the steps soundlessly and must have been listening to our entire discussion. He was dressed, as before, in impeccable elegance. His blazer was of black velvet, with a red silk foulard in the breast pocket that bore his family crest; his shirt was a pale rose silk, his slacks were an immaculate white, as were his slip-ons. I didn't think Bally made white shoes, but there they were, slim and soft and completely unscuffed, as if this was the first time they had been worn.

"It's true," he said as he stepped forward. "This is not the skull of Mary Magdalene. It is a substitute carefully selected to resemble the original."

"How did you get here?" I asked, and then, "How did you know we'd be here?"

"That's not important," he responded. "What is important is the fact that this young woman, who never viewed the relic before, immediately identified it as a counterfeit. Does that not astound you?"

"Nothing Magdalena says astounds me anymore," I said.

"Well said! She is truly a remarkable woman."

I didn't like the way he was smiling at her: an intrusive, ingratiating smile that infuriated me. Especially when my lovely, innocent young Magdalena returned his smile with one of her own.

"*Enchanté, mademoiselle,*" he said. He took her hand and very ostentatiously bowed and kissed her fingers, the sort of gesture I wished I could have handled with the practiced ease he displayed. The gallantry, which seemed so false to me, brought a blush of delight to Magdalena's face. "*Je m'appelle Jean-Claude DesRosier, Comte d'Anjou, Grand Chevalier du Templier. À votre service.*"

If I wasn't mistaken, he had just identified himself as a Templar, a Grand Knight, no less.

"How do you know it's a fake?" I asked.

"You mean other than taking the word of this lovely young woman?" he smiled at her again. "A man in my position has many sources of information. In any event, I wouldn't exactly call it a fake. It's a real skull, carefully selected to match the original. But it *is* a substitute. The original skull was removed and taken to Rome, where it was subjected to carbon-14 dating tests. Those tests established a date of death in the middle to the end of the first century."

"Which would be consistent with the date of Mary Magdalene's death," I said.

"Exactly," DesRosier smiled.

Beside me, I could sense Magdalena frowning.

"Why would such a thing happen?" she asked. "Why remove my bones from where they rested so long?"

"The Vatican, like God, works in mysterious ways," he shrugged.

"Please do not involve God in this matter," Magdalena said. "Tell me how this all happened."

DesRosier hesitated, glancing at me. His expression suggested he was uncomfortable discussing the matter in front of me. Yet he couldn't refuse Magdalena's request.

"Two months ago, an emissary from the Vatican arrived unannounced at the Basilica," he said. "He had in his possession a letter from the Secretary of the Sacred Congregation for the Doctrine of the Faith. The letter authorized the emissary to examine the reliquary containing the skull of Mary Magdalene. It also authorized him to take certain samples from the relic. At that time, of course, the reliquary contained the original Magdalene skull. I have independent confirmation of that fact. My sources tell me the rector was excited. A representative from the Vatican? That was quite extraordinary. He wanted to call his bishop, but the emissary told him he had specific instructions to inform no one. It was apparently a secret mission. No one was to be told, even after the fact." DesRosier hesitated again, glancing nervously at me, and, it seemed, behind me as if someone else was listening in. I looked back, too, but saw no one on the stairs behind him. We were alone in the crypt. "Perhaps I am revealing too much," he said.

"No," Magdalena replied. "I want to know what happened to my skull. How did it disappear. And where is it now?"

"I can assure you it is safe," DesRosier said. "Safer than the Pieta or the original manuscripts of Saint Paul. I understand it is being kept in a special vault in the Secret Archives of the Vatican Library."

"Your sources seem to have supplied you with a lot of information," I said.

DesRosier gave a shrug and went on with his account.

"If you saw the original skull, which is quite similar to what is now contained within the reliquary, you would see there was still hair attached. Not a full head of hair by any means. Just loose strands and a few small clumps. The rest had been taken through the centuries by priests and cardinals and I'm sure some of it was sold. During the Middle Ages, there was a huge trade in religious relics. I'm surprised the teeth weren't removed. In any event, it was apparently the hair that the emissary was after, at that time, at least. He took eight strands, each from a different section of the skull. The strands were about thirty centimeters in length."

About ten inches, I thought, doing a quick mental calculation.

"After removing the hair samples, the emissary swore the rector to secrecy."

"A vow he obviously didn't keep," I pointed out.

"The rector was intimidated. Vows made under duress are not valid."

"Strands of hair?" Magdalena was puzzled. "Why did they want the hair?" Her hand went to her own hair. She seemed on the verge of saying something more.

"For testing," DesRosier said.

"Testing? What do you mean?" she asked.

"Oh, of course, *pardonnez moi, mademoiselle*. I forgot you have not TV or newspapers in the *convento*. You don't know anything about DNA testing, do you? It's very complicated, but basically, all humans, animal and plants contain DNA molecules. Those molecules can be extracted and examined to determine all sorts of information, including the genetic programming of the individual."

"Even people who died two thousand years ago?" she asked.

"Longer than that," DesRosier said. "DNA testing has been used on the mummies of the Pharoahs who died four thousand years ago."

"And also the five-thousand-year-old remains of a man they found in the

Italian Alps," I interjected, my ego demanding I show Magdalena I knew as much about the subject as DesRosier. "The DNA samples they took from his hair and tissue revealed quite a bit about his medical history."

"This DNA, it lasts that long?" Magdalena asked in amazement.

I started to answer, but DesRosier interrupted. "Allow me," he said. "A few months ago, all I knew about DNA was what I learned from the O.J. Simpson trial and watching *Jurassic Park*. I've learned quite a bit about it since then."

He quickly surprised me with an explanation far more detailed than the one I was going to offer.

"There are two types of DNA that are used for examination purposes," he said. "One type is what they call nuclear DNA, which comes from the nucleus of the cell. The problem with nuclear DNA is that it can deteriorate quickly, depending on its exposure to the elements. Even under the best of circumstances, it becomes useless for comparison purposes after three or four hundred years. The other type of DNA is what they call mitochondrial DNA. If you ever have the opportunity to see a motion picture titled *Jurassic Park*, that's the type of DNA they were supposed to have used to re-create the dinosaurs."

"From mosquitoes trapped in amber a hundred thousand years ago," I helpfully pointed out. "Although how those tiny mosquitoes could penetrate the thick hide of a dinosaur was never explained."

"In any event," he continued. "Mitochondrial DNA is almost invulnerable to decay. It can be extracted from tissue and bone samples that are thousands of years old. In addition to direct comparisons of samples, it can also be used to trace ancestry along the maternal bloodline. Oddly enough, nuclear DNA follows the paternal bloodline, while mitochondrial DNA follows the maternal bloodline. Which once again proves the primacy of the female."

"All right," Magdalena said impatiently. "All right, I think I understand all that. But tell me about the hair they took. What happened to it?"

"The eight strands of hair were not sent to a local laboratory," he went on. "They were carried by the emissary to Rome, to the office of the Secretary of the Sacred Congregation for the Doctrine of the Faith, where they were turned over to a Vatican laboratory."

DesRosier glanced behind me again before continuing in a hushed voice, as if letting us in on a great secret.

"One month later, the emissary returned, with two assistants. They carried with them a large container. Acting upon their orders, the rector closed the basilica to the public, and unlocked the metal gate that protects the reliquary. He was ordered out of the crypt, so that he could not observe their actions. When they were done, he was once again sworn to secrecy, this time on the threat of excommunication. Nevertheless, after the visitors departed, the rector came down here into the crypt to see what they had been up to. That was when he discovered, after close examination, that a different skull had been substituted."

"Why?" Magdalena asked.

"That is a question that will be answered at another time," DesRosier said. "Perhaps we should proceed to lunch now. I've reserved a private banquet room for us at the Hotel Sainte in Baume."

Mystified by DesRosier's strange revelations, I followed him up the stairs into the main nave of the Basilica. It was a magnificent Gothic structure, not well maintained, yet probably the finest example of such architecture in Provence. As if on cue, the first resonant notes boomed out of the enormous pipe organ in the back of the basilica. The organist was playing Franck's *Panis Angelicus*. The sumptuous bass notes of the opening bars, magnified by the power of the massive organ, reverberated through the basilica. It was such a gorgeous sound, it stopped me in my tracks.

The distraction, if it was planned that way, succeeded. Two uniformed *gendarmes* suddenly appeared at my sides. Before I realized what was happening, my wrists were handcuffed behind my back.

Coronel Velarde stepped out from behind a column to explain what was happening.

"Mr. Theophanes Nikonos, it is my duty to inform you that you are being arrested for the act of terrorist bombing that resulted in the deaths of Spanish citizens Javier Serrano and Frederico Zangara, and for the subsequent murder of the Lebanese national Naghib Abramakian, which also occurred on Spanish soil. Due to the terrorist nature of the crimes, the French authorities have expedited the extradition process. I have all the necessary papers in my possession. You may read them if you choose."

I declined the offer, certain that the fastidious *Coronel* had carefully followed all the formalities.

"In that case," he said. "You will now return with us to Spain, where you will stand trial."

Two uniformed *Guardia Civil* officers took over from their French counterparts. As they led me out of the Basilica, I turned to look for Magdalena.

She and DesRosier had disappeared.

I could only hope he would not betray her as he apparently did me.

Sixty

I WAIVED EXTRADITION and was taken on the overnight train to Valencia, where I was delivered to the *Refugio,* a holding prison for suspects awaiting trial. It was a fortress-style structure that Velarde explained was once used as a refuge for those fleeing Saracen invaders. The front was an almost unbroken wall of massive stone blocks. The only breaks in the wall were a few narrow openings that once served as gunports, but were now disguised as windows.

Despite its impressive exterior, the inside of the *Refugio* seemed a dismally ordinary jail. The floors were scuffed, the walls bare of any ornamentation. The acidic odor of stale human sweat defied the ventilation system. Unseen cell doors opened and closed with a regularity that suggested the immensity of the place

Velarde accompanied me through the booking process, watching impassively as I was strip-searched, issued an orange prison jumpsuit, assigned a number, and photographed. He carefully counted out the remaining $5,250.00 of DesRosier's money in front of me, placed it in a grey cardboard box, along with my passport, wallet, camcorder, and voice-stress analyzer, and had me sign a receipt. My civilian clothing went into a separate bag.

"I'd like you to inform the American consulate," I said to him. "Tell them I need a lawyer."

Velarde motioned to the cell phone, which had not been packed with my other personal items.

"Tell them yourself," he said. "You can keep the telephone with you. A courtesy we extend to our more distinguished guests."

He left me then, and a guard led me through two sets of barred doors and down a long corridor lined with two-man cells. My cell was near the end of the corridor. It contained two sagging beds, a small sink, a toilet, a metal mirror, and a small bookshelf.

My cellmate was sitting on his bed, reading a thick technical manual of some sort. He glanced up at me, nodded, and returned to his book until after the guard left. Only then did my cellmate rise and introduce himself. He was a tall, emaciated man, at least six inches taller than me, and he moved with a languid ease. His scalp was completely bald, and his facial skin was stretched so tight it glistened. Narrow-lensed titanium glasses rested halfway down his nose. Holding his place in the book with one bony finger, he extended his other hand to me and introduced himself with a graciousness I never expected to find in someone whom I soon learned was imprisoned on drug charges.

His name was Orlando Panay, and the first thing he did was to accuse me of being an informer. What aroused his suspicion was the cell phone. He examined it carefully, explaining that such items were normally not allowed in the cellblock, no matter what *Coronel* Velarde said. I raised my arms to allow him to search me for hidden wires, microphones, or recording equipment. Naturally, he found nothing incriminating on me, although he continued to regard the cell phone with suspicion for the entire time we were cellmates.

Rather than call the consulate, which the travel section of the *New York Times* had convinced me would provide little assistance, I called Jean-Claude DesRosier. He was aware that I was in jail, he said, and would arrange for one of his Valencia lawyers to visit me. He seemed very helpful and more concerned with my well-being than I anticipated. He assured me Magdalena was safe, although she was worried about me. We both agreed on the importance of keeping her hidden from the police.

DesRosier's lawyer showed up later that same afternoon. Edgardo Guzman was a man with a pockmarked face, bulbous lips, heavy earlobes, and thick fingers, a rough-looking character who wore an incredibly expensive-looking custom-tailored dark blue suit and carried a shiny alligator briefcase. However rough his life may once have been, and from the scars on his knuckles and his right cheek he may have been a street fighter in his youth, he now exuded the prosperity of a man at the top of his profession. He did nothing but grunt and nod his head until we were alone in the small lawyer's conference room.

"First," he said, before even opening his briefcase. "You will never mention the name of the man who hired you. Do you understand?"

"Yes."

"If his name ever comes out of your mouth, I promise you will never see the outside of a Spanish jail again. Never! Understand?"

I was taken aback by the harshness of his tone.

"What about Magdalena?" I asked. "I'd like to talk to her."

"Impossible. We are doing our best to protect her. For her safety, we cannot allow you any further contact with her."

Apparently, he was here only to deliver that message. He made a few cursory notes and told me he would arrange for another lawyer to take over. I never saw him again. The new lawyer who turned up a few days later was a young man recently out of law school who visited me often, took a lot of notes, and kept telling me the first hearing would happen "*muy pronto.*"

My cellmate spent most of his time reading. They were technical books: chemistry and physics, mostly. During the first week, he spoke little. When he wasn't reading, he kept eyeing my cell phone. The breakthrough in our relationship came when I let him use the phone to call a few friends. Having finally determined the cell phone wasn't a police tape recorder in disguise, he decided I probably wasn't an informer, but a legitimate murder suspect. After that, we got along rather well.

Like me, Orlando was an educated man, although his background was in the physical sciences. He was born in Avila, studied molecular biology at Salamanca University, and after graduation went directly into the research and development department at DuPont Pharma S.A., one of the largest pharmaceutical companies in Spain. When someone discovered that a computer could do most of the theoretical modeling work he did, Orlando was "downsized." Six months later, the unemployed scientist was arrested on charges of producing and distributing designer drugs.

Although he exhibited a superficial veneer of trust toward me, he was careful never to admit having done anything illegal. Apparently an informant led the police to a loft in an industrial area of Valencia, where they seized large quantities of Ecstasy, Rohypnol, crystal methamphetamine, LSD, and the equipment and raw materials for manufacturing dozens of other popular drugs. The police arrested Orlando when he showed up the next morning. It was a case of entrapment, he claimed. He went to the loft simply to apply for a job, having been informed by a chance acquaintance that a small research firm was looking to hire someone with his credentials. The fact that he had a key to the door was evidence of nothing, he insisted; he had been instructed that the key was under the mat. He had similar explanations for every other possible piece of evidence the police might come up with. It sounded to me as if he was rehearsing the defense strategy his lawyers would use at the trial.

"Unlike you," he said. "I have very good lawyers."

I had to agree. Visits by the young lawyer tapered off, until in the fourth week, he showed up only once. When I told him I wanted to hire a new lawyer, he responded that such an action would delay my hearing, because all the necessary paperwork was already filed under his name. Any change in legal representation would require refiling all the required documents. I was caught up in *Cláusula veinte-dos,* the Spanish equivalent of Catch-22.

"You don't look like a terrorist," Orlando said one day. "You are not Spanish. What is your connection with the Basques?"

"I have no connection with the Basques," I replied. "I had nothing to do with the bombing at *Naranjas*."

"I am sorry," he said with a smile. "I forgot. We are all innocent here."

There was no point in arguing. Unlike him, I had no skilled lawyers to provide me with the kind of defense even an innocent man needs in Spain.

During the weeks that followed, images of Magdalena kept me company. When the hot sun streamed into our cell, I thought back to the sunny beach in Collioure, and how warm her skin felt under my hands. After sunset, when the first stars came out, I remembered those wonderful evenings in Barcelona and Arles, and how she alternated between teasing me and charming me with those sweet and innocent eyes. Lying awake late at night, I tortured myself with thoughts of what might have, could have, should have transpired between us if I wasn't so restrained by religious taboos and my own basic backwardness with women. It was ridiculous behavior, I thought. I was agonizing over being separated from a woman to whom I had never had the courage to express my feelings.

"You have a woman waiting for you?" Orlando asked me one morning.

"Me? No. Unfortunately, no."

"You were talking in your sleep," he said. "Not for the first time. You talk to her every night."

"That would be Laura," I said, a little embarrassed. The slow-motion replay of her death was indeed a nightly dream, but I was never aware that I spoke her name aloud.

"Not Laura," Orlando corrected me. "The name you call out is Magdalena. I think she is Spanish, and I think you must love her very much."

Sixty-One

AS THE WEEKS dragged on with no hearing date and fewer and fewer visits from my lawyer, I occupied my time by studying the language of my captors. While other prisoners watched the soccer matches in the exercise yard, I was in the prison library with a Spanish-English dictionary.

Orlando suggested I read the daily newspapers, and that proved to be a big help, particularly the advertisements and the comics, where the words were accompanied with illustrations.

Orlando was turning out to be the ideal cellmate for an academic like me. We spent many afternoons discussing our areas of intellectual interest, and I found that the border between science and philosophy was much narrower than I once thought. We talked of Plato and Archimedes, the relative merits of Newton and Feynman, the Egyptian and Ming dynasties. And then one afternoon, we were sitting in the cell discussing reincarnation.

"I imagine everyone tells you there's no scientific basis for reincarnation," he said. It was just after we came in from the exercise yard. He was lying on his cot, staring up at the ceiling. I was working on my Spanish vocabulary.

"The migration of souls isn't the sort of thing that lends itself to scientific investigation," I said.

"That's the common perception," he said. "But it's not entirely true."

I lowered the book I was studying. In wide-ranging conversations often extending deep into the night, I had never heard Orlando Panay make a statement he couldn't support. He was the prototypical scientist, cautious in his assessment of the facts, and not given to expressing opinions on any subject about which he didn't have adequate information.

"As far as I know," I said. "Science hasn't even proven the existence of the human soul."

"You're wrong about that," he replied. "Speaking as a molecular biologist, that's a fairly easy proof. Of course, it depends on your definition of the soul."

He had my attention, and I could tell he enjoyed it.

"All right. Just for the sake of discussion, let's take one of the most common definitions," I suggested. "The average dictionary defines the soul as an immaterial essence, an animating principle, the breath of life, which has no physical or material properties, yet is responsible for our thoughts, our free will, and our behavior."

"That's a fairly easy concept to prove, and I can think of at least two different approaches," he said. "The first has its roots at Yale University, strangely enough, which, if you believe William Buckley, has little enthusiasm for religious matters these days. Way back in the 1930s, Yale professors Harold Burr and F. C. Norton discovered the existence of what they called 'the electrical architect' in all living creatures. The experimental evidence, which was presented to the National Academy of Sciences and praised in the *New York Times*, demonstrated that an electrodynamic field exists within the human body from the pre-embryonic stage until death. The field is apparently slightly different in each human being, and is responsible for the organization of cells, which eventually determines our personalities and who we are."

It was typical of the kinds of conversations I had with Orlando. Give him a subject, almost any subject, and he'd be off and running, constructing elaborate dissertations that were fascinating to hear, even if I didn't fully agree with them.

"Now the electrical architect was an important theory at the time," he went on. "Especially since it corresponded with the idea of the *astral body,* which was then being discussed by the spiritualist movement, and certainly supported the later concept of *Kirlian photography.* Everything we've learned since then provides further proof that this electrodynamic component is the immaterial life force, without which the body can't survive. The brain and the heart both depend on a continuous electrical charge to function. And the measurement of the activity of both of those organs is with instruments that measure electrical activity . . . the electrocardiograph and the electroencephalograph. Since death occurs when these instruments report the cessation of electric activity, one can only assume the electric activity is the life force, or if you will, the animating principle."

"That sounds kind of simplistic to me," I objected.

"Some of the best science is simple," Orlando responded. "But if you're looking for a more complicated definition, let's turn for a moment to DNA, which everyone thinks has answered every question we have about how humans grow and function."

"I know a little about DNA," I offered, still smarting from the way DesRosier upstaged me on the subject.

"Then you're in pretty much the same boat as most scientists," Orlando said. "To paraphrase the great quantum physicist Richard Feynman, the more we find out about it, the more we realize how little we know."

"I know it's the acronym for deoxyribonucleic acid." I felt compelled to show I wasn't totally ignorant about his specialty. "It's the famous double helix that's supposed to be inside every cell."

"That's more than most people know. Now imagine how tiny a single cell is. So infinitesimal that you need a powerful microscope to see it. And yet the single strand of DNA coiled up in the nucleus, the center of every cell, is a strand which would measure over two meters long if it was stretched out to its full length. That would make it taller than you. Boggles the mind, doesn't it?"

I nodded. One thing I learned long ago was to listen. And with Orlando, listening was always a revelation.

"Now consider: every strand of DNA in your body is identical. Every strand contains millions of bits of information, the genes that determine the color of your eyes, the shape of your fingers, how tall you are, how much hair you have on your legs. Every scientist knows that. But no scientist can explain what causes one strand of DNA to command its cell to become part of a toenail, while another identical strand of DNA commands its cell to become part of a brain that can think, have free will, make decisions, and sit here and communicate with me about the human soul.

"Oh, they'll talk about proteins and RNA, but the basic point is that *something* commands certain genes on the DNA strand to turn on or off, which in turn causes the cell to grow as part of a liver or part of an earlobe. And when we trace it all the way back, we find that an electrical charge plays a central role in that decision. So we get back to those earlier discoveries at Yale, which predated, and as with all good science, anticipated the work of today's DNA researchers. What Burr and Northrup found in their research was that the electrodynamic field was not just some random electrical charge activating proteins. In some unknown way, their 'electrical architect' worked with a pattern in mind, deciding which cells would perform which tasks, including the task of thinking. And that, my dear fellow, not only suggests that the electrical field possesses preordained knowledge of what a human being should be, but also suggests that it is responsible for our intellectual capabilities. Which, to me, fits your definition of a soul."

Orlando was still lying in bed, talking at the ceiling rather than at me as he spun out his theory. It reminded me of some of the conversations I had in college with my roommate, an intense New Englander who went on from psychology classes to divinity school at the Moody Institute in Chicago.

"Now consider the cosmic nature of that electrodynamic field," Orlando continued with his explication. "You can measure the field, you can prove it exists, but you can't see it and you can't feel it, whether in your own body or someone else's. And when the electrical activity of that field ceases, death follows almost immediately. Now that may not completely fit your Eastern Orthodox religious definition of a soul, but it is a fairly commonly accepted scientific proof of the 'spark of life,' which can be traced back to the primordial soup of creation."

"An interesting theory," I admitted.

"It's not just a theory," he insisted. "And if you doubt it, go into any hospital and look at the ECG and EKG equipment they use to monitor life."

"Okay, okay," I argued. "Let's say I accept your electrical architect as a crude definition of the soul. Or at least part of the soul. That still doesn't provide any kind of proof of reincarnation."

"I was getting to that," he said. "Reincarnation, as I understand it, is the belief that the soul reappears after death in a new body."

"It's not just a question of reappearing in a new body," I said, not wanting to make it too easy for him to explain away. "A true case of reincarnation would mean the transmission of information, personality, even memory from the former life to the new one."

My challenge, which I thought would give him pause, didn't faze Orlando in the slightest. He rolled effortlessly on, as if he was just getting warmed up.

"Now we go back to DNA," he said. "Contained within those millions of bits of programming information in each double helix are the blueprints for the brain and the central nervous system. But these two systems, even in an infant, are not created as empty vessels. Someplace along the line, humans learned certain behavior patterns that were necessary for survival. The baby, without being taught, already knows how to suckle at its mother's breast.

The growing child, whenever it is frightened, experiences a rush of adrenaline that enables it to fight or flee more effectively. You're a psychologist. You know about instinctive behavior."

I nodded, beginning to understand where he was headed.

"So basically, the same DNA that builds the brain also imparts memories of behavior that enabled our ancestors to survive. The fact that instinctive behavior exists proves that knowledge can be transmitted through different generations."

"That may make the case for genetic memory," I said. "Which would also explain personality traits passed along from a distant grandparent to a child who might never have met that particular ancestor," I admitted. I had read the anecdotal accounts in my Behavorial Psych classes. "But it doesn't make the case for reincarnation in genetically unrelated bodies. And just to give you a totally impossible intellectual hurdle, there's the issue of the *karmic cycle.*"

"You mean the Buddhist Wheel of Life."

I guess I shouldn't have been surprised at his knowledge of reincarnation theory. It would explain why he seemed so glib and almost well rehearsed with his explanations.

"According to which we all move through a progression of lives towards enlightenment," I said. "Each new life is supposedly determined by the quality of the previous life. Only by living a good life can we finally achieve *nirvana.*"

"Which means the rebirth process is not random," he agreed. "Therefore, the good soul must somehow find a new life in which it can better itself, while the bad soul is doomed to a life in which it must correct its mistakes."

"You know more about this process than you admitted at first," I said.

"Everyone knows something about reincarnation," Orlando smiled. "Perhaps because we are all living proof of its truth."

"You haven't given me the proof yet," I pointed out.

"On a molecular level, there are countless examples of the kind of attraction that would draw a 'good' soul to a 'good' body. James Ward gave one analogy of such chemical affinities in his famous Gifford lectures at Cambridge University. He described how an atom liberated from its molecular bonds behaves in an unexpected manner. Ward identified it as the 'nascent' state, which literally means 'coming into existence.' The fascinating aspect of that nascent atom's behavior is that it does not combine with the first free atom it encounters, as scientists might expect. Instead, it only combines with an atom for which it has an affinity. And as Ward said in his lecture, if a liberated atom can do that, certainly a liberated spirit can do as well, if not better."

"Not bad," I commended him. "At least you've got one good scientific analogy."

"Oh, but there are other examples all around us." His eyes lit upon my cell phone, which was lying on the table. "It's very common for us to use computers as a way of explaining how the brain works. And that's a very good example. But you can also use the wireless cell phone as a way to explain how a soul migrates to another body. The cell phone is a physical object, just like the human body. You can see it, touch it, hold it. Yet there's a tiny electronic brain inside that phone that can send out an invisible electronic message which can be received only by the electronic brain in a single specific cell phone that might be halfway around the world. Now the human brain is a lot more powerful than the computer chip in your cell phone. And it also operates with an electronic charge. So why can't the electronic charge that leaves the body at death be transmitted to a fetus with a compatible brain?"

"An interesting concept," I mused.

"Oh, it's not my concept," Orlando said. "The credit belongs to Julian

Huxley, the great biologist. Early in his life, he didn't believe in reincarnation. But later, after studying the evidence, he wrote about 'a permanently surviving spirit-individuality given off at death the way a wireless message is given off by a sending apparatus.' He postulated that the spirit-individuality remains an unseen and unheard entity in the atmosphere, just like the wireless message, until it comes back to the actuality of consciousness by making contact with something that could work as a receiving apparatus for the mind."

Orlando picked up my cell phone and waved it to make his point more emphatically.

"And that was before the cell phone was even invented . . ."

He stopped in mid-sentence, staring quizzically at the phone in his hand. He turned it over, examining the back of the unit. Suddenly, as if it was some sort of poisonous object, he dropped it on the table and backed away. His face twisting with rage, he turned on me. Grabbing me by the shirt front, he slammed me against the bars of the cell.

"You *puta!*" He hissed at me through clenched teeth. "You son of a bitch!"

He was absolutely berserk with rage. The well-mannered intellectual who I thought had become my friend was slamming me again and again against the bars until my shoulders ached and I was afraid my skull would crack.

"You're an informer! A Goddamned informer!" He kept his voice low, barely above a harsh whisper. The spittle from his angry mouth spattered against my face. "You and your Goddamned cell phone. They've been listening in all along!"

"I don't know what you're talking about," I said.

He spun around and threw a pillow over the cell phone.

"You thought you could fool me," he said, talking louder now that the phone was covered. "Who gave you that phone? The police? The *Guardia?*"

"I still don't know what you're talking about."

"Don't play innocent with me. That cell phone has been transmitting every word that's spoken in this cell. You've been working with the police! You were sent here with that phone to see if you could get me to incriminate myself. And someplace, they've got a tape recorder taking it all down."

"No, I promise you! That's not true! It's just an ordinary cell phone. You made calls on it yourself."

He stopped banging me against the bars, although he held onto my shirt front.

"Don't take me for a fool," he said. "I know how bugging equipment works. That phone has been altered to contain a special transmitting device. Every sound it picks up, including my phone calls, is being sent to a specific receiver."

"You're imagining things," I tried to calm him down.

"Why else do you think our court hearings are being delayed so long?" he asked. "They're hoping to get me to say something they can use against me. But I was too smart for them. I suspected you from the start. *Gracias à Dios,* I was always careful what I said."

"I assure you, I swear to God," I said. "The police never gave me that phone. It was never out of my sight from the moment I was arrested."

"Then why is it warm to the touch?" he asked. "The only time a wireless phone should be warm is when the battery is being recharged or when the battery has been in use for a long period of time. Your phone has been off the charger since this morning. So if it isn't in a constant transmission mode, why is it warm?"

Sixty-Two

ORLANDO WAS RIGHT.

The back of the phone was warm, just as he said. The power button was switched off, the indicator light was off, and to all outward appearances the phone was in a dormant mode. Yet the distinct warmth on the back of the case was a sign that the battery was indeed being drained for some purpose. I thought back to the instructions DesRosier had given me. He was very precise about recharging the phone every night. It seemed at the time unnecessary, especially when I hadn't used the phone during the day. But the one time I didn't recharge, when we drove through the night to Barcelona, the indicator signaled the battery power was low. If Orlando was right, and I now believed he was, that meant the phone had been transmitting the entire time, even though I hadn't been using it. And Jean-Claude DesRosier must have been the person on the receiving end.

But why would he want to listen in on my investigation?

After all, I was working for him. He had every right to expect I would report back to him with whatever I learned about Magdalena. Was he too impatient to wait? Didn't he trust me?

Or was there some more sinister reason behind the action?

I pressed the speed-dial button. As I listened to the electronic beeps making contact with DesRosier's phone, I couldn't help thinking about Huxley's analogy of a soul searching for a new body. On each of my previous calls, DesRosier's office answered on the second ring. This time, I counted six distinct rings before I heard the familiar female voice.

"I'm sorry," the voice said. "The party you're calling is out of country and unavailable to take your call. If you care to leave a message, please wait for the tone."

A recorded message? I was stunned. DesRosier had promised he could be reached wherever he was through his switchboard.

"This is Theophanes Nikonos. I have an extremely important matter to discuss. Please call me as soon as possible."

Orlando took the phone from me and pressed the speed-dial button himself. He rolled his eyes as he listened to the recorded message. Silently, he closed the phone and replaced it under the pillow so he wouldn't be overheard.

"You were calling to tell them you have been found out," he said. "Do you really expect them to return your call?"

"Orlando, I swear. I didn't know the cell phone was rigged."

"Rigged?" He was momentarily puzzled. "I don't know that word."

"I'm sorry, it's slang. It means I didn't know the phone was tampered with."

He gave a snort to show his disgust.

"In that case, you are very stupid. Who gave you the telephone?"

"The man who hired me. He gave me ten thousand dollars in U.S. currency, the cell phone, and a car."

That elicited a low whistle from Orlando.

"And you were not suspicious?"

"He promised me another fifty thousand dollars when I finished my investigation," I said, realizing as the words came out how improbable it all sounded.

"And now you are sitting in jail and his lawyers don't even come to see you anymore."

"I should have known better," I sighed, slumping down on the edge of my cot. "That was obviously too much money for what he wanted me to do."

"And where is this girl you dream about?"

"Magdalena? As far as I know, the police haven't arrested her. She's safe."

"Says who?" Orlando asked. And before I could respond, he answered his own question. "The man who hired you?"

Defeated, I could only nod. Orlando took pity on me, sat down on the bed, and laid his arm over my shoulder.

"I believe you are not an informer, *compadre*," he sighed. "I think you are just stupid. You are very well educated, but stupid in certain areas."

"You're right. I should have noticed the phone was warm," I berated myself. "I should have been more suspicious, like you."

"Ah, but I ignored the heat myself when I first examined your phone. When you carry it on your belt, your body heat warms up the whole case. I assumed that was why it was warm. But when you left the phone on the table all morning, it should have cooled off."

"Even if I had noticed it, I wouldn't have known it was a listening device," I said. "I thought listening devices are just little circuits that don't need batteries."

"Those little circuits you read about, the ones that look like shirt buttons? Those are passive transmitters which have a very limited transmitting range." He chuckled softly and explained, "I'm very well informed about listening devices, because many of my . . . um, friends . . . have been convicted with evidence gained through wiretaps and bugs. Based on the amount of heat being generated, your telephone contains a slightly more powerful active transmitter, one with a range of perhaps five kilometers, depending on the quality and power of the receiving equipment. From the receiving point, it could be relayed anywhere."

A range of five kilometers meant everything Magdalena and I said anywhere, even in the flat open areas of the Camargue, could have been overheard without any risk of the eavesdropper's being seen.

"The smaller passive transmitters don't generate any heat, so their presence can't be detected unless you open the back of the phone," Orlando continued. "But your system has a longer range, so it requires power which it drains from the battery. The warmth you feel is actually coming from molecular activity in the battery, rather than the transmitter itself. And this Nokia has a special 2700mAH lithium ion battery that can transmit up to 20 hours on a single charge. They could be listening to you all day long, and you'd never know it. "

"But I was using the phone, making calls. If the phone was in constant transmission mode, how could I make calls to different people?"

"The transmitter is on a separate circuit. It operates independently of the phone transmission. On the other hand, it'll pick up both sides of any phone conversation that takes place."

All the explanations in the world couldn't make me feel better about being duped by DesRosier. There is nothing more depressing for someone like me than to be outsmarted by a person I considered my intellectual inferior. I had come away from the meeting at his chateau thinking he was a harmless dilettante, living on the inherited wealth of a business empire created by his ancestors. Academics like myself have a history of denigrating the mental ability, if not the moral character, of such individuals. It was hard to accept that the man I dismissed as a dilettante had successfully played me for a fool.

"I guess we should destroy the phone," I sighed. "Unless you know how to disconnect the listening device."

"No, no, no," Orlando said. "That's what I mean about you being stupid in certain matters. If we do anything to cut off transmission, other than allow the batteries to slowly die out, your friends will know their scheme has been discovered. They may not be answering your phone call, but that does not mean they are not listening for anything we say. We must find a way to use that knowledge to our advantage."

"How do we do that?"

"I don't know. Not yet. But we'll figure something out. Just be careful what you say. We can't keep the phone covered, or they'll suspect that we know they're listening. The best thing is to speak normally, and if you have anything you don't want overheard, use the pillow or write a note."

It wasn't much of a strategy, but at least it was proactive. Frankly, there wasn't much to conceal in the way of conversation. Most of what we had been talking about for the last month and a half was what now seemed to be pointless philosophical and scientific discussions that were probably a subconscious effort to make ourselves feel as if we were smarter than the run-of-the-mill criminals who occupied the other cells. It helped compensate for our disappointment as we watched how quickly those lesser prisoners were being processed, granted hearings, and either released or sent on to other prisons to begin their sentences.

The following days passed slowly. While we languished in seemingly endless captivity, the cell phone served as a constant reminder of my failure as a judge of character. I tried a few more times to call DesRosier. Each time the recording repeated its claim that he was out of the country and offered me the false hope that he would return my call. Orlando failed to come up with any plan to use the telephone for anything other than playing practical jokes on the eavesdroppers. He continued to study his technical books. And with his help, I worked on my Spanish. Not having figured out any way to use the cell phone to our advantage, I finally surrendered it to the guards, who presumably passed it along to *Coronel* Velarde.

By the end of the second month of my confinement, I was able to speak and understand enough Spanish to carry on a minimal conversation. I did even better when it came to reading. I was actually getting quite literate in the language. I was at the point where I could understand much of what I read in the newspapers on my daily visits to the library. I read about local and national politics, the sports pages, the comics, the real estate section. None of what I read had any relevance to my situation, of course.

Until the day I opened up the *Sociedad* section one morning and saw a photograph of Jean-Claude DesRosier with his fiancée. I didn't have to read the caption to recognize the beautiful woman smiling up at my devious former employer.

The bride-to-be was Magdalena.

What felt like a mild earth tremor caused the newspaper to tremble in my hands.

The overhead lights began to flicker. For some strange reason, the photograph turned grainy, blurring Magdalena's image beyond recognition. The lights grew dimmer. Suddenly, someone slammed my forehead against the hard oak table.

Sixty-Three

WHEN I AWOKE, I was lying on a bed in the prison infirmary. An automatic blood-pressure cuff was wrapped around my left bicep. A clear plastic IV tube connected a glucose bag to a needle in my right forearm. A grey-haired nurse with heavy breasts smiled down at me.

"*Buenas noches, señor,*" she said.

"*Cómo lo suciedidio?*" In my newly acquired Spanish, I asked her what happened.

She responded in Spanish spoken too rapidly for me to understand.

"*Lentamente, por favor,*" I asked her to speak slowly.

She told me I would have to wait for the doctor.

"Quisiera el periódico," I asked, wanting to see the newspaper again.

She told me again I'd have to wait for the doctor.

"Solamente las páginas de la sociedad," I said, explaining that all I wanted was the society pages.

But she was adamant, unwilling to do anything not authorized by the *médico*.

The doctor finally showed up a half-hour later. He was a bored young Spaniard, brusque and even a bit arrogant, probably because he felt his prison patients were something less than worthy of his skills.

He explained that there was nothing wrong with me. The prison librarian thought I had collapsed with a heart attack, but the doctor's examination proved otherwise. The EKG revealed no discernible malfunction. My blood pressure had been unusually low, that was true, but now it was back to normal. All my other vital signs were also in the normal range. Apparently, I had fainted. The only damage he could find was the bruise where my head hit the table.

Again, I asked for the newspaper. He frowned, as if he was unaccustomed to a prisoner having the audacity to address such a trivial request to a man of his obvious importance.

"Solamente las páginas de la sociedad," I persisted.

He shrugged and nodded to the nurse that it was all right.

When she brought me the paper, I quickly turned to the page with the engagement photograph. This time, I was better able to control my emotions.

Magdalena was even lovelier in the news photo than I remembered. She was wearing a white gown with a heavily embroidered bodice. With its low neckline and long sleeves, it was elegant enough to be a wedding gown. Three strands of pearls adorned her neck. She wore what appeared to be expensive diamond earrings. A large diamond ring, presumably the engagement ring, was visible on her fourth finger. Her hair was longer than when I last saw her, professionally styled to outline her ears and curled at the bottom where it teased her bare shoulders.

She was photographed seated, looking up with what appeared to be a loving smile at Jean-Claude DesRosier, who stood rather imperiously behind her with one hand placed rather possessively on her shoulder. The caption announced the upcoming wedding of the "well-known industrialist and philanthropist" and a young woman identified only as Mariamme Magdala. The wedding ceremony, which would be a gala event at the DesRosier ancestral chateau, was to be the highlight of the social season, due primarily, it appeared, to the number of representatives of royal houses who would be attending the wedding. It wasn't the A-list of European royalty. Although King Juan Carlos would normally be expected to attend the wedding of one of Spain's wealthiest citizens, he was out of the country, meeting with the U.S. president. In fact, no other actual crowned heads were listed as attendees. The Elizabeths and Rainiers of this world normally limit their attendance at weddings to those of other royalty or heads of state. Instead, this was a rather strange "B-List," a mixture of secondary representatives of the reigning royal families of Europe, as well as the putative heirs to some of the continent's most illustrious vacant thrones. The list included representatives from the houses of Windsor, Saxe-Coburg, Bourbon, Hapsburg, Savoy, Mantua, and Hohenzollern, along with the exiled Princes of Venice and Tuscany, Princesses of Romany, Hungary, and Bavaria, various viscounts and dukes and duchesses, and even the pretender to the throne of the Russian Empire. Rounding out the guest list was a remarkably ecumenical gathering of religious leaders, including the Roman Catholic cardinal of Bordeaux, the chief rabbi of Madrid, the Greek Orthodox archimandrite of Alexandria, the Orthodox patriarch of Leningrad, the Lutheran bishop of Munich, and representatives from the Church of England, the Methodist Church, the Reformed Baptist Church, the Mormon Church, the Church of Christian Science, and the World Council of Churches. Strangely, however, the list included none of the business tycoons or political figures or show business celebrities who normally turn up at such events. There wasn't anybody on the list who didn't have a regal or religious title attached to their names.

Except, of course, for Jean-Claude DesRosier and the woman identified as Mariamme Magdala.

No mention was made in the article that she was a *monja*, a nun. And except for a brief and adulatory mention of his business empire, no reason was given for the importance ascribed to this marriage by European nobility.

The guests were arriving today, according to the article, most by private jet. The bride would be introduced at a special ceremony immediately prior to the wedding, which was scheduled for 9 p.m. this evening, July 22. I glanced up at the wall clock. That was one hour and forty-eight minutes from now. The article went on to describe the wedding preparations at "the historic Chateau DesRosier, a magnificent thirteenth-century Crusader castle that dominates the coastline from its mountaintop setting." The adulatory article went on to describe DesRosier's ancestors as "noble knights who fought for the freedom of the Holy Lands, and returned to help defend Spain from invading enemies." It read like a typical puff piece authored by some society writer hoping to curry favor with the rich and powerful. It didn't mention that July 22 was the feast day of Mary Magdalene.

Obviously, it didn't bother DesRosier that the woman he was planning to marry was already a Bride of Christ, a woman who had taken the vow of chastity and dedicated her life in service to God. And from her expression in the photograph, it didn't seem to bother Magdalena, either. She seemed obviously smitten with her wealthy Svengali. I wondered if this had been DesRosier's plan from the start? Had he somehow fallen in love with the young nun from afar, and afraid to risk his reputation, hired me to unwittingly deliver her into his arms? That would explain the rigged wireless phone. It gave him the ability to keep track of us, to listen in on our discussions, and to know where to show up just in time to be the hero who "saved" her from the *Guardia*. That being true, I could only assume he was the one who told *Coronel* Velarde where to find me. And it was undoubtedly his instruction to the lawyers that kept me locked up in prison without bail.

Yet it seemed to be an extraordinarily complicated bit of maneuvering. DesRosier didn't need me to deliver Magdalena into his clutches. With his money and influence, he could have easily made some sort of *sub rosa* arrangements with Church authorities to achieve the same goal. Why involve me at all? And having involved me, why was it now necessary to have me imprisoned? Did he somehow fear what I had learned about Magdalena?

The clock on the wall was ticking away. One hour and forty-four minutes now. Magdalena would be making her last-minute preparations before she walked down the aisle. And here I was, stuck in a prison hospital bed more than two hours away. Even if I wanted to do something to interfere with the wedding, I couldn't. It was all over. In despair, I closed my eyes and sank back into the pillow.

Was this all the workings of *karma*? Was it some form of cosmic retribution for a misdeed in a previous life? Why else did I seem doomed to repeat this awful scenario over and over again? Two years ago, I had lost one woman I loved, without ever getting the chance to tell her of my feelings. Now an eerily similar set of circumstances seemed to be developing around me. Why, why, why had I not permitted myself to acknowledge my love when Magdalena was beside me? Why did I wait until it was too late? Why did I once again let the opportunity for love slip away? Oh, I could come up with a lot of reasons for my reticence, ranging from my religious upbringing, to professional ethics, to the private investigator's code of conduct, and probably a dozen more if I chose to think about it. But deep down, I knew none of those reasons were valid.

The truth is, it was the legacy of an unhappy marriage. Ever since my long-ago divorce, I had withdrawn from contact with women. I was celibate, living an almost monk-like existence. During my work for Professor Debray I had come to prefer the cool pleasures of cerebral activity over the sometimes unpleasant consequences of emotional involvement. Now, lying in bed in the solitude of a Spanish prison hospital, I realized that I was becoming a man who was afraid to open himself to another woman. I was afraid of intimacy. Afraid to love.

Tormented by such thoughts, I didn't hear the footsteps of the men who entered the hospital room. It wasn't until I felt a hand on my arm that I opened my eyes.

I looked up into the cadaverous face of the old priest from the cathedral.

Standing next to him was the young backpacker who had left the *Naranjas* moments before the bomb went off.

"*Buenas noches,*" the backpacker said with a smile.

They were both wearing dark brown, hooded robes.

Frightened, I reached for the nurse's call button. The old priest's hand shot out to grab mine before I could summon help. For someone his age, he had amazingly quick reflexes. His grip would defeat Sylvester Stallone in any arm-wrestling contest.

"Who are you?" I asked.

"I am Abelard de Montbrison," he replied. "This is my protégé, Lucien Poussin." French names, I thought. French accents, too. But were they French priests, or were they Frenchmen posing as priests?

"How did you get in here?" I asked, unable to disguise the fear in my voice.

"Here are your clothes." Montbrison placed a large paper bag on the bed. "Get dressed. We must leave quickly."

Sixty-Four

I WASN'T ABOUT to obey the commands of strangers, particularly these two, who seemed to have a habit of showing up whenever bad things were about to happen to me.

"I'm not going anywhere," I said.

The young priest, Lucien, took a menacing step toward me.

"What are you going to do?" I asked defiantly. "Kill me? Like you killed Serrano?"

"If I wanted to kill you, you'd be dead already," the young priest said.

"Stop it!" Montbrison ordered. The menace immediately disappeared from Lucien's eyes. Obediently, he withdrew to a position behind the old priest. "We have no time for such foolishness," Montbrison continued. "Serrano's death was the result of an unfortunate mistake. We should have been more cautious."

"Which one of you did it?" I asked. "Which one of you killed him?"

"It was my fault." Young Lucien bowed his head. "I am responsible for his death. I am ashamed of my actions. I will carry the burden of my guilt for the rest of my life."

"You murdering bastard," I swore at him.

"Lucien did not kill Padre Serrano," Montbrison said.

"Weren't you listening? He just admitted he killed him."

"He said he was responsible for Padre Serrano's death," Montbrison gently corrected me. "But he did not say he killed him."

"My job was to follow the Padre," Lucien explained. "I was there to listen and observe, to learn if I could how much the Padre knew."

"How much he knew?" I asked. "Knew about what?"

"I should not have left him when I did."

"Lucien was drawn outside," Montbrison explained. "By an accomplice of the bomber, no doubt, who knew he was there to watch the Padre. It all happened too quickly to prevent. A satchel bomb was thrown into the bar."

"If I had been inside, I would have thrown myself on the bomb," the young man said. He spoke in a deadly earnest voice, without the slightest hint of false bravado. These were not ordinary men of the cloth, I thought. The young one was clearly a militant, willing to make any sacrifice his mission demanded. The older one looked on approvingly, as if he would have done the same.

"Get dressed," Montbrison repeated his earlier command. "We must leave quickly."

"This is a prison hospital," I protested. "I'm not exactly able to get up and walk out of here."

"We spoke with your doctor," Lucien said. "You are perfectly healthy. All you suffered was a fainting spell, probably caused by a sudden emotional shock."

"You are no longer a prisoner," Montbrison added. "The necessary papers have been signed. You are being released into our custody. Please get dressed."

"Let me see the release papers," I said, still suspicious.

Lucien withdrew a thick envelope from a pocket inside his robe. It contained five separate documents, each apparently signed by Fulgencio Velarde, *Coronel*, *Guardia Civil*. Each of Velarde's signatures was embossed with an official seal to attest to its authenticity. With the Spanish I learned during my confinement, I was able to read enough of the text to confirm what Montbrison had said. My hand trembled as I returned the documents to Lucien. After two months and three weeks in prison, freedom appeared to beckon.

Still, I was in no hurry to leave the safety of my hospital bed to accompany these two into the night. Not until I had more details.

"You hesitate," Montbrison said. "Are you afraid of us?"

"Frankly, yes."

"We mean you no harm."

"You've been following me. Watching me. Why?"

"Our interest is in protecting the *Sangreal*."

"The Holy Grail . . . the chalice in the cathedral? The vessel that's supposed to have held Christ's blood?"

"What did she tell you about it?" Montbrison asked.

"About the Holy Grail? Nothing. We never talked about it."

The two priests exchanged dubious glances.

"I find that hard to believe," Lucien said. "You were with her for days. You never left her side. Surely she told you something about it."

"I have no idea what you're talking about."

"Perhaps he is telling the truth," Montbrison said.

"We must be certain," Lucien said. "The risk to the brotherhood . . ." he started to add, and then, seeing the curiosity in my eyes, stopped.

It was, however, too late. He had spoken one word too many. My mind was already making the inevitable connections that any religious historian would have made much earlier. There was only one 'brotherhood' whose mission it was to protect the Holy Grail. That group was the order of warrior monks established by Hugues de Payen in 1118.

"You're Templar Knights," I exclaimed. "Of course! I should have known."

Their faces, long accustomed to protecting secrets, remained blank, devoid of any expression.

"And Velarde . . . he was wearing a Templar pin. That's how you were able to get him to sign the release papers. He's a Templar, too. You're all working together, aren't you?"

No wonder Velarde knew what happened at the *Naranjas*. His "eye-witness" wasn't a policeman. It was Lucien, posing as the mysterious student backpacker. How foolish Velarde must have thought I was when I insisted the backpacker was the bomber.

"But if you saw a satchel bomb being thrown into the *Naranjas* . . ." I started to think it through a little further. " . . . and you told that to Velarde . . . then he knew I had nothing to do with Serrano's death. Yet he arrested me. He chased me into Spain and brought me back here and put me in jail for two months. Why?"

"It was for your own protection," Montbrison said. "Padre Serrano was dead. Professor Abramakian was murdered. We suspected you would have been next."

"But you had me arrested."

"Would you have come with us willingly?"

"Probably not."

"We were also concerned about the *Sangreal*."

"You keep talking about the Holy Grail," I said. "Has somebody stolen it from the cathedral?"

"That is not the *Sangreal*. The chalice in the cathedral is not the true *Sangreal*."

"But the Vatican authenticated it."

"That was a fiction, part of a long line of falsehoods invented to mislead the faithful."

"Then where is the real *Sangreal*?"

The old priest turned to his younger protégé as if the answer required unanimous approval. The younger man shrugged his shoulders. After looking around the room to be certain no one was listening in, he finally answered my question.

"The *Sangreal,* the true *Sangreal*, which the Templars and their predecessors have sworn to protect ever since its arrival in France two thousand years ago, is now in the possession of Jean-Claude DesRosier."

"A traitor to his ancestors," Lucien snarled.

"He was supposed to protect the *Sangreal*," Montbrison continued. "Now he wants it for himself. All for his own fame and glory. You see?" He threw the morning newspaper on the bed. It was open to the same page I had been studying. I stared down at the photograph of DesRosier and Magdalena. "We thought she would be safe with him. Now he plans to marry her!"

There was something here I wasn't quite understanding.

"We cannot permit this wedding to take place," Montbrison said. "We need your help to stop it."

Stop the wedding? I couldn't think of anything I would rather do.

"Why me? What makes you think I can help?"

"Because she trusts you."

"That may be so," I said sadly. "But she's going to marry DesRosier."

"Do you want her to marry this man?" Montbrison asked. Seeing my hesitation, he smiled and answered the question for me. "I think not. I think you love her too much to see her make such a mistake. I watched the two of you in Barcelona, the way you smiled at her. I watched you on the beach in Coullioure, when she revealed herself to you, and again as you strolled through the streets in Arles and *les Saintes-Maries-de-la-Mer*. I watched you falling in love with her, and I think she also has feelings for you."

How was it possible to see such things from a distance, I wondered? We had never embraced, publicly or privately; never even exchanged words of endearment that could be overheard. All that had passed between us were the faintest signals of affection: casual touches followed by embarrassed withdrawals, sudden silences while we stared into each other's eyes, the satisfaction of simply being near each other. The spiritual and cultural chasms that separated us made us unsure of our own behavior, much less the trembling, tentative signals each of us offered the other. If we were so unsure ourselves, how could our feelings be detected by anyone watching from afar?

"If it's true that she has feelings for me," I said, hoping that it was, "then why is she marrying DesRosier?"

"I think he has confused her, as he has confused so many others, including us. He is a man who has grown wealthy by his ability to manipulate others."

"As much as I'd like to help you," I said. "I'm afraid the wedding is a done deal."

"*Qu'est-ce que c'est 'done deal'?*" Lucien asked.

"It's American slang," I explained. "It means it's all over. It's too late to do anything. They're getting married tonight." I glanced at the clock. "The ceremony is scheduled to start in an hour. The chateau is at least two hours away. Even if we left right now, the wedding might be over by the time we got there."

"He's right," Lucien said. "Why are we wasting time with this *idioto*? We could already be halfway there. I say we leave now, with him or without him."

"*Calmez-vous, calmez-vous,*" Montbrison said, without taking his eyes off me. "You must excuse Lucien. He is young and impatient. However, his urgency is well placed. We must be on our way. Time is of the essence."

"Even if we reached the chateau there in time, how do you plan to get inside? You can't just walk onto a guarded estate, uninvited."

"We will attack the chateau directly, if necessary."

I thought of the mountaintop chateau, the guards along the private roadway, the additional security people that would have been brought in for the wedding, and the personal bodyguards who inevitably accompanied members of the various royal families.

"The three of us? Attack a heavily guarded castle?" I asked. "You've got to be kidding."

"Nine Knights defended the Temple of Solomon against the infidels during the Crusades. Three Knights should be an equal match for the defenses of Chateau DesRosier."

I didn't know whether to smile or cry as I looked into the eager faces of this ancient priest and his undernourished young assistant. They were the unlikeliest pair I could imagine to be comparing themselves to the ferocious warrior-monks of the Middle Ages. They seemed unaware that the glory days of the Knights Templar ended in 1307, when their heroes were slaughtered by King Philip's army. The modern Templar chapters, as far as I knew, bear little resemblance to their illustrious forebears, the members gathering for fraternal and business purposes rather than heading off to do battle against the enemies of Christianity. Despite their boasts, these two priests seemed to possess neither weapons nor training in the skills of war. What distorted logic convinced these otherwise rational clergymen they could do battle against the stronghold of one of the richest men in Spain?

I couldn't decide whether following them would be an act of courage or an act of madness. At the moment, however, I wasn't all that concerned about their need to rescue the *Sangreal*, or even whether the mystical Grail really existed.

All I cared about was seeing Magdalena again.

Sixty-Five

THERE WERE MOMENTS that evening when I felt as if I had stepped onto a movie set where a modern version of *Don Quixote* was being filmed. Montbrison was perfectly cast as the elderly eccentric whose mind had been addled by too many books about knighthood and chivalry. Lucien was a younger, slimmer version of Sancho Panza, with his battered black Ford sedan serving as a substitute for the donkey. And I, despite my doubts about their sanity, was a willing fellow traveler, prepared to join them in their attack on the castle in the hope I might be reunited with the woman I loved. I could only pray that morning would find us more victorious than our fictional predecessors.

"There's going to be an awful lot of security at the chateau," I repeated my earlier warning as we sped north out of Valencia. "Many of the guests will bring their own bodyguards. How do you plan to get past them?"

"We'll find a way," Montbrison said calmly.

"The security people will have guns," I pointed out.

"We've dealt with such people before," he said.

"So have I," I said, recalling that awful night in New York. "And it didn't work out so well for me."

Lucien was driving with little regard for the speed limit, perhaps assuming his priestly robes conferred some sort of legal immunity upon him.

"At the hospital, you mentioned something about the Holy Grail," I started to say.

"Not the Holy Grail," Montbrison corrected me. "The *Sangreal.*"

"Okay, the *Sangreal,*" I said. "Although I don't understand what the difference is. In most of the literature, the two terms are used almost interchangeably."

"If you understood medieval Spanish or French, you'd know the difference," Lucien said.

"It would be good to remember your vows, Lucien," the old priest admonished him. "You should not speak of these matters to outsiders."

"We are only three against many," Lucien replied. "If he is the only one left alive, he must know the truth about our lady."

"The only one who is permitted to speak of such things is our lady herself."

They lapsed into silence for the next hour. Nothing I said evoked any response from either of them. I kept looking at my watch. There was no way we were going to reach the chateau before the appointed time of the wedding. The sun disappeared behind the coastal mountains. Lucien turned on his headlights, an almost useless gesture considering that the speed at which he was driving made it impossible for him to avoid any living creature that strayed into the path of the car.

We reached Peniscola shortly after dark. Lucien slowed down, and following Montbrison's instructions, pulled off the highway so we could study the chateau. Perched on its mountaintop, it seemed an impregnable fortress, its gloomy exterior brilliantly illuminated by the floodlights.

"Now it begins," Montbrison said. "Let us pray that our efforts are successful."

And that we all survive, I silently added.

"The road up is three and a half kilometers in length," Montbrison said. "There are five checkpoints, two of them gated and clearly visible, the other three hidden. One of those three is a mobile post, whose location is changed on a daily basis."

"You've been here before," I said.

"To this particular castle? No. But I have spoken to people who have access to old maps of all the Templar castles."

"Old maps? How old?"

"As old as the castles themselves."

"We're working from a thirteenth century map? I don't believe it."

"The castle hasn't moved. The road up is still three and a half kilometers in length."

"And all the checkpoints? Were the five checkpoints on the map?"

"Only the visible ones. The three hidden checkpoints are a Templar tradition. Fortunately, these defenses are most likely being manned by Basques. They should represent no problem for us."

"No problem? I was under the impression the Basques are fearless. DesRosier told me they'll fight to the death."

"That is true," Montbrison said. "But they are not Templars."

"We fear no one but other Templars," Lucien added, with what I thought was foolish bravado.

"The first checkpoint will be the most visible," Montbrison continued with his briefing. "It will be a gatehouse located at the boundary between the public and private portion of the road. That boundary is at the point where the paved roadway ends and the gravel begins. The first hidden checkpoint will be perhaps half a kilometer after that, just about the distance in which any trespasser will begin to relax. At that point is a bridge over a small stream. It seems the ideal place for a hidden checkpoint."

I remembered passing a gatehouse at the bottom of the hill and one at the top when the Basques brought me to the chateau, but there seemed little point in mentioning it. I was more concerned about Lucien's comment.

"You say you only fear Templars," I interrupted, unwilling to let the inconsistency pass. "But this is a Templar Castle you're attacking. And DesRosier himself is a Templar. He's a *Grand Chevalier*."

"A meaningless title," Montbrison sniffed. "DesRosier is the head of the modern Fraternal Order of the Knights Templar in Spain. But that is just a social group that meets openly. He is not a warrior, like his ancestors were."

"Or like we are," Lucien added.

"He enjoys the public prestige of his position, and uses it for social and business purposes. But like most members of that modern group, he is not aware that some of us are true Templars, trained in the skills and traditions of the original nine Knights of the Temple."

"We are wasting time," Lucien interjected. "We should be attacking instead of talking."

"You are right, Lucien," Montbrison gave the rest of his briefing in a clipped voice worthy of a military commander. "After crossing the bridge, the next hidden checkpoint will most likely be at a stone cliff where the road once again narrows. As for the mobile checkpoint, I have no idea where it is. We will just have to move carefully to flush them out."

This would have been the time for any counterfeit heroes to come up with some excuse for not proceeding any further. But from what I could see of their faces in the darkness, it appeared my companions were totally serious about this attack. Which made me very nervous. It was one thing to talk about hidden checkpoints and how they feared no one except other Templars, but so far, they had displayed no weapons.

As I listened to these two priests calmly discuss the impossible task of overpowering checkpoints and attacking the castle, I wondered about their mental health. Their behavior suggested they might be suffering from a delusional disorder of the grandiose type, also known as megalomania. The usual symptoms include a sense of inflated worth, power, and knowledge, often leading the victims to identity with a deity or famous person, all of which these two displayed. They were seeing the world through a prism constructed from fragments of remembered history, and responding accordingly. The disorder poses no particular danger to the patient, except for a sense of inflated power and personal invulnerability. Such disregard for danger, when directed toward noble ends, is the stuff of which heroes are made. Usually dead heroes.

"Where are your guns?" I asked.

"We have no need of weapons," Lucien impatiently whispered.

"There'll be security cameras trained on the road. They'll see us coming."

"They will think nothing of one man in a car."

"One man?"

"Yes, you. You will be driving the car," Montbrison said. "We will be in the forest, where we won't be seen."

"So what's the plan?" I asked, not having heard them discuss any course of action beyond the description of the checkpoints.

"You will drive, and we will go on foot," Lucien said.

"Drive slowly," Montbrison said. "Slowly enough for us to move through the woods ahead of the car."

That was apparently as much of the plan as they were willing to share with me, because they quickly separated, disappearing into the shrubbery on both sides of the road.

I waited a reasonable time before putting the car in gear. This wasn't how I envisioned the "attack" on the chateau. Somehow I had the idea I'd be sneaking through the bushes alongside them, rather than driving openly up the middle of the road, where I'd make a perfect target for any trigger-happy guard who was sworn to protect the distinguished guests who were gathered in the chateau. Worse yet, I had instructions to drive slowly, which made me even more nervous. I told myself I was probably over-reacting, that no one would shoot me. Not without challenging me to stop first, which I would surely do. I wasn't about to go crashing through any gate in a hail of bullets.

The only thing that kept me going up that dark road at the slow pace Montbrison requested was the knowledge that it led to Magdalena.

The first gatehouse was right where the old priest predicted it would be, marking the place where the paved road turned to gravel. It was a small grey sentry shack, large enough to shelter a single guard. The gate, strangely enough on a night with such illustrious guests, was already raised. I slowed down even more, expecting to be challenged. But the guardhouse was empty.

No one stepped forward to challenge me.

Puzzled by the lack of security, I drove on. The road turned sharply uphill. I kept the car in low gear, trying to gauge how quickly the priests were moving through the bushes. Four miles an hour was the standard pace of a human walking on level ground, which translates to about six and a half kilometers per hour. I tried to keep the speedometer at five kph. I couldn't help wondering whether they were actually out there some-where, or whether I had been sent on a fool's errand.

Up ahead was the bridge. So far, Montbrison's description of the area was accurate. For what seemed like no reason other than security purposes, the road narrowed to a single lane at the bridge, which made it an ideal place for an ambush by anyone guarding the approach to the chateau. The glare of the headlights turned the shrubbery to a silver-gray shade, and intensified the blackness of the shadows. Through the open window, I could hear the rushing of water as it poured down the steep slope. Once on the bridge, I wouldn't be able to turn or maneuver. The side clearance was too tight for a U-turn. If I was going to be stopped by a hidden sentry, I thought, this would be the logical place.

The front tires bumped as they struck the wooden edge of the bridge. Up ahead, the road was empty. Nervously, I studied the bushes lining the road. At any moment, I expected one of DesRosier's beret-clad Basques to step in front of the vehicle. What would I do? What could I do, other than stop? A bump jolted me as the rear tires left the bridge. I was back on the two-lane gravel road. Amazingly, no one had stopped me. Every instinct I possessed, every inherited fear and acquired piece of logic screamed at me to press down on the accelerator and get out of there. But somehow, I managed to keep my anxieties from taking over. I continued at a steady five kilometers per hour up the hill and around the second bend.

Suddenly, I slammed on the brakes.

A man, a frightened man, staggered out into the road ahead of me. He was bleeding from the mouth. His eyes were wide with the blank look of unseeing panic. His right arm hung at an odd and apparently helpless position from his shoulder. Caught in the glare of my headlights, he collapsed face down into the gravel. Before I could react, a hooded figure emerged from the bushes. I watched in disbelief as old Montbrison grabbed the fallen man by the belt and dragged him almost effortlessly back into the shrubbery. I waited, heart beating wildly, for what seemed a long time before Lucien stepped out of the bushes on the other side of the road to wave me on. At the same time, he motioned with his hand for me to proceed more slowly.

He didn't seem anywhere near as nervous I was. I fumbled with the gearshift and clutch before I could get the car moving again.

Montbrison had said there would be five checkpoints. I assumed the man who had tried to escape from the old priest was from the second checkpoint. That would mean there were three more to go. Perhaps through some lucky circumstance, perhaps because DesRosier's guards were distracted by my approaching car, the priests had been able to overpower them. What did they use as weapons? Wooden clubs? Rocks? Their bare hands? They might have been lucky so far, but we were only half way up to the castle.

Ahead of me was a huge cut in the rock on the side of the road. It rose straight up, perhaps twenty feet. Atop the cliff was a large boulder. Was it placed there purposely, in position to either shut the road or crush a vehicle? Was that someone moving behind the boulder, getting into position to roll it down on me? Or was it just my continuing high level of anxiety, seeing danger in a simple rock formation? I bit into my lower lip in an effort to control my emotions and drove on. Passing the overhanging rock without incident, I relaxed. Behind me, I heard a thumping sound, almost like a pumpkin striking the ground. The red glow of my taillights barely illuminated a lump in the roadway. The lump seemed to be clothed in a shirt and pants. I decided I had just passed the third checkpoint.

As ferocious as the Basques were reputed to be, DesRosier's hand-picked crew so far seemed to be no match for two unarmed priests. What strange skills did they possess, I wondered? I had scoffed at their claim of Templar knighthood, dismissing it as the fantasy of repressed psyches. Yet they appeared to be clearing the roadway with ruthless efficiency. But the chateau was still two kilometers away, and there were still two more checkpoints along the dark road.

Through an opening in the trees, I could make out the distant glow of the castle floodlights against the night sky. It wasn't a welcoming glow, more like the harsh light of reality, beckoning me to a no-man's land of armed guards. What would happen when we reached the castle? Attacking DesRosier's isolated guards in the darkness along the road was one thing. Perhaps the Basques were poorly trained. The chateau, however, would certainly be surrounded with an elite corps of skilled professionals, brought in by the royalty who had convened for DesRosier's wedding. Given the state of near-paranoia that afflicts Europe's nobility these days, those bodyguards would be trained and equipped to repel anything from suicide bombers to coordinated nighttime assaults by armed groups. What chance would we three have against that small army?

I searched both sides of the road for any sign of the next hidden checkpoint. A shoulder-high clump of bushes on the right side of the road offered an ideal hiding place. Watching for someone to pounce from the bushes, I became aware, too late, of activity on the opposite side of the road. Through the open window, I heard a loud grunt, a rustle of branches, and then the sudden return of silence. Had another guard been dispatched? I shuddered and continued up the mountainside.

The final gatehouse was the same gray color as the first, with a white gate barring any further progress. Unlike the first gatehouse, this one was occupied by a sentry wearing the traditional Basque beret. A second sentry, also wearing a Basque beret, sat in a chair beside him.

I slowed to a stop, praying that the two priests would arrive in time to rescue me.

The first sentry waved for me to stop. For a moment, I thought of crashing through the gate in a desperate attempt to . . . to do what? It was an insane thought, I realized. Instead, I shifted into neutral and set the parking brake as the tall sentry approached.

Beyond him, on the other side of the gate, was the historic Chateau DesRosier, every square inch of which was bathed in brilliant light. On the lawn in front, neatly parked in three rows of twenty each, was the greatest single assemblage of European luxury cars I had ever seen. Unlike less expensive vehicles, these were all recognizable by their classic silhouettes: there were at least a dozen Rolls-Royces, as many Jaguar sedans and oversized Mercedes, and even, almost incongruously, a wide, knee-high yellow Lamborghini, probably driven defiantly by one of the Monaco princesses.

And everywhere I looked, walking among the cars, around the chateau, loitering under the trees, were the guards. Some were neatly dressed in suits, a few in casual clothes, and even a half-dozen in camouflage gear. It was an impenetrable defense. DesRosier and his guests could relax without fear of unwanted intruders.

Perhaps it was for the best that I was about to be apprehended, I thought. Any attack on the chateau would certainly be ill fated, if not suicidal.

Sixty-Six

WHERE WERE THE two priests?

Had they met their match at the last hidden checkpoint?

Were they lying injured, or even worse, dead, out there in the darkness?

And what would happen to me?

The man in the beret avoided the glare of the headlights. It was hard to make out his features in the shadows. It wasn't until he came up to the window and smiled at me that I recognized him. I slumped back in the seat and let out a sigh of relief.

It was Lucien!

Along with the beret, he was wearing a blue denim shirt and dark blue slacks, what seemed to be the unofficial uniform of DesRosier's Basques. To conceal the fact that the shirt was too small for him, he had rolled up the sleeves. Grass stains on the knees and elbows were the only hint that the clothing hadn't been willingly surrendered by its owner.

"Leave the lights on and the engine running," he ordered. "And follow me."

I obeyed, feeling a fool for having let my fears run wild.

"Thank God you're okay," I said as I followed him to the guardhouse, where we found Montbrison sitting on a chair, waiting for me. Montbrison rose and took off his beret as we approached.

"You did well," he said. "The guards focused their attention on the car, which allowed us to take them by surprise."

"How did you . . . what did you do to them?"

"We did what was necessary," Lucien said.

"I think they are not dead, if that's what you mean," Montbrison said. "But they will not be a threat to anyone for a long time."

"So what do we do now?" I asked. "There must be dozens of guards around the chateau. You can't sneak up on all of them."

"Put these on," Lucien said, handing me a rolled-up bundle of clothing, still warm from its previous wearer.

"And this." Montbrison placed his beret atop my head.

"Hurry," Lucien said. "We are wasting time."

The pants were a decent enough fit, but there was a problem with the shirt. A bloodstain, still wet, darkened the front. I told them I didn't want to wear it.

"Just put it on," Lucien ordered.

"The bloodstain will help," Montbrison said. "It will distract their attention from your face."

"What about the car?" I asked. The lights were still on, the engine running. "It's probably already attracted attention."

"Precisely," Montbrison said. He smeared some of the blood from my shirt onto his face. "Now let us go to meet the enemy."

The old priest, who had been strong enough to overpower the guards in the darkness, suddenly seemed to become weak, his footsteps faltering. I quickly grabbed one arm to prevent him from falling. Lucien was already at his other side. Following Montbrison's directions, which were delivered in a strong voice that belied his apparently feigned weakness, we stepped out into the roadway. The car's headlights clearly illuminated us. Up ahead, perhaps 100 meters further, two security agents watched our approach. Each held a hand behind his back, presumably hiding a weapon.

We must have made an odd trio: Lucien and I wearing the berets and garments of our fallen adversaries, and Montbrison, still clad in his now dirtied monk's robe, stumbling feebly between us.

"Who the hell's the old bugger?" one of the security guards asked in a British accent.

"*El padre es muy loco,*" Lucien replied, quickly switching to English with a heavy Spanish accent. "He says he is a missionary, here to convert the pagans."

"*In nomine Patri . . .*" Montbrison started to mutter, only to stop when Lucien shook him.

"Was there anyone else in the car?" the British guard asked.

"Just the *loco Padre,*" Lucien said.

"Looks like he gave you a tough time." The guard nodded at my bloodied shirt.

"You know these *locos,*" Lucien said. "We'll lock him up in the basement until the ceremony's over."

The guard stepped aside to let us pass. I couldn't believe the deception had worked so easily. I could only assume it was because they were foreign guards. If we had encountered any of the Basques, I'm sure they would have been onto our game immediately. I checked my watch. The wedding should have started a half hour ago. With luck, we might be able to break in and disrupt things just before the vows.

"Hold on there," the second guard suddenly called out.

We froze.

"*Cómo?*" Lucien asked, without turning.

I felt Montbrison grow tense between us, as if he was preparing to spring into action.

"You can't leave that car blocking the road," the guard said.

"*Sí.* We will move it as soon as we lock up the prisoner."

"Don't worry about it," the first guard said. "I'll move it for them."

"We're not supposed to leave our posts," the second guard argued.

"For Christ's sake, Harry, I'm just helping out with a situation. What if another big shot shows up and there's a car blocking the road, and all we're doing is watching? It'll just take a minute."

"*Muchas gracias,*" Lucien called over his shoulder as we headed up to the chateau.

Everywhere we looked, security guards were patrolling: out on the open floodlit lawn, beneath the trees, among the bushes. Two sets of guards were patrolling the dry moat with dogs, German shepherds who strained at their leashes when they saw us, probably because of the odor of fresh blood from my "borrowed" shirt.

Lucien, following Montbrison's whispered instructions, led us to the service door. The security guard stationed outside that entrance watched us approach. I expected another challenge.

He stepped forward to stop us. But possibly because he had seen us pass inspection at the outer perimeter, he confined himself to a perfunctory inspection of Montbrison, who maintained the pose of a broken man, eyes staring at the ground. Lucien repeated his explanation of the "*loco padre.*" The guard muttered something unintelligible and took the old priest's chin in his hand, moving it roughly from side to side. Montbrison kept his eyes from making contact with those of the guard. Finally the guard stepped aside and waved us in.

Although there were enough security people to protect the chateau from anything short of a tank attack, they suffered from a lack of coordination. Each of the guests had brought their own bodyguards, who were accustomed to acting independently, often in accordance with their cultural norms. The Greeks, accustomed to guerrilla warfare, melted into the shrubbery. The British, two of whom we had already encountered, roamed the outer perimeter with imperious visibility. The Russians never strayed far from the chateau. The Monagesques hovered near the parked vehicles, which provided not only cover, but fodder for conversation. The Italians and the French positioned themselves at opposite ends of the chateau. The Belgians were the ones who showed up in camouflage uniforms. And the Spanish provided the attack dogs. The only group that seemed to have a specific mission was DesRosier's Basque contingent, who were supposed to have cut off all access along the road.

The result of the lack of coordination was an overabundance of protection around the outside of the chateau, and almost no one inside. We went in through the kitchen, which was jammed with extra servants and cooks and assistants, all of whom were so consumed with their own jobs, they barely paid us any notice as we moved through. The "Hall of Flags" was unguarded. I assumed the rest of the bodyguards were in the main banquet room, where their employers had gathered for the wedding. The doors were slightly ajar. The music of a string quartet competed with the excited buzz of a hundred conversations and chairs being moved about.

Was the wedding over? Were we too late?

Lucien rushed ahead to peer into the room. He returned with a smile. "She is not here yet," he whispered.

"Upstairs, then," Montbrison said.

With no one to stop us, we dropped the prisoner-and-guard sub-terfuge and hurried up the wide, carpeted steps. Although the stairway continued up for two more floors, Montbrison stopped us at the first landing.

"She will be on this floor," he said. "The master of the castle and his most important guests are always on the second floor, where they have easy access to the main floor."

But where, I wondered? The interior design of the chateau was in the form of an "H,"with six doors on each side of each of the four lateral extensions, plus two doors in the middle span.

"These look like the biggest rooms on this floor," I said.

"We're wasting time," Lucien said, as he flung open the first door.

The room was enormous, with high ceilings, huge windows, a canopied bed, a desk, a sitting area, a sofa and a fireplace. It was a man's room. The large painting over the fireplace was a portrait of Jean-Claude DesRosier himself, astride a rearing white horse, clad in chain-mail armor with the white cloth surplice and splayed red cross that was the battle uni-form of the Knights Templar.

Montbrison let out a snort of derision, using a French epithet whose meaning could only have been obscene.

Lucien backed out and went to the next room. I was right behind him when he threw open the door. Even before I saw her, the aroma of a famil-iar fragrance told me we were in the right room.

There were three women inside. Two of them were servants, older white-haired women, clad in long black dresses. Frightened by the arrival of men who dared throw open their door without knocking, they drew back, pulling away from the woman they were attending.

She stood erect before a mirror, this woman whose marriage we had come here to prevent. She was wearing a long white tunic—not what any-one today would consider a bridal gown, but probably the preferred wed-ding garment during biblical times. The tunic appeared to be made of a single voluminous piece of lustrous white fabric, its ample folds covering her arms and reaching to the floor. A long veil of the same fabric was wrapped around her neck and covered her head.

It was Magdalena, more beautiful, if such a thing was possible, than she appeared in even my most idealized dreams.

When she turned to see me, her eyes peering out from beneath the fold of the veil, the action was an eerie replication of Savolda's haunting portrait of the myrrhophore turning to see the risen Christ.

"James," she said.

I looked around, thinking she was addressing someone behind me. But the hallway was empty. The only men in sight were me and the two priests, both of whom immediately dropped to their knees, bowed their heads, and clasped their hands to their hearts, as if before royalty.

"Tell your friends to rise," she said. Her voice was deeper and richer, more mature than I remembered. It seemed to come from a great distance.

I prodded Lucien and Montbrison in the shoulders. Reluctantly, they rose to their feet.

"I knew you'd come, James," she said.

It was the second time she had called me by the wrong name. That was when I was convinced I had lost her. For two months, I had carried this lovely young woman's image firmly fixed in my mind; thoughts of her occupied my waking hours and intruded on my dreams at night. I conjured up fantasies of a joyful reunion, of a tender embrace, loving words whispered between us . . . and now it seemed to have been all for naught. I had lost her so completely, she didn't even remember my name. That was the most stunning, most humiliating part of it all: she didn't even know my name. What had happened to her in these past few months, I wondered?

"But . . . why are you bleeding?" she asked, seeing the dark stain on the front of my shirt. "Did they hurt you?"

"It's not my blood," I replied. "I borrowed the shirt."

"You must be careful," she warned. "There are many dangerous people here." She turned to one of her attendants. *"Por favor, Elena, traiga una camisa."*

The shorter of the two women nodded and scurried off to bring me a clean shirt.

"My lady, may I be permitted to speak?" Montbrison asked in a voice that surprised me with the submissiveness of its tone.

Magdalena nodded.

"We have come here to rescue you."

"Rescue me?" Magdalena sounded amused at the idea. *"You* will rescue me? From what?"

"From this evil man who wants to marry you."

"Jean-Claude? But he is a Templar like you. A *Grand Chevalier,* no less."

She seemed to be teasing Montbrison. I didn't understand why.

"My lady, I beg of you, you must not marry him."

"And why do you give me such unsolicited advice? Without knowing what I think?"

"I am sworn to protect the *Sangreal*, with my life if necessary," he said. "I cannot let this wedding take place."

"But people have come from all over Europe," she said. "Important people. Royalty. They represent not only their nations, but also the major religions of the world. They will report back to their people what they see and hear tonight. And there are television cameras, too. Tonight's events will be recorded for history. Everyone will know what took place here."

This was not the simple little nun I had rescued from the *convento*. She spoke with an assurance and a media awareness that surprised me.

"With all due respect," Montbrison persisted. "You must not go through with this. Think what it will mean to the *Sangreal*."

"I have thought it through very carefully, I can assure you."

"Then, please, I beg of you, my lady." Montbrison's voice trembled with emotion. "In the name of all who have sacrificed their lives for you, do not go through with it."

She looked at him with sad eyes.

"I have no choice," she said. "I have been waiting for this moment for two thousand years."

Sixty-Seven

"ARE THE OTHERS here?" she asked.

"Not yet, my lady," Montbrison said.

Others? I wondered? What others?

"I can wait no longer," Magdalena said. "It will soon be time for me to go downstairs."

"Good evening," I heard DesRosier's voice behind me. Startled, I spun around. He was nowhere to be seen. "I apologize for the late start," I heard the disembodied voice say.

My two compatriots were as puzzled as I was. DesRosier sounded as if he was in the room.

"That is Jean-Claude you hear," Magdalena said. "He will be giving his speech now, at the end of which, I am supposed to make a grand entrance. It will be a remarkable speech." She turned to me. "What he has to say will answer many of your questions, James. Perhaps you would like to listen in?

"Yes, I would. But my name is Theo, not James."

"Of course it is," she said with a playful smile. I noticed the two priests looking at me with strange, almost suspicious expressions.

Magdalena directed our attention to the floor on the far side of the room.

"We are directly above the banquet hall," she said. "What you hear is coming up through the registers."

In the days before central heating, architects relied on registers, which were metal-screened openings cut into ceilings and floors to provide a flow of warm air from one level to another. Rather than remove the ornate metal grillwork when modern furnaces were installed, the registers were often left in place as quaint reminders of a bygone era. There were two of these registers in the room, one in each corner. The ducts not only enabled DesRosier's voice to drift up to us, but also, as I quickly discovered, provided a partial view of the room below.

By pressing my cheek to the floor, I could see the back of DesRosier's head. When he turned to survey his guests, I could see his profile. He was just finishing his opening remarks.

" . . . and I am particularly grateful to those of you who traveled long distances to be with me on this glorious evening."

The short attendant slipped quietly back into the room with a new shirt for me. It was tailored of blue silk, with DesRosier's family crest on the pocket.

"I stand before you tonight with the greatest humility," DesRosier said. "I am grateful to God that I have been singled out for the tremendous honor that will soon be bestowed upon me."

It sounded more like the formal acceptance speech of someone about to become a head of state than the words of a man about to be married. His figure was bathed in a harsh artificial light that suggested his speech was being videotaped for the late news broadcasts.

"As many of you have suspected, this is no ordinary marriage, no simple union between a man and a woman who love each other. It is also not, as it has been characterized in the European tabloids, a case of a lonely billionaire finally finding love, or a young woman leaving the convent to take a place on the world stage. No, my friends, it is far more than that. For those of us who believe in God, for those of us who believe Jesus Christ was the son of God, for those of us who believe our Savior will come again, the ceremony that will take place in this room, on this night, with you as witnesses, will reshape the beliefs of millions of the faithful."

Wealthy men like DesRosier were often given to hyperbole, in an attempt to imbue their activities with supranormal significance. But the religious references struck me as being a bit over the top.

"Two thousand years ago, a child was born to Mary and Joseph," he continued. "His birth, as much of his life, was shrouded in legends. Some traditions claim he was born in a stable, some say a cave; some say the birth was in Bethlehem, some say Nazareth. How many of us in this room can say with absolute certainty that we know the truth about the life of Jesus Christ?"

Now he was sounding more like a preacher than a prospective bridegroom, I thought.

"There are the missing years to deal with, of course. We have no idea what Jesus did or where he lived between the ages of twelve and thirty. The Gospels are silent on that subject. And on many other subjects, from the presentation in the Temple to the raising of Lazarus from the dead, to the final words on the cross, to the Resurrection itself, the Gospels often contradict each other.

"And to make matters worse, we have the confusing positions of the biblical scholars themselves. There are scholars who tell us that since the bible is the inspired word of God, we must take it literally; other equally distinguished scholars tell us part of it should be taken literally and part figuratively; and others believe we should take none of it literally."

His remarks caused a restless stirring among the guests. Most likely it was the religious leaders, wondering if they should take umbrage.

"I believe, as you all do, that Jesus Christ was the true son of God, sent down to Earth to become man . . . I emphasize those words, *to become man* . . . to die for our sins and to rise from the dead in glory and to ascend into heaven. But I also believe, as most modern scholars do, that advances in science, anthropology, and archeology can help us test the legends, and determine truths that might have eluded earlier generations."

DesRosier paused to take a drink of water.

"Tonight I will be pleased to reveal to you the truth of one of those legends . . . "

He paused again, but this time it was an oratorical pause to add emphasis to his words.

" . . . the true nature of the *Sangreal,* which until now has been mistakenly identified as the Holy Grail."

Beside me, I heard Montbrison suck in his breath, and Lucien muttering some unintelligible curse. Magdalena remained supremely, unaffectedly calm.

"And with that revelation, my dear friends, you will understand the true significance of the wedding you are about to witness."

"It is almost time for me to go downstairs," Magdalena said. "We rehearsed my entry yesterday. The doors will be opened for me at precisely the most dramatic moment."

"If the scriptures have left us with many unanswered questions about the life and death of Jesus," DesRosier continued, " . . . it is at the time of his Resurrection from the dead that the most intriguing question occurs. Of all the people to whom our Lord and Savior could have revealed his return from the dead, why did he not do what any loving son would do: first console his mother, who was in such terrible grief after having witnessed the agonizing death of her first-born son? Or, if Jesus was intent on fulfilling his divine mission, why did he not first appear to Peter and the other disciples, who were hiding in a room in the nearby Old City? The Resurrection from the Dead is the very foundation of our faith, the single most important tenet of Christianity, the ultimate proof of Christ's divinity. Yet the person whom Our Lord chose as the first witness to this monumental event was the woman known as Mary Magdalene."

Again a pause. This time, the audience greeted his remarks with total silence. DesRosier apparently had their rapt attention, as he did that of everyone in this upstairs room. Yet to me, the words sounded strangely familiar. I had read them before. In Valencia, I realized. In Padre Serrano's marginal notes.

"He chose this woman as the first witness," he continued, " . . . and instructed her to tell the good news to the others . . . which made her the 'Apostle to the Apostles,' the first among equals, even more important . . . with all due respect to Cardinal Amoroso, who is with us today . . . than Peter. Even the great Peter, the 'rock' upon whom Scripture said Christ planned to build his church, received the most important news of our faith secondhand. Our Lord chose Mary Magdalene to deliver his Good News to the world."

DesRosier let those words sink in before continuing.

"And then comes another great mystery of the New Testament," he said. "From that point on, after this pivotal point of Christianity, Mary Magdalene disappears. There is no further mention of her anywhere, not in the Gospels, nor in the Acts of the Apostles, nor in the writings of Paul, nor in any official history of the early Christian Church."

When DesRosier moved his shoulder, I could see he was reading from a prepared script. But was it his script, or Serrano's, I wondered?

"Many scholars attribute this strange omission to the extreme misogyny of those male-dominated times, which found expression in much of Paul's writings," he continued. "But there is another reason, one which provoked the famous wrath of Peter, the jealousy of the Apostles, and even . . . again with apologies to Your Eminence . . . determined which of the many accounts of Christ's life and teachings were selected by the fourth-century Councils of Trent and Carthage to be included in the 'approved' version of the New Testament."

That DesRosier had somehow acquired Serrano's research papers was proven by his next comments.

"I have spent the equivalent of two and a half million Euros over the past three years investigating this matter," he said. "I have hired archeologists, theologians, and private investigators. I have bribed government and church officials. I have done things of which I am not proud. But in the end, I have learned the great secret of Mary Magdalene, and the true meaning of the *Sangreal*."

I listened, fascinated. Magdalena was smiling enigmatically. Montbrison and Lucien could barely contain their anger.

"From the Canonical Gospels, we know Mary Magdalene was a woman of some wealth, who along with her friends provided for Jesus Christ and his followers out of her means. In other words, she supported Jesus and made it possible for him to preach and travel the countryside, bought his food, his clothing, and certainly even the donkey on which he rode into Jerusalem. In the Scriptures, she is always mentioned first in any list of people, which suggests her importance.

"While the apostles hid from the Romans, Mary Magdalene followed Jesus to the crucifixion, watched him suffer and die on the cross, helped carry him to his grave, and as I said earlier, was the first to witness his Resurrection. When I read those passages as a child, I thought of her as our Savior's most faithful follower. Certainly more faithful than Peter and the others, who doubted and denied and hid out of fear."

How did he get Serrano's research, I wondered? Was it through his contacts with the church in Valencia?

"But those four Gospels, which I hold in the greatest reverence, provide only the barest description of Mary's relationship with Jesus. Biblical scholars know there were many other works, other Gospels, some of them written by eyewitnesses to those events. But those documents were lost in the devastation of Jerusalem and Judea during the Jewish uprising. Any surviving Jesus documents were ordered destroyed by Diocletian in the year 303, and any documents that didn't conform to orthodox Christian beliefs were confiscated and burned by Constantine thirty years later in the year 333 . . . although my sources tell me many of those early manuscripts still survive in the Vatican Library's Secret Archives."

Perhaps more ominously, I wondered, was DesRosier's speech based on the contents of Serrano's missing briefcase?

"For the rest of us, however, it wasn't until 1945 that we began to see what some of the early Christians wrote about Mary Magdalene. At about the time the Dead Sea Scrolls were discovered, a young Arab digging for fertilizer near the town of Nag Hammadi uncovered a large clay jar containing thirty-two papyrus codices. For Christians, it was a discovery more important than the Dead Sea Scrolls, because it was an ancient Gnostic library, containing the most valuable documents of the early days of that Christian sect."

If DesRosier had Serrano's briefcase, then he must have had something to do with the bombing at the *Naranjas*, I realized.

"One of those documents was the Gospel of Philip. Unlike Matthew, Mark, Luke and John, the writer of that Gospel personally witnessed the events about which he wrote. Here is a paragraph from the Gospel of Philip." He read the words carefully from the pages in front of him. *"There were three who always walked with the Lord. Mary his mother and her sister and Magdalene, the one who was called his companion,"* he read. "But the word 'companion' is not an accurate translation of the Hellenic Greek word *koinonos,* according to the experts whom I consulted. They told me, and other scholars now concur, that the proper translation of *koinonos* is 'partner' or 'consort.' Both of these terms in biblical times meant a woman with whom a man has had sexual intercourse."

I barely listened to what DesRosier was saying. My anger was growing with the realization that he was responsible for Serrano's death.

"If that was the only such reference, it might be dismissed," DesRosier continued. "But in the Gospel of Thomas, we read the following: *But Christ loved her more than all the disciples and used to kiss her often on the mouth. The rest of the disciples were offended by it and expressed disapproval. They said to him, 'Why do you love her more than all of us?' The Savior answered and said to them, 'Why do I not love you like her?'* I could go on to cite dozens of others references to support the legends that Mary Magdalene was the lover of Jesus Christ."

Was that what Serrano died for, so that DesRosier could quote his research?

"I have not yet found any hard evidence of their marriage," DesRosier went on. "All legal records were burned during the destruction of Jerusalem. However, it is inconceivable that the moral Jesus, the pure Jesus whom we know, would have had carnal knowledge of a woman without benefit of marriage. There are a number of biblical scholars who contend that the Gospel story of the wedding feast at Cana was actually a disguised account of Jesus Christ's wedding to Mary Magdalene."

Was this the "great secret" Serrano hinted at before his death? If so, I had to confess disappointment. I had heard it all before. That such a marriage took place was never proven, of course. And there were conflicting theories of what occurred at Cana, one of which claimed that John the Evangelist was the groom on that occasion.

"As you all know," DesRosier continued. "The idea that Christ married Mary Magdalene at Cana has been rumored since ancient times, and is an article of faith among certain Christian sects, most notably the Cathars and Gnostics. Because of the primacy such a union would give to Mary Magdalene, some scholars suggest it was the reason the bride and groom's identity were omitted from the Gospels. It was also the motive, some contend, for the false portrayal of Mary Magdalene as a prostitute. That awful slander was a clever piece of propaganda designed to confuse the faithful and render it morally impossible to link her name romantically with the Savior. We now know that terrible libel was a conscious act of defamation, perpetrated by ambitious men who wanted to protect their own exalted positions. Theologians I have consulted on the matter of Christ's marriage are divided, but they insist the Church would have no problem with a married Jesus. The union between man and woman, after all, would be the ultimate expression of Christ's humanity. It would also finally explain why the risen Savior chose to reveal himself to the Magdalene before any other. As a loving husband, it would have been his most natural act to speak first to his wife."

When I looked at Magdalena, she nodded her head in confirmation.

I found it remarkable that this prestigious audience was sitting quietly through DesRosier's lengthy oration. Did they have some idea of where this was leading? And why was he being so bloody long-winded about it?

"There is quite a bit of documentation that the Magdalene fled Jerusalem shortly after the Resurrection," DesRosier continued. "We know she came to France, with Lazarus and Joseph of Arimethea and others. We know she preached in Marseilles. We know she died at Aix-en-Provence. The oral traditions of Provence, historic documents dating back to the fourth century, and the secret records of the Cathars, the Knights Templar and the Merovingian archives support that history. Which leads us, of course, to the mystery of the *Sangreal*."

For a moment, I forgot my anger. DesRosier's story was finally getting interesting. The Knights Templar were the historic guardians of the Holy Grail, and I had Montbrison and Lucien beside me, swearing they would lay down their lives to keep DesRosier from possessing the Grail. I glanced at them. They were listening as intently as I. Montbrison was moving his lips, but making no sound. Silent prayer? Or silent curses? I knew not which.

"According to the oral traditions, when Mary Magdalene came to Provence, she carried with her something called the *Sangreal*," DesRosier said. "It was described as a vessel that held Christ's blood. Until now, that is all we knew about the *Sangreal* that approached fact. The *Sangreal* promptly disappeared from sight. Myth and legend took over. No one knew for certain what it was. If it held Christ's blood, people surmised it must have been a cup, or a chalice, or a bowl. But the stories described it simply as the Holy Grail. That was the literal translation achieved by breaking *Sangreal* into two words: *San* and *Greal*. As those of us who grew up with the legends of King Arthur know, it was considered to be one of the greatest religious treasures of all time, on a par with the Ark of the Covenant and the stones on which the Ten Commandments were given to Moses. Although there are a number of cups, chalices, and bowls in the cathedrals of Europe claiming to be the authentic Holy Grail, including the one in nearby Valencia, the true *Sangreal* was hidden in a convent."

Now he had me hooked. I knew which convent he was going to name. But how could it have been hidden there, while the nuns venerated a false Grail in the cathedral?

"The convent, appropriately enough, was *El Convento de las Hermanas del Sangreal*, the Convent of the Sisters of the Holy Grail. Their mission was to protect and venerate the *Sangreal*, which they thought was the alabaster chalice in the great cathedral. In fact, the real *Sangreal* resided among them."

I felt Montbrison tense up beside me. He was ready to explode. I put a hand on his shoulder, ready to hold him back if he tried to rush down to the banquet hall before DesRosier finished his discourse.

"Breaking the word *Sangreal* into the words 'San' and 'greal' was an error, probably an intentional one, perpetrated by the protectors of the sacred object to obfuscate the truth. The early Christians often disguised their faith by using symbols intended to confuse their enemies. The symbol of the fish represented Jesus, the 'fisher of men.' The anchor was really a disguised cross. And translating *Sangreal* as 'Holy Grail' followed in that tradition of subterfuge. It was meant to send the uninitiated on fruitless searches. Which is exactly what happened over the centuries. Popes and kings and treasure seekers were deceived, while the true *Sangreal* remained hidden, protected for the first millennium by devoted followers, and for the second millennium, by a loyal band of devout priests and warriors, of whom I am proud to be a member."

"Liar," hissed Montbrison. "He was never a true Templar. He was never trained in the art of battle, never ordained to the priesthood. He is a fake, a pretender."

"Now, at the beginning of the third millennium," DesRosier continued. "It is my great honor and personal privilege to reveal the secret of the *Sangreal* and reveal how it will be protected for the next thousand years."

DesRosier took an actor's dramatic pause at that point. I could imagine him surveying his audience as they awaited his next words.

"The secret of the *Sangreal* is concealed within the word itself," I listened to him say. "The uninitiated have always divided the word *Sangreal* into the words '*San*' and '*greal*', which translates as Holy Grail. But by moving a single character, the meaning is changed entirely. *Sangreal* becomes two entirely different words: '*Sang*' and '*real*.'"

A mild uproar erupted in DesRosier's audience. With the help of the microphone, DesRosier's voice drowned them out.

"*Sang* is the French word for 'blood,' but it is also a medieval variant of the Spanish word *sangre*, which has the same meaning," he said. "And of course, *real* is the Spanish word for 'royal'. So the true meaning of *Sang Real* is 'Royal Blood.'"

There was a rising clamor from the audience. DesRosier continued to speak above the din.

"Yes," he proclaimed. "Mary Magdalene fled Jerusalem, and came to the safety of distant Provence, because she was pregnant! The 'vessel' which held the Royal Blood was not a cup or a chalice or a bowl. . . but her womb! Her womb was the vessel in which the Magdalene carried our Savior's blood in the form of his unborn child. The *Sang Real* is the royal bloodline of our King and Savior, Jesus Christ. And just like the royal blood which flows in the veins of many of you who are present here today, it must continue. It must be perpetuated."

The reference to their own royal bloodlines seemed to make it all more understandable to many of the assembled guests. But a few of the religious representatives rose to question him.

"But what proof do you have of this theory?" asked one guest.

"And if this bloodline exists, who is the heir, who carries the royal blood?" asked another.

"To answer your questions, I have four items of proof," DesRosier said. "The first is a letter from a young nun to a Jesuit priest."

I watched him reach into his pocket to remove a familiar envelope. The red wax seal identified it as Magdalena's letter. The one she had entrusted to me. He unfolded Magdalena's note, apparently to be sure he quoted it exactly.

"*Dear Padre,*" DesRosier read. "*I now know my destiny. I know who I am and why I was born again. You must help me find the man who will fulfill that destiny. I must pass along the Sang Real while I am still of child-bearing age.*"

So it was one of DesRosier's thugs who had stolen the letter. Which meant he knew its contents all the time. He knew it before he hired me. He knew it before I met Padre Serrano at the *Naranjas*.

"The letter is signed La Magdalena," DesRosier said. "This was a name given by the nuns of the *Convento de las Hermanas del Sangreal* to one of their own, Sister Mariamme. I had heard stories of this young nun before, but the letter was my first solid evidence of her royal lineage. Somehow, through what I can only conclude was some strange trick of genetic memory, she knew of her true identity, and she was determined to see that the royal bloodline endures."

DesRosier folded the letter and replaced it in his pocket.

"My investigation revealed that she was taken to the *convento* when she was a few months old," DesRosier went on. "She was raised by the nuns. In particular, by a Sister Mary Generosa, who is now deceased. What Sister Mariamme didn't know, until I revealed that fact to her, was that Sister Mary Generosa was the woman who brought her to the *convento*."

Now it was my turn to tense up. I thought I saw Montbrison begin to cry.

"Before her death in a retirement home in Barcelona, Sister Generosa wrote a letter to the young nun, explaining how the child was brought to the convent. The letter, which has come into my possession, traces the Christic bloodline back to the first century, to Mary Magdalene's arrival in France. As a sign of the sanctity of the *Sang Real*, each generation has produced only one child, always female. Until now, there has yet been no male heir, which leads to important theological questions. As the rabbi can confirm, since ancient times, Jewish law has determined heredity through the mother's lineage, not the father's. Which means the bloodline remains pure."

"But you've still given us no proof," a lone voice persisted. "All this is hearsay, letters from women who may be imagining things."

"The Vatican was looking for proof, too," DesRosier said. "In an independent investigation, they were asking the same questions I was. Eight hairs were removed from Sister Mariamme's head, saliva swabs were taken, the DNA was extracted and compared with DNA removed from the skull of Mary Magdalene, which has been on display in the Basilica at *Saint-Maximin-La-Sainte-Baume* for the last thousand years."

"But how can we be certain the skull belonged to Mary Magdalene?" another voice argued. "There was a great deal of trafficking in relics during the Middle Ages. We all know many so-called relics are counterfeits, whose purpose was to attract donations and attendance at Mass."

"Two months ago, representatives from the Vatican removed the original skull from the basilica and replaced it with a similar one," DesRosier said. "The skull was subjected to radiocarbon analysis at the University of Rome, under the supervision of Vatican scientists. At great cost, I was able to obtain copies of both the DNA and radiocarbon dating. Not only is the DNA a perfect match, but three separate carbon-14 tests conducted on the flesh, the bone, and the hair, have dated the skull to the middle of the first century, about the time the oral traditions say that Mary Magdalene died."

Invoking the Vatican seemed to satisfy the skeptic, who fell silent.

"But the greatest proof of all will soon walk through that door," DesRosier said. "When I present to you my wife-to-be, Mariamme Magdala, the direct female descendant of Mary Magdalene, the future mother of my children . . . the DesRosier children . . . in whose veins will flow the Royal Blood of Jesus Christ."

Excited whispers erupted among the guests.

"She has been released from her vows, enabling this marriage to take place," DesRosier continued. "I trust you will welcome her with the dignity and reverence she deserves. As the direct descendant of Jesus Christ, my bride will command an important position in church matters. In fact, she may become the unifying force behind which all the Christian denominations will finally unite. After all, no matter what divisions may have taken place over the centuries, no matter how varied the dogmas and rituals, the one belief that all Christianity shares is the divinity of Jesus Christ. And now we have the living proof that the Son of God did indeed become man."

DesRosier's speculation on religious unification was not as far-reaching as the one Padre Serrano had been sketching out in the margins of his books, in which he explored the similarities of all religions, but it was obviously based on Serrano's thinking.

"There will be those who try to discredit my wife, perhaps simply because she is a woman, or keep the facts of her life secret, because it threatens their authority. But the truth will prevail."

Of course it would, I thought. DesRosier had cast aside Magdalena's past-life claims in favor of scientific proof of lineage. He had chosen the easier route, tracing the genealogy of her flesh rather than the genealogy of her soul, the physical rather than the spiritual, to establish her Christic credentials. And from the lack of argument, it sounded as if the distinguished guests were buying his premise.

"I am prepared to commit my entire fortune to this great cause," he said. "With your help in spreading the word, Christianity will be restored to its original purpose. We will see a tremendous rebirth of faith, a restoration of hope, and a universal Christian Church with the direct descendants of Jesus Christ at its center."

Now I finally began to understand what DesRosier was up to.

It was a breathtaking claim, a grasp for power over Christianity that hadn't been seen since the days of Constantine. And I, through my foolishness, had helped make it possible.

Sixty-Eight

FROM DOWNSTAIRS CAME the sound of the string quartet launching into Mendelssohn's *Wedding March*.

"It is time," Magdalena said.

She led us out to the top of the stairway, where two young acolytes awaited her, slowly swinging covered incense burners to sanctify the air through which she would walk. In front of them, a little girl in a white dress had already started down the grand stairway, strewing rose petals from a wicker basket. Also waiting in the hallway was a thin man with a scar on his left cheek. It was Tito, the Basque. He stiffened when he saw me. For a moment, I thought he was going to reach for a weapon. Instead, with the insolent calm of a man who feared nothing, he waited for me to make the first move.

"Step aside," Magdalena said to him, in a voice that commanded obedience. "They are with me."

Tito hesitated, glancing from her to me and the two Templars who stood behind us.

"They are part of the wedding party," she said. I was amazed at how confident she sounded. She stared down Tito until, with a crooked grin masking his misgivings, he complied with her command.

Magdalena brushed past him, leading the way down the winding stairway. I fell in behind her two attendants, followed by Lucien and Montbrison, who had once again pulled his hood over his head. Tito took up what I assumed was a guard position in the rear.

The music increased in volume as we descended the stairs. The faces of ancient Templar warriors stared down at us from their paintings on the wall. Overhead, like parade bunting, hung the tattered battle flags of DesRosier's ancestors, their colors long faded. We passed the armor-clad figures that flanked the landing, turned to the right, and were greeted by a pink-cheeked and well-fed cleric wearing the scarlet cap and robes that identified him as a Roman Catholic cardinal.

"I am Joseph Cardinal Amoroso," he said. He held out his ring to be kissed, a standard formality for princes of the Church.

Magdalena ignored the proffered ring.

The cardinal pretended to ignore the fact that she paid no attention to his extended hand.

"How wonderful to finally meet you, my dear," he said in a fraudulently sweet voice. "I shall be escorting you to the altar."

The doors to the great banquet hall opened slowly. The music continued to swell in volume. Inside, the guests all rose to their feet, watching expectantly for their first look at the woman DesRosier had just described, the woman in whose veins flowed the sacred Royal Blood. Cardinal Amoroso smiled and nodded toward the guests, obviously enjoying his moment of glory. Magdalena remained out of their direct line of sight. Mistaking her reticence for shyness, the cardinal offered her his arm.

"Do not be afraid, my child," he said. "Take my arm. I will fill the role of your absent father, and give you away in holy matrimony."

"I will walk alone," she said.

"But . . . I was told . . ."

"I will walk alone," she repeated. "You have no right to give me away."

"It's purely symbolic, of course . . . to have someone give the bride away is a traditional part of the wedding ceremony. And on an occasion as important as this, what could be more appropriate than to have a representative of the Holy Mother Church accompany you down the aisle?"

"You may walk behind me, if you wish. But not before me, and certainly not beside me."

"With all due respect, may I remind you that I am a cardinal of the Catholic Church, bishop of Bordeaux, member of the Apostolic Committee for the Propagation of the Faith? I represent your church."

"You represent Peter's church," she said bluntly. "And please take off that cross." She indicated the large crucifix which the cardinal carried in his cincture. "It offends me to see such reminders of the suffering of Jesus my Christ."

The cardinal scowled and sucked in his breath, rising to his full height, as if to intimidate her. "What offends me is your attitude, my child. Christ died on that cross for our sins."

"I know," she said. "I was there."

The comment, which was perfectly understandable to me, visibly perplexed the cardinal.

"His death on the cross was the central element of our faith," he said.

"Dying didn't prove he was divine," she countered. "It was his rising from the dead that proved he was truly the Son of God. You should be carrying a symbol of his resurrection, rather than his death. Now get behind me."

The paraphrase of Christ's words to Peter was not lost on the cardinal. Deflated, he stepped aside to let her enter the room before him. She moved slowly, her bearing more regal than any of the royal guests who stood up to applaud as she entered the room. She walked on rose petals in a cloud of air sweetened with the scent of incense.

Without warning, an intense, almost supernatural white light appeared to settle around Magdalena. She seemed to be the focal point of the beam, which followed her as she moved. The source of the light was the television photographer, who back-pedaled a few meters in front of her, recording every step she took with a shoulder-mounted video camera. A still photographer also walked backwards before her, clicking away furiously. While the video camera remained trained on Magdalena, the still photographer also shot dozens of images of the distinguished guests, who were as excited by her entrance as teenage fans waiting in line for hours to see their favorite music stars. The women, in particular the heavily jeweled princesses and duchesses, strained to get a better look at Magdalena's face, which was partially hidden by her veil.

She walked gracefully, slowly, to the center of the room, where DesRosier was waiting for her. He stood before the enormous fireplace, which had been skillfully camouflaged with the help of hundreds of cut roses and candles and statuary of Jesus and the Blessed Virgin and Joseph. In front of the elaborate *faux* shrine was a lace-covered table on which stood an ornate golden monstrance holding a white Communion host. The resulting display was worthy of a small church. I noticed, reassuringly, there were no images of the crucified Christ to offend his bride. DesRosier had planned the wedding well.

With everyone's attention focused on Magdalena, Lucien, Montbrison, and I were able to slip into the room unnoticed by anyone except Tito. We found a place to stand where we would be partially hidden by some suits of armor. Tito followed close behind, remaining within striking distance.

The long banquet table had been removed from the room to make way for five rows of twenty chairs each. The hundred chairs must have come from some enormous cache of antiques. They were identical ebony armchairs, elaborately hand-carved, with red-velvet cushions to comfort the distinguished posteriors of his guests. Despite the wedding decorations and seating alterations, the room remained an homage to the chateau's Templar heritage. The crossed swords and axes and other weapons of war remained on the walls, along with the enormous oil paintings of battle scenes, renderings of Templar cathedrals, and battle flags. No one was paying attention to the museum-quality artifacts, however. All attention was focused on Magdalena.

She stopped to say a few words to the rabbi, greeting him in what sounded like the Aramaic tongue that had so impressed Professor Abramakian. The rabbi reacted first with a stunned expression, which quickly melted into a delighted smile. He bowed his head and kissed her hand, before replying in what sounded like Hebrew. She responded in kind, leaving him glowing with pride at having been singled out first. To the archimandrite of Alexandria, she spoke in Hellenic Greek, another language I recognized from her interview with Abramakian. The archimandrite, apparently a language student himself, understood the ancient tongue, although he responded in modern Greek. She turned to speak again to Cardinal Amoroso, smiling sweetly as if the tense encounter before her entrance had never happened. Her words to him this time were in fluent Latin, which drew an uncomprehending silence from the cardinal. It was a language he probably never used conversationally even before it was abandoned by his church. Magdalena was moving along the row of clerics like a queen greeting the leaders of her Commonwealth, bestowing upon each the incandescence of her smile and warm words in the languages of their forefathers. It was a combination that was impossible for the holiest of men to resist. She was confirming, in her own very human way, the extraordinary nature of the woman they were greeting. All the while, Jean-Claude DesRosier watched from his position in front of the altar, beaming with pride at the great prize he was about to win.

The *patrón*, resplendent in his custom-tailored white tie and tails, was a world figure himself, accustomed to having his photograph in both the business and society pages of the major European newspapers. He was the owner of the chateau, the host of this spectacular event, the bridegroom-to-be. The aura of wealth and prestige that surrounded him, however, was no match for the powerful charisma exuded by the woman in the simple white tunic. Her smile, when she turned to look at the guests, seemed to touch each of them on some deeply personal level. The room fell silent. Even the photographers ceased their annoying activity. I could sense the expectant mood as they waited, actually seemed to yearn, for her to speak. Was this how it was in Provence, when hundreds gathered wherever she preached; where everyone from the poorest widow to the governor of Marseilles sought her intercession? Was this why kings and queens and popes built monasteries to her memory? Why hymns were still sung to honor her throughout Europe? Why the people of dozens of cities paraded through the streets on her feast day every year? Looking at the response of these jaded jet setters and religious leaders, I marveled at the power the legend of Mary Magdalene still exerted two thousand years after her death. I tried desperately not to get swept up in the strange euphoria that seemed present in the room. As anyone who ever studied mass psychology or attended a rock concert is aware, the mood of a crowd can have profound effects on both consciousness and perception, leading to mind-altering experiences that can mimic the effects of various drugs. One trigger, I thought, one phrase or action, carefully timed, could tip this room into a state of mass hysteria to rival that of the sightings at Lourdes, Fatima or Medjugorge. I could see the beginnings of it in DesRosier himself, who stared at his prospective bride with a glazed look in his eyes.

The moment, as I anticipated, came when Magdalena decided to speak.

"The Lord be with you," she said in a gentle voice.

With those words, all of us, priests and princes and princesses, dukes and duchesses, rabbi and cardinal and archimandrite, Muslim and Protestant, even the Basques, fell to our knees and bowed our heads in homage before the *Sang Real*. All except Jean-Claude DesRosier, who remained standing, who coolly surveyed the room and seemed to glory in the idea that all these powerful people would kneel before his bride. DesRosier took a deep breath, the image of a man reveling in the rarefied air of conquest. A thin smile appeared on his lips.

I knew by now why this marriage was taking place. DesRosier was truly marrying for love. Not the love of Magdalena, as beautiful and blessed a creature as she was. It was the love of power that motivated him. Despite having reached the pinnacle of wealth, controlling the destiny of dozens of companies and thousands of workers and their families, earning the respect and even in some cases the obeisance of pliable politicians, he still hungered for new power, new glory. And what better way to achieve it than to possess the fabled *Sang Real,* the spiritual treasure, the supreme mystery that had seemed to be forever beyond mortal man's reach? Having eluded the searches of figures as mythical as King Arthur and Percival and as real as Richard the Lion-Hearted and yes, even Hitler himself, the legendary *Sang Real* was now within the grasp of Jean-Claude DesRosier. He seemed barely able to contain his joy. His slender body seemed to quiver with anticipation of what was about to take place.

Whom does the Sang Real serve?

That was the question posed in Malory's Arthurian tales.

The answer tonight appeared to be Jean-Claude DesRosier. For even if one disputed the mystical power of the *Sang Real,* there was still the very real issue of Magdalena's ancestry to deal with. Reasonable people might dispute theories of reincarnation, finding minor flaws in the most convincing evidence. But the purloined Vatican documents, the mitochondrial DNA and carbon dating tests had convinced the highest levels of the Roman Catholic Church that this young bride-to-be was directly descended from Mary Magdalene herself. And in all the Canonical and Apocryphal Gospel references, there was only one man with whom the Magdalene had any close relationship, one man she supported with her wealth, one man for whom she wept, one man who "kissed her on the mouth" and "loved her above all others."

That man was Jesus Christ.

Whether she was his "consort," as the Gospel of Philip proclaims, his concubine, as the Gnostics were convinced, or his wife, as many modern theologians believe, Jesus Christ was the only man who could logically have fathered the child who was Magdalena's ancestor. The *King of the Jews* left his legacy to mankind in a royal bloodline. And now this power-lusting billionaire was about to usurp that bloodline, adding his seed to the divine genes, becoming the father of the descendants of Jesus Christ and Mary Magdalene. This marriage, when its real significance was known to the world, could reshape the configuration of the competing systems of Christian religious beliefs. That was the reason why this fascinating array of European nobility and religious leaders were assembled here. They came to witness the historic event that DesRosier had promised them: a matrimonial union that would produce a new heir to the reign of God. What Catholic pope, what Orthodox partriarch, what Protestant leader would not bow down before this new Holy Family? With six billion Christians in the world, what political leader would not seek the approval of these new leaders of the faith?

No wonder DesRosier was so excited. He was about to put himself at a pinnacle of power unmatched since the days of Julius Caesar, Alexander the Great, or the Emperor Constantine. It was a temporal position to which even Jesus Christ himself never aspired. But clearly, Jean-Claude DesRosier was on the verge of achieving it.

And what of Magdalena, I wondered? Was that what she wanted, too? Had I misjudged her so horribly? Was she as hungry for power as DesRosier?

Sixty-Nine

"I CONSIDER MYSELF a widow . . . ," she said into the microphone, " . . . the widow of Jesus my Christ."

Total silence in the room. No one moved. Everyone, including the Basques, who had silently taken up positions on both sides of us, waited to hear the first public statement of the woman about whom DesRosier had made such remarkable claims.

"A few weeks ago, Jean-Claude told me I was the direct descendent of the union between Mary Magdalene and Jesus my Christ. He says the Vatican in Rome has the physical evidence to prove that I carry the Royal Blood, the *Sang Real,* in my veins."

Her voice was warm and husky, the amplification of the microphone adding a false sense of intimacy. It was the kind of voice men dream of hearing in dark rooms on warm nights, when in their loneliness, they fantasize about the eternal feminine.

"He speaks of my body with reverence, and tells me tales of secret sects and hidden places, and of those many brave knights and holy men and women who gave their lives to protect the sanctity of my bloodline."

DesRosier's triumphant smile faltered when he saw us in the back of the room. But perhaps reassured by the way Tito and Manolo had us bracketed, he quickly resumed his triumphant expression.

"I remember nothing of that," she continued. "What I remember is my life with Jesus my Christ. My body, you see, may be that of a young woman born in 1982. But my soul, my emotions, my memories, are all those of a woman who walked the Earth and shared the bed of our Savior."

She was slipping now into reincarnation theory, and the guests, whatever skepticism any of them might harbor about such matters, were enthralled. They came here not just for a wedding, but wanting to be part of a great religious revelation, to learn the secret of the *Sangreal,* and if the ancient belief in the karmic cycle of rebirth was part of that mystery, then so be it.

"I am Mary Magdalene," she proclaimed. "I stand before you, reborn in a new body, prepared to be married and fulfill my sacred mission, which is the continuation of the royal bloodline of Christ the King."

Even for me, by now a believer in her claim, it was an audacious statement. Yet it drew not the slightest challenge from the audience. It was a classic demonstration of group behavior, in which the most ardent skeptic's normal disbelief was submerged by the majority's unwillingness to question what it was hearing. Add to that, of course, the influence of the religious role models in the front row who remained silent, thus giving their imprimatur-by-default, and the situational influences were overpowering. I had no doubt that these guests would leave DesRosier's castle convinced of everything they heard, ready to spread the word among their peers and followers.

DesRosier had masterfully arranged the moment and the setting to impart a Pentecostal atmosphere to the proceedings, converting both secular and religious guests into believers, into the Apostles of his new family's reign.

And yet, it was hard for me to believe that Magdalena, the woman with whom I had fallen in love, was playing a willing part in all this. I waited for her to continue. She seemed to be looking around nervously, searching the room, until finally her eyes settled on me, and her lips spread in the most beatific smile I ever saw.

"I was married to Jesus my Christ in a wedding performed according to the Jewish tradition," she said. "He was crucified, died, was buried, rose again from the dead and ascended into heaven, leaving me behind to carry his seed."

She was momentarily overcome with emotion. When DesRosier stepped forward to comfort her, she waved him off and continued.

"I consider myself a widow," she said, her voice rising in strength, like that of an evangelist proclaiming the word of God. "And since I was married in accordance with the Law of Moses, my fate as a widow must be determined by the Law of Moses."

She focused her eyes directly upon me.

"The law requires that, if a man's brother dies and leaves his wife behind him, his brother must take the wife and produce offspring to carry on the name of the brother who died. That is the Law of Moses."

DesRosier frowned. In the front row, I could see the rabbi and his fellow religious leaders nodding appreciatively at this biblical reference.

"The wife of the dead man shall not marry unto a stranger; her husband's brother shall go unto her and take her to wife. That is the Law of Moses."

What was she talking about? DesRosier jumped to her side, placing his hand over the microphone while he angrily whispered something to her. The uniform quiescence of the crowd was beginning to break down. The priests were murmuring to each other, particularly the rabbi and the Russian Orthodox partriarch.

Magdalena pushed DesRosier aside and took the microphone again.

"Therefore, in accordance with the Law of Moses, I cannot marry anyone but my husband's brother," she said.

"They're all dead!" DesRosier exclaimed. "Christ's brothers all died two thousand years ago."

"Yes!" Magdalena said. "But like me, one of them was reborn of new flesh. I recognized him when I first saw him. He is James, the younger brother of Jesus."

The backs of my knees felt weak when I heard that name. She kept her eyes focused on mine, raised her hand and pointed at me with her extended palm.

"That is James," she said. "Look at him. It is he who will assure the survival of his brother's line. In accordance with the Law of Moses, James is the man I must marry."

Seventy

SOMETHING SNAPPED INSIDE DesRosier's mind.

"No!" he screamed. "Noooo!"

To have his magnificent plan thwarted, to see his chance for immortality slipping away was something he refused to consider. He was, after all, a billionaire, a man of noble descent, unaccustomed to being denied anything he wanted. For years, he had schemed and worked on this glorious plan, this bid for unparalleled power, and yes, even immortality. To have it snatched away from him at what should be his moment of greatest triumph, and to have it happen in so public a manner, in front of so distinguished an audience, was impossible for him to accept.

He grabbed Magdalena and shook her violently. His face reddening, his nostrils flaring, the veins at his temples throbbing, he thundered at the stunned audience.

"She is mine!" he raged. "Not his! Mine!"

Turning his murderous rage on me, he screamed out, "Manolo! Tito! Get rid of him!"

He shouted out something else, too, something in their native Euskadi that sounded like a more ominous command. Manolo responded instantly.

One of his massive hands wrapped itself around my neck. I thought he was going to strangle me, until I saw the gun in his hands. It wasn't one of those slender semi-automatic weapons that look so deceptively elegant. Such a weapon wouldn't be suited to Manolo's huge hands. This was a brutal, large-caliber, Dirty Harry type of revolver, big and bulky, heavy enough to kill by crushing my skull if he chose not to waste a bullet on me.

"Shoot him!" DesRosier shouted. "Now!"

Magdalena screamed.

The strange calm that often envelops those facing certain death settled over me. Time seemed suspended. Sounds stilled. I stared in fascination at the source of my impending demise, my attention focused on the fat, copper-coated bullets whose rounded tips were visible in the cylinder. Manolo aimed the gun at my left eye. The trajectory, I thought with clinical dispassion, would take the heavy slug right through the center of my brain, exploding it and tearing away the back of my skull. Unlike the last time I was shot, there would be no possibility of recovery. The pain would be brief, over almost instantaneously. Having already died once, I had little fear of what awaited me. My only regret would be leaving Magdalena behind.

As the cylinder slowly turned, I was aware of a blur of movement behind Manolo.

It was the old priest, Montbrison, who moved with the speed of a feral creature attacking its prey. He snatched one of the heavy two-handed Templar swords from a display on the wall as easily as if it were a plaything. His hands wrapped themselves comfortably around the grip as he let out a roar in a language I never heard before—a roar that echoed through the hallways of the castle—screaming out in a blood rage that must have been familiar to the warriors whose portraits hung on the walls, and had been heard in the scene of slaughter in the painting above me. It was the battle cry of the Templars, stilled for centuries and now back in full glory—a blood-curdling sound that froze Manolo and brought a fear into his eyes that was supposed to be unknown to Basques.

Manolo could have shot me then. But perhaps wondering if he might yet bargain for his own life, he hesitated. In an almost liquid, silvery blur, the sword sliced down through his wrist, the Toledo blade cutting through flesh and tendon and bone with an astonishing ease. Manolo's face went pale. The gun, with his hand still attached to it, clattered to the floor. He screamed and sank to his knees, scrambling after his severed hand. Montbrison promptly kicked it out of reach.

Another shout came from behind me, this one in the Basque language. Tito, the smaller of the two, had taken the second sword from the display and was raising it above his head. While he struggled with the weight of the sword, Montbrison spun around to face him, swung his own bloody sword above his head and was ready to attack, when Magdalena's voice rang out.

"Stop!" she cried. "In the name of Jesus my Christ, stop!"

The two swordsmen hesitated.

Montbrison looked back at me, looked at the guests, and finally looked at Magdalena. He nodded his head in obedience and lowered his sword.

With his enemy defenseless, Tito attacked.

He slashed his sword across Montbrison's chest, pulling it in a cutting motion that knocked the old priest against the wall. The blade sliced through Montbrison's brown robe, exposing a wide band of crimson just below his heart. In what seemed like a particularly bloodthirsty act, Tito raised the blade again, ready to slash even more deeply into Montbrison's chest. The old priest was spared a second blow when Lucien came up behind Tito, and grabbing the attacker's shoulders from the rear, delivered a knee into Tito's spine that appeared to break the thin man's back. He collapsed in agony at Lucien's feet.

"Securité! Securité!" I heard DesRosier calling out over the microphone in French. In his excitement, he switched to Spanish. *"Seguridad! Ayuda! Es terroristas!"* And finally English. "Hurry! We're being attacked!"

Lucien was bent over the old priest, cradling his head in one hand. DesRosier held Magdalena by the arms. I could hear the front doors of the castle thrown open, followed by the thunderous footsteps of what sounded like a small army coming in response to DesRosier's call.

The invading force crashed through the banquet hall doors on the run. Dozens of them poured through the opening. They seemed a highly disciplined group, quickly fanning out around the room until they had all of us surrounded. To my surprise, these were not the well-dressed bodyguards I had seen outside. They appeared to be priests, wearing brown hooded robes identical to that worn by Montbrison, and earlier, by Lucien. As they took up positions along the walls, strange metallic sounds emanated from beneath their robes.

If I was surprised, DesRosier was absolutely dumbfounded by the appearance of these peculiar creatures who had responded to his call. Two of the hooded men bent down beside Lucien to minister to Montbrison. There wasn't much they could do, I knew. The large red slash ran directly across the old priest's chest. That large and bloody a wound would be fatal, even for a younger man.

In response to some silent command, the invaders threw back their hoods, revealing heads and necks covered with glistening mesh. Like heroic statues being ceremoniously unveiled, they removed their sash cords and allowed their robes to drop slowly to the floor. None of us was prepared for what we saw. The scene was a throwback to medieval times. In this great banquet hall with its heraldic displays and Crusader artifacts, we were surrounded by two dozen men clad in chain-mail armor, with large swords at their sides. Draped over their chests were white linen tunics emblazoned with the blood-red splayed cross of the Knights Templar.

I felt light-headed. I was convinced I had just lost touch with reality. These weren't men who had dressed up in costume for some spectacular practical joke. These were powerful men with broad shoulders who seemed perfectly comfortable wearing their custom-fitted suits of flexible armor. All wore beards, in the traditional Templar style. Some of them were young men, probably in their twenties; the beards of others were already greying. One thing they all had in common was the grim, determined expression of men willing to fight to the death. Right here. Right now, if need be.

I heard a groan from the floor. It was Montbrison, who, incredibly, still appeared to be alive. Not strong enough to get up, but alive nevertheless. When the men helping him removed his robe, I could see why. Although he wasn't wearing the mesh headgear of the others, Montbrison was clad in the same chain-mail armor. Tito's thin arms hadn't been able to put enough strength into his blow to penetrate the protective woven metal. What I had thought was a bloody wound was, in fact, the horizontal bar of the red Templar cross on his linen tunic. He might have suffered a broken rib or two, had the wind knocked out of him, but he was alive!

In unison, the Templar Knights removed their swords from their sheaths, held the blades aloft, and saluted Magdalena.

"Nous saluons le Sang Real!" They called out in unison, saluting the *Sang Real* and vowing death to her enemies. *"Et la mort à ses ennemis."*

But if twenty-four armored Templar Knights who seemed to appear out of some strange time warp thought they could intimidate Jean-Claude DesRosier, they were mistaken. He still held the prize in his grasp. The presence of the Knights probably confirmed in his mind the power he could achieve by marrying Magdalena. He wasn't yet prepared to surrender his chance at immortality. A small stiletto appeared in his hand. He pressed it against Magdalena's neck. The point had not yet drawn blood, but it was already making a small indentation in her flesh.

"We will proceed with the wedding," he whispered to her. The microphone picked up his words and amplified them across the room.

"No! I will never marry you."

"You will bear my child."

"I would rather die than allow a murderer to taint the royal bloodline."

"Then die you will," DesRosier said in a quiet voice. "If I can't have you, no one will."

"Do you not fear the wrath of God?" shouted the rabbi. "If you kill the *Sangreal,* you will be killing the unborn descendants of Jesus."

"It is her choice," DesRosier said. "She is the one making the decision, not me." He turned back to Magdalena. "What will it be?"

"Death," she murmured.

"So be it."

"Wait!" Cardinal Amoroso jumped up. "Kill me instead! I will gladly exchange my life for hers."

"Keep back," DesRosier warned him.

Another cleric, the tall thin Anglican bishop rose, and in a courtly voice said, "Kill me, too. I will gladly join the cardinal and die for the *Sang Real*."

"And me." An African Baptist minister rose. I watched in awe as Coptic and Methodist, Anglican and Jew, Greek and Russian Orthodox, the entire front row of religious leaders put aside their historic differences and rose to stand united for a cause in which they all had a common interest. "Kill us all," the cardinal said. "We are all willing to die so that she might live."

They were joined by a slender young Bavarian princess in the back of the room. "And me," she said in a trembling voice. "I am willing to die for the *Sang Real*, also."

Another princess arose, and then an elderly couple, and then groups of two and three at a time, until finally, everyone in the room, royalty and religious, was on their feet, all expressing their willingness to be martyred so that the bloodline of Jesus Christ would survive.

It might not have been what DesRosier expected. But this moving expression of faith had little effect on him.

"You think I care about your silly lives?" he responded. "I wouldn't trade all of you for the *Sang Real*. Not even for ten times as many as you."

He started to edge toward the door. With his knife pressed against Magdalena's throat, the imposing company of Templars could do nothing but watch. Sirens outside announced the arrival of the *Guardia Civil*. There were more shouts and footsteps rushed into the castle. *Coronel* Velarde, handgun drawn, entered the room, only to stop when he saw the threat to Magdalena. The SWAT team behind him took up positions outside the doorway.

"So you're on their side, now?" DesRosier said to him.

"I am on the side of justice," Velarde responded.

"You were my friend once," DesRosier said.

"Put down the knife."

"And what then? Allow you to arrest me? I'm not that stupid."

"A man with your wealth and influence has little to fear from the law," Velarde said. "I'm sure your lawyers will see you spend little time in prison."

"Your laws are of no concern to me," DesRosier said. "Now step aside, and tell your men to drop their weapons."

He pressed the stiletto's point harder against Magdalena's throat. She let out a little cry.

The knife had pricked her skin; a drop of blood formed at the point of contact. It grew thicker and slowly began dribbling down her neck, leaving a trail of red behind. It was royal blood, I thought. *Sang Real.* DesRosier had set out on the quest that so many others had pursued, but unlike the untold hundreds of knights and kings and emperors who preceded him . . . he had succeeded. He had learned the deepest secret of the Templar's Inner Circle, outwitted them, and now had the precious *Sang Real* within his grasp. I knew he would never willingly give her up. If he was able to get out of here—and with Magdalena as his hostage, that was looking very likely—he could use his wealth to disappear from sight. He could buy a venal official in some foreign country, arrange the marriage he desired, and father the child that would make him master of the royal bloodline. Nine months would be all the time he needed, and then he could emerge as head of the most important family in Christendom.

To rephrase the Arthurian question: *who, then, would the Sang Real serve?*

I couldn't allow that to happen.

But how could I prevent it?

With his knife against Magdalena's throat, no one dared stop him. Even the heavily armed Templars were rendered powerless by the threat to her life. There was nothing I could do. The *karmic* wheel was turning. Once again, I could only watch helplessly as an evil creature took control of a woman I loved. Was this some form of cosmic retribution for having allowed Laura to sacrifice her life for me? Was I to be forced to live variations of this scene over and over again, as I did in my dreams? I stared in disbelief as the faces of Magdalena and her captor changed to the faces of Laura Duquesne and her murderous husband. Call what I saw a flashback, a waking dream, a stress-induced hallucination; whatever it was, it presented an exact replay of the awful images that had haunted my dreams since that awful night in New York. Spellbound, I watched the sequence play itself out exactly as it had a thousand times before: the final fatal embrace as Harrison Duquesne held tight to Laura's left arm before both of them plunged to their deaths. But as I watched, the flow of my dream/flashback/hallucination, which had always been identical, suddenly took on a new ending.

In this new version of the dream, I saw Laura pause and turn to me at the last moment. Harrison Duquesne disappeared. For the first time, the dream moved on into the afterlife, where Laura explained why I couldn't remain with her. Speaking in an ethereal otherworldly voice, she had whispered, "You still have work to do."

And just as it happened when she spoke those words before, I was instantly transported back to the world of the living. The hallucinatory episode, despite how long it seemed to play in my unconscious, probably took no more than a half second of real time. Laura's image was replaced with that of Magdalena. DesRosier was still moving her toward the door. And I was watching helplessly, just as I always did in my dream.

Before DesRosier reached the door, however, I found myself stepping forward to block his way. I had no plan. I had no idea what I would do. For the first time in my adult life, I was making a move that I hadn't carefully thought out beforehand. All I knew was that I had to stop him from taking Magdalena through that doorway.

"I'm the one you want to kill," I said, offering myself to him.

"You! You bastard!" he spit out the words. "You should have died with Serrano."

"If I did, who would have delivered Magdalena to you?"

"I would have found another way," he said. "You weren't that important to me."

"Then why didn't you kill me after I survived the bombing?"

"Two attempts on your life would have drawn too many questions. In the end, the information you developed was useful. But perhaps you are right. Perhaps I should have killed you when I had the chance."

"That was probably the greatest mistake you ever made in your life," I said. I was making it up as I went along. He hadn't loosened his grip on Magdalena. The knife was still drawing blood from the small cut on her neck. The Templars and *Guardia* were still afraid to make a move against him. He was still in control of the situation. But he was listening to me. He had paused, and he was listening to me. My mind raced desperately to improvise something.

"By not killing me," I said. "You lost your chance to become the father of Magdalena's firstborn child."

I had him! I could see I had him! His eyes flared with fury. He looked from me to Magdalena, and back again.

"What do you mean by that?" he asked.

"I thought you already knew," I said as innocently as I could. "Magdalena is pregnant. She's carrying my child. I am going to be the *Sang Real's* father. Not you. The holy child will bear my name, not yours."

Seventy-One

IT WAS AS cruel a blow as I could possibly deliver.

To be told on his wedding day that his bride-to-be was pregnant with another man's child would be devastating to any bridegroom. To have the news delivered in so public a manner, before so distinguished an audience, had to be the most humiliating moment of DesRosier's life. It caught him totally unprepared. He had so carefully engineered this moment. He had devoted years of his life and vast amounts of money to unraveling the secret of the *Sang Real,* in the process betraying the most closely guarded secrets of his Templar ancestors, bribing Vatican and government officials, hiring thugs to intimidate and even murder those who got in his way, to finally reach this moment of glory: when he would publicly take his place as head of a new Holy Family, and rewrite the future history of Christianity.

And I, with just a few well-chosen words, had destroyed it all.

It was a lie, of course.

An awful, wonderful, exquisitely effective lie that came unbidden from somewhere in my subconscious.

And I enjoyed watching the effect it had on him. His face morphed through a series of emotions as his mind tried to cope with what her pregnancy would mean to his plans.

"I'm sorry, my darling," I said to Magdalena. "But this is too important to keep secret."

"You lie!" DesRosier said. "You were being monitored electronically. I heard everything the two of you said, everything you did. You never went to bed with her."

"We made love that night in Arles," I said, thinking quickly. "I left your wireless phone in my room and went to hers. Your phone transmitted the sounds of an empty room."

"One night in a hotel room doesn't mean she's pregnant."

"You can tell from a woman's face," I said. "When I saw her tonight, I knew she was carrying my child, even before she told me." Magdalena's face was indeed fuller, as was her figure. But that was undoubtedly due to the change in her diet from convent food to castle fare, not because of anything I had done.

"If you don't believe me, ask her yourself," I said. It was a tremendous risk I was taking. As if the knife at her throat wasn't motivation enough, both DesRosier and I knew the *Sang Real* would never allow herself to be caught in a lie.

"Is it true?" he asked her. When she didn't respond, he shook her roughly. "*Puta!* Is it true?" He used the harsh Spanish slang for a woman's private parts, the word often used to describe whores. The crude insult drew gasps and protests from the guests behind me. DesRosier didn't care. He was waiting for an answer that didn't come.

In nineteen years of convent life, Magdalena had undoubtedly never heard the pornographic word voiced aloud before. To have it directed at her, personally, left her confused and frightened. She couldn't find her voice. Her eyes filled with tears of shame. In an incredible accident of feminine body language, her right hand went to her stomach. It was a normal enough posture for a frightened woman, but in the context of the situation, it seemed an almost maternal gesture, a confirmation of my lie.

"She's carrying my child, DesRosier," I taunted him. "My child, not yours."

I took a step forward, deliberately trying to provoke him, to divert his anger from her to me. He watched as I brought myself within range of his blade. I could see him calmly judging the distance. I knew what he was going to do, but I wasn't afraid. Inspired perhaps by a hallucination, I was no longer the cautious academic, weighing risk against reward before taking action. None of this had been planned in advance. It could result in my death. But I took another step forward, bringing myself within arm's length. How much taunting would it take before he attacked?

"My child," I repeated. "Not yours."

When the thrust came, I was ready.

Rather than retreating, I stepped forward, turning slightly, but still allowing the knife to penetrate my right side. Getting stabbed on purpose might not seem like a very ingenious plan. But it was the best I could come up with at the time. I let out a grunt when the blade pierced my side. I always thought a knife wound would be a searing sort of pain. What I didn't expect was to feel as if I had been punched in the ribs. Maybe it was due to the violence of his thrust, or the hilt of the stiletto slamming against my flesh when the blade reached its deepest penetration. At that point, he must have twisted the knife, because I almost passed out from a sudden excruciating bolt of pain. The edge of the blade scratched against a rib bone. It felt as if I was being skinned alive from the inside. I would have gladly exchanged that knife wound for another bullet in the chest. Yet I had asked for it. A knife in the ribs was the price I had to pay to get the blade away from Magdalena's throat.

DesRosier tried to pull the knife out, to stab me again. But I grabbed his wrist with both my hands, clasping him to me in a death grip. I would not let go. I pushed forward, separating him from Magdalena, who by now must have been screaming. Lost in my own agony, I heard nothing. I continued pushing stupidly against DesRosier, until we both collapsed on the floor.

He continued tugging at the knife, sending jolts of pain through my side. He seemed determined to kill me, and I no longer had strength enough to resist.

Death held no fear for me. I quit fighting, closed my eyes and let out a long sigh, preparing myself for the journey to the Other Side.

Seventy-Two

THE ARREST OF Spain's most prominent billionaire dominated the media for weeks.

The existence of a descendant of Jesus Christ and Mary Magdalene was never mentioned. All references to the *Sang Real* and the Christic bloodline were expunged from the stories, presumably due to the influence of the Templars. The sanitized version of the news gave credit for solving the case to *Coronel* Fulgencio Velarde of the *Guardia Civil* in Valencia. As one account described the events: *"Acting on an anonymous telephone call on the day of DesRosier's wedding, Coronel Velarde led a SWAT team to the castle north of Valencia, where he effected the billionaire's arrest. In attempting to escape, the suspect stabbed a guest who has not yet been identified. A link between DesRosier and the Basque separatist movement ETA has been established in the bombing of the Naranjas Café in Valencia, which resulted in the deaths of a Spanish priest and a café employee. The billionaire is also being charged in the asphyxiation death of a Lebanese linguistics professor in Barcelona."*

The television stories invariably showed views of the now-empty castle, intercut with footage of a shackled DesRosier being escorted from a police van into the *Guardia* headquarters. The only reference to Magdalena was a cryptic reference that "DesRosier's fiancée has gone into seclusion."

The knife wound, though serious, healed quickly, requiring only a five-day stay in the hospital. After a return visit a week later to have the stitches removed, the doctors gave me permission to resume normal activities. For me, that meant leaving Valencia.

I was in my room at the *Pension Adriatica*, packing up Serrano's books for shipment, when *Coronel* Velarde came to visit me.

"Speaking on behalf of the Templars, we are very grateful for your assistance," he said. "We could have handled the situation ourselves, of course. But you displayed great initiative and personal courage."

I had been expecting this visit for the past three days, ever since the surveillance of my activities was resumed.

"The Templars will pay your hospital bills, of course," he added.

"Of course," I said. "Will you hold the top of this box for me, please?" I ran a wide strip of shipping tape across the open ends of one of the cartons, and then sealed the sides.

"And we will also pay your hotel bills," he added. "Which as you know are quite substantial."

"That's very generous," I said. I printed my father's Athens address on two sides of the carton with a black felt-tipped marker. Having already addressed three cartons, the marker had left pungent chemical fumes hanging in the air.

I started packing the next box of books.

"Does your wound still give you pain?" he asked.

"It's still tender," I said. "Especially when I get up in the morning."

"The doctors are surprised by the speed of your recovery. And I must say, so am I. You are a remarkable man, Mr. Nikonos."

"It's just another scar for another policeman to question," I said, unable to avoid reminding him of his earlier suspicions.

"You are too modest," he said. "Your actions that night impressed many people. Your willingness to sacrifice your life to save another's displays the nobility of purpose and purity of soul the Templars have always valued."

I didn't trust this sudden, effusive praise.

"As a result of your heroic actions, I am pleased to inform you that you have been appointed an honorary member of the Knights Templar." In his hand was a black velvet cloth, which he slowly unfolded to reveal a lapel pin bearing the gleaming image of two knights on a single horse.

"You are now entitled to wear the same gold pin I do," he said. "We are now members of the same brotherhood, dedicated to the protection of the *Sang Real,* a task to which you have already proven your commitment."

I listened as he explained that, for her own protection, Magdalena was safely sequestered somewhere in the Languedoc, the legendary stronghold of the Templars, where the local French population still owes its allegiance to the ancient ways. For a thousand years, the Templars had been the guardians of the *Sang Real*, and he assured me they would continue that tradition for the next thousand years. Her exact location, however, must remain a secret from all but the Inner Circle.

I took the pin and studied it, the tiny figures gleaming in the morning sunlight. It seemed a bit larger than the pin Velarde wore.

"You will find there are many courtesies extended to those who wear this pin," he added. "Our members reach into the highest levels of government, finance, and industry. Doors will be opened for you, opportunities will be presented, access provided."

"But you say I won't be permitted any further contact with Magdalena?" I murmured as I turned the pin over and studied the back.

"The *Sang Real* must be protected," he said. "Surely you understand the need for secrecy. You saw what happened with Señor DesRosier . . . the greediness that arises when men hunger for the power and prestige that can be derived from the *Sang Real*. That is why men have searched for it through the ages."

"DesRosier was a Templar," I reminded him. "Hold the top of this box for me, will you?"

I put the pin in my shirt pocket and taped up the top of the next box. He watched as I printed my father's address on the carton.

"You will be leaving Spain now?" he asked.

"There's nothing keeping me here, is there? I mean, I don't have to testify at DesRosier's trial, do I?"

Although I assumed he would have hired a phalanx of Spain's most expensive lawyers and perhaps attempt to buy off judges and juries, DesRosier inexplicably offered a complete confession to all charges. But he wasn't the type to give up his freedom without a fight. What deal had he worked out in exchange for his silence about the *Sang Real* and the activities of the Templars, I wondered. Perhaps a short term in jail. A quiet release on some spurious medical claim. And ultimately, perhaps, even the restoration of his financial empire. In return for which the Templars would avoid having their activities subjected to the intense public scrutiny that would accompany so sensational a trial.

"No, there will be no need for your presence," Velarde said. "The documents Sister Mariamme passed along to us convinced Señor DesRosier it would be useless to contest the charges. He is relying on the leniency of the courts."

A sudden pain in my side reminded me I wasn't fully recovered. Seeing me stiffen, *Coronel* Velarde helped me to the bed.

"Are you certain you are healthy enough to travel?" he asked, uncharacteristically solicitous. "Perhaps you should stay in Valencia longer."

"I'll be all right," I said.

Holding my side, I took a deep breath. The pain eased, and soon I was able to breathe normally again. Velarde seemed in no hurry to leave.

"The newspapers made you out to be quite the hero," I said.

"That is the doing of the *Guardia's* public relations people. They have very good connections with the media."

"Are they the ones who managed to keep any mention of the Templars out of the story?" I asked. "Or do the Templars control the media, too?"

He gave a helpless shrug. "Some things are beyond my understanding," he said. "Unlike you, I do not seek answers to every question."

"Nevertheless, there are still some answers I'd like," I said. "Now that I'm considered a Templar . . ."

"An honorary Templar," he reminded me.

"Yes, an honorary Templar. But one who has knowledge of the role the Templars played in this matter, and also knows the secret of the *Sang Real* . . ."

"Is this some sort of threat, Mr. Nikonos?" He shifted uneasily. "Because I do not threaten easily, particularly in such important matters."

"I'd just like some background," I said. "If I tried to tell this story to anyone, they wouldn't believe me. Not as long as the Vatican doesn't release the results of their DNA testing. And you and I both know, that will probably never happen."

The pain hit again, causing me to wince. Perhaps that elicited enough sympathy to loosen his tongue.

"You're right," he said. "No one would believe you. Sometimes I myself find it hard to believe. I am just a small player in these events. But I am proud of my role. And I admire the role you played. You suffered greatly, and perhaps you deserve to know some . . . some of what transpired."

He didn't realize I already knew almost all of it. Like any researcher, however, I wanted to hear the story from another viewpoint, to check certain facts, in case I someday decided to write about it.

"Much of what I tell you is confidential," he said. "As an honorary Templar, you are not bound by our vows. But I ask you to respect them, nevertheless."

"I promise to reveal nothing of what you tell me," I said. "Except that which defends the faith." It was an enormous loophole, and from the expression on his face, I'm sure he recognized it. Nevertheless, like Serrano before him, he seemed glad to have someone with whom he could share his secrets.

"Over the centuries, many people have guessed at the 'Secret Knowledge' the original nine Templars brought back from the Holy Land," he said. "As you may have already suspected, part of the 'Secret Knowledge' they brought with them was documentary proof of the marriage of Jesus Christ and Mary Magdalene. It was in the form of a Jewish marriage contract, which is still in the possession of our brotherhood. It was that document that inspired the Templars to seek out and protect the descendants of that marriage. It is the most sacred vow of the Templars. And one that we have faithfully fulfilled at the risk of our lives."

He was making it sound much more altruistic than I now knew the facts to be, but I didn't argue with him.

"It was thought at one point that the royal bloodline had died out. However, we knew of the existence of one more child, the last remaining child who was descended from the divine marriage. As protectors of the *Sang Real,* we were eager to find her. We knew the child was female. We knew the year in which she was born. But we had no idea where she was living. Our chapters in Europe, Africa, and North and South America regularly sent information back to the Languedoc headquarters. Emissaries were sent out to investigate the most promising leads. They were very careful, even skeptical, like you, Mr. Nikonos. We didn't dare risk a misidentification in so important a matter."

Unknown to Velarde, my camcorder was running, making a permanent record of everything he said. At some point, I believed, his statements might be used to "help protect the faith."

"When we learned of Sister Mariamme's odd behavior, Abelard Montbrison and Lucien Poussain were sent to investigate. There had been many false leads before, and they were instructed first to watch her from a distance. I helped in this surveillance by making *Guardia* personnel available."

"You posted your men outside the *convento.*"

"Yes."

"Wasn't that risky, using official *Guardia* personnel for Templar business?"

"As I told you, the influence of the Templars reaches into the highest levels of politics, Mr. Nikonos. I had no reason to fear for my actions."

He sat on the window ledge, which put him in the camcorder's direct line of sight.

"As one of our most prominent members in Spain, Señor DesRosier offered his services and influence. At first he was helpful, absorbing some of the costs of our twenty-four-hour surveillance. But at some point, his personal ambitions got the better of him. He went outside our agreed-upon methods and began bribing church officials. He learned that Padre Serrano had been appointed Sister Mariamme's therapist. His fear that the Padre might discover her great secret led to the bombing at the *Naranjas*. I honestly thought it was a Basque act of terrorism, and in fact, the bomb was placed by one of DesRosier's Basques. But I never suspected him.

"I knew he was monitoring your activities with the telephone he gave you. That was a wonderful piece of initiative on his part, and I welcomed it. That was how we traced you to the hospital in Barcelona. Unfortunately, his men reached Abramakian's bedside before we did. We now know that one of them was posing as a male nurse."

"But why would he kill Abramakian?"

"Because, like Serrano, Abramakian was getting close to the truth about Sister Mariamme's identity."

"All right, then. Why didn't he kill me as well?"

"For one thing, he felt you were going up what you Americans call "a blind alley" with this reincarnation business. And he was using you, Mr. Nikonos. You think you are a smart man, but he is much smarter. He was using you to deliver Sister Mariamme to him. When we arrested you in Saint Maximin, Magdalena thought she was being rescued by a benevolent patron. And frankly, at that point, so did we. DesRosier was a Templar. We thought he would return . . ." he quickly amended himself. "We thought he would see that she was safe."

The Templars had an odd definition of the word "safe," I thought.

"Unknown to us, DesRosier had other plans. Sister Mariamme was naïve to the ways of the world, and easily manipulated. He told her you were released from jail, and that you had already returned to America."

That part of the story was identical to the one I heard. It explained why DesRosier arranged for me to be kept in prison with no contact with anyone other than his lawyers.

"Sister Mariamme was convinced you had abandoned her, and remembering all the good things you said about DesRosier, she welcomed his attention. For a young woman so innocent in the ways of love and so alone in the world, it was an easy progression from gratefulness to admiration to infatuation and eventually, betrothal. DesRosier promised to use his wealth to correct the public image of Mary Magdalene, which Sister Mariamme felt so strongly about. The campaign would start on their wedding day, he promised."

"Which was why the wedding was scheduled for the feast day of Mary Magdalene."

"Exactly. The date was chosen for its obvious symbolism. He said he would gather religious leaders and royalty from around the world. He would have his speech recorded and distributed to television stations around the world."

"But his reason for the big campaign wasn't the same as Magdalena's reasons."

"He invited all those important guests and the television cameras for his own glorification. He was willing to reveal the most sacred secrets of the Templar Knights, the bloodline we had so carefully protected for a thousand years . . . and he was doing it brazenly, openly, in the effort to set himself above all others."

"To become the father of the new generation of Christ's descendants," I murmured. "That was a lot more important than being a mere billionaire."

"And everything would have happened the way DesRosier planned," Velarde went on. "Except for one thing. His fiancée overheard him speaking to the Basques on the afternoon of the wedding. She learned that he had ordered Serrano's death."

At least Velarde was being honest about this part of the story. It confirmed the story that had been told to me two days before.

"You can imagine her horror when she realized she would soon be married to a murderer. Evil blood would be entering the Christic bloodline. But what could she do? She was trapped in a castle, surrounded by Basque guards, and if she tried to escape, DesRosier had ways to deal with her. Her only hope was you, Mr. Nikonos."

Once again, as I did when I first heard this part of the story, I gave thanks that I had explained the workings of the wireless phone to Magdalena.

"She found DesRosier's cell phone and pressed the speed-dial number that was supposed to reach you, as you had told her, wherever you were in the world."

"But I didn't have the telephone," I innocently played along. "I gave it to the guard a month earlier."

"Who naturally passed it along to me. The telephone rang on my desk, where I was keeping it. When she explained what she had learned about her future husband, I contacted Templar headquarters in the Languedoc. Since they couldn't reach the castle in time, Montbrison suggested I free you from prison. The three of you would form an advance party to stop or delay the wedding until reinforcements could arrive."

"So the real hero in all this was Magdalena," I said. "And what reward did she get for her efforts?"

It was a question purposely designed to put Velarde on the defensive. I knew exactly where she was, which was more than he did. But I didn't dare let him suspect that.

"It's really quite incredible," Velarde said, ignoring my question. He sat on the window ledge, watching me stack the boxes on a dolly, but not offering to help, even when he saw me wince with pain. "To think that all these years, this incredible woman . . . the *Sang Real* herself . . . was growing up right here in a *convento* in Valencia, and no one knew her identity!"

"Except for one old nun," I reminded him.

"Ah yes, the nun in Barcelona. Whatever happened to her letter, do you think?" He tried to make it sound like an innocent question, something incidental that had just occurred to him.

"You should ask DesRosier," I said. "His men got to the letter before I did."

In fact, I did know what was in the letter. And I knew why he was much more interested in its return than he was letting on.

"And there was also the note intended for Serrano . . ." he said, as if remembering it for the first time.

"I'd say you should search DesRosier's castle. It was one of his goons who mugged me."

"Unfortunately, we haven't located either of those documents. Not yet. They weren't with the papers Sister Mariamme turned over, and DesRosier claims he has no idea where they are. But we'll keep looking, you can be certain of that."

"With all the evidence you've already got, why are you so worried about those two letters?"

"Just tying up loose ends, Mr. Nikonos," he said with a phony sigh. "Policemen in Spain are much like your policemen in America. We don't like loose ends, no matter how insignificant they might seem to others."

As a lie, it was quite effective, since it was built around a truism. However, I knew what he was after. I knew the real reason he was here, and it wasn't just to inquire about my health and pay me some phony compliments.

"DesRosier knew what was in both documents," I said. "He read Magdalena's letter aloud to his guests. He can tell you what was in the other one."

"He told us his story. The only way to corroborate it would be to find the documents themselves."

"What did he say? What was his side of the story?"

"Unfortunately, that's privileged information."

Of course it was, I thought. And that's why he wanted to find the originals. The old nun's letter would be devastating for the Templars if it was ever published.

In her letter, Sister Generosa described the circuitous route by which the newborn Magdalena was brought to the *convento*. It was the dying wish of her mother that the child be raised away from the influence of the Templars. Protecting the *Sang Real* seemed a noble cause when viewed from outside, but the reality was that in the name of "protection," the women who were Magdalena's ancestors had been imprisoned in remote Languedoc fortresses for a thousand years. Years in which every aspect of their lives was totally controlled by their "protectors," including the selection of their husbands. Because only the seed of a Templar was deemed worthy of the *Sang Real*, once every generation they would nominate one of their own to father the next holy child.

Not wishing the same fate for her daughter, Magdalena's pregnant mother had arranged with a devoted maidservant to spirit the newborn child to freedom. Hunted down by the Templars, the devoutly religious servant sought refuge in the one place she knew that no men, not even the most influential, were permitted to enter: the *Convento de las Hermanas del Sangreal*. In a marvelously fortuitous closing of an ancient circle, the newborn *Sang Real* would grow up in religious anonymity, surrounded by nuns devoted to the preservation of a spurious *Sangreal*. The servant herself took Holy Vows, and became *Hermana Maria Generosa,* the "nanny nun" who supervised the child's upbringing.

She recorded it all in her letter, which was intended for Magdalena's eyes alone. If the Templars learned that I knew the contents of the letter, it could cost me my life. I was certain that was one of the reasons Velarde had come here, to find out how much I knew.

"I wish I could help you, *Coronel.*" I chose my words carefully, trying to sound as if I had no further interest in the matter and was only casually interested. "But I never saw either of the letters, and as far as I'm concerned, the case is closed."

Watching him out of the corner of my eyes, I could see my answer didn't completely satisfy him. The case should have been closed, but we both knew, without admitting so, that it wasn't.

How the Templars must have rejoiced that night on their private train, when they took Magdalena back to their Languedoc fortresses. Their marauding Crusader ancestors had often carried back treasures in the past. But these modern Crusaders were returning from an expedition into Spain with the greatest prize of all, the treasure that had been the source of the Templars' spiritual authority, the mystical center of their very existence. Without possession of the *Sang Real*, their hold over hundreds of thousands of followers whose influence reached into the highest levels of power and influence in dozens of countries would inevitably dissipate. What a great moment it must have been when they recovered Magdalena, their sacred treasure, and took her back to France!

The Templars thought they had outsmarted her, but I knew they were wrong. Magdalena was not with them. She had escaped from their fortress that very night, using the same secret passage and route that Sister Generosa had described in her letter. And that was the real reason for the resumption of surveillance and Velarde's visit, I knew. Without indicating his motive, he was searching for some clue, anything in my room or in my manner that would indicate I had been in touch with Magdalena. Finding nothing, he had given me the Templar pin and the ridiculous little speech designed to hide its true purpose.

"Perhaps I am intruding on your preparations," he said, still trying to maintain a facade of civility. "I can see you are busy. Perhaps I should take my leave." He made no effort to leave, however. "Before I go, there is something very important I must discuss with you."

His voice remained calm. He spoke briefly, but politely, not in any threatening manner, although what he had to say devastated me. His words, when I played them back later on the camcorder, took up less than three minutes of videotape. In that short period of time, he totally destroyed my dreams, my hopes, my plans for the future.

"I am sorry," he said before leaving. "I came here not to disturb you, but to thank you for your help. I am just a policeman, doing my job. And once again, the Templars will not forget your assistance."

When he left, I sat down on the bed with my head in my hands, making no attempt to hide my despair.

The Templars had exacted their revenge on me.

Seventy-Three

I WAS NEVER a very emotional person. In my adult life, I remembered crying only twice before: at my mother's funeral, and when I saw Laura Duquesne fall to her death. Now, realizing the enormity of what I was about to lose, I began to sob. Slowly at first: the hesitant, stiff-jawed sobbing of a man unaccustomed to tears. But alone in that room, knowing that no one could see me, I abandoned myself to my anguish and wept unashamedly. Whoever said crying is good for the soul must have been a masochist. My tears didn't wash away my sorrow. If anything, I felt even worse when I looked at myself in the bathroom mirror. How could I face my beloved Magdalena with the reddened eyes that stared back at me? How could I find the words to tell her what Velarde had so coldly explained to me?

She was waiting for me upstairs, in my room at the *Pension Toledono*, where Alfredo had taken her when we saw the *Guardia* car pull up. Before going upstairs, I soaked my face in cold water, combed my hair, and hoped she wouldn't notice the redness that lingered in my eyes.

She was waiting for me, watching through the peephole. Before I could knock, she threw open the door and rushed into my arms as if we had been separated for years rather than minutes. Her body molded itself against mine. She squeezed me tight and kissed me on the cheek. Alfredo and his girlfriend were standing in the doorway watching, probably disappointed that I didn't respond with a passionate kiss of my own.

"I was so frightened," Magdalena said. "I thought he was here to arrest you."

She was dressed in tight-fitting jeans, and a blue cotton blouse that was opened two buttons too low, revealing a bright red bra. Probably the work of Alfredo's girlfriend again, I thought. When she pulled back to look at me, her smile turned to a puzzled frown.

"What is it?" she asked, staring at my reddened eyes. "What's wrong?"

"Nothing," I lied. "Just some old allergies acting up.

"Was it Velarde?" she asked. "What did he say to you?"

"It's you he's looking for, not me," I said. "He never mentioned anything about your escape from the Templars, but I'm sure he thinks you'll show up. He left two people behind to watch me."

"How will you get out of here, Señor?" Alfredo asked.

"He left me this Templar pin," I showed them the golden emblem. "He said it would open doors and create opportunities for me."

Magdalena made a sour face. She obviously wanted to hear nothing more about the group that had imprisoned her ancestors. "Don't trust them," she warned.

"I'll use the pin, but not in the way he intended."

I fastened the emblem to the inside of Alfredo's shirt, where it wouldn't be visible to anyone.

"I don't understand," Alfredo said.

"This will be my last assignment for you, Alfredo. I don't have much money left to give you . . ."

"Please, Señor, you have already given me too much." He removed the pin from his collar and tried to give back to me. "I can accept no more money and no valuables from you. And it will be my pleasure to help you and your lady escape from the *Guardia.*" To protect Alfredo, I hadn't told him anything about Magdalena's true identity. "Please, you need not give me your pin."

"It's not an ordinary pin," I said. "It's really a tracking device. That's why they gave it to me. They assume that sooner or later I'll lead them to Magdalena."

"No comprendo, señor. What is this 'tracking device?'"

I turned the pin over to show him a small line where it had been soldered along the edge.

"There's a tiny transmitter inside," I explained. "It sends out a radio signal that allows them to follow the pin."

"But why give it to me?" he asked.

"Stupido!" his girlfriend laughed and slapped him on the arm. "He wants you to lead them away from here, so he and his woman can escape. Here, give it to me." She removed the pin from his shirt and fastened it to her bra. "I will take the bus and lead them all around the city for three hours, and then leave the pin in the ladies' room of the fanciest hotel in Valencia." Looking at me brightly, she asked. "Will three hours be enough?"

"More than enough," I said.

For the young couple, it was an opportunity to play a joke on the unpopular *Guardia.*

For Magdalena and me, it should have been our opportunity to begin a new life together.

Seventy-Four

WE LEFT VALENCIA that evening on the *Cyclades*, a magnificent 80-foot fiberglass-hulled yacht capable of transatlantic crossings. The yacht was owned by Spyros Kyrinos, a Greek shipping magnate. It was made available to us through the intercession of Athanasius, the archimandrite of Alexandria, who helped me plot this escape route.

"They'll come after us," Magdalena said softly. "The Templars won't give up easily."

"This time will be different," I said.

We were standing on the stern deck that evening, watching the skyline of Valencia recede in the distance. Shivering in the cool sea air, she sought shelter in the warmth of my arms. Her body nestled itself against mine, her head finding comfort in the hollow of my chest.

"Where are we going?"

"To a place where they won't find you."

"I don't think such a place exists. They have members and friends everywhere."

"Not in the Eastern world," I assured her. "The Templars made blood enemies in the Eastern world during the Crusades."

I explained that the yacht was taking her to the one place in all the world where the Templars would never think of looking for her . . . the sacred Mountain of Athos, where no woman has been allowed since the days of Constantine the Great. Through the intercession of the archimandrite, a special exception was made for Magdalena. She would be given a small house with a servant and a garden on the eastern slope, where the breeze comes across the sea from the Holy Land. She would be allowed to remain there in prayer and meditation for as long as she wished, and then, with the help of the Greek Orthodox community, disappear into the anonymity of the Eastern World.

"Meanwhile, the religious leaders you met at DesRosier's castle are warning the Templars to stay away from you. Otherwise the organization and its members will be condemned from the pulpit of every Christian church in the world. I'm sure they won't bother you anymore."

I felt her body stiffen and start to shiver.

"Are you still frightened?" I asked.

"Not as long as you're with me, James," she said, once again using that name from her past. "When they took me back to the Languedoc, I thought I had lost you forever."

The boat swayed gently in the trough of a sudden wave.

"But now we're together, and nothing else matters." She wrapped my arms tighter around her body. "Together we will continue the sacred bloodline. As the brother of my dead husband, I belong to you, James. You will be the father of my children."

To hear those words coming from a woman of such spellbinding beauty, yet one I now knew I could never possess, was almost more than I could bear.

No woman had ever spoken to me so directly, so intimately, offering herself so completely. She had escaped from violent men to be with no one but me, and here we were, together on a luxury yacht cruising the Mediterranean, and she was mine for the taking. My body yearned for her even more now than it did during those months in prison, when her image filled my dreams and occupied all my waking hours. I wanted to turn her around in my arms to behold her radiant face, inhale the lovely lavender fragrance that always enveloped her, and taste the sweetness of her sacred lips. It would have been so easy to lead her downstairs to the stateroom where Kyrinos had entertained some of the world's most beautiful women.

And yet, I couldn't.

She, the most physically desirable female I had ever met, was offering herself to me. A woman so important to Christian history that men sacrificed their lives to protect her, was telling me she wanted to bear my child. What greater honor could any man have than to be responsible for fathering a direct descendant of Jesus Christ? To have his seed become part of the royal bloodline? To become the spouse of the fabled *Sang Real*? To succeed at a goal for which the kings and emperors of the ages would have gladly given up their thrones?

And yet . . . and yet . . . I dared not.

I tried desperately to suppress the passion she aroused in me and to withstand the force of the testosterone surging through my veins. I had not been intimate with a woman for almost five years, celibate not by choice but by the depressing circumstances of my life. At any time in that period, I would have gladly thrown myself at half the woman she was.

How could I withstand the allure of this nubile young virgin who stood radiant before me in the moonlight, eyes sparkling, lips moist, mouth open with anticipation? Her physical charms alone made her a woman worthy of the Savior of Mankind.

And that was exactly why I held back.

As much as I loved her, I knew I could never permit myself to weaken in these last moments we had together.

"Please don't call me James," I said. "My name is Theophanes."

"But in a past life, you were James, the brother of Jesus my Christ."

"I have no memories of any past life," I responded stiffly.

"Perhaps not yet. But the memories will come flooding back to you, just as they did to me."

"I don't think so," I said. "Your case was unusual. Most memories of past lives exist only in young children, and fade away within the first ten years."

"James . . . Theo . . . why are you talking like this?" She drew away from me, pulling herself out of my arms and moving to the railing, but still facing me. "I thought surely by now you believed in me."

"Do I believe that you are Mary Magdalene, born again two thousand years later in the body of one of her descendants? Yes I do. All the evidence supports it. Do I believe I lived a previous life, too? That I'm also an old soul in a new body? Based on your case and thousands of others, I believe that I probably am. I've experienced instances of *déjà vu*, unexplained knowledge, and other reincarnation markers. But unlike you, I have no memories of any previous lives. And more specifically, I have no memory of ever having been the man you think I am."

"But you look exactly the way you did when you accompanied your mother Mary and your brother Jesus my Christ to Cana. Your eyes, your chin, the shape of your face, you look exactly the way I remember. When you approached me in Valencia Cathedral, I knew it was you. That was why I selected you to carry my note to Serrano."

The sea breeze was turning colder. Now it was my turn to shiver.

She reached out for my hand.

"And this scar of yours . . . "

"It's just a birthmark," I lied.

"Do you remember when we were having dinner in Barcelona? That night, when I took your hand in mine, I noticed the same mark appears on both sides of your hand." She turned my hand over and back to show me something I already knew. In the center of my palm was a long red mark that corresponded perfectly with the vertical mark on the back of my hand.

"I never heard of a birthmark that appears on both sides of a hand," she said.

It was the same thing the doctors had told me during my hospital stay. They insisted some sharp object had penetrated my hand. I told them I couldn't recall any injury to my hand, even as a child.

"It resembles a stab wound, and it's on your right hand, in exactly the place where the spear penetrated James' hand."

When the doctors pointed it out to me, I immediately wondered if it could be a mystic reminder of some past life wound? But the Stevenson protocols attribute such birthmarks only to fatal wounds. A stab in the hand certainly wouldn't qualify as a biological marker of reincarnation.

"Take off your shirt," Magdalena suddenly said. She started to unbutton my shirt. "Take if off! Now."

"What are you doing?" I asked, pulling away from her.

"I want to see your chest. The brother of Jesus my Christ died as a martyr. They stoned him at first. Then they put a big rock on his chest and put a heavy weight on it to suffocate him. When he didn't die, they ran a spear into his heart. People who were there said that he tried to protect himself, and the spear was driven right through his hand into his heart."

"No!" I shouted, clutching my shirtfront.

"If there's a mark on your chest, a mark over your heart that matches the one on your hands, there can be no doubt. You are James, the brother of Jesus, the man I must marry."

"No!" I was afraid to allow her to look, afraid that she might see the karmic residue of a brutal death in a prior life.

"I have to see," she insisted. "I have to see if it's true."

"No!" I shouted. "It doesn't matter whether I lived a previous life, or who I might have been. What matters is that I can't marry you."

She stopped, stunned by my outburst.

"Why not?" she asked.

"Just . . . because I can't," I said, buttoning my shirt.

"Are you afraid of me?" she asked.

It was a prescient remark, I thought. An insight worthy of a trained psychiatrist. In fact, there was a certain element of fear involved in the turmoil I felt.

"Is it my memories you fear?"

I hesitated to answer. It might seem peculiar to fear another person's memories. Yet the idea that she might compare my touch, my kisses, my caresses with her memories of the man who "loved her above all others" was a fearsome prospect. Did I dare think that in the most intimate moments of married life, I could ever replace Jesus in her thoughts?

"You're not . . . jealous? Are you?"

How could anyone be jealous of the Son of God, I wanted to ask. Intimidated was more like it. Intimidated and frightened. If I hadn't been raised as a Christian, if I hadn't been brought up to revere God the Father and the Son and the Holy Ghost, if I hadn't partaken of the Body and Blood of Christ in Holy Communion all those Sundays, perhaps I might have been able to overcome my fears. But the love of Christ was too deeply ingrained in me for me to ever think I could replace Him in this woman's heart. And yet, that wasn't the reason I would have to deny myself marriage to a woman I so dearly loved.

"Is it my reputation?" she asked, her voice filled with pain. "All those evil things that were said about me being a prostitute? A sinner? A woman of the streets?"

It was growing harder for me to keep track of which woman was talking to me. The innocent voice of the young nun had been taking on more and more of the rich maturity of the woman who addressed the wedding guests with such authority. It was an astounding transformation, nothing less than an identity shift with seismic philosophical implications, which raised serious questions about the plasticity of identity. The Behaviorists contend that human identity is nothing more than the sum total of memories and experiences acquired over a lifetime, and is by definition, relatively immutable. The Reincarnationists, however, argue that it takes more than one lifetime to achieve perfection as a human being, with the actions of each lifetime determining the nature and personality of the next. The memories of Magdalena's past life had become so vivid, so clear in her mind that they had overcome the barriers of time and space and death to transform her very identity.

"How can you refuse me?" she asked. "How can you refuse to continue the bloodline of Jesus my Christ?"

How indeed, I thought, as I tried to avoid looking into her eyes. What words could I possibly use to refuse the Apostle to the Apostles, the consort of Christ, the biblical figure, the venerated saint, the woman who had the ability to rewrite Christian history?

I would have given anything to spend the rest of my life with her, but knew I couldn't. Her eyes pleaded with me for an explanation, but the words stuck in my throat.

I decided to let *Coronel* Velarde speak for me. His words and his image were preserved on my camcorder, which had recorded his entire conversation earlier that day. I fast-forwarded the tape to the place where he forever put Magdalena beyond my reach.

"Sister Mariamme may attempt to contact you at some time in the future," the camcorder reproduced Velarde's voice with a tinny quality. "I know you are deeply attracted to her, but I must caution you about any involvement."

"You take your advice from a Templar?" Magdalena shouted. "How can you?"

"Please," I said. "Listen."

"Sister Mariamme is not an ordinary person," Velarde's voice continued. "She can never be treated as an ordinary human being. She is, as you know, the *Sang Real,* the sacred vessel that carries within her the unfertilized eggs that contain the DNA of Jesus Christ. That fact alone makes her a woman of enormous theological significance. That is why the Templars would lay down their lives to protect her."

"Protect?" Magdalena said. "He means imprison. Keep as a possession. And decide who among them will impregnate me. How can you listen to this . . . this obscene man?"

I paused the tape. "Please, Magdalena. This isn't easy for me, but you have to listen. What he says is important."

"Sister Mariamme herself realizes she is not an ordinary human being," Velarde's voice continued. In the little square viewing area, his image moved in and out of sight as he paced the room. "When she stood at the microphone and told the wedding guests she must follow the Law of Moses, she was not inventing a convenient excuse to get out of a marriage she did not wish to consummate. Don't you think it was because she really believes in following the Law of Moses?"

"Well . . . yes, I guess she does," I heard my voice say.

Listening to the tape, Magdalena nodded her head in vigorous agreement.

"And don't you think there are other religious laws . . . ," Velarde's voice said, " . . . that she probably feels she is required to follow?"

"I imagine so. Yes."

"The rules that Jesus Christ established through his teaching?"

"Yes. Definitely yes," Magdalena interjected, partially overlapping my taped response.

" . . . are obviously very important to her," my answer ended.

"In fact, any violation of those teachings would be unthinkable for her."

"I imagine so. It would be a desecration of Christ's memory."

"Exactly!" Listening to the *Coronel*'s voice, I could hear the sense of satisfaction he felt as he was leading me into his trap. Despite my feelings about him and his Templar relationship, it was not an evil-intentioned trap. In a strange way, he was even serving a noble purpose. But it was a trap nevertheless, one from which even now I couldn't find a way to extricate myself.

"And any violation of Jesus Christ's teaching would diminish not only Sister Mariamme's moral authority, but her very identity. I ask you, Mr. Nikonos, during your investigation, if she had repudiated the teachings of

Jesus or acted in a manner inconsistent with them, would you have believed for one moment that she was the reincarnation of Mary Magdalene?"

"I doubt it," my taped voice murmured.

"Of course not. And neither would any of the skeptics and critics who will certainly attack her."

"But the DNA tests . . ."

" . . . would mean little if she was perceived as betraying Christ's memory."

"But she hasn't betrayed his memory. Magdalena is as devoted to Jesus as . . . as you are."

"And what about you, Mr. Nikonos?"

"Well . . ." my voice hesitated on the tape.

"We've looked into your past, Mr. Nikonos. And I'm very troubled by what we found."

"You mean the murder trial in New York? You know I was acquitted."

"The mere fact that you were charged with so serious a crime could certainly represent a problem to any priest asked to approve your marriage to a woman of such sacred ancestry. But I'm speaking of something far more serious. Something which would place Magdalena in direct violation of the teachings of Jesus."

I glanced at Magdalena. She was listening intently, her face suddenly serious. I wanted to turn off the tape recorder, to try to explain it myself, but it was too late for that. And I might find it harder to repeat the words face-to-face.

"I haven't been to church in a few years," the tape revealed me saying. "But I'm prepared to start going again."

"I'm not talking about going to church. I'm talking about something far more serious in your past. In our investigation into your past, we learned of a woman named Elizabeth Ann Malatesta . . ."

As the tape revealed my groan of despair, Magdalena's eyes widened.

" . . . Her married name was Elizabeth Ann Nikonos."

Magdalena's face went white. She let out a gasp and clutched the railing. I tried to reach out for her, but she waved me away.

"You were divorced in New York State . . ." *Coronel* Velarde continued.

Magdalena looked up in anguish, her eyes asking me if it was true. Helplessly, I nodded.

"Now you may argue that times have changed," Velarde's voice said. "That today's morality and church teaching allows remarriage after divorce. But we are dealing here with a very special person."

"I know," my voice on the tape said. It was flat and emotionless, the voice of a man suddenly bereft of all hope. Velarde had destroyed me. With simple, basic police work, he had found a way for the Templars to work their vengeance on me. Magdalena would forever be beyond my reach.

"Magdalena, as she will undoubtedly tell you herself, is committed to following the literal words of Jesus." Velarde's voice went on. "And Jesus said, 'Whoever divorces his wife and marries another, commits adultery against her.' In the eyes of Jesus, you are still married, Mr. Nikonos. Therefore, you can never have anything more than a platonic relationship with Sister Mariamme."

I switched off the tape, unable to listen to any more.

I bent down to Magdalena. I was afraid to touch her, afraid she might push me away.

"I'm sorry," I said. "I forgot what the divorce could mean. But he's right, isn't he?"

With tear-filled eyes, she nodded her head.

"You didn't have to play that tape," she sobbed. "You could have kept the divorce a secret. You didn't have to let me know."

"I know I didn't," I said. "And I have to admit, I was tempted to destroy the tape. There are men who would tell any lie, commit any fraud, to claim you as their wife. But I can't do that. I can't do that to you, my beautiful Magdalena. Not to you."

I took her tear-stained hands in mine.

"No matter how much I love you," I said. "No matter how much you may love me, we can never marry," I told her. "The sanctity of the Christic bloodline would be destroyed by a union Jesus would consider adulterous." Feeling my throat tighten and the tears welling up in my own eyes, I whispered, "I'm sorry."

Our hands were trembling together.

"I'm sorry," I repeated.

"No. Don't be sorry." She tried, but failed, to smile through her tears. "You were willing to sacrifice your life for me." She gently touched the wound in my side. "And now, you are willing to sacrifice your heart for me." She placed her hand on my chest, sliding it inside my shirt so that she could better feel the sorrowful throbbing. "Jesus my Christ loves you as much as I do. Those of us who followed him left behind everything we owned, everything we cherished. He taught us that the greatest act of love is to be willing to give up that which we love most."

And then, with infinite tenderness, she leaned forward to kiss me on the cheek. "You will be rewarded for this in your next life."

There wasn't much to say after that. I remained sitting at her feet, with my head on her lap. She gently stroked my hair and began to hum a lovely melody. After a while, she began to sing, a melancholy song whose words were foreign to me. In that lovely, untrained soprano voice, it was a song, I thought, that might not have been heard in two thousand years.

A feeling of contentment settled over me. The breeze died down. The sea grew calm. The powerful engines hummed beneath us as we headed out into the middle of the Mediterranean.

I had set out to authenticate someone else's past life, only to discover I had found one of my own. Birthmarks that suggest the manner of a previous death are among the most important markers of reincarnation. Instead of finding such biological proof on Magdalena, I found it on myself. The death mark was on my chest, right where she said it would be. The doctors had pointed it out to me in the hospital. It matched perfectly with the marks on my hand

To this day, whenever I look at the telltale marks, I wonder whether it was possible that Magdalena had correctly identified me as James, the younger brother of Jesus. As a psychologist, it would be easy to dismiss that idea as a classic case of transference, in which she was projecting her fantasies upon me. Yet the physical manifestations, whatever their origin, could not be denied.

And if I was the reincarnation of James, had I not fulfilled the Law of Moses by taking responsibility for the widow of Jesus? Had I not delivered my brother's descendants from a thousand years of captivity?

And if I wasn't James? Well, I had authenticated the reincarnation of Mary Magdalene and found the "Holy Grail."

"You still have work to do," I was told when I was sent back from the afterlife. Surely now, I thought, that was work enough for one lifetime.

About the Author

William Valtos has been writing since his childhood, when his plays were performed by fellow students in grade school. As an advertising executive, Valtos won the coveted *Clio* award. His novel *Resurrection* was the subject of the HBO film *Almost Dead*.

Hampton Roads Publishing Company

. . . for the evolving human spirit

Hampton Roads Publishing Company
publishes books on a variety of subjects including
metaphysics, health, complementary medicine,
visionary fiction, and other related topics.

For a copy of our latest catalog,
call toll-free, 800-766-8009,
or send your name and address to:

Hampton Roads Publishing Company, Inc.
1125 Stoney Ridge Road
Charlottesville, VA 22902
e-mail: hrpc@hrpub.com
www.hrpub.com